The Pirate's Curse

DANNY GUNN

© Danny Gunn 2023

danwritesbooks@outlook.com \ @danwritesbooks

ISBN: 978-0-6456418-3-7

eBook ISBN: 978-0-6456418-4-4

Cover Design by designticks.com

Chapter and page break images by designed by macrovector / Freepik

Homemade Apple font by FontDiner via Google Fonts

Published by Danny Gunn

(https://facebook.com/dannygunnwrites)

It is a blessing for a man to have a hand in determining his own fate...

~ Blackbeard

Prologue

Ocracoke Island, North Carolina
November 22, 1718

Night had fallen. Stars dusted the sky, and there was not a cloud in sight. The chirping of crickets in the reeds and creaking wood as the sloop ship *Jane* rocked gently in the lapping water were the only sounds to be heard. Lieutenant Robert Maynard stood port side on the *Jane* staring out at the dark horizon, his mind on the battle earlier that day and the dead body that lay below deck.

So many men lost for one pirate.

"Lieutenant."

Maynard turned to see his captain, George Gordon, approaching. Captain Gordon was a solid man and dressed in a blue navy jacket with golden epaulettes.

Maynard gave an exhausted salute.

"Good work capturing that brigand," Captain Gordon said. "Governor Spotswood is most pleased."

As he should be.

"Thank you, sir."

"Have you completed the final summary of what was in the hold?"

Maynard shook his head. "I am waiting for the men to complete the final count, but we know he was carrying cocoa, indigo, sugar and cotton and in large quantities."

Gordon nodded. "Excellent. That should satisfy Governor Spotswood."

"You can thank Odell for that, sir."

"Samuel? Why?"

Maynard expelled a breath, the air misting in front of him. "It seems one of the pirates we captured was instructed to blow the *Adventure* if it looked like they were going to lose. Samuel stopped that."

Gordon raised an eyebrow. "Is that so? It seems like Samuel Odell not only provided the necessary distraction, but saved the lives of many men as well."

"Indeed," grumbled Maynard.

"And the body?"

"Below deck, sir. I was just about to examine it."

Gordon nodded. "Take Smith with you."

"He's injured, sir."

"Then take—"

Maynard cut him off. "The men need rest, sir. I can handle it."

Gordon considered this for a moment, but the night's chill seemed to remove any desire for an argument. "See that the report is finalised and brought to me as soon as you have finished the examination."

"Yes, sir."

"Excellent," Gordon said. He paused, as if contemplating something.

"Sir?" Maynard prompted.

"I have received word from Governor Spotswood. He told me that the reward will be paid out from the loot below once it is sold at auction, and…," he paused, and Maynard could tell it was going to be bad news. "…it will be split evenly between your crew and Captain Brand's."

"Sir!"

Gordon held up his hand. "Lieutenant, I've read the initial report and I understand how you must feel—"

"My men were the ones on the ship fighting for our lives. Captain Brand and the crew of the *Lyme* tallied behind and boarded the ship once we had secured it." His voice was raised now, and he didn't care who overheard his insubordination. "They can just sit back and enjoy the spoils of our hard work? I lost good men out there!"

"Lieutenant."

"I strenuously object!"

Gordon gazed at Maynard and said, "Lieutenant, your objection is noted. I will make it known to Governor Spotswood and will ask him to reconsider—"

"You know he won't."

"He may not, but I will still take it to him. Now I suggest you take a moment to calm yourself before your examination. When you are done, come see me on the *Pearl* with your final report of what was in the hold and anything of note on the body."

Maynard took a deep breath and saluted. He stewed over his raging thoughts while he watched Gordon head to his own ship, the *HMS Pearl*.

Calm yourself, he admonished. *Think of the bigger picture.* Taking deep breaths, he turned to walk along the deck intending to head down, but he was intercepted by Jones, one of his midshipmen.

"What is it?" he snapped. He was tired, sore, and needed sleep, and the news from Captain Gordon did not help. However, he still had much to do, and he felt the anger building inside of him again. He took another deep breath.

"Final count of the dead, sir," the young man said.

Maynard waited, but the midshipman did not speak. "And?" he asked irritably.

"Ten of our men dead, twenty wounded," he replied, "including Hyde and his second-in-command, Baker, and subordinate, Hill. Samuel Odell as well."

"Ten!" Maynard said, aghast. They took sixty men for their assault on the pirates and half were either dead or wounded.

"And the pirates?" he asked.

"Ten dead and nine captured."

Maynard considered this. Ten good men died, and another handful were wounded in return for ten dead pirates and another nine who would likely see the gallows. Was it a worthy trade-off to take down one of the most notorious pirates of all time?

Ultimately, Maynard realised he didn't care that much, at least not now. He was too exhausted. He bore multiple cuts and bruises from the encounter earlier that day.

Descending the steps, he walked past the crew quarters to the aft of the ship where the body rested on a wooden table, candles burning brightly around it.

Edward Teach was his name. The former pirate captain lay with his eyes closed with dried blood from a gash on his cheek covering his neck and famous black beard. Subconsciously, Maynard ran his left hand over the bandage around his right, the fingers bruised and bloodied. Seeing the pirate's face brought the memories of the day to the forefront of his mind.

Intelligence acquired from Teach's former quartermaster William Howard indicated the pirate was anchored near Ocracoke Island. With Captain Brand and the *Lyme* stationed far away, Maynard, commanding the sloop-of-war *Jane*, and his second-in-command Jonathan Hyde, commanding the *Ranger*, approached the island where Teach was entertaining his guests, including Samuel Odell. Teach, Odell, and his crew remained on Teach's ship, the *Adventure*, while his second, Israel Hands, had taken more than twenty of Teach's men to the town of Bath, leaving the pirates drunk, outmanned, and too ill-prepared to notice them moving in.

After spending the night deliberating with his subordinates on what to do, and concerned he would run aground in the unfamiliar waters, Maynard decided to wait out the night and begin their attack at daybreak. He reminded his crew that he, and he alone, would engage Teach.

The next morning, he intended on sneaking up on the *Adventure,* but both the *Jane* and the *Ranger* grounded in shallow water. Furious with the misfortune, Maynard ordered his men to toss heavy materials overboard. They worked frantically to lighten the sloop and eventually freed themselves and sailed toward the *Adventure* with the *Ranger* close behind. With the element of surprise lost, though, the *Adventure* cut its anchor and tried to escape through the channel through which Maynard had entered. Teach fired upon both Maynard and Hyde's sloops.

The attack was devastating.

Maynard remembered the barrage of cannon balls whistling past his ears, smashing into the ship. The sounds of splintering wood and explosions became entangled with the cries of men both injured and dying. The *Jane* took the brunt of the barrage, stalling under the heavy losses. The *Ranger* made a direct course for the *Adventure*, which was heading straight for the *Jane*.

When the pirate's ship came within earshot, Maynard heard Teach call out, claiming he was a supporter of King George and that if Maynard would let him go, he would harry them no longer.

Maynard replied that he intended to board his ship and capture him, dead or alive.

At an impasse, Teach unleashed a broadside attack that decimated the *Ranger*, killing Hyde as well as the second and third officer, leaving the ship leaderless and a non-factor.

In the return fire, Maynard's crew hit the jib halyard,

disabling it and slowing the *Adventure* down.

"Prepare for boarding!" Maynard bellowed, watching the pirate ship get closer. Before heading to his cabin, he again reminded his men below deck to leave Teach to him. Meanwhile, the *Adventure* crashed into the *Jane*, causing it to heave back and forth. Ropes and sails got tangled, and Maynard watched from his vantage point as Teach and a dozen of his motley crew boarded the *Jane.* The pirate chuckled, thinking he had the battle won as he stood at the head of the group. He wore long white breeches and a blood-red coat over a sling with three flintlocks holstered in it. But his appearance was dominated by his unkempt waist-length black beard with colourful ribbons twisted into it. His beard complemented the black hair that peeked out from his tricorn hat.

Before Teach could order his men to attack, Maynard screamed, "Now!" and emerged from his cabin while his crew burst out of the hold and they attacked the pirates.

His crew and the pirates exchanged gunfire, and Maynard felt bullets whizzing past his ear. Men on both sides went down, but Maynard ignored it, firing once more at the pirates. He tossed his flintlock aside, let out a primal roar, and charged at the pirates with his men following behind.

He unsheathed his cutlass and engaged with Teach, who blocked with his own cutlass and parried. All around them the battle ensued in the smoky haze, the sounds of gunfire and swords clanging against swords echoing in the morning air. More men fell, the naval men soon becoming outnumbered. Teach forced Maynard back until he hit the mizzenmast.

Maynard pulled a dagger from his belt with his free hand and sliced Teach along the arm.

The pirate laughed and knocked the dagger out of Maynard's hand. Maynard parried a blow from Teach and stepped back, giving himself some room.

Teach was covered in blood, oozing from holes and cuts in his jacket and arms. He flashed a row of blackened teeth in what Maynard later assumed was a smile, and Maynard smiled back and winked, knowing what was coming next. The faint yet growing noise of footsteps made Teach pause and cock his ear. Suddenly, the backup units Maynard had deliberately held back burst out from the hold, shouting and firing their pistols. The fight was turning in Maynard's favour.

Teach snarled and backed off, ordering an escape, but it was no use—the pirates were surrounded.

The battle raged on and Maynard's crew pushed the pirates back toward the bow. He found himself in space and engaged the pirate captain again. He felt like a gladiator in battle as he and Teach swapped blows. Maynard thrust, catching the pirate's cartridge box and bending the cutlass. Teach hit him with a devastating blow that broke the sword's guard, and Maynard cried out in pain as his fingers were crushed. They grappled before one of Maynard's crewmen, Demelt, interfered, forcing Teach to release Maynard to engage with him. Demelt landed a cut along Teach's neck, which the pirate grabbed at, blood leaking through his fingers, and he fell to his knees.

Demelt, a highlander from Scotland with fiery red hair, was going in for the killing blow when Maynard shouted, "Stand back!"

Demelt looked at him, confused, until he saw the pistol Maynard held pointed at the pirate's chest. He pulled the trigger, and the notorious pirate known as Blackbeard collapsed, dead.

Maynard stood over Blackbeard's body and sighed. The adrenaline of the fight had long left him. He was exhausted and in desperate need of sleep, but Captain Gordon needed the report for Governor Spotswood. Rolling up the sleeves of his shirt, Maynard examined the body. The pirate's red coat was torn and his white shirt blood-soaked and the body was riddled with cuts, twenty of them by his count. The cuts were mostly around the torso, but there were also three on his right arm and shoulder and two on the left, and the final one on the neck courtesy of Demelt. He also noted four holes in the coat and shirt, and another on the left thigh. Blackbeard had been shot five times.

Twenty cuts and shot five times. He must have been possessed by the devil!

Next, he checked the pockets of the coat, finding a couple of round bullets and a gunpowder pouch. He put them aside and flipped open the jacket with the tips of his fingers, careful not to get any blood on them. There was one inner pocket on the left side and, carefully opening it, he pulled out a handful of documents. He quickly leafed through them, finding letters from people he'd never heard of until the last one. It was from Tobias Knight, a government official in North Carolina.

What was Tobias doing fraternising with a pirate? Captain Gordon will be interested in this, he thought.

Putting the letters aside, he lightly ran his fingers over the inner left linings of the jacket and found a small bag. He pulled it out and opened the drawstring. Inside was a mixture of silver and gold coins. He poured the coins out and counted.

Almost ninety pounds!

He put the coins back in the bag and shoved it in his pocket. "You don't mind, do you, old chap?" he said to the body. It wasn't much, but after being told that the reward was being split between both crews, he thought giving this money to his crew might make up for it.

He continued searching the pirate's coat.

What's this?

There was a slight bulge along the seams that ran down the right side of the coat. Grabbing a thin knife from the table, he pried the stitching loose and pulled the seam open, revealing the secret pocket. He wrenched out its contents with two fingers, exposing some sort of metal device the size of his palm.

He tried to open it, but it was stuck. He examined it, rotating it in his hands, trying to find a clasp or a way to unlock it, but there was nothing. He would have to inspect it later in his own time.

"What is it, sir?" came a voice from the darkened doorway.

Maynard looked up and saw Smith, one of Gordon's sergeants, enter. He was tall, with dark hair and a pale, pinched face. He held up the device. "I don't know."

Smith peered at it and then held out his hand. "May I?"

Maynard handed him the device, and Smith held it to a

candle. He examined it much like Maynard had. He tried to open it and failed, eventually handing it back to him.

"I can't open it."

"Yes, thank you," he replied drily.

"Why do you think he had it?"

"Unfortunately, I didn't have time to ask him during the battle," he said sarcastically.

Maynard put the device to the side and continued his examination.

"Are you not adding it to the report?"

Maynard sighed. He didn't like the sergeant. He was Gordon's lapdog and would report everything he saw to him. In fact, Maynard was certain he would swim to England if Gordon asked him to do it. Picking up his quill, he scribbled a couple of words down.

"That doesn't say anything," Smith complained.

Maynard looked up and narrowed his eyes at the sergeant. "If Captain Gordon seeks clarification of my writing, he can ask me himself."

Sergeant Smith was about to protest when Maynard held up his hand, stopping him before he spoke. "Get me a saw."

"A saw? For what?"

"For cutting," Maynard said, as if he was speaking to a dim-witted child.

"But... why?"

Maynard turned his head slightly. "Are you questioning me, *sergeant*?"

Despite being Gordon's lapdog, Maynard outranked him and

could order him around as he pleased.

"No, sir."

"Then get me a saw."

"Yes, sir!"

Smith snapped a salute, turned on his heels, and left the room. Maynard watched him go, and when he heard the telltale thudding of boots on stairs, he grabbed the device and put it in his pants pocket. Then he paused, listening intently for sounds of anyone coming. He heard nothing but the creaking of timber and lapping water against the hull, allowing him to pull a syringe from his coat pocket quickly and uncap it. Just as he was about to plunge it into the pirate's thigh, he paused, the syringe hovering in mid-air. He thought about the choices he'd made this day that led him to this moment. Then, shaking his head of such thoughts, he jabbed it into the pirate's thigh, depressing the plunger.

Smith returned later, saw in hand, to find Maynard had finished his examination of the pirate.

"What took you so long?" Maynard asked, taking the saw from him.

"Sorry, sir. I had to get one from the *Lyme.*"

"There is my report if you want to take it to Captain Gordon."

Smith collected the documents, and looking at the dead body, frowned.

"What is the matter, sergeant?"

He pointed at the body. "I could have sworn he was taller

than this, and didn't he have a cut on the right side of his neck?"

Maynard looked at the sergeant but said nothing, the silence becoming uncomfortable until Smith continued. "I must be more tired than I thought."

"We are all tired, sergeant. Take the documents to Captain Gordon. There is some information on there that he will find very interesting."

The documents connecting Tobias Knight to Blackbeard would be enough for Governor Spotswood to dismiss any suspicions about a broken trinket.

"Yes, sir. Thank you, sir."

Suddenly, there was a loud thud. Maynard heard it but didn't give any indication that he had. Instead, he watched Smith intently. The sergeant's head lift as he squinted into the darkness behind the lieutenant, where a row of storage cupboards had been built into the inner hull.

"Did you hear that?" Smith asked, his hand instinctively going to the sword at his belt.

"Hear what?"

"Sounds like something fell."

Maynard shrugged, unconcerned. "Probably one of the men above. Tripped or something."

"No, I am sure it came from behind you."

Maynard turned around and looked at the cupboards in the gloomy candlelight. "There's nothing there, sergeant."

"But—"

"Sergeant, if you please. I've had a long day and want to get back to my cabin sometime this night."

The sergeant continued to stare over Maynard's shoulder, as if ready to argue the point, but thought better of it and nodded.

"Good," Maynard said, and held up the saw. "Now, unless you want to soil your uniform, I suggest you step back."

Smith did, and Maynard placed the saw on the pirate's neck and started cutting.

One

Burnie, Tasmania, Australia
Present Day

The loud banging of metal-on-metal startled Ethan awake.

"Jackson!" the police officer said. "Get up."

Ethan lay on the flimsy bed, his head pounding. The thin mattress and springs sticking into his back made sleep impossible. As did spending the better part of the night with his head in the toilet, throwing up the meagre contents of his stomach. When he was sober enough, his mind ticked over the previous night's incidents and his poor life choices. Eventually he was tired enough to doze off, though it felt like he had been asleep for all of two minutes before being disturbed again.

"What is it?" he groaned and then winced, his jaw stiff and sore. He touched his cheek. It felt tender.

"Time to go."

Ethan opened his eyes and immediately closed them. Despite the dim lighting in the cells, it still pierced his eyeballs and went straight into his brain. He groaned again.

"Come on."

"Just give me a minute, Davies."

Constable Davies gave him exactly one minute before he banged on the steel bars, each hit a piercing scream that worsened his already horrible headache.

"Okay! Okay!" he said, rubbing the tiredness out of his blue eyes. He sat up and slowly moved his hands away, allowing his eyes to adjust to the light. It didn't help much, but it was enough that he could see, even if it was a little blurry around the edges.

"Jesus, Ethan, you look like shit," the constable said while opening the cell door. Ethan said nothing and walked out. "You smell like it, too," he added.

"Missed you, too, Jason," Ethan said.

Leaving the cell door open, Constable Davies directed Ethan down the hall toward an opening that led back to the main offices of the Burnie Police Station.

"You also look like you're wearing shit."

Ethan looked down and saw his shirt was covered in mud and vomit and possibly actual shit as well.

"You sound like you want a hug," Ethan said, turning around and opening his arms.

"I will throw you back in that cell," Davies said, his hands up but his mouth turned in a half smile. He pointed to the cell they passed where a skinny homeless man in tattered clothes lay on the ground. "Or maybe I'll put you in there with Barry. You like hugs, don'tcha, Barry?"

Barry giggled and said, "The younger, the better."

"That's disturbing," Ethan said.

Davies rolled his eyes. "Barry's as harmless as they come."

"Totally explains why he's in a jail cell."

The constable ignored him and led him to his desk, where he handed Ethan the possessions that were taken from him the night before, his wallet, watch, keys, and phone. He strapped the watch to his wrist, then grabbed the phone and keys and put them in his pants pocket. Just as he reached for the wallet, Davies pulled it out of his reach and said, "Pete wants to see you before you go."

Ethan groaned. "What now?"

Davies shrugged. "Just told me to tell you to see him before you go."

"All right," Ethan said, and Davies held out the wallet for him. Ethan grabbed it, but the constable held on to it. "You *will* see him, right?"

Ethan held up his other hand. "Scout's honour."

Giving him one final look, the constable let go of the wallet, and Ethan put it in his pocket with the rest of his items. "Anything else?" he asked.

The constable shook his head. "You're free to go. Just keep out of trouble, will you?"

"You're one to talk," Ethan said, giving him a mock salute. He stood up and left the officers' pool. He made for Senior Sergeant

Peter Miller's office, but took a left just before the office and proceeded out the door into the reception area. Just as he was about to leave the building, a familiar voice called out to him.

"Ethan."

Ethan stopped and closed his eyes. *Just give me a break, would you?*

He turned around to see the six-foot-tall, slightly greying senior sergeant of the Burnie Police Station looking at him with a mix of amusement and annoyance. "Thought you could leave without saying goodbye?"

"Didn't want to take up any more of your valuable time," he replied.

Peter Miller was a friend of his parents and unofficial carer for him while he was growing up after they died. He did as good a job as anyone could have, considering he was at a crossroads in his life and could have strayed far from the path his parents had mapped out for him. He did stray, but not to the point where he was a lost cause. He still caused trouble, and Peter had bailed him out or saved his ass more times than he deserved, but he wasn't a career criminal. At least not convicted as an adult, and his record was clean enough that he might be able to get a decent job shoving dirt or holding a slow/stop sign for construction workers.

"Come on. I just need a minute."

Ethan ran his fingers through his wavy brown hair and followed him back into the bullpen and through to his office, where he shut the door. "Take a seat," he said.

Ethan did, and Peter took his own seat on the other side of the paper-strewn desk. Rather than look at him, Ethan focused on the framed certificates hanging on the wall behind him. Certificates that showed successful completion of various training modules, leadership courses, as well as police awards. Below the certificates was a low-lying cabinet with framed photos of his wife and two boys, both who would be in high school now.

"How are you feeling?"

"Fine," he said, still looking at everything but him. His headache was worse in the bright office lights, and he slumped in the chair, willing himself to submerge into the darkened fabric.

"You don't look fine. You look like—"

"Shit, I know. Jace mentioned that."

Peter clasped his hands together and asked, "What happened last night?"

Ethan was now focusing entirely on a crease in his pants and said, "I don't know. Someone was talking crap, causing trouble, and I told him to knock it off."

"By socking him in the jaw?"

Ethan pointed to his cheek, which was red and swollen. "It was all hazy at that point, but I'm sure there was a bit of pushing and shoving going on, and obviously he got one in."

"Yeah, they told me it was a modern-day Ali versus Liston," Peter scoffed.

"I assume he isn't pressing charges."

"I talked him out of it. Convinced him it was two guys who were too drunk, and both got in their shots."

"Thanks," Ethan mumbled, meaning it.

There was a long silence, and Ethan knew what was coming.

"I know what today is," Peter said.

"Thursday?"

"The bank takes the house today."

Ethan finally looked at him. "So they are."

"Do you need any help?"

Probably. But not the kind you can provide.

Ethan shook his head. "Nah, they got a removalist. I just gotta sign something and then I am done with it."

"Can I trust you not to cause a scene?"

"They've been dead for ten years, Pete. I haven't lived in that house for eight, and it's been boarded up for five. Frankly, I'm surprised it's still standing."

"Given the... unique nature of your parents... ah... profession and the publicity of their deaths, we have had security monitoring it since the news came out."

Ethan knew he wasn't talking about their mysterious deaths, rather, how after their deaths, news came out that they were involved in the black market trade of rare and priceless artefacts. Considering they were archaeologists and historians teaching at the University of Tasmania, it caused a bit of a scandal among their peers. An inquiry into their activities, which lasted months and had him questioned like a common criminal, revealed these allegations were true, and Ethan's whole life came crashing down around him. He received interview requests, bricks through the windows, and even death threats because of what was discovered. If he was honest with himself, he was surprised he didn't just lash out at every kid at school who teased or questioned him. Or the smartasses who called him 'Indiana Jones' and said stuff like, "Hey, Ethan, how much did they sell the Holy Grail for?"

He also wasn't surprised that he didn't go down the drug rabbit hole that half the kids in his class did. Of course, there were the other half—those who got jobs and did well. Jason Davies was one of those kids. He was a bully in school, but he pulled his head in after year twelve and became a cop.

"You alright?" Peter asked.

"Just thinking about how funny life can be," Ethan said. "I'll be fine. I've moved on. They were criminals and now they are dead. What can I do?"

Peter smiled at him and said, "Maybe spend less time parkouring at that old paper mill and picking fights with every dumbass at the pub and more time applying yourself to something that interests you."

"Parkouring at the paper mill and picking fights with dumbasses *does* interest me."

Peter's smile turned stern. He had the type of face that when he got serious, you would shrink in your seat. "I'm being serious, Ethan. No more trespassing and no more fights. Find something to do with your life, because I won't be around to protect you from your destructive behaviours forever."

"Anything else?" Ethan asked. He'd been on the receiving end of these lectures before. His teachers, his principal, old bosses, and even Peter on occasion—they were all the same.

Peter shook his head. "Sarah would like you over for dinner soon."

Ethan stood up and said, "Maybe," before walking out the door.

Two

The representative from the bank arrived at exactly midday, and Ethan took an immediate dislike to the little man, with his cheap suit and pasty skin.

"Mr. Jackson?" he asked, approaching Ethan, who sat on the first step leading up to the three-storey colonial sandstone house set on top of a hill overlooking Emu Bay. His childhood home was one of the grandest in all of Tasmania and was steeped in history. It was built in the 1870s and used as a customs house. Though officials quickly realised that it was pointless to have the customs house so far away from the bay, and they sold it to a rich landowner who made his money from high costs and indigenous slavery. The owner was murdered sometime in the late 1880s, and the house was used as a private residence ever since. Ethan's parents bought it a few years before he was born, and he spent his first fourteen years living there. He loved to explore the old halls and rooms, creating fantasies and adventures with his parents' encouragement. What they didn't encourage was climbing out the casement windows and along the ledges into locked rooms, but he did it anyway.

Ethan stood and nodded at the banker.

"I'm Nigel Witts, pleased to meet you," the man said and offered his hand.

Ethan ignored the proffered hand and asked, "What happens now?"

"Well, I go in and check to make sure all is in order while we wait for the removalists. We will then take possession of the items inside and sell them at auction." He pulled a key out of his pocket and said, "I'm afraid you must wait outside until I have finished my inspection."

Ethan shrugged and sat down, ignoring the man as he made some excuse about being required to follow the rules set by the bank. He soon realised Ethan wasn't listening and walked up the steps to the double entrance doors. He slotted in the thick brass key and turned it, pushing the doors open. They squealed, protesting at being opened for the first time in five years. Then the man disappeared into the darkness of the house and Ethan returned to brooding.

Half an hour later, a removalist truck arrived, and two men got out just as Nigel Witts appeared from inside the house. He'd spent his time opening the curtains to let some light in and checking the house for damage and any other noticeable issues.

"You can go inside if you'd like, Mr. Jackson," Nigel told him as he walked past to greet the removalists.

With nothing better to do other than watching them take away all he grew up with, he went up to the house and paused at the threshold, hand on the doorframe. This would be the first time he had entered the house since he had been caught breaking in five years ago. He looked in, the familiarity of the foyer washing over him, and hesitation warred in his mind. Then, taking a deep breath, he entered his childhood home.

The foyer was a three-story open space with a grand staircase directly in front leading to the second floor. The floor was covered in a layer of thick dust, though beneath it was a simple white ceramic tile. Wood-panelled walls spread through the entryway, and a large chandelier hung above. To the left and right were doors that led into entertainment areas and the kitchen, and more doors beyond the staircase led deeper into the house. Ignoring the first floor, he took the stairs to the second, where they switched back on both sides to the third. Here was the study, guest rooms and a large entertainment room they had converted into a place to display artefacts they had found during their searches.

Or at least ones they hadn't sold to bored rich people all over the world.

He went up to the third floor and turned down the hall to the far end where his old bedroom was located. He grabbed the dusty handle of his door, turned it, and pushed it open. The door creaked loudly as he stepped into his former bedroom.

It was empty. Everything he'd owned was removed when he moved out, and all that remained was dust, dust, and more dust. He walked to the far corner of the room and pulled back the thick, moth-eaten curtains, revealing a corner window that looked out over the bay. He unlatched and pushed them open and was welcomed with a chilly breeze. As he gazed down on the town centre, the port, and the bay beyond, memories flooded back to him: He was a child pretending he was a king lording over his subjects below, or a sailor trying to spot whales with his mother, or an astronomer looking at the moon with his father through a telescope.

A wave of nostalgia washed over him at the thoughts of a happier time, and he wiped at his eyes, the threat of tears overwhelming him. He left the room, closing the door behind him and heading down the hall to the room at the other end.

His parents' bedroom.

His hand hovered over the doorknob and he almost turned around, but he swallowed the lump in his throat and opened the door. The curtains had been opened and sunlight illuminated the room, the walls, and floor, seeming to drink in their first taste of natural light in years. Motes of dust danced in the beams and the white walls almost glowed.

Unlike Ethan's room, his parents' room at least had some traces of life. Against the far wall, covered in dust, was a king-size four-poster bed, the canopy drawn. Ethan remembered many mornings as a young boy when he would climb into bed with his parents, feeling warm and safe. Opposite the bed was an armoire, too heavy to move when the initial clean-out was done. Sitting on top of it was a ship's bell.

Ethan froze when he saw it. He'd forgotten about that bell. It was made of brass, an oxidised dull blue-green, and stencilled into it was the word '*Swallow*'. The bell had been discovered off the Blythe Head bluffs the day his parents went missing.

He knew this because he was the one who discovered it.

Three

Blythe Heads, Tasmania
Ten Years Ago

The water was freezing cold, but that didn't bother Ethan. He'd grown up in these waters and acclimated to them in his fourteen years, though he still wore a seven-millimetre wetsuit and neoprene hood. It was Tasmania after all, and the weather was rarely hot enough to warm the waters of the Bass Strait in summer, let alone in the middle of winter.

Equipped with a snorkel, mask, and fins, he glided through the waters just off Blythe Heads. He avoided the worn rocks that made up most of the terrain along this area of the coast until he was about a kilometre from the beach. Taking a deep breath through the snorkel, he submerged, kicking strongly to propel him deeper until he reached his targeted area: a cluster of large boulders ten or fifteen metres below the water.

Reaching the rocks, he steadied himself on them with one hand while checking his dive watch with the other. The time was 10:13 a.m., and he was almost twenty-five metres below the surface.

Holding his breath, he explored among the rocks, knowing he had five or so minutes before he would need to surface. That was the benefit of growing up near the ocean—he could explore deeper than most without the need for scuba gear. While he was a keen scuba diver, he preferred freediving. It felt liberating to be so far underwater with no equipment, no reliance on external devices. It was akin to a weightlifter benching a personal record or someone completing an ultra-marathon; just his body pushed to the limits.

The boulders were bare, anything attempting to grow on them blown away by the constant currents. But beneath them in the cracks, crevasses, and valleys created between boulders were grasses, soft coral, and kelp shielded from the currents. Ethan probed them, parting them gently, careful not to dislodge them while he searched.

After close to four minutes of searching and finding nothing, he kicked up. The day was overcast, and a icy wind was blowing when his head broke the surface. Ethan took in deep lungful's of air while the unprotected parts of his face stung like they were being assaulted by tiny pricks of ice.

Once he felt rested enough to return to his search, he took a deep breath and dove back down.

This time, he kept close to the floor, probing the rubble until he reached another cluster of boulders. He surfaced again and repeated the same process as before: recovery, rest, deep breath, dive. Another fifteen minutes of this process revealed nothing, and he surfaced one more time, disappointed.

The wind was still blowing relentlessly when his head broke the surface, and he shivered.

"I should have tried this in summer," he mumbled, wading in the water. Though he was accustomed to the cold Tasmanian waters, his body still lost heat, and he risked hypothermia.

Ethan put his face into the water and looked around. Thankfully, visibility was excellent, and he could map out his next route. The next set of rocks were deeper, starting at twenty metres and sloping down, further out to sea. This concerned Ethan. If what he was looking for wasn't here, it might have tumbled deeper than he originally anticipated, which would require a wider search area and the need for scuba gear. He didn't want the search to go on for much longer—he wanted to find it now.

He dove and reached the first rock, exploring around it but finding nothing but a school of blue-throated wrasse that scattered as soon as they saw him. He moved further along, following the decline of the rocky ground. He explored around each rock and crevice but found nothing except schools of fish and long grasses swaying in the currents and it was time to surface again.

Feeling dejected, Ethan hovered above one of the larger boulders, scanning the area. He felt his lungs beginning to burn and wondered how long he had been down on this dive.

Must be pushing five minutes now.

He sighed, letting out a flurry of bubbles that raced to the surface. It seems like it was going to be another failed search.

As good a time as any to go.

The water suddenly grew lighter as the sun broke through the clouds above the surface and traces of light moved along the rocks in a frantic dance. Lungs burning, he sighed again. Just as he was about to begin his ascent, a flicker of something shiny caught the corner of his eye. He turned and studied a rocky reef that led to a steep drop, maybe thirty metres deep. Only the strongest of grasses could cling to rocks with that type of drop.

There!

Buried among the rocks, something flashed each time a streak of sunlight passed over it. Despite his burning lungs, Ethan moved closer, staring at it. Whatever it was, it was extremely small, easy to miss among the rocks. The light rolled over it again and it flashed. Ethan caught the sight of metal and his heart skipped a beat.

That must be it!

His heart was racing. Despite the desperation to get a closer look, he noted the location of the item and kicked back to the surface. Ethan's lungs were close to bursting when his head emerged from the water. He spat out the snorkel mouthpiece and gasped for air, his chest heaving as his lungs tried to take in oxygen.

"Idiot!" he admonished himself, still sucking in deep breaths. But despite his anger at himself, he felt a familiar excitement building up in him. The idea that he had found it had his heart

34

racing, and he was giddy with joy. Even the increasingly cold water couldn't change his mood.

When his chest felt looser and his breathing was back to normal, he put the mouthpiece back in and looked down, trying to see if he could find the glinting metal. But the sun retreated behind the clouds, and he only saw the cluster of dull-coloured boulders, and the grasses and soft coral dancing among them.

"Okay, one more time," he said and took another deep breath through the snorkel and dove back under. He kicked hard until he reached the area where he had seen the metal and explored, parting the grasses and soft corals.

It was when he glided over a tall section of rocks that he saw it. A small piece of metal was buried beneath a pile of rocks. Ethan moved so close his mask almost touched it, and he saw the metal was attached to something larger. He ran his hand over it, the brass a dull blue-green and rough from corrosion, and began pulling the rocks away from it. They fell away like a pile of children's blocks until the top and side of a bell were exposed.

The rest of the bell was corroded, but not as bad. The little protection afforded by the rocks did enough that the stencilled-in name could be read: *Swallow*.

This was it. This was what he had been searching for these last four months. The bell of the schooner ship known as the *Swallow*.

The *Swallow* wrecked on October 14, 1876, after popping a plank and filling with water. The crew safely disembarked and watched the ship sink. It was one of almost a thousand wrecks that had happened in Tasmanian waters over the past two centuries. This was the last remaining element of the ship. The rest of it would be long gone, the wood rotted by the ocean water and destroyed by the strong current.

Ethan pried more rocks off, revealing more of the bell where molluscs had attached themselves to the lower portion of it. He tried to pull the bell out, but it was wedged solidly between three larger rocks. With his lungs burning, he decided he would have to come back with a boat and winch it out. He quickly piled the rocks back around it, giving it a little more protection and to ensure it didn't loosen before he came back, and then kicked to the surface.

When he was above water, he let out a little whoop of joy, happy he could finally claim a find all on his own. He noted the location using visual markers and the coordinates on his watch, and he made his way back to shore.

Ethan was halfway to shore when he heard the buzzing of a boat's motor. He looked back toward the open ocean, and speeding along the water, skimming the waves and spraying water behind it, was a police boat.

It was heading right toward him.

Four

Ethan raised both arms and waved, making sure the police boat saw him. He watched the officer standing near the bow point at him and yelled at the driving officer to slow down.

Ethan frowned. What did they want with him? He was doing nothing illegal.

Yet.

He waited as the boat throttled back and approached slowly. On the boat were two stern looking officers—one was driving the boat, the other Ethan knew.

"Sean," Ethan greeted as he waded in the gentle waves.

Sean Stirling was a constable with the Devonport Police Department. His brother, James, was a friend of Ethan's.

"Ethan," Sean returned. He was muscular and tall with brown eyes and short, brown hair. He looked like an older version of James.

"What's up, Sean?" Ethan asked.

Sean looked down at him with a grave face, and Ethan knew something was wrong.

"You better come with us."

Something was definitely up.

"What's wrong?"

Sean looked at him, chewing his lip, as if deciding whether to tell him the secret he currently held. After a minute, he said, "It's about your parents."

Ethan's heart shot up into his throat. "My parents? They're overseas at the moment."

"Look, just come with us," he said, holding out his hand. "It's better if we explain it down at the station."

Heart hammering, Ethan looked at the constable. A small part of him wondered if this was some kind of school prank. It was such unbelievable news. He wouldn't put it past some of the boys he knew to do something like this. But then he thought the better of it—this was a police officer, and there were no boys from school in sight. There was no way they were playing a trick on him.

He took the constable's hand and boarded the boat. Sean introduced the boat captain as Sergeant Matt Peterson.

"Do you have any clothes?" he asked him.

Ethan pointed toward the beach where the pack he'd brought with him was laying on the sand. "Over there," he told him.

"Put this on then," Sean said, handing him a blanket. "I'll get someone to pick them up."

Ethan took it and wrapped it around his shoulders as the boat swung around and headed west toward Burnie.

An hour later, Ethan was sitting in an interview room, still in his wetsuit. He'd declined the offer of clothes, but he had his hands around a hot chocolate that someone had made for him. It tasted terrible, like hot, flavourless water, but he appreciated the warmth it gave him. The room was bare, with cracked white walls and a cold metal table with metal chairs. It was functional but not comfortable.

Probably a tactic to make suspects feel ill at ease.

When he had arrived at the station, Sean brought him to this room and told him to sit tight. He said they would be as quick as they could and someone would be in with his pack as soon as possible. While he was waiting, Ethan wondered why Sean was even here. He was a constable at the Devonport cop shop, which was a forty-minute drive west of Burnie and wouldn't have had anything to do with his parents.

Then his mind turned to his parents, and his heart raced again. They were overseas, somewhere in England for work. He wondered what had happened to them. It couldn't be a plane crash since they were not due back for another week. An accident, then? Car? Robbery? Theft? Heart attack?

His mind was running through every possible scenario when the door opened and Peter Miller entered, followed by a stone-faced Sean Stirling.

Peter sat down opposite of Ethan and placed a manila folder on the table while Sean stood in the corner behind him.

"Ethan, thanks for coming in," Peter Miller said and held out his hand.

"What's this about?" Ethan asked, shaking the hand. "Something about my parents?"

Peter opened the envelope, picked up a pen, and said, "Can you please just answer a few questions before we get to it?"

Ethan nodded, but said nothing.

"First, who is looking after you at the moment?"

"My grandpa," Ethan said. Though "looking after" would be a gross overstatement. His grandpa was in his seventies and was losing his marbles, sometimes calling him David, his dad's name, or forgetting things. His driver's licence had been taken from him after he ran his car into a fence on an empty stretch of road.

"Can I call him? He will want to be here for this."

Ethan shook his head. "Don't bother. He's probably half cut at the pub by now."

Peter turned to Sean and there was some silent communication between them. Sean nodded and poked his head out of the room.

"Let's start with your full name," Peter said once Sean was back and leaning against the wall in the corner.

"Ethan Hannibal Jackson."

"Hannibal?" Sean asked, and then immediately looked abashed when the senior sergeant gave him a stern look.

"Mum and Dad love the story of Hannibal crossing the Alps...." He trailed off when he noticed neither Peter nor Sean had a clue what he was talking about. "Never mind."

Peter wrote his answer on a notepad and continued, "Can you confirm your home address?"

Ethan told him.

"And your parents' names?"

"You know this," Ethan said.

Peter put the pen down. "It's a process we have to follow."

"Then can we skip to the point?" Ethan said, exasperated.

Peter held up a hand. "A couple more questions. Please, bear with me."

He sighed. "David and Gemma Jackson."

"What do they do for their jobs?"

"They are archaeologists," he said. "And lecture at UTAS."

"And obviously they have the same address as you?"

Ethan nodded.

"And you said they were overseas?"

"That's right. In England."

"What were they doing there?"

Ethan shrugged. "I don't know. Something to do with their work."

"A dig?"

"Kind of. They were going to look at artefacts discovered underwater near Norfolk, I think. They were scarce with the details this time."

Peter raised an eyebrow. "'This time'? Do they normally tell you what they are doing on their trips?"

"Usually, yes."

"Why not this time?"

"I don't know," Ethan snapped. "Can you tell me what the hell is going on? Why are you asking about my parents? What happened to them?"

If Peter was affected by Ethan's outburst, his face didn't show it. Instead, he asked, "When are they due back?"

Ethan sighed. "Next week."

Peter wrote this final answer and then put his pen down. He clasped his hands together and suddenly had the look of a doctor about to deliver bad news. Ethan felt sweat drip down his forehead, worried what Peter would say.

"We've received word from London authorities that your parents have gone missing."

Ethan's eyes widened. "Missing? What do you mean *missing*?"

Peter flipped a page over in the folder and said, "Your parents were meant to meet someone yesterday, a woman named Andrea Gatting. Do you know her?"

"I've heard her name mentioned before," Ethan told him.

"But you don't know her?"

He shook his head. "She's visited once or twice before, but she and my parents always went into the study and locked the door. I've said hello, but that's about it."

Peter wrote this down in his notepad and then continued. "She said she'd collaborated with your parents in the past and that, according to her, your parents didn't show up to a planned meeting. She tried calling them, but there was no reply. She told the police it was unusual for them to miss a meeting without calling ahead, so she went to their hotel thinking they may have been delayed or caught up in something else, but the calls to the room were unanswered. The concierge was unable to help, so Andrea went to the police."

Ethan's heart felt like it was about to burst out of his chest. This could not be happening. There has to be a reasonable explanation for it all.

"Wh—what did the police find?"

"They took down all Andrea knew, which was very little, and searched your parents' hotel room. Everything looked pretty normal. Suitcases were there, unlocked. Beds had been slept in, there were toothbrushes and other toiletries in the bathroom—"

"What about CCTV?" Ethan interrupted, understanding that they hadn't left the hotel with their luggage.

Peter shook his head. "Nothing."

Ethan slumped in his chair, astonished. "How is that possible? What happened to them?"

"London police are trying to figure that out. They are trying to piece together the series of events leading up to their disappearance. The concierge said they left yesterday morning, and their schedule confirms they had a diving expedition planned in Norfolk. It was confirmed with the British Museum that they were working in collaboration on a discovery and they were confirmed to be on site, but stayed behind after everyone else for 'one last look.' The boat captain confirmed he took them back to land, and they got into their rental car, but that was the last time anyone could account for them."

Ethan felt cold all over, and it had nothing to do with just wearing a wetsuit. The rest of the interview was a blur, with Peter giving him as much information as he could and guaranteeing that the police were doing everything they could to find them.

Then he was suddenly back home, still in his wetsuit, his pack on the ground near the door. Sean waited with him until his Grandpa Mike got home.

Ethan remembered his grandpa's lack of reaction to the news and thought it was strange. He mumbled something about how it was "only a matter of time" before passing out drunk on the couch. Ethan convinced himself that it was just Grandpa being two sheets to the wind. He spent the rest of his time at home or at school feeling numb while waiting for news on his parents.

A week later, Peter informed him that the boat captain couldn't be found for follow-up questions.

Two days after that, Peter called him again and told him that the captain's body was found behind a pub dumpster in a Liverpool alleyway. The cause of death was a heart attack.

After that came the reporters. They appeared at his house and at school. They asked pointless questions about how he was feeling, and if there was any news about their disappearance, as if he alone possessed these answers.

Peter kept them at a respectful distance, and they mostly obliged.

Then they turned on him.

It was two or three weeks after the boat captain's death that Ethan went from having lost parents to having lost parents who were actually criminals. He was walking to school alone. The reporters observing from afar in the last couple of days. With no news to report, their interest was waning, but suddenly a man stuck a camera in Ethan's face while a woman walked with him step for step, microphone in hand, asking questions about the latest updates on his parents.

Then more appeared, as if out of nowhere, with more questions.

Thinking they'd been found, he stopped and asked with high hopes if they had been located, but the reporters only asked about their criminal activities. Rapid-fire questions assaulted him from all directions and didn't let up despite his confusion and repeatedly saying he had no idea what they were talking about. Eventually, he ran off into the safety of his school, leaving them behind.

Rumours swirled around school. Kids whispered behind their hands as he walked past, but no one let him in on the secret. Later that night, a visibly distressed Peter Miller visited and told him that the investigation into his parents had led them to discover evidence that they were selling artefacts on the black market. There was going to be a thorough investigation into their accounts, lives, and the lives of their family, including Ethan and his grandpa.

Learning that his parents had lied to him his entire life had rocked Ethan to the core, while Grandpa was unsurprised and later (after getting drunk) explained to Ethan that his parents had been involved in the black market since before he was born.

"How else could they afford this house?" he groused.

Ethan's life was turned upside down. He lashed out at anyone who he thought deserved it. Peter Miller tried his best to reel him in and encourage him to work it out of his system by doing something he enjoyed or would wear him down. Ethan tried exploring in the bush, away from everyone, or breaking into the abandoned buildings around the city centre or the abandoned paper mill.

It was a month later when he started searching for the bell again, feeling the need to do something to get his mind off everything that was going on. Once he found it, he hauled it out of the water and took it home. He put it on the armoire as a present for when they came home, his naïve fourteen-year-old mind still believing they were alive.

The next day, his dad's body—clad in his wetsuit—washed up on a beach in Hunstanton, not far from where they had dived. An autopsy performed on the body revealed the cause of death to be water in the lungs leading to suffocation.

The body of Ethan's mum, however, was never recovered.

She was officially considered lost at sea.

Five

Present day

Ethan left the bedroom and walked down the hall. He heard voices coming from the ground floor. He peered over the balcony to see Nigel talking to the removalists. Ethan took the stairs down one level and went into the study. Like the rest of the house, the study was laid with polished timber, though dull and dust-covered, with floor-to-ceiling bookcases lining the walls. A moth-eaten square rug the colour of spilled wine filled the centre of the floor, leading to a large mahogany desk in front of a rectangular window. The curtains were open and sunlight filtered in through the dirty window, dust motes dancing in the rays of light.

Ethan ran a hand over the desk's surface, leaving a trail in the thick dust. He remembered being in here as a child, reading while his dad did some paperwork, or sitting on his mum's lap while she explained the history behind a find they'd made or something she was researching. It was in this room that he developed his interest in, and love of, history and spoke with his parents of his desire to follow in their footsteps.

He snorted at that thought. "So much for that," he muttered, and sat down in the high-backed chair. The leather creaked and dust puffed up, but he didn't care. He ran his hand along the surface and the sides of the desk, feeling the mountains carved into the legs. His mind wandered as his fingers probed the carved peaks and valleys of the mountains and the engraved elephants. He remembered his parents had this desk custom made after one of their trips, a decision that seemed sudden. He was lost in that thought until his finger depressed a notch in the desk.

Ethan frowned and looked at where his finger was resting on the depiction of a man standing at the head of the herd of elephants. The man was dressed in thick winter clothing and seemed to lead the elephants. Thinking it was a broken piece, he pushed it again, and it clicked in like a button. A small, rectangular panel popped open on the left side, just above the first mountain peak.

Behind the panel were four rotatable disks depicting the numbers zero through nine.

A combination lock?

"They must have had this built in. But why? And what's the code?" Ethan wondered.

He tried several possibilities—birth years, anniversaries, but each code produced no result. Frustrated, he sat back and looked at the carvings in the desk. He was about to give up when he saw a carving that gave him an idea. He noticed there were four mountains engraved in the desk and there were elephants under three of them, all of them facing toward the man, who was waiting for them. The first peak had zero elephants underneath it and the second had two. On a hunch, he turned the first dial to zero and the second to two. The next peak had one, so he turned the third disk to one. The last peak, the one closest to the man, had eight elephants moving toward him. Rotating the final disk to eight, he heard a click, and a drawer popped out from the skirt of the desk.

"I should have known… 218 B.C.," he muttered. That was the year Carthaginian General Hannibal Barca crossed the Alps with his war elephants and march into Northern Italy during the second of the three Punic Wars.

He pulled the drawer out, and inside it was a book. Ethan picked it up and placed it gently on the desk. After checking for anything else but finding nothing, he closed the drawer and turned his focus back to the book. It was cracked with age and encased in brown leather with a plain front.

He opened it and instantly recognised his dad's handwriting. He scanned the pages and realised it wasn't a book but his dad's journal, filled with his musings and thoughts about various projects he'd worked on over the years. Ethan was browsing near the end and wondering why his dad had hidden it when a sketch caught his eye. It was a drawing of a chest. Ethan's dad, much like Ethan himself, liked to draw and sketch things he had seen or imagined. Ethan had books full of sketches of architecture and famous buildings, and even the mundane things he'd seen around town. His dad had drawings of artefacts, sites, and discoveries he'd made and used them to chronicle his finds. Some of those journals had been used to write now-discredited books and texts (though there was an immediate surge in sales after the news came out about their illegal activities), while the original journals were now in a box at Ethan's place, some of the few items he took with him when he moved out of the house.

The chest looked like a treasure chest you'd see in movies and kids' books, though this one was finely detailed with swirls etched into the sides and had five panels on the front. The panels had images carved into them, but they were faint and vague. Ethan couldn't make them out.

Beneath the picture was the word 'Spanish?' with an arrow pointing to the chest. Taped below that was a receipt from a place called Sotheby's Auction House, in Marylebone, England. It was only dated a few months before his parents died. The receipt didn't say what was bought, only the item number 83450-3512-329, and that it was purchased for… "Seventy-five thousand dollars!" he said, almost shouting it. "What the hell did they buy?"

Pulling his phone out, he searched for the Sotheby's Auction House website. Selecting the "Closed Auctions" tab, he put the number in the search field and submitted.

The result came back listed as "The Diary of Robert Maynard," with the following description:

Own a piece of rare British naval history as we put up the diary of eighteenth-century Lieutenant Robert Maynard of His Majesty's Royal Navy for sale. Lieutenant Maynard was famous for defeating the infamous pirate Blackbeard in a bloody battle on November 22, 1718.

This diary documents the fantastical details of his life, his beginnings in the navy to the end of his life in 1751, and gives the reader a rare look into the life of a British naval officer and life in the eighteenth century.

The diary has been maintained to the highest standards and is in exceptional condition. Don't miss out on your chance to have this unique piece of history.

Est. value: $1500

Fifteen hundred dollars? Why did they pay seventy-five thousand for it?

Knowing his parents, it was important. There was no way they would spend so much on a journal from a British officer— even if he had his place in history—if they weren't working on something related to it.

He went back to the auction house homepage and found their email address and sent them an email, explaining that his parents purchased the diary and he was wondering why it went for so much over the estimated value.

Pocketing his phone, he returned to the journal. The next few pages were his dad's notes on Maynard and his life after North Carolina and the death of Blackbeard. One note read:

History says that Maynard essentially disappeared from public life, but I'm not sure I buy it. After such a successful, if not brutal, defeat of Blackbeard the pirate, he would have become a favourite of the Royal Navy, but, instead, he stagnated and retired almost two years after the events at Ocracoke Island. It doesn't make sense.

There were notes added to this in his mum's handwriting, questioning if Maynard found something and pursued it.

He flipped over the page and found the last entry:

Gemma and I are on to something here, that much I am sure of. We thought it strange that Maynard disappeared from all records after he killed Blackbeard, and we know nothing of what happened to him between 1718 and his death in 1751.

We did some research into his life between those times. There is so little record of him that when we saw his diary was up for auction for such a measly sum, we decided it was worth looking into, even if it just satisfied our curiosity.

But then the bidding began. The bids got higher, and we thought something strange was going on. We were knocked out of the race when our bid of seven thousand dollars was upped to seventy-five thousand by the opponent. We couldn't match that bid and we suspected the mysterious bidder would have gone even higher.

Our interest was too piqued to leave empty-handed. Before the winning bidder took possession of the diary, we managed to acquire it along with a copy of the receipt.

The diary was a gold mine of information, but it brought heat that we never expected.

Ethan stopped to take in what he had just read.

"They stole the diary?"

He thought back to before they died and tried to remember if they took any trips overseas, but nothing came to mind. However, he remembered a long weekend when he stayed with Grandpa Mike while his parents went on a quick getaway. Was that an excuse? Did they go to Sotheby's and steal the diary then?

Pulling his phone out again, he searched for "Sotheby's" and "theft" and the year the diary was sold. The top news article was dated not long after the auction of Maynard's diary. It was titled:

Theft at Sotheby's Auction House.

Police are appealing for witnesses who might have any information on a break-in that occurred at Sotheby's Auction House over the weekend. Police have confirmed that only one item was stolen, the diary of eighteenth-century naval officer Robert Maynard, legendary for his defeat of the pirate Blackbeard.

The rest of the article talked about Maynard and who to contact if they had any information.

He put his phone away and sat in stunned silence. With everything that had happened since their deaths and the allegations involved, he knew this shouldn't be a surprise, but it was. It seemed all too surreal.

Was it all related to their death?

He continued reading his dad's journal:

While he did not outright say it, it seems that Maynard was involved in something big. Something to do with a treasure. He worked for decades hiding it because he feared the repercussions if it was found. He called it a "voodoo-cursed treasure."

This has both of us stumped, and we cannot find anything on Maynard's travels after 1718. British history isn't our forte, so we have asked Andrea for help. If she doesn't know, she will know someone who does. While she is no longer in the game, we think this will pique her interest. Gemma and I have an upcoming trip to an underwater site in Norfolk to investigate. While we are there, we will meet up with Andrea and see what we can brainstorm.

"Andrea," he murmured the name, remembering it coming up in the interviews and subsequent investigation.

She'd been cleared of any involvement in their disappearance, but that didn't mean she didn't know something. It was known that his mum and dad were going to meet with her, but she said it was for business, which was technically true. Now, with this information, Ethan wondered if he might be able to get more out of her. Ask her why she didn't mention the real reason for their planned meet.

And what game was she no longer a part of?

"What were you guys up to?" he murmured.

He was about to continue reading when he heard footsteps thudding on the floorboards. Ethan quickly shut the journal as Nigel entered the study, followed by two burly men wearing blue coveralls.

Nigel barely gave Ethan a passing glance as he said to the two men, "Everything in here as well."

Then he turned and left the room, followed by the removalists.

Ethan sighed and felt despair setting in. This chapter of his life was closing, and he didn't want to be here for it.

Night had fallen, and Ethan was sitting at the bar of the only pub in town that would have him as a patron. He'd been kicked out or banned from the others, so the Spring Street Pub across the road from the TasRail rail yard was his only choice to get a drink.

An untouched beer sat in front of him as he pondered the

journal that sat on the bar. His phone buzzed, breaking him out of his thoughts.

It was a reply from Sotheby's, which politely but curtly stated they could not divulge any personal information regarding that sale.

Ethan wasn't surprised. It was a long shot, anyway. He flipped open the journal. Now that he knew they went to England for another reason, he wondered if investigating Maynard was what got them in trouble. He never believed they died while diving. They'd been diving for decades in the toughest and coldest environments. They knew how to handle themselves.

It never made sense to him.

Despite the news of their black market dealings coming as a shock to him, he still knew them well enough to know that equipment malfunction, as the official report stated, seemed unlikely. He thought back on the report, which stated that because of the theft of their equipment from their hotel room, they had to use borrowed equipment from the dive company. The report said the equipment was not maintained to appropriate standards and was the likely reason for their deaths.

But Ethan remembered being told by Peter that the dive operator swore their equipment was serviced and of the highest quality. He didn't believe the man, but the British police did, and there was nothing that could be done, no matter how many times he asked Peter to try. Now, with all this new information, maybe Peter was telling the truth, but it just left more questions. Who did they steal Maynard's diary from? And did they find out his parents stole it? If they did, did they break-in and steal their dive gear and sabotage their rental equipment?

Then there was the boat captain who said he brought them back, which was clearly a lie. He was found dead not long after. Was it a coincidence, or was there something more sinister going on?

After years of questions and getting no answers, Ethan started believing in the stories that it was just a freak accident. David Jackson had washed up on shore and Gemma Jackson had sunk to Davy Jones' locker—he had accepted those as fact. Now, with the discovery of the journal in his dad's desk, he started rethinking it all over again.

He flipped the diary to the last page, rereading the last entry. They stole a diary and discovered something about Maynard, but the only person they mentioned it to was Andrea. It was strange how she mentioned nothing about Maynard in the reports. Pulling out his phone, he logged into his dad's email and browsed through his contacts. Finding Andrea's name and a number attached to it, he rang it and, after a couple of seconds of silence as it connected to the UK, he was greeted with an automated voice telling him the number was no longer in service. Finding an email address in the contacts, he sent off an email explaining who he was, and that he wanted to speak to her about his parents, though he didn't mention anything about Robert Maynard or the journal he found.

After flipping through the journal yet again, Ethan found another page that gleaned more information—an entry written by his mum. Her swooped handwriting read:

Maynard frequently wrote about Jesus in his diary, focusing a lot on

Him being a Martyr and comparing it to his own plight. It seems Maynard believed that after his success in defeating Blackbeard he was due more than his share of the reward since his crew did the dirty work.

He wrote about how he took ninety pounds from Blackbeard's body and distributed it among his own men—something he thought was a noble act. However, once it was discovered that he had taken the money, he was reprimanded and passed over for any promotion within the Royal Navy.

Maynard believed he was made a Martyr for all things that happened afterward. When examining Teach's body, Maynard discovered a letter from Teach to Tobias Knight, the secretary to North Carolina Governor Charles Eden, indicating Governor Eden was colluding and profiting from Blackbeard's piracy, perhaps receiving a cut of the booty.

Governor Eden was tried and found not guilty. Since the Governor was untouchable, Maynard believes they blamed him for the greater good of the Royal Navy and the British Occupation of the Americas and Caribbean.

It's clear this did not sit well with him, and in the immediate aftermath of Governor Eden being found not guilty, Maynard writes about an opportunity presented to him. If this offer was what he believed it to be, it would make him wealthier than any Naval Commander could ever be. He didn't mention who had presented the opportunity to him, but whoever they were, they were planning on working together.

In one of his last entries before he died, Maynard writes about his great regret in the discovery but does not go into detail what the discovery was or where he made it—only that he had no means to destroy it, so he had taken great pains to hide it so it will be lost to history forever.

David and I are sure Maynard discovered a vast treasure, but he believed it to be cursed or 'voodooed' as he called it. We believe Maynard

made notes in his diary during his search for the treasure, and notes after
the discovery. These notes have been torn out and presumably destroyed.
Whatever he discovered, it spooked him enough to hide all traces of it.

In his final entry, two years before his death, he wrote:

Attached to the diary was a photocopy of the entry Ethan's
mother was referring to. It said:

13 August 1749

I have returned home from my voyage to hide that voodoo-cursed
treasure. Everyone who knows about it has been eliminated, except the
Blue Men of the Desert, but they will take care of themselves. That is the
nature of the curse after all. I am the last remaining person alive to know
of its whereabouts and its secrets and I will happily go to my grave with
God at my side before I speak of its ultimate resting place.

I can live the rest of my life knowing that what started out as a journey
for greed has ended as an act for the greater good. Like Jesus AND his
disciples, I will always be BORN A MARTYR and will be BURIED as
one.

His mum's notes continued afterward:

We believe Maynard hadn't completely eradicated the treasure from
history. While he may not want to speak of it to anyone, there are clues to
its whereabouts, and it starts with his burial site.

We will have to be careful. I don't know if I am being paranoid since the
trip to London, but I feel like we're being followed…

"Followed," Ethan murmured. "By whom? The original
owner of the diary? If so, did they have anything to do with their
deaths?"

Ethan read and reread his parents' entries, trying to find any
clues or hints, but after an hour, he realised he was just stalling.

He took one last swig of his beer, as if he needed the courage to confirm what he was going to do next, and picked up his phone. He had one new email, but it was a bounce-back stating the email address for Andrea Gatting doesn't exist.

There was nothing he could do from Tasmania, but he had new information and a tenuous spark of hope that was at risk of being extinguished by the slightest breeze. But maybe it would lead him to some answers. If he followed in their footsteps, maybe he would find out who murdered his parents.

He dialled a number, and when it was answered, he said, "Yes, I need a ticket on the next available flight to London, please."

Six

London, England

The flight to London took Ethan from Launceston to Melbourne, then Singapore, before landing at Heathrow Airport. It was another two hours before he checked into his modest motel in Bedford Place, almost thirty-five hours after he departed.

Exhausted, Ethan was grateful to check in immediately, and he crashed on top of his bed, fully clothed, and slept like the dead.

The next morning he was still jet-lagged but feeling fresher. After a shower, he left his motel in search of something to eat.

The day was cool and crisp, with clear blue skies. The sounds of cars and horns echoed off the tall, Georgian-style brick buildings that lined both sides of the street. The ground floors were all painted white, while subsequent floors exposed the brown brick with white, rectangular windows.

Ash trees alternated with standing streetlights along the footpath, and Ethan crossed into Russell Square. Named after the fifth Duke of Bedford in 1804, Russell Square was a square park surrounded by holm oak and yew trees. A paved circle with a fountain sat in the centre of the square, with benches spread around the perimeter.

Nearby was a coffee van where Ethan bought a cup and a muffin and took a seat on a bench. He pulled out his phone and opened his email app. Before his flight, he found another email address for Andrea Gatting in his dad's contacts and sent another email. It didn't send a bounce-back, so he had hope it was current.

There was nothing from her, so he sent off another and, with nothing else to do, waited. As he watched people hurrying across the square, coffee in their hands, heading to work or the tube, he wondered what he would do if Andrea didn't get back to him.

She was the last person to hear from his parents, and she worked closely with them from time to time, according to Dad's notes. While he was sure the police did a thorough job of questioning her, she didn't mention anything about Maynard's diary. Even if she wasn't involved, it sounded like she had knowledge of its theft. Maybe if he confronted her about it, she could connect some dots for him.

He knew it was a long shot, but he had to try, otherwise he was down to one last option: the gravesite of Robert Maynard himself. He couldn't imagine what that would do to help him, but his parents noted it down for a reason, so it must have meant something.

Although apparently, they were black market dealers, so maybe I didn't know them at all.

That thought left a bitter taste in his mouth, forcing him to throw his almost empty coffee cup into a nearby trash can. He pulled his phone out of his pocket and checked his email again, but there was still nothing from Andrea.

"Another useless email," he complained. "Christ, I have no idea if she is even in London or what she does."

Opening his internet browser, he searched for "Andrea Gatting" and turned up hundreds of social media accounts. Groaning, he added "London" to the search string and, while still getting social media profiles, there were fewer this time.

He switched from search results to image results, hoping he might find her from a photo from a business profile or something. He wasn't sure he would be able to recognise her. The two or three times she came to the house, he barely caught of glimpse of her before she was rushed into the study. As far as he was concerned, she was one of many, and frequent, acquaintances that visited the house to talk shop.

Scrolling through the photos, he stopped on a picture of an attractive, middle-aged woman with pale skin and long, dark hair. She was wearing a suit and standing with her hands clasped in front of her. She had a faint scar that ran from the temple to the top of her cheekbone on the right side of her face, and she wasn't shy about it, showing it off rather than hiding it. But it was her eyes that caught his attention: almond-brown, and even from the portrait photo he could see they were intense, as if they were judging his every move. It jolted a memory loose in his head.

It was ten years ago, just before his parents died. His mum and dad had just come back from a long weekend away and told him they were heading to England in a week or two. He asked if he could come, but they said no. He was downstairs in the lounge room, focused on a video game, when he heard a knock at the door.

"Ethan, where are you?" his mum called out.

Ethan, still sulking at being told he couldn't go to England with them, didn't reply.

There was another knock at the door.

"Ethan?" His mum appeared at the entrance to the lounge. Upon seeing him heavily involved in his game, she sighed and said, "Your father and I will be upstairs for a while. Lunch is on the counter if you want it."

He grunted but kept his eyes on the game.

Sighing again, she slid the doors closed, and he heard her footsteps retreating down the hall.

Ethan paused the game and looked at the closed doors, frowning.

Must be someone important.

He got up from the couch and approached the doors, sliding them a crack. Just enough that he could see his mum and dad greeting someone at the door.

They stood back, and a woman entered. Ethan couldn't see much of her, as she was hidden behind his parents, but he guessed she was in her thirties. She had long, straight, black hair and wore a dark business dress and carried a briefcase.

"Andrea, it's been too long," his father said, shaking her hand.

Ethan thought she looked like a lawyer and out of place among his parents' other friends. They usually consisted of archaeologists wearing dirty khakis and hiking shirts, or scholars wearing vests and slacks. If it were one of their usual friends, Ethan would have gone back to his game, but seeing someone new proved more interesting.

"David, you are looking well," Andrea said in a London accent. She turned to his mum. "And Gemma, gorgeous as ever."

Gemma laughed and said, "You always were a flatterer, Andrea. Would you like a drink?"

They headed down the hall, and Ethan ducked back as they passed the lounge doors. He poked his head back out as Andrea said, "That would be great. It's been a long day, and I am feeling a might tired."

"Did your talk at the university go well?"

"As well as could be, Gemma. You know students—don't have quite the attention span to listen to me drone on about business for three hours."

They moved into the kitchen where his dad said, "If what we have to show you is what we think it is, then it will be the pick-you-up that you need."

Andrea laughed. "That sounds both mysterious and enticing, David."

There was silence and then Ethan heard glasses clinking together and the telltale squeak of the liquor cabinet being opened. It was followed by the thud of a bottle on the bench top and then a call of cheers before they clinked glasses.

After another moment of silence, Andrea asked, "I'd like to hear about this purchase you made."

Purchase?

Ethan was usually aware of any artefacts his parents had bought to display in the house, or donations they had made to various museums and collections around the world. As far as he was aware, they hadn't made any purchases for a long time, and nothing big had arrived at the house recently.

His parents, followed by Andrea, emerged from the kitchen and headed to the staircase. "It's in the study. We'll talk there," his mother said, and they headed upstairs.

Ethan exited the lounge and stopped at the foot of the staircase. He heard the thudding of footsteps on the floor above and then a door closing. Slipping his shoes off, Ethan padded noiselessly up the stairs in his socks. Once he reached the landing, he turned and walked down the hall to the study.

The study door, like every other door in the house, was made of oak, with a faded brass handle and warded lock. He grabbed the handle and gently turned it, but it resisted. It was locked.

Strange, he thought. In the past, when his parents wanted privacy to talk to someone, they would come in here, but Ethan could always open the door a crack to listen. This was the first time he could remember it being locked.

Ethan peered through the keyhole and could see the corner of the ornate desk that sat in the centre of the room and the open window beyond, but nothing else. He placed his ear against the door and listened, but the door blocked out all sound except the muffled conversation.

Intrigued by the secrecy of this meeting, Ethan hurried back down the hall and up the stairs to his room, grabbing a pair of hiking shoes. Then he went back down to the second floor and into a guest bedroom next to the study. He pulled on his shoes and pushed open the double-bay windows. He was greeted with a gust of fresh air and a view of the Burnie docks where ships were unloading cargo. Beyond that, he saw boats making their way out of Emu Bay and into the Bass Strait.

Ethan stepped out of the window onto the cornice that ran around the entire length of the house. The cornice was made of stone and was about the width of his shoe. Closing one of the bay windows so he could move past it, he slowly shuffled across the ledge, hands, and back against the rough and irregular stone surface.

It wasn't the first time Ethan had climbed across the outside of the house and the thrill it gave him now was identical to the first time he tried it out of boredom. He shuffled across until he reached the study. The bay windows were open, allowing him to hear his parents and their guest talking inside.

"This is an interesting theory, David. But do you believe it?" It was Andrea talking.

"I'm not sure. It sounds fantastical, but this wouldn't be close to the strangest thing we've discovered. If it is true," his dad replied.

"Do you have any other evidence, or is this page all there is to it?" Andrea asked.

Ethan peered into the room and saw his dad sitting in a chair with his mum peering over his shoulder while Andrea sat in the chair next to him. They were looking at something on the desk, but Ethan wasn't tall enough to see what it was.

"We are working on different theories and plans," his mum said. "This is just an investigation into the possibility of it being real."

Andrea took a drink and said, "Don't get me wrong, you guys are some of the best at what you do, and I am not trying to discourage anything here. But Paititi is just a rumour. There isn't any evidence to suggest it exists, just a lot of wild goose chases. It's another Atlantis."

"You could be right," said his dad. "But it's worth checking out. This script is written by Pope Clement IX himself and it details the evidence obtained by Spanish conquistadors in the late sixteenth century."

Ethan stood on his toes and leaned over a bit more, trying to catch a glimpse of what they were looking at when Andrea spoke again. "This might be real," she began, "but it's quite a stretch. It's information the Spanish stole, translated into Spanish from Incan, and then translated again into Italian. *After* it was locked in a vault for a century. It's third-hand information. I'm not sure my clients would be interested, but I will pass it on to them."

"And the fee?"

"If they find it, they will cut you in for fifteen percent."

"Fifteen? But you said twenty-five," his dad argued.

Andrea held out her hands. "The best you'll get is twenty."

His dad sighed and said, "It will have to do."

"You said there was something else."

"Yes." It was his mum speaking now. "This is off the books, right?"

"Of course," Andrea said.

She pulled something out of the desk drawer. "We… recovered this diary of an old British naval officer."

"Is that right?"

"Yes."

"I heard through the grapevine that a diary was stolen from an auction house last week. A diary of an eighteenth-century navy lieutenant."

"We wouldn't know anything about that," his mum replied, but Ethan could hear the smile in her voice. She flipped open the diary and turned it around to show Andrea. "This was in it."

"You mean you think this leads to—what the?" she yelped.

Ethan looked up from the desk, and his eyes locked with hers.

The last thing he saw were those intense almond-brown eyes before he slipped from the ledge.

Ethan stared at the photo on his phone. It was her. It had to be. The dark hair, the business suit, the intense eyes. Only the scar was new. Clicking on the photo, it took him to a "Meet the Team" page of a consultancy firm called Provolution, where Andrea Gatting was an executive.

Heart racing, he pressed on the "Contact Us" page and found a number for the firm.

He dialled the number and waited as it rang and rang and —

"Good morning, this is Amy from Provolution speaking."

"Ah… hi," Ethan said, suddenly aware he had no idea what to say. "I'm… um… looking to speak with Andrea Gatting."

"I'm sorry, sir. We don't accept unsolicited sales calls—"

"I'm not a salesman," Ethan interjected before she could end the call. "I'm a friend. My name is Ethan, and it's very important I speak with her."

There was a pause at the other end of the line, and Ethan wondered if she was about to hang up on him.

"Eric, did you say?"

"No, Ethan. Ethan Jackson."

"Hold please."

Ethan waited as he was put on hold, recognising the hold music to be from the opera "Il barbiere di Siviglia" by Gioachino Rossini. He thought this firm must be fancy if they were using something other than the standard hold music or common classical hold music like Beethoven's Fifth. Moments later, Amy came back and said, "I'm sorry, Mr. Johnson, but Ms. Gatting is busy all day with meetings and has asked not to be disturbed. Goodbye."

"But—"

The phone went dead before he could protest.

"Shit," he muttered. He fiddled with his phone, considering calling back, but he replayed the conversation in his head. There was a notable difference in Amy's voice after she came back, making him wonder what had happened while he was on hold.

Sitting back on the bench, he thought about what to do next. He could call back and lie, saying he was someone else, but even if he got through, Andrea could hang up on him once he told her who he really was. He was willing to give her the benefit of the doubt in that she didn't realise who he was, given his parents died ten years ago and she barely knew he existed.

No, he thought. *I need to see her in person.* She had no chance of distancing herself from him that way. Browsing back to the "Contact Us" page on the firm's website, he found their address and put it into the maps app on his phone. It wasn't that far away.

Wasting no more time, Ethan pocketed his phone and left Russell Square, heading for the tube.

Seven

Ethan took the tube from Holbrook to Liverpool Street, and less than an hour later, he arrived at Broadgate Tower in London's Financial District.

His mind turned back to the day he spied on Andrea and his parents in the study, more memories coming back to him. After he slipped, he had managed to grab hold of the ledge and his parents hauled him in. Andrea had disappeared, and Mum and Dad had scolded him for doing something so stupid. Later that night, after they had calmed down, he asked them what the meeting was about, but they told him it was nothing, just business.

Another sign that naïve fourteen-year-old Ethan missed. His parents always included him in their work, keeping him involved with their historical research. It was why he always got straight A's in history and had a natural curiosity that led him to exploring and climbing in places he shouldn't be.

Like the secret compartment in the desk, this is just another secret they kept from me. All those allegations about them were true. I guess I didn't know them at all, he thought bitterly.

Broadgate Tower was built in the early 2000s and consisted of a narrow, thirty-three-storey building with a similar thirteen-storey building next to it called 201 Bishopsgate. Both buildings were panelled in glass from bottom to top on all sides, providing a 360-degree view overlooking London.

Ethan walked into the courtyard that separated Bishopsgate and Broadgate, where it was busy with corporate types discussing business as they headed to lunch or whatever meeting they had next. There were restaurants and pop-up stores littered about the undercover walkway. The smells from the variety of foods reminded Ethan that he hadn't eaten anything except for a muffin. Leaving the walkway, he passed through the revolving doors into the Broadgate Tower foyer.

The foyer was bright, clean, and functional, and busy with people walking to and from the escalators leading further into the building. Ethan checked the building's index and found Provolution occupied the thirtieth and thirty-first floors. He went up the escalators to a bank of elevators and pressed the up button.

The elevator arrived, and he entered, pressing the button for the thirtieth floor. The button light flashed briefly before going dark. He tried it again, but the same thing happened.

"Is something wrong?"

Ethan looked up to see a middle-age lady in a business suit looking at him.

"I'm trying to get to level thirty," Ethan told her.

She gave him an appraising look, noting his jeans and jacket, and asked, "Do you work there?"

Ethan shook his head. "I'm… meeting someone."

More people were getting into the elevator now.

"You'll have to speak to the receptionist then," she told him.

Ethan nodded his thanks and left the elevator, heading back down the escalators. He approached a curved reception desk where he was greeted by a well-groomed man who gave him a smile.

"Hello, how may I help you?"

"Hey," Ethan said, "I'm trying to get to the thirtieth floor to meet someone."

"Provolution? I'll have to call up. What is your name and who are you meeting?"

"Ethan Jackson, meeting Andrea Gatting."

"One moment," the receptionist said. He put on a headset and dialled a number.

"Hello. It's Gary at reception. I have a Mr. Ethan Jackson here to see Andrea Gatting." He paused for a breath and then said, "Sure."

Gary looked up at Ethan. "Just a moment," he repeated.

Ethan nodded.

"Yeah?" Gary said into the headset after half a minute. He looked at Ethan. "Do you have an appointment?"

"Ah… no," he said sheepishly.

Gary frowned. "I'm sorry, Mr. Jackson, but Miss Gatting is very busy and cannot take cold callers."

"What? I'm not trying to sell anything."

Gary looked him up and down, clearly not believing him.

Ethan sighed. "Fine," he grumbled, and stalked away.

Leaving Broadgate Tower, he took a seat near a pop-up food van selling Mexican food. The smell made his stomach rumble, and he decided he needed to eat and think about what to do next. He ordered a burrito and a drink and slumped down at a rickety metal table with uneven legs. Staring forward at the building's revolving doors, he willed an idea to come to him.

He supposed he could wait here until the workday finished, but without knowing how Andrea travelled to work, it would be pure luck if she happened to leave through the front entrance. He wondered if there was a basement she might use instead. The risk was too great. He had to see her before heading to Maynard's gravesite, which he thought would be less likely to reveal anything about his parents than Andrea walking out of those revolving doors.

"Hey, buddy, your order is up," a voice said, breaking Ethan out of his reverie.

Ethan went to pick up his order but was cut off by a man wearing cycling gear carrying a heavy satchel strapped diagonally across his shoulder.

"Hey, Juan, can I have the usual and extra quick, if possible? I got a ton of deliveries to make before the day is out."

Ethan was about to say something when an idea struck him. After the messenger moved aside, he said to the chef, "Hey, can I get this to go?"

Ethan sat in the foyer of Broadgate Tower waiting for Gary the receptionist to leave his desk. At his feet was a brown bag with his now-cold lunch in it. It was almost one o'clock when a young girl approached Gary. They spoke for a few seconds before Gary got up, grabbed a bag from under the desk, and walked around the counter, waving to her as he left.

Seeing his opportunity, Ethan grabbed his lunch bag and approached the counter. The new receptionist looked up at him and smiled. She was young, about Ethan's age, with bright blue eyes and blond hair, the nametag pinned to her top reading "Jasmine."

"Good afternoon," she said with a bright smile. "How may I help you?"

"Hello," Ethan said quickly, as if in a hurry. "I have a lunch delivery here for a—" he pulled out his phone and pretended to read off the screen, "Andrea Gatting, at… Provolution?" he looked at her as if seeking confirmation that he got it right.

Jasmine nodded and reached out her hand. "I can take it and call to have someone pick it up."

Ethan shook his head. "Usually I would, but the last guy who made a delivery to her almost got fired because she thought he stole food from her. He denied it, but considering he handed it over to reception, there's a lot of 'he said, she said' going on. So I have to give it to her myself and she has to confirm everything and sign off on it. It's annoying, I know, since I have a ton of other deliveries to make today, but we have to protect ourselves, you know?"

Jasmine smiled at him. "I get it. I'll call her now and see if she can come down."

She picked up the phone and dialled a number. "Hi, Amy. It's Jasmine at reception. I have a delivery here for Andrea Gatting that she needs to sign for. Yep. Okay. Thanks, Amy."

She hung up the phone and said, "She will be down shortly if you want to wait over there," pointing off to the side.

Ethan nodded his thanks and walked to a row of seats to wait.

Five minutes later, Ethan saw a woman with black hair and a scar near her eye approach Jasmine. She spoke to her and Jasmine pointed at Ethan.

Andrea nodded and walked over to Ethan. "You have something for me?" she asked.

Ethan handed her the brown paper bag. She looked at it wearily, which was understandable considering it didn't look at all official, and opened it.

She looked in the bag and then back at him. "Is this some sort of joke?"

"Actually, it's my lunch," Ethan said, snatching the bag back from her.

"Who are you?" she asked, brown eyes narrowed, as if trying to work out where she had seen him before.

"Ethan Jackson," he told her.

"Ethan…" Her eyes went wide. "Gemma and David's boy?"

He nodded. "That's right. I've been trying to get in contact with you."

"You were the one who called this morning? But Amy told me it was an Eric… Johnson or something."

"She must have gotten my name confused, but yes, that's right. I need to talk to you about Mum and Dad."

Andrea's eyes softened. "Ethan, it's been ten years. I told everything I knew to the police. I don't know what else I can tell you."

"Why didn't you mention Maynard's diary?" he asked, more sharply than he had intended.

She looked at him, as if weighing something in her mind, before she finally said, "I think we should talk in my office."

Eight

Calling Andrea's office, an office was like calling a sword a butter knife. It was set in the corner of the thirty-first floor and had a sprawling view of London through two glass walls that looked out as far as the Thames and St. Paul's Cathedral. The office itself was quite spacious. A desk with a laptop and screen sat along the glass back wall. A small table and three chairs sat along the glass wall to its right, looking out toward Fenchurch Street and the Gherkin, one of London's more famous contemporary buildings. On the wood-panelled wall to the left of the desk was a large bookshelf filled with blood-red leather-bound books and business awards that surrounded a mounted television. In front of it was a brown leather couch.

"Please take a seat, Ethan," Andrea said, leading him into the office and gesturing to the couch. He took a seat while she shut the heavy glass door.

Ethan admired the office. "What is it your company does, Miss Gatting?" he asked, curiosity getting the better of him.

Andrea took a seat on the couch and said, "We're a consultancy firm. Advising to businesses, getting them on track, stuff like that. It's not very interesting."

"The perks seem to be worth it, though," Ethan commented.

Andrea nodded absently. "Would you like a drink? Coke? Juice?"

"I'm fine, thanks," he said.

"Gosh, I can't believe you're all grown up. I remember the last time I saw you was when you were out on that ledge at your parents' place." She chuckled, shaking her head. "I swear Gem had a heart attack when she saw you."

Ethan smiled at the memory. "I got in a lot of trouble for that."

"Gem and David always said you were getting into mischief, harmless though it was, and trying to get into places you were not meant to be. I remember David saying if you were denied access somewhere that you would always find a way in, and it usually involved climbing something to get there. I see not much has changed, though I hope you aren't still climbing things," she mused.

Ethan shrugged. "If it requires it," he said coyly.

Andrea smiled again and said, "What can I help you with?"

"Miss Gatting—"

"Please, call me Andrea. Miss Gatting makes me sound like a schoolteacher," she said with a laugh.

"Did you know what my parents were involved in?" he asked.

"I… am aware of them."

"Is it true? Were they heavily involved in black market dealings?"

Andrea chewed her bottom lip while she considered her answer. "It's true," she admitted.

"Were you ever involved with them?"

Andrea considered his question. "I had—have—a lot of contacts. People who are interested in historical artefacts for their personal collection and pay a lot of money for them. I was a middleman between them and your parents."

Ethan leaned forward, arms folded over his stomach. Even though the allegations had been made all those years ago, he'd never met anyone who was involved with them. Because the investigations never involved him directly, he felt like he was always at arm's length from it all. But Andrea, a person who was a friend of theirs, confirming it made it feel more real, and it hit him like a truck.

"Ethan, are you okay?" Andrea said with concern in her eyes as she kneeled in front of him, holding his hand in hers.

"Yeah… just shocked. It's weird, you think you know your parents, but it turns out they have this secret life that I wasn't a part of—that I never knew about."

Andrea patted his hand. "Oh, Ethan, if they didn't tell you, they had good reasons for it. You were young, and they were protecting you."

Ethan shrugged, removing his hand from hers. "Maybe you're right, Miss Gatting. I just wish I knew more about what they were doing before they died."

"The police told me they died while diving at a site in Norfolk."

Ethan nodded. "That's the official story, but I don't believe it. They were experienced divers, and I just cannot believe that they would have gotten lost at the dive site."

"Maybe they went back out?"

Ethan shook his head, and she took her seat next to him. "As much as I want to believe you, even professionals make mistakes that prove costly."

"And the boat captain who said he brought them back was found dead in Liverpool," he added, ignoring her. "He lied about bringing them back."

"Maybe he lied to protect himself? As cold as it sounds, maybe he figured they got lost at sea. The bodies were gone, so he could claim he brought them back instead of bringing any insurance issues to himself and the company."

"I doubt it."

"What do you think happened?"

"They were murdered."

Andrea stared at him. "Ethan, I know loss is difficult to accept, but the police investigated it. They declared it an accident. I think you are trying to find something that isn't there."

Ethan shook his head, staring at the lush office carpet. "This whole thing has been shrouded in secrets and lies." He looked up at her. "Why didn't you tell the police about Maynard's diary?"

"How do you know about that?"

"Why didn't you?" Ethan repeated, ignoring her question.

She paused for a moment and then said, "It didn't seem relevant at the time."

"Why not?"

"Do you know how they got the diary?"

"They stole it."

She nodded. "They said they had a passing interest in Maynard, wondering why he went incognito after he defeated Blackbeard. They thought maybe he made a discovery or spent time somewhere else. They were curious, so they wanted to get his diary to see if he had written about it. But the bidding went crazy, and it solidified their belief that they were on to something."

"Why?"

"Because it wasn't worth that much. They thought there was more to it. Otherwise, why else would someone pay out the nose for it? Anyway, when the police interviewed me, they indicated it was a diving accident, so I didn't bring up the diary. I didn't need to throw dirt on their names when it wasn't relevant."

Ethan looked into her eyes, trying to see if there was any possibility she was lying. But they were hard to read, and he felt brittle under her gaze, like he would crumble at any moment. Finally he said, "I see."

"Ethan, I'm sorry. If I thought the diary would help in shedding any light on their deaths, I would have told them."

"No. No, it's okay. It's not your fault." He was silent for a long time, thinking about all she had told him, then asked, "Did you see the diary?"

"Only what your parents showed me back at the house. I didn't think much of it, but I don't have their knack for discovery… or puzzles."

"When they disappeared, the police interviewed you, right? You were meant to meet with them?"

Andrea sat back. "Ethan, this sounds like an interrogation."

"Please, anything you tell me might be helpful."

Andrea sighed. "Yes, we were meant to go out for dinner. They wanted my advice on something."

"It had to do with the diary, didn't it?"

She nodded.

"But they didn't turn up?"

"That's right."

"Do you know where Maynard's diary is?"

She shook her head.

"Do you know what advice they wanted?"

She looked up at the roof, thinking, before glancing back at him. "It had to do with what Maynard wrote in his diary."

"The voodoo treasure, right?" Ethan said.

"That's right… how do you know?"

He pulled out his dad's journal and showed it to her. "There's an excerpt of his diary in here. He mentions a cursed treasure and that he took great pains to hide it forever."

She blinked. "Where did you get this?"

"I found it at home."

"I see." She held out her hand. "May I?"

He opened it to the page with the copy of Maynard's writing and handed it to her. She flipped through it and said, "Maynard's diary was more than what met the eye. There were some historical references, people searching for this treasure that Maynard mentioned, but it went nowhere and they thought he was just a crackpot. But your parents truly believed Robert Maynard had found, and hidden, a great treasure because he believed it to be cursed."

Ethan's heart raced as his excitement grew.

"You should give this to the police," she said, handing back the journal.

"Not a chance."

"Why not?" she asked with a frown.

He shrugged. "Miss Gatting, the case is closed. They're just going to think it's a desperate son trying to clear his parents' names."

"They're not going to think that," she said. "You should have more faith in people doing the right thing."

"Did they think the treasure was in London?"

"I don't believe so."

"You're in consulting. I don't understand what kind of business you and my parents could have had that could overlap."

"I am a consultant now, but back then I was a… broker of sorts. As well as the connections I mentioned before, I helped them get permissions, permits, or workers when they wanted to go to places that sometimes were not easily accessible."

"Grease a few palms?"

She nodded. "If it came to that."

"Did they make any enemies from doing this?"

"I imagine they made many."

"Dangerous ones?"

"I tried to dissuade them from going into war zones or paying off warlords, but they were headstrong. They had a goal in mind and they wanted to achieve it no matter the costs." She looked at him and cocked her head. "And I don't think the apple has fallen far from the tree in that regard."

Ethan looked abashed. "I'm sorry," he said. "I'm just not convinced the real story has come out, and finding Dad's journal has solidified my belief that they were murdered. And... Mum was worried they were being followed not long before they died."

Andrea sat back, eyes wide, stretching the scar. "How do you know that?"

He held up his dad's journal. "Mum wrote about it in here, right before they left for London. Did they mention anything to you?"

"No, not a thing," she said and stood up, walking to a small bar fridge and grabbing a bottle of water. She offered him one, but he declined. She took a sip and replaced the lid, turning to look at him. "Ethan, what they did came with certain risks. They understood and accepted that. But in saying that, I doubt anyone would have known they stole the diary."

"Why?"

"They were very good at what they did," she said plainly.

Ethan stood up, brushing off his pants.

"What are you going to do?"

"I'm going to find out what they were looking for. Maybe it

will lead me to some more answers."

"Do you even know where to start?"

He held up the diary. "I'm going to follow in their footsteps."

"You know where they went?" she asked.

He nodded.

"Where?" she asked, her eyes alight with excitement.

Ethan considered how much to tell this woman. He didn't know her at all, but she was a family friend, and his parents trusted her enough to tell her about Maynard's diary. And maybe with her old life, she had contacts that might be able to help, if it ever got to that stage. But she could also get the police involved, and he didn't want that—not yet, at least. Not until he had some proof.

In the end, he took her advice on having faith in people.

"They visited Maynard's gravesite."

It was as if the room had deflated, and Andrea visibly sagged. "That's not much of a lead, Ethan."

"Maybe. Maybe not. But it's something, and I have to try."

"No stone unturned, huh?"

"Something like that."

She grabbed his hand in her own again, and he noticed how soft they were. "Ethan, are you sure about this? I don't mean to be a wet blanket, but look at it logically. You're only excited because you found something new, something that gives you hope, but are you sure you're not trying to fit a square peg into a round hole?"

Shrugging, he said, "I don't know, maybe. But I have to find out. It's the best option I have so far. If it turns out to be nothing, then I will go home, but as far as I am concerned, it's low risk and high reward."

Andrea let go of his hand. "If you are right, then it could be dangerous. If Gemma was right and someone was following them, then it is possible they might now follow you."

"Maybe," Ethan said. He hadn't considered that whoever was following them might be interested in him. "But it's been ten years. Surely, if there was something sinister going on, that would be over with by now."

"Look, Ethan," Andrea said. "If your parents ran afoul of one of their collectors, then there is nothing they won't do to get retribution or revenge. Especially if they catch wind of you looking into this Maynard thing. There are incredibly dangerous people in this line of work and I couldn't, in good conscience, let you go out there and get yourself killed."

"I appreciate the concern, Miss Gatting, but I need to find out what happened to them."

Andrea sighed. "I see you have inherited your mother's stubbornness." She walked to him and handed him a card. "If you insist on following this through, will you at least keep me updated? This card has my private number on it. Call me anytime, day or night, and let me know you're safe. Okay?"

"Sure," he said. "I can do that."

She gave him a smile, and to his surprise, hugged him. "Thank you, Ethan. Is there anything else you need?"

"No, I'm good. Thank you, Miss Gatting."

"Can you do me one more thing, please?"

"What's that?"

"Call me Andrea."

He laughed as she moved to hold him at arm's length. "I truly hope you find some answers."

"I appreciate that… Andrea," he said.

Leading him out of the office and to the bank of elevators past reception, she hugged him one more time and said, "Remember, keep me up to date."

Nine

Great Mongeham, Kent, England

Ethan hired a car and drove east for two hours until he reached the village of Great Mongeham. Located near the east coast of the United Kingdom, and just north of Dover, the Great Mongeham settlement dated back as far as 761 A.D. and currently had less than one thousand people living there. The drive into the village had Ethan navigating narrow roads bordered by grassy hillocks, brick walls, or brick houses. The village centre was a mismatch of brick and timber buildings with sharp gabled roofs, a Dutch influence, with no consistency in design.

The sun was on its way down when Ethan turned off Northbourne Road into a side street that led to St. Martin's

Church. Parking the car on the street, he got out and zipped up his jacket, the air misting as he breathed. He picked up a backpack with supplies he'd prepared on his way out and walked to the gate leading into the church grounds.

The iron gates were chest high and attached to a brick fence. Ethan pushed on the gates but they were locked, rattling like gunshots in the silent night. He looked around and saw only a handful of houses lining the street, chimney smoke twirling lazily into the sky. He grabbed the top of the gate and launched himself over it.

Amused, and wondering what the point of locking the gates was since anyone with two functional legs could climb over them, Ethan moved further into the grounds. He passed the trees and stepped into a clearing, where he was greeted by St. Martin's Church. The church was a mediaeval-style stone castle built in the thirteenth century. It had a tall, rectangular tower on the west side with crenellated parapets and gabled, tiled roofs of various heights flowing toward the back. Norman and tracery windows ran along the north and south walls and into the chapel that sat off the nave. And on the west-side transept was a stained-glass window of Saints Peter and Paul.

Littered around the church grounds were gravestones. With the sun nearing the horizon, Ethan shrugged off his pack and pulled out a sturdy flashlight that he'd purchased on his way out of London and turned it on. The beam of light cut through the gloom like scissors through dark cloth, and he moved on, swinging the light side-to-side over the grave markers, trying to read the names. But they were mostly faded and worn away by time and weather. Searching toward the back of the church, he stopped at a well-maintained, above-ground stone grave. In front of it was a plastic marker. Using his light, Ethan read:

Here is the burial site of Captain ROBERT MAYNARD of His Majesty's Royal Navy, best known for his heroic actions in defeating the famous pirate Blackbeard.

There was more beneath it that delved into Maynard's life, and Ethan silently read it to himself, his breath misting before him as he read.

This is it.

He ran his hand over the grave. The stone was rough and cold to touch, but otherwise, it was like every other stone grave he had seen. At the head of the grave, etched into the lid, was the lieutenant's name and a testimony beneath it:

In memory of
Captain Robert Maynard.
Faithful and Experienced Commander
in the Royal Navy.

There was more, but it had faded with time.

Beneath the testimony was an engraving. Ethan leaned in closer, brushing off dirt and shining his light on it. Despite it having worn away in the elements, he could make out the image of an anchor with a piece of rope curled around the shank in the shape of an 'R'. Ethan thought it looked familiar and then realised why. He flipped his pack around and unzipped it to grab his parents' journal, turning to one of the last pages. In the page's corner was a sketch of the same upright anchor and R-shaped rope. He'd done some research and found this symbol was like the anchor on the flag of the British Lord High Admirals, except Maynard's anchor was facing upright. The traditional Lord High Admirals anchor was side on, which made Ethan wonder if Maynard created his own symbol or flag based on that design.

Strange, I never saw this symbol in any of the research I did on Maynard. What does it mean?

He closed the journal and stood up. Staring at the grave, he hoped something would pop out at him, but in the darkness, nothing stood out as unusual. He moved on to circle the church, passing by more graves and tombstones to get an idea of the place, wondering what his parents were doing here. *What did they find?* He returned to the front of the church, none the wiser. Approaching the wooden double doors, he pushed on them and was surprised to find they creaked open. He stood at the threshold and shone his light around the door and walls, looking for any sign of an alarm. Finding nothing, he entered the church.

The light played across the narthex, the entryway into the church, passing over a small table with a crucifix of Jesus mounted to the wall directly above it. Across from him was a set of stairs winding its way up the tower and disappearing into the darkness above. Taking a right turn, he entered the nave. It was narrow, lined with rows of wooden pews on either side. Above were twin sets of arcades running toward the crossing at the far end, where the left and right transepts led into the chapels. The roof was gabled with old timber beams.

Ethan approached the altar, admiring the geometrical tracery window with a statue of Jesus above it. Then returned to the nave and took a seat on the front pew. He shone his flashlight around;

the light reflecting off the stained-glass depiction of St. Peter holding the keys to heaven on the left side and St. Paul holding a sword as a reminder of his beheading on the right.

Flipping open the journal, he turned to the last of the written pages, the one with the receipt and his parents' final message. He'd read and reread it obsessively during his flight here. If there was something, it would be in this church.

As he read it, a passage from the photocopy of Maynard's entry stood out to him:

Like Jesus AND his disciples, I will always be BORN A MARTYR and will be BURIED as one.

Every time he read it, trying to find the clue his mum left, he wondered why Maynard had emphasised the words he had. It made no sense. The writing was neat and clean, but this was an outlier in his handwriting. Ethan glanced down and caught his mum's last entry, stating that it *'starts with his burial site'*.

Burial site…

"Maynard's burial site is why they came here, but what did they find?" he murmured.

His eyes returned to Maynard's symbol, thinking that it seemed like a weird way to sign off. He wondered if he did it to all his entries in his diary. A thought suddenly jumped out to him—he'd *just* seen that symbol. It was on Maynard's gravesite, but he'd also seen it somewhere else, somewhere in the church. He pointed his light up and around, first on the chancel and the choir and around the transept. Then he directed the beam of the light over the tracery window at the rear, a statue of Jesus standing on a small ledge above it, and—there!

Above the statue of Jesus and just below the point of the vault was not a piece of art, but Maynard's symbol. The R coiled around the anchor, but it was facing the wrong way. The R and anchor's crown were facing right, like that of the Lord High Admirals, but it made the coiled R look like a random tangle of rope. Ethan wondered if anyone ever saw it and wondered why it was incorrect. *Did they just assume it was a version of the Lord High Admirals' flag? To the untrained eye, it did look similar.* He also wondered if it was designed to look that way—perhaps a design fault—or deliberately turned that way for another reason.

When he was younger, his parents would talk of their discoveries of secret rooms in temples and pyramids by finding a slight deviation in the norm. Correcting it would reveal levers or secret rooms filled with treasures, scrolls, and artefacts lost to time. One day, when he was seven, they told him there was a secret room in their own house. Much to their amusement, he roamed around the house, knocking on walls, pulling books out of bookshelves, pushing against cabinets, trying to find the secret passage. After weeks of searching, he got so frustrated that he couldn't find it, he started acting out. Then his dad picked him up and told him to keep trying, that sometimes the key hides in plain sight.

With that in mind, he continued his search, vowing to keep trying every day until he discovered his house's secret. Two days later, he was in a long hallway on the ground floor when he noticed the clock on the wall skipped time. He'd always assumed it was broken but was too nice to throw out. The problem with the clock was that the hands would always skip the 3 and the 9, so it would never be fifteen, or forty-five-minutes, past. Rather, it would sit on fourteen or forty-four for two minutes before going to sixteen or forty-six. And it would never be three or nine o'clock, but two or eight o'clock for two hours before moving to four or ten o'clock.

Thinking this could be the key his dad talked about, Ethan grabbed a chair and climbed on it to examine the clock. It was a Vienna wall clock. The circular clock face was encased in ornately carved and hand-polished timber, with a glass panel and iron hands. Below it were two golden weights that hung from the body. Ethan tried to take it off the wall so he could better examine it, but found it was permanently mounted. So he opened the glass panel and ran his fingers around the face, seeing if there was anything movable. Finding nothing along the clock face, he moved to the hands. The current time was five forty-nine p.m. and he thought about how the hands never sat on the three or nine, so he gently pushed the minute hand, surprised to find little resistance, and circled it back up to the three. He expected the minute hand to skip to the sixteenth minute, but after a couple of seconds of watching, the hand seemed to recess a little into its position. He wobbled it and found it was much more resistant now.

His heart beating heavily in his chest, he moved the hour hand, circling it around to the nine position. Again, after a few seconds, the hand recessed in. The clock hands looked like a handle to Ethan, so he grabbed it and rotated it, expecting them to snap off, but instead they turned smoothly, as if well-greased. He turned until the hour hand was on the six and the minute hand was on the twelve.

The clock let out a loud gong. Beside him, the wall slid aside, revealing a dark entrance.

"It's always six o'clock now."

Ethan swung around, almost toppling off the chair. His dad stood in the hall's gloom, a smile on his face. "Alice in Wonderland was always a favourite of mine."

Ethan got down from the chair and peered into the opening where there were stairs leading down into the darkness. "What is it?" he asked.

"The Rabbit Hole," his father replied mysteriously. He handed Ethan a flashlight. "Shall we?"

The Rabbit Hole turned out to be a secret passage his dad discovered not long after they moved into the house. His dad let Ethan lead the way down the stairs to a landing where a crude tunnel supported by old beams of timber disappeared beyond their lights. They walked for almost an hour before they emerged on the shore west of Emu Bay. His father told him it was an escape tunnel built in the late 1800s that was probably used for the movement of illegal goods. Stored in the house and then moved to boats on the bay, they were then transferred down river or on to bigger boats heading for the mainland or New Zealand.

That was the moment Ethan knew he wanted to be an explorer. Discovering lost passages and lost treasures gave him a thrill like nothing else. It was only a year or two after that he started studying shipwrecks of Tasmania, desiring to discover one of the thousands of wrecks sitting undiscovered beneath the

Tasmanian waters.

Ethan shook his head, bringing him out of his reverie. *Not the time*, he admonished. He stood up, his light still directed at Maynard's symbol. Instinct was telling him it was deliberately put that way and, like the clock, there was a reason for it.

He walked toward the altar, deciding to make his way to the anchor. With little light shining through the windows, Ethan clipped the flashlight to his pocket and climbed onto the altar. He examined the tracery window and was confident he could find enough handholds to climb up to the Jesus statue.

He grabbed a hold of the cusp on the window and, bracing himself on the hood mould, pulled himself up until his feet were on the bottom transom between the mullions. Then he climbed, grabbing hold of the cusps between the dagger-shaped holes as best as he could, and moved up at a slow pace. Balancing on the narrow cusps, Ethan was soon below the ledge where a statue of Jesus stood, overlooking the pews with arms outstretched, as if embracing the congregation.

He reached up, grabbing hold of the stone robes around the thigh area, and hoisted himself up until he was standing on the ledge, face to face with the Son of God, looking like they were about to hug.

"Jesus," he greeted the statue.

Looking down, Ethan was at a height where a fall probably wouldn't kill him but could seriously injure—if not paralyse— him. The thought didn't scare him, since he had been in higher and more precarious positions before and came out of them unscathed. He was confident in his climbing ability, but not so much that he was careless or didn't recognise that he hadn't had any close calls in the past.

Placing his hands on Jesus' outstretched arms, Ethan lifted himself until his feet were on the stone arms and his midsection in Jesus' face. He chuckled to himself at the thought of someone suddenly appearing and finding him in such a compromising position.

Looking around just to be sure, he saw that the church was now pitch black aside from the glow of his light, and realised he would have to be extra careful climbing back down.

"Excuse me," he said to the statue, placing one foot, and then the other, on the stone head of Jesus Christ, and stood up. He was near the point of the vault now and face to face with the symbol of Robert Maynard.

Running a hand over the anchor, Ethan noted it was made of metal, possibly brass or iron. It was cool to the touch with a dull metallic sheen and any colour it might have had was lost in time.

"Ouch!" Ethan gasped, pulling his hand away sharply. He looked at it in the light to see blood trickling down from a cut on his fingers. The colours might have dulled, but the anchor's bills were still sharp. The anchor was attached to a metal shaft that ran into the ambulatory wall. Ethan grabbed a hold of it to steady himself with one hand and grabbed the stock with the other hand. The anchor crown was pointing right, like the Lord High Admirals symbol, but Maynard's pointed down—well, at least it did on his grave and the sketch in the journal.

"Here goes nothing," he muttered and said a silent prayer for help, given his location. Then he turned the anchor.

Nothing happened.

He turned again, harder this time, and the anchor jolted. Ethan flinched, thinking he'd snapped the anchor off the wall and was about to fall off the head of Jesus, but instead, it rotated. Grabbing the anchor at either end of the shank, he twisted it. The anchor resisted at first, the metal shaft grinding as he rotated it, but he finally got it into place, the R in the correct position.

As soon as Maynard's symbol was in place, there was a loud grinding sound, as if gears were turning behind the wall. The sound echoed around the church, and then a muffled thud, like wood smashing against wood, followed it.

Ethan, one hand still grasping the anchor, grabbed the flashlight with his other hand and directed the light toward the sound. The beam crawled across the timber floor until it crossed a black void in the narthex.

He frowned. *What is that?*

After a few moments of examining the void with his light, he realised what it was.

It was a *trapdoor!*

Ten

Despite his excitement, Ethan forced himself to take his time climbing down from his spot above the tracery window. The thrill of discovery coursed through his veins, and it was all he could do not to jump off the transom. He reached the altar and hopped off it, eager to reach the trapdoor in the centre of the narthex. The trapdoor was square, about the same size as a manhole. He approached it cautiously, flashlight in hand. The light glinted off a metal ladder that was bolted into the wall, traces of rust flecking each rung. He followed it down with his light until it couldn't pierce the inky black darkness below.

Getting to his knees, he grabbed the top rung and tested its strength. The rung didn't move, so he put his foot on it and pushed down. Confident that it wasn't going to snap or break apart, he hung his legs over the edge and lowered himself down until his feet touched the ladder and began his descent.

The air was stale and dusty, having been trapped for so long. The excitement within him soared as he realised he was probably the second, maybe even the first, person to use this ladder in centuries.

He climbed down; the torch keeping the suffocating dark at bay, until his foot hit something solid a couple of minutes later. He'd reached the bottom, where a floor made from perfectly cut square stones was set into the ground. The walls were made of the same stone and, despite the age and lack of maintenance, they still held up the tons of dirt and the church above.

"Did you guys make it this far?" he wondered out loud as he thought of his parents, his voice echoing off the stone walls.

Shining his light around the passage, Ethan noticed it was bricked in on three sides and that an impenetrably dark passage led off to his right. Seeing no other way to go, he took a deep breath and moved forward.

Ethan followed the passage, cutting through thin curtains of cobwebs, as it curved to the left. If his sense of direction was correct, he was passing underneath the church.

He'd been walking for five minutes before his eagerness turned into impatience and his mind pondered whether this tunnel was built during Maynard's time or if it was even older.

Ethan knew the church was built in the thirteenth century, but he was certain the stonework wasn't that old. It wouldn't be in this good of condition after eight hundred years. But it could have been constructed any time between then and when Robert Maynard used it.

If he actually did use it.

For all Ethan knew, this had nothing to do with Maynard. It could be a coincidence that his symbol opened the trapdoor. It could be something the church knew about and was using for storage. Ethan tempered his expectations, and his enthusiasm waned. Even if his parents had come this way, it could still be a dead end.

After another few minutes walking in the eerie silence, the passage opened up into a room. This one was designed with the same square stones for the floor, walls, and roof. It was about five metres wide by ten metres long, and the floor was thick with dirt and dust, with puddles and cobwebs in the corners.

Opposite was him was a door.

Ethan approached it. The door was made of timber, banded with iron along the top and bottom and framed in thick timber posts. Ethan grabbed its iron ring handle and tried turning it like a doorknob, but it held firm. He then tried pushing and pulling the door, but still no luck.

It was then that he noticed that on the door, etched in thick block letters, were words that read, "I WILL ALWAYS BE."

Beneath it were a series of blocks with letters etched into them. The letters spelled "ROBERT MAYNARD." Ethan poked the first block letter and found it rotated on its axis. The letter R rotated to B first, then T, and then B, before going back to R.

On the posts on either side of the door were lanterns hanging on hooks. Ethan opened the lantern door, the hinges stiff from lack of use, and sniffed the wick. It smelled faintly of oil.

Leaving the door open, he swung his pack around and pulled a box of matches from it. His parents always told him to be prepared and carry an emergency survival pack with him wherever he went, because you never knew when you would need it.

Thankful for the sage advice, Ethan struck the match and held it to the wick, which whooshed to life. Bathed in the red-orange light of the fire, Ethan turned to the other lantern and repeated the process. Now the doors were illuminated in the glowing lantern light.

With enough light to work with, Ethan turned off his flashlight and put it into his pack, along with the matches. He stood up, leaving the pack on the ground, and examined the door. He fingered each block, rotating them and examining each letter before returning them to their original positions.

"I will always be Robert Maynard," he murmured, reading the blocks. "Yeah, no kidding, mate."

Pulling out his journal, he flipped to a fresh page and jotted down all the letters for each block into a four-by-thirteen table. Then he sat down, back against the door, and studied them.

There were thirteen blocks, one lot of six (ROBERT) and one lot of seven (MAYNARD) with four sides to each block, meaning there were only... "sixty-seven million possible combinations," he groaned. "This might take a while."

He was certain it was an anagram, but with so many letters, he could spend months down here trying to work it out. He knew the first letter had to be R, T, or B, and that the fourth, fifth, ninth, and thirteenth letters had blank sides, which he thought could be a space in the words. If so, that narrowed down the possibilities.

Ethan sat in the glowing firelight and worked on potential strings. Time seemed to have no meaning in the gloomy room and before he knew it, it had been more than an hour since he started working on it, yet he still had nothing.

"Crap!" he growled, tossing the journal aside. Frustration getting the better of him, he stood up, kicked the door, and started pacing in front of it like a caged lion.

Maybe his parents' notes had something. He picked up the journal and flipped it to the last pages and reread what he had already looked at multiple times.

It was when he was reading the photocopied page of Maynard's diary that he realised the answer was right there the whole time, hiding in plain sight.

"I can live out the rest of my life," he read aloud, "knowing that what started out as an act of greed has ended as an act for the greater good. *Like Jesus AND his disciples, I will always be BORN A MARTYR and will be BURIED as one.*"

"I will always be born a martyr," he repeated, and then looked at his notes with the letters and quickly jotted down a combination. "Oh, I'm an idiot!" he groaned, mentally kicking himself. The clue was right there in Maynard's diary!

He turned to the door and began rotating the blocks, turning the first to B and the next to O and so on, until it read:

I WILL ALWAYS BE

BORN A MARTYR

There was a clicking sound coming from behind the door. "So

simple," he muttered. He should have known, remembering he thought the capitalisation was odd when he first read that passage. He knew his parents would have easily remembered and recognised it and answered it in no time.

Don't do that! You're not them, and you still worked it out.

Taking a few deep breaths to reset, he told himself to forget about it. Everyone starts somewhere.

Opening his pack, he stowed the journal and grabbed the flashlight, slinging it back over his shoulder. He pushed the door, and it creaked open a tiny bit, years of neglect having rusted the hinges enough that it had become stubborn. After putting his shoulder against it and pushing again with all his weight, the door opened inch by inch until he created enough of a gap to slip through.

Eleven

The door led Ethan into a square room that was almost double the size of the one before, but this one had clearly been used. Immediately before him was a thick rug. It was dirt-stained and tattered, and his light followed it, piercing the inky blackness until it revealed a desk sitting against the back wall. On either side of it were tall bookshelves, and on the left wall was a cot. Attached to the roof was a timber chandelier, hanging by a single chain. The other two chains had broken, and the chandelier hung lopsided, ready to crash at any moment. Below it were more moth-eaten rugs and spots of hardened candle wax. Ethan wondered if Maynard spent a lot of his time down here. It was very isolated.

And if he did, what was he doing down here?

Along the walls were more lanterns, and he circled the room, lighting each one until the room was bathed in orange light.

He crossed the space from door to desk and examined the bookshelves. The shelves were packed tight with books on various topics, including naval warfare, world history, and even books by Descartes, Eliza Haywood, Daniel Defoe, William Chillingworth, Marquis de Sade, and many others. Ethan realised this was a veritable goldmine of first editions. He pulled out *Fantomina* by Haywood, opened the leather-bound cover, and turned to the first page, but it disintegrated in his hand.

"Shit."

He picked up another, *The Adventures of Peregrine Pickle* by Tobias Smollett, and again the pages disintegrated with his touch. Deciding it was best not to handle any more books, Ethan moved to the other shelf and found more books, both fiction, and nonfiction, along with rolled-up maps and charts.

How long had Maynard been spending down here?

He moved away from the shelves and examined the desk. On it, he found a brass candleholder, the candles long burned away with globs of wax splattered about the base. There was also a gold ink pot whose ink dried away long ago, and no sign of the quill. What caught Ethan's attention the most, though, was the dust-covered leather satchel setting on the desk. He wiped his hand across the front of it, brushing off the dust, and found Maynard's symbol stamped into the leather.

Unbuckling the straps, Ethan flipped open the satchel and looked inside. Holding it up to the light, he saw a book and something that looked like a wooden block. It was a device the size of his palm and as thick as a book. It was five-sided, like a pentagon, and made of wood with inlaid brass. He laid it flat on his palm and saw a seam running across the middle, as if it could open like a clam. He tried to pry it open, but it wouldn't budge.

It looked like it had been through a rough time, given its scratched casing and dents all around. The top was smooth and overlaid by dozens of raised bumps that reminded Ethan of braille. He turned it over, revealing a plain back with something scratched into it.

Ethan brought it up closer to his face and squinted in the dim light. It looked like initials.

B.I. . . B.T. . . E.T. . . F.T. . . E.I. . . F.I. . . might even be a J or L.

He pocketed the device, deciding he could examine it later in better light, and pulled out the book from the satchel. He immediately dropped it in shock.

The book was bound in dark leather, aged over the centuries. The title read:

Robert Maynard.

Beneath it was his symbol.

Maynard's diary! Mum and Dad must have been here!

Ethan's heart skip a beat. His parents had been here! They were here looking for Maynard's treasure.

But why was the diary here? Did they leave it? Why would they?

Needing to process this new discovery, Ethan decided he needed to think, but he couldn't do it here in this cramped room and oppressive darkness. Taking a couple of deep breaths, he calmed his mind and then picked up the satchel and tipped it over. Something fell out of it and landed with a metallic clink on the table, followed by another.

Ethan's eyes widened. "Are they—?" He picked up one of the fallen items. It was weighty and roughly circular. The orange glow of the fire seemed to illuminate the gold colour. "A Spanish real," he breathed.

He examined it closer: one side was stamped with the words 'PHILIPPUS • V • 1709' around the circumference, and the profile was of a person facing right.

"Philip V, minted in 1709," Ethan said. He flipped the coin over, where the words 'HISPANARIUM REX', which meant 'King of Spain', was stamped around the outside with the image of a shield and crown in the middle.

He picked up the other coin, which was similar in shape and design, but the words were different. On one side, it had 'EL MAL • 1516' written around the profiles of a crowned king and queen facing each other. On the other side, the words 'MUERTE • REAL' curved around a similar shield and crown.

Ethan rolled the coin in his fingers, thinking.

Two gold coins minted almost two hundred years apart.

If his barely passable Spanish was correct, 'El Mal' meant 'evil' and 'Muerte Real' meant 'death coin' or 'coin of death' or something like that.

"The evil and the death coin?" he said. "What does that mean?" He'd never heard of such coins and wondered if it was a mistake. "Was this part of the treasure Maynard found?" he added. Yet another question to ponder.

He was about to put the coin down when he noticed something. Squinting, he brought the coin closer, turning it in the light to get a better look.

Is that…

A black X was marked over the eyes of both the king and queen. Ethan rubbed his finger over it, thinking it was dust or dirt but he felt the groove and realised it was deliberate.

His frown deepened, and he tapped the coin with his finger.

Why is there an X on the eyes?

"Was this what Mum and Dad were looking for? Is this the treasure he hid? Is there more of it somewhere?" He thought back to his mum's note about Maynard writing about a discovery that would make him wealthy. Was this what he was talking about? Based on his research, Maynard wasn't wealthy. Was this all he found? Two Spanish reals? This wouldn't make him wealthy at all, but he wrote about a cursed treasure—was this part of it? If so, where did he hide the rest? And did the discovery of this bunker and the gold get them killed? Was there more and did they take it?

"What is going on here?" Ethan growled, frustrated that he had come here seeking answers but so far, all he had were more questions. He searched the desk, but there were only faded papers that broke apart as soon as he touched them. He growled again and turned to leave when he noticed the map on the wall opposite the cot.

Turning his flashlight back on, Ethan walked to the map. It was caked in dust, and he wiped it free to reveal not a world map like he thought, but a giant star map consisting of a dozen constellations stencilled into the wall. Ethan didn't know much about stars and constellations, but he recognised the North Star and the Southern Cross. Along the middle, cutting the map in half, was a horizontal line that he assumed was the equator. Just below the North Star was the image of a Romanesque chariot with a ship next to it. Underneath the chariot was a date: 14/3/19.

A line ran down from the chariot to a picture of a lion with the date 7/4/19.

From the lion, the line continued south until it connected to a picture of a bear, dated 19/5/19.

Then the line reached the equator, where there was the image of an eagle dated 5/8/19. It continued heading south, connecting to a jar pouring out a liquid dated 13/10/19, after which it ended at a picture of a centaur next to the Southern Cross with no date. Beneath the centaur was a cluster of islands where the ship was docked.

In the top left corner near the North Star was a set of numbers: 16/20/15/12/5/13/25.

Everything about this was foreign to Ethan, but his instinct told him this was important. He wanted to stay and study the map more, but he was already suffering from information overload and the onset of claustrophobia. He drew a rough sketch of the map in his journal, noting the dates next to the pictures. Then he grabbed his phone and, with the flash enabled, took photos of the map. They didn't come out great, but along with the sketch it should be enough. He took a moment to look around, making sure he hadn't overlooked anything, and then thought about his next steps. He summarised what he'd discovered: Maynard's hidden bunker, his diary, two Spanish coins, and a strange star map. Were the coins part of the cursed treasure he had discovered and hidden? They had to be—that was the only part that made sense so far. Mum and Dad had found the bunker, and for whatever reason left Maynard's diary down here. Were they worried about being captured? Whoever was following them may have been here as well.

All he knew was that they were here, and they were on to something, and he was going to find out what it was.

Thrilled he had another lead to follow, Ethan glanced over the room one last time and, satisfied he hadn't overlooked anything, adjusted his pack, and exited the secret bunker of Robert Maynard.

Twelve

London, England

It was almost nine at night when Ethan arrived back in London. It was Saturday, so London was lit up and crowded with revellers socialising at restaurants and going to clubs. Ethan dropped off his car in Camden Town and grabbed his jacket from the back seat and put it on. Then he shrugged on his backpack and, wanting time to think, decided to walk to his hotel.

Camden Town was famous for its eccentric style, and that was evident as Ethan walked down Chalk Farm Road toward the Regents Canal when he stopped at the Camden Market.

The market was hidden behind a tall, dark-brick fence with two-story buildings made of the same brick in the middle. Inside the buildings and out were stalls selling everything from food to clothing to crafts. The entire market had been retrofitted with glass roofs and modern buildings. This, combined with the brick facades, gave it a mix of old school and new age.

Music blared from various venues and clubs, and as Ethan browsed, he realised he hadn't eaten anything since the cold burrito after speaking to Andrea.

I should probably call her, he thought. But the smells of hot food coming at him from all directions made his mouth water, so he decided he could call her when he got back to his room. He stopped at a food stall selling pizza just outside the market. Something quick and cheap, since his wallet was looking empty.

While he was reading the menu board, he noticed someone standing next to him, just on the edge of his periphery.

"Can I have a slice of tropical with pineapple?"

Ethan continued reading the board, trying to decide what he wanted.

"Can never have enough pineapple on a pizza, right?" the man said in the Queen's English.

Ethan grunted, not at all interested in discussing pizza toppings.

"I understand your parents were not big fans of pineapple on pizza."

Ethan's head shot around. The man who spoke to him had jet-black hair, dark eyes, and a hint of hair growth along his jawline. He was shorter than Ethan by a couple of centimetres and dressed in a dark pin-stripe suit that looked like it cost more than some cars.

"What did you say?"

"In fact," the man continued, as if Ethan hadn't said anything, "I don't think they were particularly fond of pizza."

There was a calmness about this man that unnerved Ethan, talking about his parents like they were still here, like they were friendly.

"Who the hell are you?"

"My name is Felix Graves, Mr. Jackson."

"You knew my parents?"

Graves nodded, and two burly men in suits appeared out of the crowd and took positions on either side of him. Graves gestured to a round metal table with colourful metal chairs. "Take a seat, Mr. Jackson."

Given the two six-foot-tall walking trucks standing on either side of the man, Ethan decided it would be best to do as he said. He took a seat, and Graves took the one opposite him, placing his pizza plate carefully on the table while his two cronies remained standing, arms folded.

"I did know your parents," Graves began, taking a bite of his pizza. He watched Ethan as he chewed slowly and swallowed. "And if you wish to avoid their fate, I suggest you give me everything you found in Great Mongeham."

"What do you know about my parents?" Ethan asked.

Graves looked at him expectantly but said nothing.

Ethan stared back at the man. "I wasn't in Great Mongeham," he hedged.

Around them, people walked, talking and laughing, completely oblivious to the man in the suit and his two henchmen who were obviously trying to intimidate Ethan.

Graves swallowed another bite. "Don't play dumb with me, Mr. Jackson. We have had our eye on you since you were growing up in that backwater shithole in Tasmania. We know everything about you—where you've been, what you've been doing. Your entire life has been under our watchful eye. And you have been quite the mischievous little boy, haven't you? Building yourself a nice criminal record." He gave Ethan a wicked smile. "I guess the apple doesn't fall too far from the tree."

Ethan glared at him. "What the hell do you want?"

"I told you, Mr. Jackson. Everything you found in Great Mongeham."

"So if I give you everything I found there, you'll tell me about my parents?" Ethan said.

"That's right."

"Sounds fair." He grabbed his backpack and unzipped it, rummaging around inside until he found what he was looking for. He grabbed it and placed it on the table.

Graves glanced at the item. "What is this?"

"All I found in Great Mongeham."

"It's a magnet."

Ethan nodded. "Yep. It has a wooden bike on it. You know they were known for building the first wooden bike in history?"

"Don't play games with me, Mr. Jackson."

Wish to avoid their fate…

"What happened to my parents?" Ethan asked, ignoring the threat.

"They're dead." He paused and then said, "Well, one of them

is."

Ethan's heart shot up into his throat. "What? What do you mean by that?"

"Exactly what I said."

"Tell me what you know!"

Graves gave him a cold smile. "We know you left Provolution after speaking to Andrea Gatting and immediately drove to Great Mongeham. I want to know what you spoke about. And what did you find in Great Mongeham? We know you went into the church and you were in there for an extraordinarily long time, so what did you find?"

He punctuated the last four words, each one feeling like a hammer blow. Ethan decided that this was an unsettling and dangerous man and that he had to tread carefully.

"Tell me what you know and I'll tell you everything," Ethan said without thinking, not even sure if he was bluffing or not. This guy had information on his parents, and he had to find out what it was.

Graves sighed and checked his watch. It was gold and looked expensive. "I don't have time for this, Mr. Jackson. I gave you an opportunity to do this peacefully, but it seems you are just as obstinate as your mother and father."

He signalled to his goons, who unfolded their arms and moved to stand on either side of Ethan. Graves stood up and adjusted his tie. "I hope you remember that." He looked at one of his men. "Take him somewhere quiet." He paused. "But don't kill him."

Ethan looked from one henchman to the other. They were

actually cracking their knuckles, and they both looked far too happy at the idea of beating him to a pulp. As Felix Graves walked away, the one on his left said, "Don't make a scene, kid," and then put a hand on Ethan's shoulder, squeezing it until he felt a sharp pain.

"Okay, okay!" Ethan said. "I'll give you what I found."

Felix Graves stopped, turned around, and looked at him expectantly.

"It's in my backpack."

Ethan slapped at the hand on his shoulder and the goon removed it, tense at the brash action and ready to retaliate.

"Relax," Ethan admonished. "I told you it was in my backpack."

Picking up his pack, he put it on the table and unzipped it.

"Hold it," Grave said, walking back to the table. "No more games, Mr. Jackson. Just give me the bag."

Ethan let go of the bag. "Take it," he said and took a step back, still sandwiched between the two men.

Graves grabbed the bag and unzipped it, pulling out Ethan's survival kit, a spare jacket, a drink bottle, and other miscellaneous items. He tossed the bag aside and narrowed his eyes at Ethan. "What is this?"

But while all eyes were on Graves searching the bag, Ethan was slowly stepping back until he was out of arm's reach, and before the men realised it, he was off like a shot.

"Get him!" Graves shouted.

Having been involved in a few skirmishes and run-ins with the law, Ethan had developed the athleticism to run from those who were chasing him, and now he ran as fast as he could in the crowded market, pushing and squeezing past people who protested as he did his best to separate himself from Graves' men.

Looking back, Ethan saw the goons shoving past people, but the men weren't built for moving through a dense crowd, which allowed Ethan to widen the gap.

He passed a clothes shop when someone crashed into him, blindsiding him and sending him tumbling into a rack of shirts. The store owner cried out as shirts and coat hangers went flying and Ethan got tangled in the rack. Another man in a black suit grabbed Ethan by the arm, trying to haul him up, but Ethan kicked him in the stomach, and he let out an "oomph," doubling over in pain. Untangling himself from the rack of shirts, Ethan stood up, shoving the guy he just kicked, and sprinted up a set of stairs leading into the market.

Risking a look behind him, Ethan saw three more men in black suits chasing him.

Where the hell are they coming from?

He passed through the doors that led into the market and was surrounded by tall brick walls and stalls that created crowded, narrow walkways. Above was a glass ceiling to protect the area from the elements.

Crashing down the walkway, Ethan knocked over stands of clothes and jewellery, causing store owners to curse at him. Shouts of protesting shoppers told him that his pursuers were still behind him, struggling to get past the obstacles Ethan had knocked over. He reached a cross section when another man in a black suit tried to tackle him, but Ethan spun out of the tackle, sending the man crashing into a book stand. Using the momentum from the spin, Ethan sprinted down another passageway and up a set of stairs, his bearings completely gone, hoping he wasn't heading for a dead end. He turned another corner, crashing into a couple of ladies. He called out an apology as he hurried past them, their angry protests following him.

At the end of this passageway were doors to another set of stairs, this time leading back down to the ground floor and back outside. He crashed through the doors, the chilly night air wicking away his body's warmth, and took the stairs two at a time before he stopped, momentum almost causing him to topple over his own feet. At the bottom were two more of Graves' men. They called out and pointed when they saw him and began climbing up.

Ethan turned to go back up, but the three pursuing men had caught up and were heading toward him now.

"Shit!"

They were closing in on him from both sides, so Ethan did the only thing he could: He leapt over the bannister. He fell several metres onto the roof of a stall selling kebabs, the weight of his body crumpling the roof, making the cook cry out in surprise. Ethan rolled off the roof and landed on his feet on the ground. A crowd had formed, staring in a mixture of awe and disbelief, while the kebab cook yelled at him.

Ethan gave the henchmen a grin and ran off, sliding in between the still-gawking crowd while Graves' men scrambled down the stairs.

Heart pumping, lungs burning, and chest heaving, Ethan

headed toward the exit and took a right into Gin Alley. He ran down it and emerged at the intersection of Chalk Farm Road where it changed into Camden High Street and Castlehaven Road.

He scurried under the train overpass. Just as he was about to cross the bridge over Regent's Canal, the screech of tyres caused him to turn around and he saw a black sedan roaring down the street. It jumped the island at the intersection of Camden High Street and Castlehaven Road, taking out a signpost and fracturing the windshield. But that did nothing to slow the car as it headed down the one-way street in the wrong direction before skidding to a halt on the far side of the bridge.

Graves and one of his buildings in a suit got out of the car.

"Jesus, how many of these guys does he have?" Ethan muttered. He had his hands on his knees and was taking deep, gulping breaths.

"Give it up, Mr. Jackson," Graves called out as a crowd of people milled about, watching the scene unfold. "You have nowhere to go."

Ethan said nothing, backing away from the car. Behind him there was a crowd, but none of his goons—yet.

Graves sighed. "Get him, would you, Mr. Grassi?"

Grassi grunted and walked around the car, his meaty paws clenched at his sides like he was ready to punch holes in a brick wall. Ethan backed away until his back hit the black and red steel barrier that separated the road from the bridge's pedestrian walkway. He leapt over the barrier, giving himself some space from Grassi, though he was still cornered with Graves at one end and a crowd of onlookers at the other. He peered down at the cold, dark, uninviting water of the canal. Lights from the nearby buildings danced in the gently lapping water.

He turned back just as Grassi swung one leg over the barrier. He got his other leg over and lunged at Ethan. Ethan ducked under his arms and threw a punch at the man's side. Pain ran up his wrist and arm, and he felt like he'd just punched a slab of stone. Grassi backhanded Ethan, and he went sprawling to the ground.

The crowd cheered, and Ethan rolled out of Grassi's grasp. He got to his feet and tried to scurry away, but Grassi was quicker than he looked and grabbed Ethan by the collar. Ethan tried punching and hitting the goon's arm, but he held firm and started dragging Ethan back to his boss.

Ethan grabbed hold of the barrier and held on tight. Grassi let go of him and threw a punch at Ethan, but he ducked, and Grassi's hand thundered into the barrier. He let out a grunt of pain, and Ethan took advantage of the distraction to kick at Grassi's leg, causing it to buckle at the knee. Grassi grunted again and fell to one knee and Ethan shoulder-charged him with all the strength he could muster. It was like running into a slab of meat, but Ethan put enough force into it to knock Grassi, who was off balance, over the side of the bridge.

The watching crowd let out an "ooh" of surprise, delight, and pain as Grassi splashed into the canal.

While everyone's attention was on Grassi, Ethan ran, turning left and hurrying down the ramp until he was on the Regent's Canal Towpath. He squeezed through the crowd that formed at the bottom, watching Grassi as he struggled to swim to the edge.

Ethan switched back from the ramp, heading underneath the bridge, and followed the towpath along the canal. He passed by closed stalls and docked canal boats until he reached the Kentish Town Road Bridge a couple of minutes later.

He took the brick steps two at a time until he was on Kentish Town Road, a couple of blocks away from Camden Market. He crossed the road and entered Camden Gardens. The gardens were simple in design and style, a triangle shape enclosed by metal fencing with an arched bridge made of brick that the overhead rail crossed. It was laid out with grass and trees and paved walkways and Ethan crossed through the empty park, emerging on to Camden Street.

Heading across the Camden Street Bridge and over the canal, Ethan passed more Georgian-style townhouses until he reached the Greek Orthodox Cathedral Church of All Saints on the corner of Camden and Pratt Street. The church, built in the early 1800s, was rectangular and built from yellow brick. Sticking out of the top of the church like a beacon was a cylindrical stone tower designed to imitate the Choragic Monument of Lysicrates in Athens. A semicircle portico with three pillars greeted Ethan as he tested the church's double doors and was relieved to find one of them unlocked. He passed through it and quietly closed the door behind him.

Ethan moved out of the narthex and into the nave, where lush red carpet bisected rows of pews stained a deep mahogany.

He took a seat in the darkest corner of the church, his eyes on the entrance, praying no one had followed him.

Thirteen

It was almost two in the morning when Ethan returned to his room. He asked the night manager if anyone had asked for him, especially any suspicious people in dark suits. The manager shook his head, but he was so involved with his phone that Ethan wouldn't have been surprised if an entire army of Graves' black-suited goons marched in and he didn't notice.

Taking the stairs to the second floor, Ethan peered around the corner into the hall to see if anyone was there. Seeing the coast was clear, he headed to his room.

Before he swiped his key, he put his ear to the door and listened. It was silent except for his breathing, though he wasn't sure what he expected to hear. If there was someone waiting for him, they wouldn't exactly be having a party. Ethan swiped his key and pushed open the door, switching on the light.

He let out a sigh of relief. His room was just as he left it, with his small pack on a chair in the far corner and a pile of clothes he'd worn on the flight at the foot of the bed. He crossed the room and picked up the clothes, stuffing them in his pack.

If Graves had been following him, then he knew he was staying here, and if he knew he was staying here, then he had to get the hell out of here before they came for him. Heck, they could be watching the hotel right now.

He checked his jacket, feeling the comfort of the two gold coins, the device, and both his journal and Maynard's diary safely zipped up in the inner pockets. He'd snuck them out of his backpack just before Graves and his men took it. Doing a final sweep of the bathroom and bedroom, he shrugged on his pack, thankful he travelled light.

He opened the door and peered out into the hallway. Gasping, he immediately withdrew his head.

"Shit!"

He peaked back out. There were two men in the hall wearing black suits. One of them was on a phone while the other was looking at a floor plan.

He looked down the other end of the hall where it ended at a T-intersection. Above it was a green exit sign that pointed right.

The end of the hall isn't that far. Ethan peered back at the two men. They were still distracted, so Ethan burst out of the door, sprinting as fast as he could down the hall.

Behind him, Ethan heard the men yell out in surprise and

then footsteps thudding on carpet as they chased after him. But Ethan was already turning down the hall and in a few short steps he burst out of the emergency exit door and onto the fire escape.

The fire escape was a pair of metal stairs bolted to the building, one set leading up to the third floor and the other leading down to the park behind the hotel. Ethan looked down. Below, the park was dimly lit but empty of all but a couple of trees and gardens. One path led out to Montague Street, with other paths disappearing behind the other buildings that lined Bedford Place. It was too exposed—they would see him the moment they came out the door.

Instead, Ethan leapt over the railing beside the emergency door and climbed down until he was hidden, hanging by his fingers on the platform with his legs dangling in mid-air. He felt his fingers slipping when the door burst open and the two goons headed down the stairs, believing Ethan went that way.

Ethan hurried to pull himself up and leapt over the railing again. He grabbed the emergency door before it shut and slid inside. Giving himself a moment's reprieve, he thought about what to do next while he flexed his sore fingers and tried to settle his racing heart. If there were two guys in the building, there would be more around, most likely waiting somewhere out front. He couldn't go back through the emergency door since those two were likely to double back as soon as they realised he had given them the slip.

Frustrated at a lack of options, his eyes landed on the red fire alarm. Without a second thought, he hurried to it, broke the glass, and pulled the alarm.

Immediately, a loud ringing pierced the halls and, moments later, doors were opening and bleary-eyed guests were looking around quizzically.

"Fire!" Ethan shouted. "Fire! Come on, let's go!"

That seemed to break the guests out of their haze. They poured out of their rooms dressed in pyjamas and dressing gowns, and headed for the emergency exits and stairways leading to the lobby. Ethan hurried them along, acting like he was a fire warden, and then filed in with the group heading to the lobby. When they reached the lobby, the night manager was still behind his desk, shouting over the sound of the alarm, "Stay calm and... uh... congregate at the meeting point."

"Where's the meeting point?" someone called out.

The night manager stared dumbly before realising he was in charge. He started talking about a green sign somewhere along the road, but most of what he said was ignored by the guests as they filed out into the street. The sound of the alarm was blaring out in Bedford Place, and lights in nearby buildings turned on and people peered out from behind curtains to watch the scene unfold. The wailing of a fire engine siren echoed off the Bedford Place buildings, creating an almost unbearable ringing. The street was crowded with guests and onlookers, and Ethan was certain he had created enough of a distraction to slip away. When the first fire engine screeched to a halt, Ethan slipped behind it and hurried down the street, using the darkness as cover.

Ethan slumped into a booth at an all-night cafe near Liverpool Street Station. He checked his watch. It was past four in the morning.

"What a day," he moaned, happy to be sitting down.

Once he'd left Bedford Place, he was looking over his shoulder every minute until he jumped on the twenty-four-hour train service at Holborn. The train was empty, and he was confident that he wasn't being followed, and rode it to Liverpool Street.

Once there, he found the all-night, three-story cafe sandwiched between two other stores on Bishopsgate.

The cafe was like an American-style fifties diner but with a retro British touch. The red leather Chesterfield booths were a stark contrast to the subway tiled walls lined with newspaper headlines, and other random memorabilia that made some sort of chaotic sense. The cafe was empty except for a group of tipsy—if not drunk—girls laughing loudly in one of the corner booths.

Certain that the danger had passed, Ethan sat back, exhausted. He ordered a coffee and a plate of bacon and scrambled eggs. When the waiter left, Ethan thought about what Graves said about his parents.

Well, one of them is.

Did that mean his mum was alive? The thought of it made his heart race. He didn't want to get his hopes up, but he couldn't help thinking about it. Felix Graves was clearly a dangerous man and he might have had something to do with his parents' death.

Or was it just Dad's death he was talking about? But if Mum was alive, why wouldn't she have contacted me? And why was Maynard's diary in the bunker?

He felt hope rise in him. *They are the only ones who possessed it, and it wasn't found among their things. Did Mum leave it there? Is she alive? Was Graves the one following her?*

He shook his head. *No! Don't think about it. He's just trying to mess with you! He can't be trusted.*

He closed his eyes for a moment, trying to clear his mind of what Graves told him—that they had their eye on him, that he knew where he had been. It was all too much.

"Excuse me?"

Ethan opened his heavy eyelids. The waiter was staring at him with a plate of food.

"Sorry," Ethan muttered as the waiter set down his plate. "Long day," he added, as if that would matter to the disinterested waiter.

Taking a sip of his coffee, Ethan dug into his scrambled eggs. Famished beyond any time he could remember, he cleaned off his plate in a matter of minutes. Once the waiter returned to take away his plate, he sat staring at the table, coffee cup warming his hands.

He thought back on the day's events, wondering how he crammed it all into one day. He went from the meeting with Andrea and thought about how, aside from confirming his parents' career choices, it yielded no results. St. Martin's Church, on the other hand, provided a boon of information and hope of picking up his parents' trail.

Looking around to make sure he was alone, Ethan grabbed his pack and pulled out Maynard's diary, the device, and the two

Spanish coins. Hiding the Philip V coin under the diary, he studied the other one. It was very similar in shape and size to the Philip coin, but he'd never seen or heard of anything like it before.

"El Mal," he murmured, rotating the coin in his fingers. What was so evil about this coin? It certainly depicted some sort of evil with the crosses over the eyes of the king and queen, suggesting their death, but otherwise, it seemed like any other coin.

"Why are you evil?" he asked the coin absently.

He grabbed the other coin and compared them. The Philip V coin seemed to shine a bright gold, while the El Mal coin was dull, as if it were shrouded in shadow.

"Weird," Ethan said, putting the coins in his pack.

Next, he picked up the five-sided device, his instinct telling him it had something to do with the star map, but he wasn't sure what. Now that he had a better light, he examined it properly. The top was plain, with braille-like bumps dotted all over it. He turned it over and checked the scratched initials, but even in the light, he still couldn't make out the letters. They looked like an 'F' and an 'I', but he wasn't sure.

"What do you mean?" he asked the device.

He examined the sides, seeing if there was a way to open it he missed in the bunker, but there was no clasp or button. He ran his finger around the seam, trying to pry it open, but he wasn't able to get his nail in enough to leverage it. Looking back at the top of it, he ran a finger over the raised stars and then pressed one. To his surprise, it popped into the casing like a button. He pressed another and, like the first, it popped in. He pressed all the buttons until they were all popped in. He then tried to open it, but it remained as tightly closed as before.

It's a key code, he realised with excitement. Press the stars in a specific sequence and it will unlock the device. Unfortunately, he didn't know the sequence or how many stars were in the sequence, and with so many possibilities, it was almost impossible to guess.

There was a single button at the top of the casing, away from the rest. He pressed it and all the stars popped back out. "Must be the reset button," he told himself.

Maybe Maynard's diary would shed some light on it. He opened it and spent the next hour scanning the pages. Before 1718, Maynard talked about his personal life, aspirations, and joining the navy. But from 1718 onwards, there were almost thirty years missing, ripped pages in the spine the only evidence of their existence. Then he came to one of his last entries, dated a year before he died, where Maynard wrote:

I have spent a year at home, reflecting on what I did. I rue that day thirty-three years ago when I came across that brigand and found that infernal contraption. I should have tossed it into the water and been done with it. But curiosity, and then greed, got the better of me.

Afterward, I convinced myself that I would hide it from the world — that I would bury it forever and leave it to history, that it was too dangerous to find. But I was fooling no one but myself. If I wanted to be rid of it, I would have dumped it in the middle of the ocean, yet I was compelled not to. Was it a sense of the greater good? Greed? I do not know. But someone will figure out what we did. They always do.

They will follow the stars.

It is my only hope they will have the courage to do what I could not.

Nothing stays hidden forever.

The "brigand" must be Blackbeard, since the dates fit. But what was the contraption he found on the body?

It must be this, he thought, looking at the five-sided device in his hand. What else caught his attention was the phrase, *'Someone will figure out what we did'.* Ethan wasn't sure why he thought Maynard worked alone, but admitting he had accomplices to help him hide the treasure was a bit of a surprise. The next sentence, *'They will follow the stars',* made him think that the star map was the clue he was looking for. But how was it meant to help him?

Since he had no idea how to open the device, he put it back in his pack and opened his journal, turning to the page where he copied down the star map. His eyes were drawn to the number in the corner: 16/20/15/12/5/13/25.

They weren't coordinates—that much Ethan knew. Maybe dates?

He looked at them, but if they were dates, he couldn't make any sense of it. There weren't enough numbers to be a set of dates.

He felt his eyes go blurry after minutes of staring at them. Then a thought struck him: *Maybe it's a code or cypher.*

Grabbing a pen, he tried using the common A1Z26 cypher on the numbers, in which each number represented the corresponding letter of the alphabet. One being A, two being B, and so on. *It couldn't be that easy, could it?*

He wrote the letters for each number and got the word "Ptolemy." Ptolemy, if he correctly remembered high school science, was an astronomer.

He pulled out his phone, grateful the battery was still more than a quarter full, and asked a passing waiter if he could have the Wi-Fi password.

Once he was online, he set to work trying to figure out what this map led to.

It was more than an hour later when Ethan worked out that the images were representations of constellations. He was right about Ptolemy. Claudius Ptolemy was an astronomer and astrologer who was famous for describing the forty-eight initial constellations in his treatise, 'The Almagest' in the second century. Figuring it had something to do with constellations, Ethan cross-referenced the images on the wall with each of the forty-eight constellations Ptolemy identified. When he finished, he had worked out each image and its corresponding constellation:

The Chariot — 14/3/19 — was the Auriga constellation.

The Lion — 7/4/19 — was Leo.

The Bear — 19/5/19 — was Ursa Major.

The Eagle — 5/8/19 — was Aquila.

The Jar — 13/10/19 — was Aquarius.

The Centaur — no date — was Centaurus.

Now he had that information, but he didn't know what it meant. But he had a feeling these constellations were directions. He swiped through the photos he had taken. The ship on the map was likely to be Maynard's ship, and these constellations were the route he took. He looked at the image of the ship next to the islands, thinking that was where he landed, but there were dozens of islands in the southern hemisphere. Where Maynard went and where he started, Ethan didn't know. He researched how to navigate star maps until his phone went dead, and he was again at a loss. All he had were guesses, and his best guess was that Maynard travelled from the northern hemisphere, probably England, and crossed the equator, most likely along the west coast of Africa, before stopping at the cluster of islands.

Despite his third cup of coffee, he was nearly falling asleep at the table. He checked the time on his watch—it was almost six.

The dirty looks he was getting from the cafe staff told him they were going to kick him out soon, and he had to find somewhere to sleep. He couldn't go back to the hotel—not with Graves' men crawling about. Plus, he would probably be in trouble for pulling the fire alarm.

From his pocket, he pulled out the card Andrea Gatting gave him. Could he call her? Would she help? She wanted him to keep her updated, but was that just a courtesy? He had the feeling she didn't really think his quest to find his parents would bear any results. Though now he had found Maynard's bunker, the star map, and had encountered Felix Graves, who knew something about his parents. That was information she couldn't pass up.

He sighed, his mind feeling like it was shrouded in fog. He desperately needed sleep and a place to think without worrying if Graves, or his goons, would come bursting through the door. Tapping the card on the table, Ethan ordered one more cup of coffee and then made his decision.

When the waiter returned with his coffee, he asked if they had a phone he could use.

Fourteen

Rain was threatening to fall when Ethan arrived at the address Andrea gave him. He stood at a row of five-story apartments sandwiched together on the Chelsea embankment overlooking the Thames. Despite his sleep-deprived mind, Ethan had to admire the red-brick Victorian architecture. He approached the landing stoop and looked at the door phone, searching for Andrea's name. He eventually found it and pressed the buzzer.

Despite his jacket, he shivered in the chill air, and the first drops of rain started pattering the stoop. The intercom crackled and Andrea's voice came over the speaker. "Ethan?"

"Yeah," he said.

"Ethan, are you there?"

He frowned. "Yeah," he repeated, a little louder.

"Ethan, press the button so I can hear you."

Oh.

He pushed the button again and said, "Can you hear me now?"

"Yes. Ethan, are you okay?"

"Yeah, I'm fine."

"Okay, I'll buzz you in. Head straight for the elevator. I am on the fifth floor."

There was a short, sharp buzz, and Ethan pulled the door open. Inside was an empty reception area with photos of various parts of London lining the walls. Dark-grey tiles led Ethan to a black and gold elevator. He pressed the up button and the elevator doors slid open.

Pressing the button for the fifth floor, the doors closed, and the elevator began its ascent, and he leaned against the wall and closed his eyes. His chest felt tight. He was tense from constantly looking over his shoulder, so now he allowed himself to breathe, willing the anxiousness away. When the doors opened, Andrea, who was dressed for work in a black business skirt and white blouse, greeted him.

"Ethan!" she said, pulling him into a hug. Standing back, she asked, "Are you okay? What happened to your face?"

He touched the red welt near his eye where Grassi had backhanded him the night before. "It's been a long night, Miss Gatting," he explained. She stood back, and he exited the elevator, expecting to follow her to her apartment, instead…

"This is where you live?" he blurted, dropping his pack by

the elevator doors.

Straight off the elevator, he found himself in a tastefully designed living room with white walls leading to high ceilings. A couch sat in the middle, facing a television, and beyond that was a kitchen with an island bench and three casement windows overlooking the Thames.

The room was decorated with artefacts from around the world. There were African tribal masks, indigenous totem poles, and pedestals with statues of various religious gods such as Ganesh, Huitzilopochtli, and Osiris.

Andrea noticed him studying the statues. "One benefit of being friends with your parents was access to these types of artefacts."

Ethan frowned. "Are these black market?"

Andrea chuckled. "Oh, gosh, no. Like I told you before, I knew they were involved, but had very little to do with that aspect of it. I just made introductions to the right people so they could go where they needed to."

"Then you're a collector?"

Andrea nodded. "I am a history buff. It's how I met your parents, actually."

"Oh?"

She nodded and indicated for him to take a seat on the plush couch. He did and sank into the cushions. It felt like he was sitting on a cloud.

"They were doing an unveiling for the British Museum, and I was there on company business and we got to talking. I showed them my collection, they showed me theirs and, well, we hit it off.

Would you like a drink?"

"Water, please, Miss Gatting."

While she headed to the kitchen to get his water, Ethan closed his eyes and rested his head on the palm of his hand. For the first time in the last twelve hours, he felt like he was safe.

"Here you go."

Ethan opened his eyes and took the offered glass. He took a sip, savouring the cool water while Andrea sat next to him.

"Tell me what happened."

Taking another drink of water, Ethan explained his trip to St. Martin's Church and finding Maynard's secret bunker.

Andrea grinned at him. "You are your parents' son, Ethan. They've told me many stories of finding entrances following clues left out in plain sight."

Ethan got up and grabbed his backpack. "I was just lucky," he said, though the compliment gave him a sense of pride.

"Don't sell yourself short, Ethan. They always spoke highly of you and your intelligence."

Ethan shrugged as he pulled out the two coins. "They're parents, they have to say that."

Andrea laughed.

"This is what I found in the bunker," he said, handing her the coins.

She examined both coins, flipping them over. "Spanish?" she asked.

Ethan nodded, pointing to the Philippus coin. "Minted in 1709 under Philip V's reign."

She looked at the other one. "'El Mal'… 'the evil'?"

"Yep."

"An evil coin?"

She looked at him for an explanation, but he didn't have one.

"Apparently," was all he said, giving her a look that said he didn't know any more than that.

She flipped it over, noting the illustration of the man before handing both coins to Ethan.

"Why did Maynard have Spanish coins on him?"

Ethan shrugged. "I'm not sure. Maybe it has something to do with the cursed treasure he wrote about."

"How so?" she asked.

Ethan put the coins back in his pack. "He has two coins, minted two hundred years apart. One of them looks to be a normal coin, but the other is an 'evil' coin. But what made it evil? As far as I know, 1516 was a relatively normal time for Spain, so I don't know why they minted it."

"Maybe they didn't," she said. "At least, maybe not officially. Not from their treasury."

Ethan considered that. She could be right, but it was only a theory, so he put that thought aside.

"So, you found two coins, one of them labelled as evil, but you don't know why. Was there anything else?"

He considered telling her about the five-sided device and star maps, but decided he would keep that a secret. While he trusted her, he didn't know her that well and wanted to keep something up his sleeve.

Just in case.

"No, that's it." He felt guilty for not having enough faith in her, especially after all the help she'd given him, but he was also aware that she was one of the last people to speak to his parents.

Ethan thought she stiffened a little, but might have imagined it. She looked disappointed, and the pang of guilt seemed to tighten its grip around his stomach.

"What about your parents?" she asked. "Any sign they were there?"

This time he smiled and nodded.

Andrea's eyes widened. "What makes you so sure?"

"Because I found this." He pulled out Maynard's diary and handed it to her.

"Is this…?"

He nodded. "It was in the bunker."

"Why would they leave it there?"

"Just another question to be answered," he sighed, shrugging.

She put a hand on his shoulder. "We'll figure it out, Ethan. You've already accomplished more in a day than anyone else has since your parents died," she reassured him.

Something jolted loose in his tired mind. "I ran into someone afterward. He said he knew my parents and that only one of them was dead."

"What? Who said that?"

"A man named Graves. I was getting something to eat at the Camden Market when he threatened me, said I was just like my parents and that only one of them was dead."

Andrea sat down, her face incredulous. "Tell me everything that happened."

Ethan went into the events of last night. From leaving St.

Martin's Church to encountering the man named Graves in Camden Town. He mentioned Graves' threat and how, if he wished to avoid his parents' fate, he would give him everything he found at the church.

"My God, Ethan. You have to go to the police about this… what was his name?"

"Graves."

"You have to go to the police about what he did."

Ethan shook his head. "And tell them what? That he threatened me? It would be my word against his. Besides, if I come forward, he will be back on my trail, and I can't have that. Not yet anyway. He knows something about Mum and Dad, but I am not giving him anything unless I have to."

Andrea seemed to think about that. "Then you did the right thing coming here," she told him. "You'll be safe."

"Have you ever heard of this guy before?"

She shook her head. "Can't say I remember anyone named Graves."

"Neither have I. I looked him up, but he's a ghost."

"That's not surprising," she said, looking at her watch. "The people who make those threats aren't the social media type. Look, I have to go to work, but you look dead on your feet. We can talk more about this when I get back. Why don't you have a shower and take a nap? You can use my bed."

Ethan nodded. The idea of a shower and sleep was very inviting.

"Come on," she said. She took him down a hallway and showed him the shower and her bedroom, which had a queen-sized bed. "There's food and drinks in the kitchen, so make yourself at home. Just stay put and you'll be safe. I'll be back by six."

"Thank you," he said, gratefully. "Truly, I don't know what I would have done without your help, Miss Gatting."

She gave him a smile, crinkling her eyes and creasing the scar. "How many times do I have to say call me Andrea? And no need to thank me. I would do anything for David and Gemma, and that includes helping you. See you later. And remember, don't leave."

After saying goodbye and hearing the elevator doors close, Ethan headed straight to the bathroom to have a long, hot shower.

It was past four in the afternoon and Ethan, still tired but feeling better after a deep sleep, was sitting on the couch in Andrea's apartment. He had his journal open on the coffee table, working out what to do next.

It had been raining all afternoon, and the steady patter on the windows helped Ethan think about his next move. He had the star map, and if his estimation and research was right, it provided a route from England to some God-knows-where island in the South Atlantic Ocean.

If Maynard left from England and not somewhere else.

The route didn't bring him north of the equator, so that leaves everything south of it. That cut out the Caribbean and most European- and American-claimed islands, but still left at least thirty-five possible islands by Ethan's count.

He shut the journal and tossed it on the table. He knew there was no way he could figure this out without help. He could ask Andrea if she knew of someone, but he didn't want to get her too involved, and asking her would mean he had to tell her about the map. He was still reluctant to tell her about it, and he wasn't sure why. This was all new to him, and he felt like he was floating alone in the middle of an ocean. Felix Graves' involvement meant danger, and he didn't want to put Andrea at risk. For all the help she had given him, he couldn't in good conscience put her in harm's way when Graves was around. No, it was best to keep her out of it.

He grabbed his phone and opened his dad's list of contacts. Maybe there was someone they knew who could help. All he needed was the location.

He had the 'evil' coin in his hand, turning it between his fingers while he browsed the contacts. Most of them were friends' back home, others were colleagues from various museums. Some of them might be able to help, he thought, though it would have been a stretch.

He was near the end of the list when he stopped on a name: Richie Richardson. Ethan had never met him, at least not that he remembered, but the name sounded familiar. His mind turned back to his parents talking about a guy they knew, a boat captain on a sea freighter. He would ship their finds across the ocean for them. He was pretty sure it was this guy.

Next to his name, there were three addresses crossed out: Portchester, England; Si Racha, Thailand; San Miguel de Azapa, Chile. There was a fourth address not crossed out listed in Cape Town, South Africa.

There were no contact numbers or email addresses for him, and Ethan was concerned that Richie Richardson was a nomad and had moved on from Cape Town.

With the trail leading out of England, there was no point in staying here. He was sure the next location was in the southern hemisphere, so even if Ritchie had moved on, Ethan could find someone down there who might help him. Money was an excellent motivator, and even with his dwindling bank account, he was sure he had enough to get to Cape Town and grease a palm or two to get the information he needed.

Decision made, he booked a ticket on the next flight to Cape Town. Then he picked up his phone and dialled Andrea's mobile number.

Andrea answered on the third ring. "Ethan? Is everything okay?"

"Yeah. I've decided to leave England, and I just wanted to say thank you for all you've done for me."

"Leave? Where are you going to go?" she asked, surprise evident in her voice.

"I can't say."

"Why not?"

"I don't want to put you at risk."

Andrea paused and Ethan thought she might hang up, but she said, "At least tell me why you're leaving."

Her voice was pleading now.

Ethan paused, still undecided on whether to fully trust her. "I found some information in my parents' journal. Someone who might have been able to help them determine why Maynard had the gold."

"Ethan, I'm not sure this is a good idea. Those men might still be after you."

"Let them come," he said. "They have information I need and I won't let them stop me uncovering what happened to Mum and Dad."

"I should come with you, at least."

Shaking his head, he again explained, "Sorry, Miss Gatting, but no. I can't put your life at risk. You've done more than enough for me. Goodbye, and thank you."

"But—"

He hung up before she could say anything, then grabbed his pack and left.

Fifteen

Cape Town, South Africa

Ethan took the next flight from London to Cape Town. Fifteen hours after he hung up from Andrea, he was in a taxi leaving Cape Town International Airport and heading into the city centre.

Founded in 1652, Cape Town was South Africa's second most populous city behind Johannesburg, and one of its most popular tourist destinations. Situated on Table Bay, it sat in the shadows of Table Mountain. Given it was along a major shipping corridor for transport around the world, Ethan figured it would be the best place to find Ritchie.

It was a sunny morning with clear skies as the taxi turned off Nelson Mandela Boulevard just out of Cape Town CBD and headed to the Victoria and Alfred Waterfront. He had spent the flight studying the star map in his journal and playing with the sequence on the device, still failing to open it. After trying and failing yet again in the taxi, Ethan pocketed the journal and device when the taxi dropped him off near the shopping centre.

Ethan zipped up his jacket against the brisk wind that blew off the Atlantic. He passed through the busy waterfront packed with tourists and locals, shopping, and eating lunch along the many dockside restaurants, until he reached the V&A Food Market. Near the Cape Wheel, the brown brick, multi-story former power station had over forty vendors selling local produce, drinks, and street food. He was passing straight through, weaving his way through the boisterous crowd haggling down prices, when he heard his name.

"Ethan!"

Ethan turned, surprised anyone would know him here, and was doubly surprised to see it was Andrea Gatting.

"Ethan!" she called out again, trying to get past a couple who were arguing with a greengrocer. She was casually dressed, wearing jeans and a dark jacket with her black hair tied in a ponytail. Ethan was shocked at how casual she looked, a welcome change from the sterile, corporate front he'd seen her in previously.

"Ethan," she repeated when she caught up to him. "Finally."

She put her hand against a stall selling ceramic bowls, trying to catch her breath. "I'm not as fit as I used to be," she gasped. "I saw you back at the Waterfront and ran after you."

"What the hell are you doing here?" he growled, surprised at how angry he was with her. He thought he was clear that it was too dangerous for her, and he didn't want her help.

"I couldn't just let you go on your own," she said. "It's dangerous out there, you said so yourself. I'm not letting you do it without help."

Ethan sighed. "No offence, Miss Gatting—"

"Andrea."

"But how can you help? What can you do?"

Andrea snorted, looking indignant. "I am not some corporate slave, Ethan. I know some martial arts. I've shot a gun before, and I've trekked deep in the Congo to see the Silverbacks. More to the point, I have money and I am resourceful. I got here at the same time you did, and I wasn't on your flight."

"How *did* you get here?" Ethan asked.

"Private plane."

Ethan raised his eyebrows. "You have a private plane?"

"I have access to one," she said with a mysterious smile.

"How did you find me?"

The mysterious smile stayed on her face, but she said nothing. Looking at his watch, Ethan sighed. "Fine," he said. "We can talk about this later. This shouldn't be too risky anyway."

Andrea grinned at him like a child who had conned a parent into buying them a toy they wanted. He turned and walked off, and she fell into step beside him.

"Where are we going?"

"The docks," he told her.

With Ethan in the lead, they made their way out of the Food Market, turning left before the Watershed—another popular Cape

Town market that sold arts and crafts—and crossed over a sluice gate. There, they passed by a shipyard where a container ship was dry-docked for repair.

It was quiet, and Ethan realised there was no one around when they crossed over a bascule bridge and into the dock's parking lot.

"We seem to have found the quietest part of Cape Town," he joked.

They were halfway across the lot when Andrea asked, "What are we looking for?"

Ethan, still ahead of her, stopped and turned. "I am looking for a family friend who might be able to help."

"Who?" she asked, shielding her eyes from the sun.

"His name is Richie Richardson. His name was in my parents' contacts. He's moved around a bit, but the last address they had was somewhere in Cape Town. Do you know him?"

She shook her head. "How do you think he can help?"

Ethan hesitated, still not willing to part with the information about Maynard's travels. Finally, he said, "He's a boat captain. I remember he used to help Mum and Dad transport large artefacts home or to other countries. I figure if he helped them legally, he might have helped them illegally, too. Maybe he has some information on what they were up to."

They were out of the parking lot and on West Quay Road, passing by a hotel that overlooked the marina and the various boats and yachts docked there.

"But what is his connection to your parents' disappearance?" Andrea asked.

Ethan shrugged. "Probably nothing," he lied. "If they were on to something and needed to get out quietly, maybe he helped them."

It was a weak reason, but before she could reply, a shout came from behind them. They both turned around and saw two black-suited men running toward them. Each of them was carrying a handgun.

"Oh, shit!" Ethan said, grabbing Andrea's hand. "Run!"

They turned and were running down West Quay Road as the first shot rang out in the silence. A bullet ricocheted off the stone block wall of the hotel, chipping it, and another shot followed, thudding into the trunk of a parked car.

"Come on!" Ethan shouted, pulling her along. She ripped her hand free of his as he veered off the road and through a small parking lot to a high brick fence with anti-burglar spikes running along the top of it. Ethan charged forward, running toward the steel gate.

"What are you doing?" Andrea called from behind him as another two bullets whizzed past them. "That gate's locked!"

In front of the fence on either side of the gate were stone planter boxes about as high as his hip. Ethan leapt onto one of them, planting his foot on the edge, and then pushed off it and grabbed the top of the iron gate. He pulled himself up and over, dropping into a parking lot on the opposite side.

He reached for the latch but Andrea, a few metres behind, saw what he did and followed his lead, leaping onto the planter box and jumping on the gate. She climbed over and landed beside him.

He was impressed. "Let's go!" he said, and they hurried away from the gate.

Behind them, the men arrived and tested the gate, rattling it as hard as they could, but it didn't open. One screamed an obscenity while the other talked into a radio.

"That's not the last of them," Ethan said, slowing his pace so Andrea could catch up.

They were out of the parking lot and turned left at a building into another dockyard. There was a fishing trawler and a luxury yacht in drydock. The sleek white yacht looked like it was under maintenance, but the trawler looked old and dinged up, like it was going through some major repair work. A score of workers were on or around the boat, with forklifts moving supplies back and forth.

Ethan stopped before a stack of shipping containers and looked around. Seeing they were alone, he held a hand out to Andrea, indicating they should stop and catch their breath.

"He was talking into a radio or walkie talkie, which means they have more guys around. We need to keep our eyes open and find Ritchie before they find us."

Andrea was bent over, trying to catch her breath. She nodded and said, "So don't get seen. Just like hide and seek in school."

"Yeah, just a bit deadlier. You good?"

She nodded again and stood up.

Ethan moved around the container and to the dry-docked boats, Andrea behind him.

"Told you," she said.

Ethan looked at her. "Told me what?"

"That I could handle myself."

He grinned. "I believed you."

"You did not!"

"I wouldn't have made that jump if I didn't think you could do it," he told her.

"Yeah, right," she replied.

They were just past the trawler when something whizzed by Ethan's head and clanged off the boat. He ducked out of instinct, and another bullet dinged off the trawler's hull.

"Run!" he shouted. But Andrea didn't need any prompting and already had a good head start on him. Following her, Ethan looked around and saw five more guys coming from the street side of the dock, each with handguns out.

"Toward the boats!" Ethan called, taking the lead.

The distance between them, and that Ethan and Andrea were moving targets, made it hard for their pursuers to fire accurately, especially on the run. But it only would take one lucky shot for things to end badly, and Ethan didn't want to push his luck.

Ethan led Andrea up the ramp into the trawler. Once topside, they passed a set of stairs leading down into the hold, dodging workers' tools, coils of rope, and pieces of metal left lying around haphazardly. Ethan avoided a pile of nets and a stack of crates and skirted around a gap in the deck that opened into the hold where they stored their catches in freezers. The floor of the hold had been removed, exposing the hull and ribbing where there was a long, jagged gash along the bottom. The metal was twisted, and Ethan wondered what the boat had hit to cause such damage. Through the tear in the hull, he could see the bilge and keel blocks holding up the ship. An idea came to him.

He stopped and turned to Andrea. "Keep going. I'll catch up."

"What are you going to do?" she asked.

"We can't keep running. They'll catch us or corner us, and either way, they'll probably kill us. I'm going to buy us some time."

She looked ready to protest, but thought better of it. "Be careful," she said, kissing him on the cheek and hurrying off.

Ethan looked over the starboard side of the ship and saw the five men approaching. Hiding behind the stack of crates, Ethan peered through a gap and watched the men approach. They were cautious, guns held down, and stopped at the ramp.

One man pointed to three of them and said, "You three keep going. See if they passed through." Then he pointed to the other one and said, "Come with me."

The three men hurried off toward the far end of the dockyard while the other two slowly ascended the ramp. Ethan lost sight of them as he crouched behind the crates, waiting.

Moments later, he heard the metallic thudding of feet on metal as the two men boarded the trawler.

"Check up here, I'm going to look downstairs," said the man who gave the orders before.

The sound of shuffling feet got louder as one man went down into the hold of the ship.

Left alone with the other, Ethan waited for what felt like an eternity until, finally, the man appeared from around the crates. The man was looking forward, gun still down, and didn't see

Ethan until it was too late.

Ethan charged him. The man, seeing Ethan out of the corner of his eye, didn't react in time, and Ethan shoved him as hard as he could, pushing him into the hold. The man cried out as he disappeared from view, his screams echoing around the hold before cutting off suddenly.

Ethan looked over the edge and blanched. The man was impaled on a twisted piece of metal, piercing him through the top of his shoulder and went out through his hip. Blood leaked from the body, trailing down the metal and dripping out onto the drydock.

"Oh, god, Barry!"

Ethan heard more metallic thuds as the other man came into the view along the walkway and bolted into the hull. He stopped and leaned over the railing, looking at the body of his colleague. He looked up and Ethan pulled away, but he wasn't quick enough.

The other man's gun fired, and the sound boomed around the ship's body, but the bullet flew harmlessly into the air. Ethan took off, heading for the ramp, but skidded to a stop when he saw two of the other men charging back from the far end of the dock.

"Shit."

Ethan turned back toward the aft and stopped just before the opening into the hold. Coming up the stairs was the other man, the top of his head visible. Ethan looked around to find a way out, but he was trapped.

Then he noticed that on both the port and starboard side of the ship, the ribs of the trawler curved around the hull and attached to the deck under his feet. From where he stood, he could make out horizontal ladder-like rungs on the steel ribs. It might give him a chance.

He dropped and lowered himself over the lip of the hold opening until he was suspended over the gash in the hull.

Don't slip. Don't slip! He silently prayed and then reached out and grabbed a rung set into the half-metre wide rib. Taking a deep breath, he let go of the lip and grabbed onto the rung. Holding on as tight as he could, Ethan hung in mid-air, while above him, he heard the men converge. He began slowly climbing down, using all the upper-body strength he could muster while he moved rung-to-rung, descending into the hold.

Above, the three men were talking, sounding confused.

"Did you see him?" asked one of them.

"No, Johnny and I ran over after you radioed, but saw no one come down the ramp."

"Then he must be here," said the other.

"What are the orders?"

There was a pause. "Shoot to kill."

"But Graves said—" began one.

"Screw Graves. The kid killed Barry—look!"

Ethan was climbing down to the railing when they all looked down and gave a shout in surprise when they saw him.

Of all the bad timings.

Ethan swung his legs over the railing and crashed into the walkway just as shots rang out. Bullets thudded into the hull, pinging off the railing and walkway. He was just out of their sight, but as soon as one of them changed the angle, he was a goner. Ethan was about to get to his feet when he saw the handgun on the walkway. It was Barry's, a SIG P229, a compact handgun handy for concealment, which is exactly what these guys were going for. Ethan picked it up and scrambled to his feet, the bullets pinging in his wake as he sprinted along the walkway. He blind fired behind him up at the opening with no intention of hitting anyone, only to give himself some time and space.

The bullets stopped and Ethan charged across the walkway toward amidship, passing through a bulkhead door and across a gutted common room. Water marks and rust stained the cream-coloured, while wind whistled like a kettle through the opening where the portholes used to be. To his left, the clatter of shoes on metal told him the men were heading down the stairs. Ethan fired another shot toward the stairs, trying to buy time.

There was a shout of surprise, but they kept after him.

Ethan ran, heading toward the bow. He charged through a second bulkhead door, pulling it closed behind him, and ran down a hallway. He passed through a third door and skidded to a stop.

"Oh, no…"

The entire lower half of the ship's bow had been removed. Whether it was torn away at sea or deliberately removed, Ethan didn't know. Behind him, he heard the heavy groaning of the bulkhead door opening. He turned and saw the three goons hurrying toward him. He reached out and pulled the bulkhead door closed. Bullets rang out in the hallway, but they bounced off the door and walls.

He jammed the door with a length of metal pipe just as the

men arrived. He could hear them try to open it, but the metal bar held—for now.

Ethan turned around to check his options, limited as they were.

He was in a bunk room. Portholes lined the wall and there was only one door in and out. There were beds attached to the floor and sides, though some were dismantled and others twisted and ruined. A gust of chill air blew through the hull's opening, which revealed a view of the V&A Waterfront and the waterways leading to Table Bay.

The goons were working on the door, and the metal bar was bending. With time running out, Ethan approached the edge of the hull where it opened to drydock. He couldn't jump—the boat was too high up—and if Ethan tried, the impact would break his legs at best, or, at worst, kill him. And a gunfight was out of the question, seeing as they outnumbered him. Fighting down his panic as he heard the metal bar groaning, his eyes followed the edge of the boat, trying to find a way down.

There!

On the starboard side of the hull plates had been stripped away, leaving a gap between two of the horizontal steel beams. If Ethan could get there, he could climb down to the exposed beams along the ship's bilge and then down the keel blocks into the drydock.

The problem was getting there. The wall plates in the bunkroom had yet to be removed, which meant he had no way of getting to the steel beam.

Unless...

Putting the gun in his waist belt, Ethan backed as far away from the beam as he could and said a silent prayer before he sprinted towards it. He was halfway across the room when the bulkhead door burst open and the three goons charged in. They fired their guns just as Ethan launched himself from the edge. Bullets flew past him as he soared through the air and slammed into the steel beam, the air exploding from his lungs, but he held on. With no time to rest, Ethan pulled himself up, his feet scrambling on the slick wall, and over to the outer side of the hull just as another spray of bullets clanged off the steel wall.

Shielded from the bullets for now, Ethan hung from the outside of the hull. He put his feet against the wall and shimmied across the beam toward amidships where the hull plates had been removed. Ethan let go and dropped to the next beam below.

Legs hanging in the air, he shimmied back toward the bow below the waterline. When he was over the bow where the engine room used to be, he found a horizontal beam, similar to the one he climbed down to get into the hold. Ethan grabbed the inside rung and climbed down as quickly as he could until he was just above the keel. He let go and fell the final few metres onto the empty drydock, landing with a thud.

He was now under the trawler, weary of how precarious his position was below a boat held up by blocks and braces, with three gunmen no doubt on their way there to kill him.

Removing the SIG from his waistband, he crept under the bow to the port side, using the keel blocks as cover. The blocks towered over him like a concrete forest as he moved from one to another, trying to get to the edge of the drydock where a ladder was mounted into the wall. He had almost made it when he heard a shout, and bullets slammed into a nearby keel block, spraying him with chips of concrete. Ethan dove behind the block and peered around. The three men were approaching from underneath the stern of the ship, spread out wide to prevent him from getting around them.

He looked around. He was stuck between the sluice gate behind him and the goons in front. He tried to get a shot off at them, but they were taking cover behind the blocks, and when they moved, the others provided covering fire.

It was then that he noticed an idling forklift, carrying a pallet loaded with debris, sitting near the stern of the ship. The driver evidently had abandoned the vehicle when the shooting started. It was facing away from Ethan, and he could see the large gas cylinder mounted behind the driver's seat.

With the men getting closer and closer, time was running out. Ethan had no place to go, so he did the only thing that came to mind.

"I hope this works," he said and leaned out with his gun raised, firing three shots at the gas tank. The first missed, going wide right, and the second thudded into the frame. The third hit its mark, and the tank exploded in a ball of fire, rocking the dock.

The explosion destroyed the braces, and four of the keels crumbled. The three goons stopped in their tracks, frozen in disbelief, as they watched the ship groan and then lurch along its port. The keel blocks shattered under the sudden weight and the ship shuddered, leaning precariously on the remaining blocks.

"Run!" one man shouted, and that broke Ethan out of his

reverie. He turned and ran toward the sluice gate, but the shadow of the lurching ship loomed over him as more keel blocks collapsed. He realised he wasn't going to make it and he veered right just as the ship's bow crashed down in a shriek of screeching metal. Ethan stopped and turned around, seeing the dockyard covered in a cloud of dust. The ship seemed to hold upright on its bow for a minute before it groaned and creaked and started listing toward him.

"Oh, no, no, no!" Ethan cried out and took off like a rocket. He felt the ship coming down on him as he dove for the drydock wall, trying to squeeze himself into the corner of it and the floor as tightly as possible.

He covered his head and closed his eyes tight as the trawler came crashing down on top of him in a thunderous cacophony of groaning and twisting metal.

Sixteen

Ethan's ears were ringing. He opened his eyes, surprised to find himself alive. He was facing the drydock wall, his nose so close he could smell the years of oil and dust that imprinted itself into it. Uncurling from the ball he had made himself into, Ethan checked himself over and, to his relief, found everything was there and working.

He rolled over, groaning and coughing in the dust cloud that had formed around him, and gave a start.

Above him, leaning precariously against the drydock wall and held up by broken keels and timber braces, were the twisted remains of the trawler. It loomed over him, creaking and groaning, like it was about to collapse on top of him.

Even with the ringing in his ears, he could hear the faint sounds of sirens. He couldn't tell whether they came from police cars or ambulances or fire trucks. In his head, it all sounded the same.

"I gotta get out of here," he mumbled, getting to his feet. He felt lightheaded and stumbled forward, heading along the drydock wall and away from the bow of the trawler. He was almost to the ladder when a metal screeching rang out through the silent air. Ethan looked up and his eyes went wide. "Oh, shit!"

The shrieking grew louder, and the trawler trembled as the remaining keels crumbled, the braces splintered, causing the ship to slip and grind down the wall.

Ethan ran, stumbling over fallen debris, while the trawler fell all around him. A steel beam slammed into the ground before him, inches from crushing him, and he jumped over it and dodged a piece of railing. He dove just as the bow thundered down behind him, kicking up another cloud of dust.

Coughing and spluttering, Ethan got up, looking at the mangled remains of the fallen fishing vessel. "Holy shit," he puffed, hands on his knees. "I really need to get out of here."

He quickly checked himself over again. He found some cuts and the beginning of bruises on his arms and legs, and his jacket ripped down the side, but otherwise, he was unharmed.

The sirens were getting closer, and Ethan hurried to the ladder built into the drydock wall. He climbed it as quickly as he could and the closer he got to the top rung, the better he felt.

He reached the top where, waiting for him, was a man in a black suit and dark sunglasses. He held a gun pointed straight at

Ethan.

Ethan sighed. "Damn."

On the other side of the dock, a crowd of people, along with emergency service personnel, were hurrying toward the drydock. Having forgotten the gunshots and emboldened by the strength of numbers, the crowd was no doubt drawn by the explosion and crashing trawler.

The black-suited man tried his radio, but all he got was static in return. He looked around, as if deciding what to do, and then said, "Get up."

He had a gruff voice and seemed unsure of himself. "Come on," he demanded when Ethan hesitated.

Ethan climbed up, and the man grabbed his jacket and pushed him forward.

"Take it easy," he said. "It's my first time, too."

The man pointed with his gun toward an empty part of the marina near a low-lying office building in the opposite direction of the crowd. Ethan headed that way with his arms raised at shoulder level, his mind racing as he tried to figure a way out of this mess. Maybe someone would see him walking away, realise he was being held at gunpoint, and alert the authorities, but he doubted it. Not with all eyes on the fallen trawler.

He chanced a glance behind to see if he could jump the guy, but he was too far away. The gun was pointed at him, arm at a right angle and tight to his body, obscuring it from anyone else's view.

"Eyes forward," he grumbled.

Heart pounding in his chest and sweat pouring down his face, Ethan scanned the immediate area, looking for a way to break free, a weapon, anything that would give him a fighting chance. But there was nothing but open space, and he knew he needed a miracle.

Maybe Andrea will find me.

His thoughts turned to her, and he wondered if she was alive. It was possible that this guy found her and shot her before coming back. *Maybe that's why he wasn't with the others.* Guilt threatened to overwhelm Ethan, but he forced it down. He could feel guilty once he was out of this.

Even if she were alive, there was little chance she would find him now. They were now beyond the building and out of sight of anyone looking over from the drydock.

"Stop here," the man ordered.

Ethan stopped. They were standing in the shadows of the building, hidden away from any onlookers, right near the edge of the seawall.

"Walk to the edge," the man commanded.

When Ethan hesitated, the man shoved him. "Move!"

"Come on, man," Ethan pleaded, moving to the edge of the seawall. "You don't have to do this."

"On your knees."

Ethan's knees buckled as he stood at the edge of the seawall. Even if he wanted to stand, he couldn't, his body betraying him when he needed it the most. The dark, oil-stained water lapped at the wall as if trying to get at him, to pull him down into their depths. This couldn't be happening, there *had* to be some way to get out of this. He couldn't die before finding out about his parents.

"Look, do you want money? I'll give you money. Just walk away and we can forget all about this." He was babbling now, anything that came to mind spouting from his lips in a desperate attempt to stop this man from killing him.

"Shut up," he said, and Ethan heard the cocking of the gun's hammer.

"P-please," Ethan stammered. He closed his eyes tightly, waiting for the end.

There was a moment of silence, as if the world was holding its breath in anticipation of what was to come, and then the shot came and the silence was broken. The sound echoed off the building and Ethan tensed his body, waiting for the pain or the darkness to overcome him. To feel the force of the bullet pushing his body off the edge and into the water's depths.

But none of that came.

He waited, but nothing happened. He felt nothing but the sea breeze on his face. Heard nothing but the lapping of water.

Then the goon crashed down on top of him. Ethan cried out in surprise as he was almost pushed off the seawall. He shoved the man off him and had his fist clenched, ready to fight for his life, but he realised the man wasn't moving. The goon was staring at the blue sky with lifeless eyes, dark blood blooming across his white shirt.

"What the?"

Still on the ground, he looked up and saw a woman dressed

in jeans and a dark-green top with a gun pointed at him.

Ethan's hands immediately shot into the air. "Whoa, now," he said. "Do you guys fight over who wants to kill me the most or something?"

She had blue eyes and long brown hair tied into a ponytail. "What?"

Ethan nodded his head at the gun she still had pointed at him. "Are you trying to kill me as well?"

"Oh," she realised, and put the gun in her belt holster. "Sorry."

Ethan got to his feet. "First day on the job, officer?"

"No, just not used to someone being a smart mouth after I saved their life," she said with an accent he couldn't place.

Despite his body shaking almost uncontrollably, Ethan chuckled, more out of relief and the release of adrenaline. "Thank you," he said.

The officer nodded but said nothing. Ethan continued, "Who is he?" he asked, gesturing to the dead man.

She shrugged, approaching the body and checking for a pulse, probably out of habit from training rather than any concern she might have that he might be alive. They both knew he was as dead as a doornail. "No idea."

"Who are you?"

She stood up and pulled a black wallet from her pocket. "Agent Abigail Myers," she said, showing him her ID.

Ethan looked at it, seeing words written along the top in Hebrew with a file photo of Abigail below it. Next to it was the unmistakable blue Star of David, which meant… "You're

Mossad?"

Abigail nodded.

"You're not from Israel, though."

She frowned. "How do you know that?"

"Your accent. It's not Israeli."

A smirk crossed the Mossad agent's face. "They said you were clever, Ethan."

He groaned. "Of course you know my name. Which means you being here isn't a coincidence, is it?"

Her smirk turned into a smile. "Like I said, clever. You're right, Ethan, I'm not here by happenstance. I need to talk to you."

"About?"

"What happened in Camden Town yesterday, and a man named Felix Graves."

Ethan sighed inwardly. He didn't have time for this. "I wasn't in Camden Town yesterday, I don't know any Fester Grapes, and aren't you a little young to be working for Mossad?"

"Mr. Jackson—" Abigail began, but he cut her off.

"You must be, what, twenty-one?"

She rolled her eyes and ignored him. "Ethan, I need to speak to you about this man and what happened last night. We can do it peacefully or I can arrest you and take you in for questioning."

Ethan chewed his lip, knowing he had to get away from this woman. If these guys were Graves' men, then he wasn't far away. He needed to find Ritchie, work out the star map, and get the hell out of Cape Town. He smiled at her. "As appealing as you putting me in cuffs might be, I think I'll go for option one."

Abigail visibly relaxed. "Great. Will you come with me now,

then?"

"Once I get a lawyer."

If looks could kill, Ethan would have been burnt to cinders by the fire in those blue eyes. She stared at him long enough that he felt like a child about to be told off by his parents. Finally, she reached a hand into her jacket and pulled out a card. "Get a lawyer and call me. We can meet at one of the Cape Town stations."

Ethan took the card, seeing that it was plain white with 'Abigail Myers' printed in block letters with a phone number underneath. "Sure thing."

"I will be expecting your call before the end of the day," she said.

Ethan crossed his fingers over his heart. "Scout's honour. By the way, you might want to check underneath the ship over there. You might find more of his friends," he said, pointing to the dead man.

"Under the ship?"

"Yep."

"How did that happen?"

Ethan shrugged. "Oh, you know those drydocks aren't always up to code…"

Abigail stared at him.

"Anyway," he said cheerfully, waving her card. "I'll call you later." Before she could say anything, he hurried off toward the docks.

Clouds were rolling in off Table Mountain as Ethan made his way down the Cape Town docks. As soon as he was away from Abigail Myers, he called Andrea, checking to see if she was okay.

He was relieved when she answered and told him she had evaded her pursuers in the crowds.

He told her it was too risky to be out right now. To his surprise, she agreed with him and said she would book a hotel room and wanted to meet up with him later. He agreed and hung up, relieved he didn't have to argue with her. He spent the rest of the afternoon around the docks asking around for a man named Ritchie, but was met with shrugs and shakes of the head. If he was around here, no one seemed to know him. He explored the Yacht Club, walking amongst the luxury yachts and asking anyone he saw if they knew Ritchie, but he had no luck there either.

Ethan moved on to the Duncan and Ben Schoeman Docks further north of Cape Town. These docks housed container ships, tankers, bulk carriers, and other larger ships used to move freight around the world. He headed down Vanguard Road until he reached the end and passed the guardhouse, going through the open gate and onto the wharf. There were four ships docked along this part of the wharf. He passed by two tugboats and a research vessel, none of them manned, and reached the last one. Ethan groaned.

"Not another trawler," he muttered.

It was a Eurocutter. Longer than a tugboat, it had twin masts with a series of pulleys attached to them for manoeuvring fishing nets to the hatch on the deck. Heading along amidships toward the aft were the cabins and mess with the bridge on top. A radar array lined the top of the bridge, and at the stern was the revolving drum, used to pull the nets in. Flapping in the breeze were the green, white, and orange vertical bars of the flag of Ireland.

The ship had seen better days. Faded black paint ran along the gunwale. The cabins and bridge were once white, but sea spray and sun damage had turned it a sickly yellow with rust streaks running down the walls. Stencilled along the gunwale was the name 'Here Comes the Jibboom'.

It didn't look like anyone was aboard, but Ethan called out anyway.

"Hello?"

There was no answer and Ethan headed back down the wharf, disappointment setting in, when he heard a loud noise coming from the boat. He turned around and watched two men come crashing out of the cabin. They had a hold of one another and looked to be in an awkward embrace—that was, until, one of them swung his fist at the other.

Ethan watched as a middle-aged man with black hair and a heavy belly held the other in a headlock. He pulled him around the deck until the other man broke free and pushed back at him.

"Don't think you can get out of this," said the man with black hair. He had a South African accent and was dressed in stained trousers and a thick woollen jumper.

"Get schuffed, Graeme," the other retorted, clearly drunk, and charged at him.

Graeme ducked a swing and threw his own punch, which landed square in the drunk man's belly. He let out an "oof" and doubled over in pain. Graeme lined him up and punched him once, twice, and then a third time to the cheek, but the drunk man stayed up, although with the way he was rocking, Ethan was sure the next one would floor him.

Graeme lined him up again and landed a punch flush on the drunk's eye, knocking him down. He writhed on the ground, groaning in pain while Graeme stood over him. "Pay up, Ritchie, or we'll take the boat."

Ritchie!

Ethan hurried back to the boat and up the gangway just as Graeme was kicking his boots into Ritchie's sides.

"Hey!" he yelled, startling the man.

Graeme turned and looked Ethan up and down. "The hell are you?"

"No one you care about, but if you want your money, you sure as hell won't get it if he's dead."

Graeme seemed to think about it for a bit, chewing on the wisdom of Ethan's words, before he turned to Ritchie and said, "You got one week, you fat slob. Get the money or not even the kid will save you next time." He put one more kick into his stomach before storming away, shoulder checking Ethan on the way out.

Ethan hurried to Ritchie, who was on his knees, groaning.

"You ok?" Ethan asked, crouching down beside him.

Ritchie looked up at him with bloodshot, hazel eyes. "Yeah," he groaned, and then turned his head and vomited bile all over the deck.

The stench of it hit Ethan like a hammer, and he almost

vomited himself.

"Jesus," he said, backing away. "What the hell is wrong with you?"

Ritchie groaned.

"Come on," Ethan grumbled, trying to breathe out of his mouth. He helped him up. With one arm around his shoulder, he guided him to the cabins.

The cabin was a mess. Empty bottles lay scattered around the floor, on tables, on the bed, everywhere. Ethan kicked them aside until he reached the table and helped Ritchie into a chair.

"Thanskhh lad," he said, easing himself back into the chair. He grabbed a bottle off the table and took a swig. Scowling, he eyed the bottle and tipped it over, but nothing came out. He swore and tossed it aside, then eyed Ethan.

"Youuuu look fa-fa-familiar," he stumbled. "Are yoooou one of mine?" Then he laughed a drunken laugh. "Nahhh, too gooood-lookin' to be mine."

Before Ethan could answer, Ritchie belched once and his eyes rolled back in his head. He fell asleep in his chair, snoring.

Ethan sighed. "Jesus Christ."

Seventeen

The sun had set by the time Ritchie startled himself awake by his own snoring. Ethan sat at the table, now cleared of the empty bottles, playing with his phone. He contacted Andrea again to say he'd be awhile and to make sure she was safe, while also convincing her he was fine.

She gave him the name of the hotel she was staying at, one of Cape Town's more upper-class ones that probably cost more than his flight over, and said goodbye.

After that, he waited. He grabbed his journal from his pocket and opened to the page with the star map. He wasn't sure what he was hoping to achieve, but it was something to keep his mind occupied while he waited for Ritchie to come out of his drunken sleep. When the snoring got too much for him, he took a chair out on deck and played with Maynard's device, pressing different sequences in the stars in the idle hope that he might stumble into the solution. The sun sank over the Atlantic and it got cold. He went inside and found Ritchie still snoring. Ethan grabbed a pair of socks off the floor and threw them at him. It stopped the snoring for ten blissful minutes before he started again, which thankfully startled him awake.

"Oh," he groaned, clutching his ribs. Then he looked around. "What the hell am I doing in bed?"

"I dragged you into it, you heavy bastard," Ethan grumbled.

Shocked by the presence of someone else in his cabin, Ritchie yelped out, "Who in God's good graces are you, lad?" He spoke in a heavy Irish accent.

"My name is Ethan, and I need your help."

Ritchie sat up in his bed, groaning again and cupping his head in his hands. He jerked back, exclaiming, "Christ, what happened to me eye?"

"Some guy named Graeme mistook you for a punching bag," Ethan said, watching Ritchie get up and stumble into a small bathroom.

"That slimy little shyte always knew to find me when I'm pissed," he said, stumbling back out of the bathroom and propping himself against the wall. He grabbed at his ribs. "Bastard could have laid off the ribs, though." He winced and looked at Ethan. "Ethan you said your name was, eh?"

Ethan nodded.

Ritchie eyed him through bleary, bloodshot eyes. "You look

familiar—you're not one of me bastards, are you?" He shook his head before Ethan could reply. "Nah, you're not ugly enough to be one of them."

Ethan sighed. "You already said that."

"I did?"

"Just before you passed out."

Ritchie chuckled, and Ethan took a good look at him. He was slightly taller than Ethan, with matted, fiery red hair and a slightly paunchy belly, likely from drinking too much.

"But you do look familiar. What's your last name?"

Ethan hesitated, wondering if he should tell him the truth or not. He would have to hedge on his answer being the right one to get this drunkard to help him. He decided the truth would be his best bet right now. "Jackson," he said.

Ritchie thought for a long moment, murmuring "Jackson" to himself, as if trying to recall a long-lost memory. Then his eyes went wide and all traces of the hangover evaporated. "Dave and Gem's kid?"

Ethan nodded.

"You're shittin' me?"

"Wouldn't dream of it."

Ritchie pushed himself off the wall and sat on his bed. Then he stood up again and paced the room. "What're you doing here, lad?"

"I'm trying to find my parents," he said. "Or, at least, what they were looking for."

Ritchie stopped pacing and furrowed his brow. "But they're dead."

Ethan nodded. "They might be," he conceded. "If so, I want to find out *why* they are dead."

"How do you plan on doing that, lad?"

Ethan shrugged. "I'm working on it. How did you know them?"

"I… uh… helped them move artefacts," he said, moving to the fridge and grabbing a beer. He popped the cap off and took a swig. "That's about all, really."

"I need the truth, Ritchie. I know they were involved in the black market and some shady shit. If that led to their deaths, I need to know so I can find out what actually happened."

Ritchie was silent for a long time, picking at the label on his bottle. When he finally spoke, he didn't meet Ethan's eyes. "Lad, I hadn't seen your parents for five years, maybe longer, before they died. I dun know anything about it." He looked up from his bottle. "But the stuff your parents did… it was remarkable. The places they visited and the dangers they faced to recover secrets of the past was nothing short of heroic."

"Except they were criminals."

"Aye, that they were," Ritchie admitted. "Though not always."

He stood up and walked to a bookshelf, searching the spines until he found the one he was looking for. Returning to the table, he opened it and handed it to Ethan.

The book was a photo album. Ethan's eyes went wide when he saw the photos of his parents and Ritchie sitting atop camels in the desert, the tip of a pyramid poking out of the sand behind them. There was another photo of them. This time wearing jungle gear and standing in front of the remains of a temple. Below it were the words 'Temple of Quetzalcoatl, South of Santa Cruz Tepetotutla, Mexico'. Another depicted them inside an enclosed space beside an open door with a skeleton peeking out of it. His mum looked like she was in her twenties and was acting as if she was frightened, while his dad had a big grin on his face. Written beneath it was "Hidden entrance in Pyramid of Unas, Egypt."

"Gem discovered the hidden entrance in that pyramid," Ritchie said. "One of the first discoveries we made together."

Ethan flipped through the pages, seeing more photos of his parents, some of them with Ritchie. They were all pictures of his parents at different ages, from their twenties to older. Tears came to Ethan's eyes.

"There were legit finds?" he asked.

Ritchie nodded.

Ethan wiped his eyes, smiling at how happy his parents were. He went to close the book when a photo fell out.

He picked it up. It was a torn photo of his parents with Ritchie. They had their arms around each other, and there was a dusty building in the background. He noticed his dad had his arms around his mum on one side and someone else on the other, but he could only see their arm in the photo. Ritchie was next to his mum.

"A tenth century Umayyad Mosque they discovered in Jordan," Ritchie explained, taking the photo and putting it back in the album. He gently pushed the photo album aside and said, "They were remarkable, your parents. But it was a dangerous job, and they dealt with some very dangerous people."

"Why though? Why the black market stuff?"

"Because they were human, lad. When they made their first major discovery, people expected more from them. They were highly sought after, hired out by other universities and museums to find some lost site or artefact. It wasn't a normal job, Ethan. They put themselves in incredible danger doing what they did, and they had no help, no medical benefits. If they got bit by a snake somewhere in remote Central America, they had to survive on their own. They couldn't call in a helicopter to pull them out. And they did all of this making very little. So, when these private companies and people came to them, offering more money than they could dream of, they took it. They had the opportunity to make more on the side—an extra reward for the dangers they put themselves through. It seemed reasonable to them. And then the risks got higher, the payments got bigger and, like with the universities, the expectations were greater."

Ethan remained quiet, and the room filled with a heavy silence. He appreciated Ritchie's honesty and how it gave him a sense of why his parents did what they did. He questioned whether he would have done the same. After a moment, he gathered himself, wiping another tear from his face and opening the journal. He turned to the picture of the star map he drew with his annotations. "Can you find out where this leads to?"

"Lad..." he said quietly.

"Can you?"

"You're not going to be talked out of this, are you?"

"Can you?" Ethan insisted.

Ritchie sighed. "Gimme a look."

Ethan handed him the journal, and Ritchie barely glanced at it before handing it back. "No."

"You didn't even look at it."

"Look, lad, they wouldn't have wanted you involved in this."

"Involved in what?" Ethan asked.

Ritchie's eyes darted around the room. "Uh… following in their footsteps," he said, obviously flustered. "You know, treasure hunting, dealing with psychopaths. Investigating their deaths," he added lamely.

Ethan glowered, unsure if Ritchie was still drunk or if he was hiding something, but he pushed his uncertainty away. This man was his best lead right now. "I'll give you five grand if you tell me where the map leads to."

Ritchie inhaled sharply. "Wha?"

"You have money troubles, right?"

He nodded.

"How much in the hole are you?"

"Eighty grand."

Jesus!

"Then it sounds like you could really use five thousand dollars," Ethan said.

Ritchie huffed and took a long swig of his beer before setting it down gently on the tabletop. He ran a hand through his matted red hair. Ethan could see he was weighing his options and decided to push him further. He stood up, collected the journal and device, and headed toward the cabin door. "Fine. I'll find someone else who could use the five grand."

"Wait!"

Ethan smiled.

"Where did you get that?"

His smile fading, he turned around. "Get what?"

Ritchie pointed at the device. "That. Where did you get it?"

"I found it."

"Where?"

Ethan sighed. "What does it matter?"

"Just humour me, lad."

Curious about where this conversation was going, Ethan took a seat, placing the device and journal on the table. "I found it in England."

"Where, exactly?"

"St. Martin's Church."

"Is that right?"

"Yeah, why?"

"Curious."

"You're being cagey," Ethan told him.

Ritchie shrugged, but said nothing.

"I think Mum left it there after she was meant to have gone missing in Norfolk."

Ritchie raised an eyebrow. "'meant to have gone missin'? What makes you think that?"

"I came across some information that suggests she might be alive."

"Seriously?" he asked, sitting forward.

Ethan nodded. "I don't know how reliable the information is, which is why I'm here. I'm trying to find out the truth."

Standing up, Ritchie got another beer from the fridge and

offered one to Ethan, who declined.

"Mum and Dad were looking into the possibility that a British naval officer named Robert Maynard had obtained a great—but dangerous—treasure and hid it from the world," he continued. "That's what they were looking into before they… died.

"They stole his diary from an auction house and began investigating the possibility. A couple of days ago, I found some information on what they were doing and it led me to St. Martin's Church, where Maynard had a secret bunker. In there, I found this star map, this thing," he pointed to the five-sided device, "some Spanish gold coins, and Maynard's diary. I believe they got as far as the bunker, seeing as the diary was there, but I don't know what happened after that."

Ritchie finished his drink, wiped his mouth with the sleeve of his shirt, and said, "Jaysus lad, you have your parents' tenacity, don't you?"

"So I've been told."

He stared at the device for a long time before he said, "Eight grand and I'll take you."

"You can read the map?"

Ritchie snorted. "Of course I can."

"I'll give you five and I'll fly there."

Ritchie shook his head. "You can't fly there, lad. You'll be lucky to get there by boat."

"Where does it lead, then?"

"Eight grand and I'll tell you."

"Six," he countered, offering money didn't have. "And if it leads me to what I think it does, you'll earn more than eighty thousand."

"Seven. And if what you say is true, you can have it back. I won't need it."

Ethan smiled at that. "Done," he said. "Now, where does it lead to?"

"It's an island six days west from here. A place called the Inaccessible Island."

Ethan laughed. "The Inaccessible Island?"

"Aye."

"You're not joking?"

"No, lad. It's an extinct volcanic island surrounded by sheer cliff faces and jagged rocks. No one goes there. Well, no one sane. It's too dangerous." He paused, then said, "There is one way in, though, but it ain't easy."

"You can do it?"

"Aye."

"Then let's go."

Ritchie raised his hands. "Settle down, lad. Like I said, it's six days west. I have to prepare, get supplies, all that fun stuff."

"Then when can we go?" Ethan asked impatiently.

Ritchie let out a long breath. "Meet me here tomorrow morning. I should be ready by then."

"All right," Ethan said, putting the journal and device into his jacket pocket. "I'll be here tomorrow morning," he added, heading for the cabin door.

"Lad…"

Ethan stopped and turned.

"If it's anything like last time, it's going to be a rough trip,"

Ritchie said gravely.

Ethan nodded and left, wondering if he meant the boat ride or something else.

Eighteen

The hotel Andrea picked was the height of luxury. Situated in Cape Town's old city, and across from St. George's Cathedral, the Paarl granite building was formerly the city's reserve bank before it moved in the late 1980s.

It was raining when Ethan passed through the former bank's original wooden doors into the reception area with its high-vaulted roof and four marble columns. He approached the concierge and told him he was looking for Andrea Gatting. After looking up her details, the concierge smiled at Ethan and handed him a key card, telling him the room number and wishing him a pleasant stay.

"It's not like that," Ethan told him.

The concierge smiled at him. "If you say so, Mr. Jackson."

It did not surprise Ethan that the room Andrea booked was on the top floor. He stepped out of the elevator into a well-kept hallway, key card in hand, and hesitated when he reached the room, wondering if he should knock or just enter.

In the end he knocked, deciding it would be politer.

The door opened a crack, and he saw Andrea peer at him before opening it fully, relief evident on her face. "Ethan! Finally! Are you okay?" she said, hugging him tightly and pulling him into the room.

"Yeah, I'm fine," he said as she shut the door behind him, put the chain on, and flipped the safety latch. He took a seat at the table near the rain-streaked window that looked out at Table Mountain, though, at the moment, it was hidden in darkness and clouds.

Andrea sat beside him. Ethan noticed how close she was and was very aware that she was wearing nothing but a loose, fluffy white robe. Her black hair was wet and hung loosely around her face, hiding the scar. "What happened?" she asked.

He told her all that happened at the docks after they split up.

"That was you?" Andrea exclaimed. "I heard the explosion and the crashing, but I had no idea it was the same boat you were on. It's been all over the news. The police know there were armed men seen in the area, but they are asking for witnesses to piece together what happened."

"That's good then," Ethan said. "By the time they work it out, we'll be out of South Africa."

"What do you mean?" she asked.

"After the ship almost came down on me—"

"Wait, what?"

"The last of Graves' men found me…"

Andrea gasped. "He did? I thought I had led him away. Three of them were chasing me and then two peeled back. I thought he was trying to cut me off. I switched back toward the markets and lost him in the crowds. I thought he would keep looking for me. I never thought he would go back. Oh, Ethan, I am so, so sorry. I should have made sure…"

"Don't be," he told her. "We're not trained for this. Instinct told you to keep going, so you did. Besides, I'm still here, aren't I?"

"But still—"

Ethan held up a hand. "Don't. No point worrying about it, right?"

She sniffed and nodded. "What happened?"

"He held me at gunpoint and forced me away from the wreck just as the police were arriving. Someone shot him before he shot me," he explained, a sick feeling forming in his stomach. This was the first time he really thought about how close he was to death today. Even when he was waiting for Ritchie to wake up, he was still running on adrenaline as he focused on the star map, and so frustrated at the drunkard that he didn't think about his near-death experience. But now he felt like he was about to crumble into a heap.

"Who was it?"

He hesitated, deciding whether to tell her about the Mossad agent. It was an added complication to his search. Besides, she was looking for Graves, not him. "A police officer. She must have seen me being led away and followed us. I didn't stick around, though. Once I realised I was clear, I bolted."

He closed his eyes, the day's events flashing vividly before him. The sound of the hammer of the gun being cocked echoed in his mind and he let out a gasping sob. "Oh, God," he cried, tears coming to his eyes.

Andrea was beside him in an instant and pulled him into an embrace. "Ethan, it's okay," she soothed. "This is a normal reaction to a traumatic experience."

He buried his head in her shoulders, the cocking hammer still echoing in his mind, and he silently begged for it to stop. If Abigail wasn't there, he would have been dead for sure.

His body shook uncontrollably, and he heaved, tears running down his face. He didn't know how long he was sobbing—time meant nothing as he processed everything that happened in the past two days. But when he finally had control of himself, he found he was lying on the bed. How did he get there? Andrea was resting next to him, running her hand through his hair, soothing him.

He blinked and sat up on the edge of the bed. "Well… that was embarrassing," he said, trying to bring levity to the situation, impossible as it was with tear-streaked cheeks and red-rimmed eyes. "Hard to be the macho tough guy when you cry like a baby."

Andrea giggled, still running her hand through his hair. He became acutely aware of her touch, his body reacting to it.

"It's not embarrassing at all. Plus, women like a man who is in touch with his emotions."

Ethan swallowed. "They do, do they?"

She made an approving, almost purring noise, her hand moving from his hair to his neck, rubbing it. "What you went through was incredibly traumatic. The fact that you want to continue is nothing short of heroic. You are determined to seek out the truth, and with that comes great danger."

She moved her mouth to his ear and whispered, "You're doing fine."

Her hands were warm, and the touch of her fingers on his sent chills down his spine, her words honey to his ears. He looked into her eyes, expecting to find the intensity he saw when they first met, but instead, he found something else… curiosity? Compassion? He couldn't tell.

"Maybe," he said, unable to think of something clever.

She moved closer to him, her body touching his. "You also saved my life," she whispered. "Drawing them to the boat allowed me to get away. I owe you my life."

Her hair was damp and smelled faintly of lavender and vanilla. He noticed her robe coming loose.

"I—I just did what anyone would do," he stammered, his body shaking again, but this time with nerves.

She was so close to him now that he could feel her warm breath. She gave him a salacious smile. "Trust me," she whispered, brushing her lips against his.

Ethan moved his head forward slightly, hesitated, then kissed her. Her soft lips returned the kiss, and he wrapped his arms around her, pulling her on top of him.

It was past midnight, and they were lying in bed, fingers entwined. Even this high up, he could hear the faint sounds of passing cars and music playing at a nearby club. Andrea's eyes were closed, and he wasn't sure if she was asleep, but he was wide awake and staring at the roof of the room, only the glow from the bedside clock providing any illumination. Ethan wasn't sure what to make of what had just happened. Maybe it was just the culmination of the day's events and the emotions that led to them sleeping together. He wasn't sure and wasn't sure he even wanted to work it out—not now, anyway.

All he knew was that it was great. Getting the raw emotion out was exactly what he needed, and he suspected Andrea needed that as well. She was equally passionate, aggressive, tender, and loving, and he reciprocated as best as his limited experience allowed him.

"How did he find us?" she asked suddenly.

"Who?"

"Graves."

Ethan played with her hair, twirling it around his index finger. "He seems like a man with many resources, and I travelled under my passport. It probably wasn't too hard for him to track me down."

"Then where to from here?" she asked, untangling her hand from his and walking her fingers up his bare chest.

Ethan's heart seemed to stop. "You mean with us?" he

murmured.

She giggled. "No, Ethan. You didn't tell me what happened after the cop saved your life."

"Oh," he said, glad the darkness hid the blush he could feel glowing on his cheeks. Deciding he owed her an explanation, he said, "I told you I was going to see Ritchie, a guy who my parents knew who helped them ship their finds."

"Yep."

He got out of bed, flipped up the light switch, and rummaged through his jacket until he found the diary. He returned to bed and, sitting with his back against the headboard, he opened the diary to the page with the map on it.

"What I didn't tell you," he continued, "was that back in Maynard's bunker, there was a star map on the wall leading to an island somewhere in the South Atlantic Ocean."

He turned the diary around and showed it to her. Andrea sat up and grabbed the diary, staring at the map. "This was on the wall?"

Ethan nodded.

"Where does it go?"

"That's why I went to see Ritchie. I couldn't read the map, but I figured it was south of the equator, because of this line." He pointed to the equator. "So, rather than following it the entire way, I banked on skipping to the end. Given that Ritchie was friends with Mum and Dad and he was already south of the equator, I went to see him if he could help."

Andrea traced a finger along the route. "And did he?" she asked, looking up at him.

"Reluctantly. He's a drunk."

"Is he trustworthy, though?"

Ethan shrugged. "I wouldn't trust him to drive a golf cart, let alone a boat, but he told me the map leads to the Inaccessible Island. He also showed me some photos of him with my parents back in the day. It seemed like they were close."

"People change though, Ethan. Did he reach out to you when they disappeared? Did you even know about him before?"

Ethan shook his head, acknowledging the point. "I've given him incentive to help. Besides, he said he's the only one who can get us there. It's so dangerous that others won't try it. If what he said about the Inaccessible Island was true, then he might be the only one crazy enough to take me there."

"What incentive did you give him?"

"He owes some people eighty thousand dollars. I offered him seven to take me to the island."

"Do you have that kind of money?"

Ethan shook his head.

"Then what are you going to do when he asks for it?"

"I have enough for half. The rest I'll worry about later."

"I have money—"

"No" Ethan interrupted.

"But—"

"No," he said again. "I appreciate it, but this is messy enough as is. I'll figure something out."

Andrea looked concerned. "Are you sure about this?"

"Not really, but I have no choice. What Graves said about my parents and then finding Maynard's diary in the bunker tells me that one, or both, of my parents got that far."

"Ethan, Felix Graves cannot be trusted. He's telling you what you want to hear so he can get what you found. He must know that only David's body was discovered. He's using the fact your mother's body was never found as a bargaining tool. He's creating doubt and false hope. You cannot take his word."

Nodding, Ethan said, "I know he can't be trusted, but as much as I try not to, I can't help thinking he's telling the truth."

Andrea tapped his head. "I cannot imagine the torment going on in there," she said.

"Anyway, they would have seen the star map and worked out the next destination. The best thing I can do is keep going, hope to get a definitive answer one way or another. I don't know why they left the diary in the bunker, but if they went this way, then I have to follow them. I have to know what happened."

She nodded and kissed him passionately. "I understand," she said, breaking off the kiss. "If I were in your shoes, I would do anything to find out what happened to my parents."

He smiled. "Thanks," he said. "I appreciate your support, even though I've kept things from you."

She paused, then leaned away and asked, "Why did you?"

He shook his head. "I don't know. I just don't know who to trust, and when Graves approached me at the market, it kind of freaked me out. I've never done this before. I don't know if there is some conspiracy going on or if I am just ignoring Occam's Razor in a desperate hope that Mum is still alive."

"Ethan, this is normal. Wanting answers to what happened is a perfectly normal thing to want. And I am here to help you."

He nodded. "I know. I can't thank you enough for what you have done for me."

"I'm not stopping now," she said.

"You want to come?"

She nodded emphatically. "Absolutely. They were my friends, too. I want answers as well."

Ethan nodded, seeing no point in arguing with her. "Then I guess we are in this together."

Smiling, she hugged him and kissed him on the cheek. "In more ways than one," she whispered in his ear.

He chuckled. "I guess so."

"Was there anything else?" she asked between kisses on his neck. Her hot breath sent chills through his body.

"Hmm?" he moaned.

She kissed his neck, "In—" and again, "the—" and again, "bunker," giving him one last kiss on the neck, lightly sucking it.

"You know it's hard to concentrate when you do that?"

"I can stop," she teased.

He snorted and got off the bed to grab his jacket, which he had tossed over the couch. He unzipped a pocket and pulled out the five-sided device and tossed it on the bed.

"What's this?" she asked, picking it up.

"No idea, but I believe it's a clue."

Andrea raised an eyebrow. "You 'believe'?"

"I can't open it," Ethan said, looking sheepish.

Andrea picked it up and rotated it in her hand. "What are these scratches? Initials?"

"I think so."

She squinted at them. "I can't really read them. Is it a B and a T?"

"Not sure. It's too faint. It could be a B or a T or an I. It's too hard to tell."

Andrea tried prying it open with her fingers, but, like Ethan, couldn't get her fingers into the seam. "Why can't it open?"

He pointed to the stars on the front. "It's locked. The stars are the key. You just have to press the right ones in the right order."

"And you don't know the right order."

"That's right."

"But you think it's important?"

"It was in Maynard's bunker in a satchel, along with the coins and his diary. I am certain it's related to his hidden treasure, and I think Mum left it there."

She gave him a hug and a big smile. "We're on the right track, then?"

He returned the smile. "I'm not trying to get my hopes up, but yes, I think so."

"Amazing!" she exclaimed, putting her arms around his neck and kissing him deeply. He kissed her back before pulling away. "I really need to shower," he said.

"Later," she purred, pushing him down into the bed and climbing on top of him.

Nineteen

The next morning, Ethan woke up to find fresh cuts and bruises all over his body. He was stiff and dirty and decided to have the shower he was meant to have last night. Uncurling himself from Andrea's sleeping form, he grabbed his pack and pulled out the only set of spare clothes he had: brown cargo pants and a t-shirt. He tossed the clothes on the bed, then headed into the bathroom.

The jet of hot shower water was a welcome relief, and Ethan felt his muscles loosen as he washed the dirt and grime away. Wishing he could stay in there for the rest of the day, he reluctantly turned off the taps and hopped out of the shower.

As he was drying himself, he heard a noise from the other side of the door. Putting his ear near the door, he listened intently and was relieved to hear it was just Andrea. She must be on the phone.

"No… we'll deal with it when the time comes… you'll work it out… we'll be fine."

He opened the door, towel around his waist, and smiled at her. She smiled back, listening to whomever it was on the other end of the call. Finally, she said, "That's fine. Look, I have to go. I'll call you when I'm back, okay?"

She ended the call and put the phone into the pocket of her robe. "Work," she said, answering the questioning look Ethan gave her. "I told them I'm taking a couple of days' leave, and naturally the whole place goes into shambles when I'm not there."

"Fair enough," he said, pulling on his clothes.

She approached him, kissed him, and disrobed, letting it fall to the ground. "I'm going to have a shower," she said. "I hope you left me enough hot water."

He admired her lithe body as she walked into the bathroom. Before shutting the door, she gave him a wicked smile. When he heard the shower going, Ethan started packing what little clothing he had into his backpack. He made sure he had his journal, Maynard's diary, the device, and the coins secured away. As he was picking up the clothes left on the floor from last night, he heard Andrea's phone ringing. He picked up her robe, and just as he pulled it out, it stopped ringing.

He was about to put it on the bed with the robe when curiosity got the better of him. He swiped up on the phone screen, surprised to find she hadn't locked it. He opened the phone app and checked the recent calls. There were the ones he made to her yesterday, and she had calls from Provolution, but the most recent one was from a number that wasn't saved in her phone. The prefix was +44, which he knew was from England. He frowned. Why did she say it was from work? Surely, she would have the work numbers saved—or maybe not. It could be someone's new phone number or personal phone, or there could be any number of reasons. He put the phone back into the robe's pocket, feeling guilty for breaching her trust. Andrea emerged from the bathroom just as he finished packing his things.

"All good to go?" she asked.

"Ready when you are," he said with a weak smile.

The taxi splashed through a puddle and stopped just outside the docks on Vanguard Road. Ethan led Andrea past the security gate and down the wharf. The two tugboats from the day before were gone, but the red research vessel was still there, as was Ritchie's. Heading up the ramp, Ethan called out to Ritchie, expecting him to be passed out drunk somewhere but instead, was greeted by a blond-haired girl who emerged from the cabin. She looked to be Ethan's age and had piercing emerald green eyes.

"Hello," she said with a distinctly South African accent.

Ethan froze in his tracks. "Who are you?" he demanded.

"I'm Hannah. You must be Ethan? Ritchie said you'd be coming by sometime this morning."

Ethan could only stare dumbly at the unexpected guest.

She looked past him at Andrea. "But he didn't mention there

would be two of you."

Andrea walked past Ethan, hand out. "Hi, I'm Andrea," she said.

"Nice to meet you," Hannah said, shaking her hand. "You're British?"

"I am," she confirmed.

"Where's Ritchie?" Ethan asked, finally finding his voice.

"He's in the wheelhouse," Hannah said, pointing above the cabins. Ethan dropped his bag on deck and climbed the ladder to the wheelhouse. Below, he heard Hannah say, "Come, I'll show you the bunks."

Up in the wheelhouse, Ethan found Ritchie in surprisingly good shape. His red hair was still unkempt, though, and hidden under a baseball cap, and he wore a stained wool jumper with equally stained pants. The main difference was that today he seemed alert, his eyes not as bloodshot as last night. He was sitting on his chair, feet up on the console, eating an egg and bacon sandwich.

"Mornin' lad," he said cheerfully, taking a bite from his sandwich. "Want one? It's the second-best hangover cure there is."

"What's the first?"

"Don't stop drinking," he said, his laughter booming jovially around the cabin.

"Who's the girl?" Ethan asked, ignoring the joke.

"Who? Han? She's me first mate."

Ethan stared at Ritchie. "Are you joking?"

"Not at all, lad. She's been with me for the last two years.

Handy lass to have, knows her way around a boat."

"She can't come," Ethan said, folding his arms.

"And why is that?"

"For one thing, it's too dangerous. And second, far too many people already know what I'm up to, and I can't have her mentioning it to anyone when we get back. There are people after me, and I don't want her getting in the middle of it."

Ritchie finished his sandwich and took a swig of his coffee. Ethan wondered if it was Irish or not. "I suppose that makes sense," he said after swallowing.

"So, you'll tell her she isn't needed then?"

Ritchie shook his head. "Sorry, lad, can't do. I need her. Can't handle this boat on me own."

"Jesus Christ," Ethan sighed, rubbing his forehead.

"Don't do that. You'll wear a hole in your head." Ritchie got up from his chair and slapped Ethan on the back. "And if it makes you feel any better, she already knows what's going on."

"You told her?" Ethan said incredulously.

"Aye, lad, I don't keep no secrets from Han. Doesn't make for a pleasant working environment."

"You have got to be kidding me!"

"Han's a tough lass. She can handle herself."

Ethan took a deep breath and then another. "Fine, if she knows, then she'll be safer with us, especially with Graves' men roaming around out there."

"Graves? You mean Felix Graves?"

"You know him?"

"Aye, lad, that little shyte rates about as well as the stuff that clogs up me shower drain."

"Did my parents know him?" Ethan asked.

Walking back to the chair, he opened the door to a mini-fridge underneath the ship's console and pulled out a carton of juice. He held the carton out to Ethan, who shook his head, and then took a swig. Ethan had the feeling he was stalling. When he finished drinking, he put the juice back in the fridge and said, "I'm not sure. I imagine they would have crossed paths given they had similar interests. What does he want with you?"

Ethan shrugged. "He wants what I found in England. I guess he is looking for the same thing my parents were."

Ritchie snorted and walked past him to look out the window. "No surprise there. He never could do it on his own."

"Could they have worked together?"

Ritchie shrugged. "Maybe. In that business, you could be friends one day and enemies the next."

"He also hinted that he knows what happened to my parents."

Ritchie whirled around at that. "He does? Well, if I find the little snot, I'll beat it outta him." He turned back to the window. "He's a dangerous man, lad. Stay well away from him."

"I'm doing my best to do just that," he replied. "If we get out of here undetected, he won't find us."

"Good," Ritchie said. "And don't worry about getting through undetected. I've sorted that out. Greased a few palms," he chuckled. "And speaking of that, lad…"

The implication hung in the air, and Ethan tossed a brown paper bag on the console. "Here's half."

"And the other half?"

"You get it when you hold up your end of the bargain," Ethan said.

"Don't you worry about that, lad. I'll do what needs to be done." Ritchie's head suddenly shot up and he craned his neck to look out the window. "Who's the lass?" He'd spotted Andrea on deck, talking to Hannah.

"Andrea. She was a friend of Mum and Dad's. Know her?"

"I wish," Ritchie said, staring at her. "She's a fine one, she is."

"When are we leaving?" Ethan mumbled, a hint of fire building in his belly.

Ritchie turned back and pointed to the cabin door. "As soon as you're out of me cabin, lad!"

Twenty

34°27'46.8"S 15°19'14.2"E, South Atlantic Ocean

They departed soon after. The engines rumbled to life, and Hannah told Ethan and Andrea they were free to roam the ship but to avoid straying too close to the railings during rough seas. Thankfully, the seas were calm as Cape Town disappeared behind them. The day was clear and all traces of the overnight rain had disappeared. Ethan was standing on the forecastle deck, leaning against the rail, watching the bow slice through the water and throwing up sea spray.

His mind was on what Ritchie told him earlier—that Felix Graves was a treasure hunter and possibly had worked with his parents.

In that business, you could be friends one day and enemies the next. If that was the case, then the opposite could also be true.

If he was looking for Maynard's cursed treasure, then could he have had a hand in their deaths? Or was it just a coincidence? What was it he said back in Camden Town? Something about avoiding their fate—Ethan couldn't exactly remember. But that didn't mean that Graves knew what happened. Maybe Andrea was right and that his comment about only one of them being dead could have meant Dad, since his body was recovered. Maybe Graves was hedging his own bets.

Andrea said he would use what he knew to get at me.

Doubt was creeping back into his mind. Maybe they were dead, and they didn't get this far.

"Penny for your thoughts?" Andrea said, coming up from behind.

"Just the usual. I'm thinking that if Mum somehow survived and came this way, it was after Dad's body was found. I keep holding on to the hope that Mum is alive, and it's all based on what Graves said. But I'm just setting myself up for disappointment, aren't I?"

"As long as we have something to go on, then it's worth continuing," she said. "Sure, you might be setting yourself up for disappointment, but there is also a chance that you might find out what happened to them. The worst that can happen is you don't find out, but at least you won't die wondering. And you might get some closure."

"Yeah… maybe," he said. He pulled the mysterious device from his pocket and started fiddling with it.

"No progress with that?" she asked.

"Not yet."

She put her hand on his. "You'll work it out. You have their brains and determination."

Ethan smiled weakly. "Maybe."

He turned and left, heading into the mess, a rectangular room with fading wooden walls covered with posters of bands and environmental issues. There was a kitchenette and small fridge on one side, and a worn two-seater couch on the other. In the middle was a small table where Hannah was sitting, reading a book. There was another book on the table, with a notepad and pen next to it. She looked up at him and smiled. "Hi, Ethan."

"Hey," he replied, opening the fridge and taking out a bottle of water. He took a seat opposite her, putting the device on the table and taking a swig of water. "Listen, about before. I'm sorry I was such a dick."

She waved it away. "No need. Ritchie told me what you're going through. And for what it's worth, I hope you find the answers you are looking for."

"Thanks," he said with a smile. He picked up the device and began fiddling with the stars again. "What are you reading?" he asked.

She held the book up for him to read the title: *Gray's Anatomy: 41st Edition*.

"You're in school?" he asked.

"University. I'm studying medicine."

"No kidding?" he said, surprised and impressed. "How are you finding it?"

"It's tough and a real challenge, but I love it."

"So you'll be a doctor when you're done?"

Hannah nodded. "That's the plan. I want to help in countries where people don't have easy access to medicine."

"So like Doctors without Borders?"

Hannah nodded.

"That's really admirable," Ethan told her, taking a sip of water.

"Thanks," she blushed. "My parents were well off, so I was lucky enough to get the health care I needed, but I've seen a lot of suffering, especially in South Africa. I want to do what I can to help those who desperately need it."

"And no one needs helping more than me, aye, lass?" Ritchie said, coming into the mess with Andrea following behind.

"If you keep up your drinking, that will stop being a joke," she admonished.

"Bah, me livers still got a bit of life in it yet," he laughed.

Andrea took a seat next to Ethan with a drink in her hand.

"Now that you're all here and chummy, I thought I'd give you an update on our progress," Ritchie announced at the head of the table. "We're making good speed with the calm waters and wind in our favour. So far, the weather is looking good and is scheduled to stay that way. But that can always change, so I'll keep you updated as we go. In the meantime, play nice," he said and laughed. Then he added, "Han, can you check the hold? The door's stuck again."

"Sure thing, Captain," she said, closing her book. She got up and followed Ritchie out, leaving Andrea and Ethan alone in the mess.

"Are you hungry?" she asked.

"I'll eat later," he said, getting up from his seat. "I'm actually going to lie down for a bit. Didn't get much sleep last night," he added with a sly grin.

Ethan's attempts to rest were interrupted with visions of the man he pushed into the hold of the ship, his body mangled on the jagged metal below, and of the man with the gun walking him to his death. The cocking of the gun's hammer still echoed in his mind. Or he was running away from the falling ship, but he could never get away quickly enough, safety just out of reach before it crashed down on him. He woke up with sweat pouring down his face and feeling worse than he did before.

Night had fallen, and he sat on the edge of the bed in the darkness, head in his hands, taking deep breaths and reminding himself that he did what was necessary. The men were trying to kill him, and he did what he had to do to survive. It wasn't cold-blooded murder; it was survival.

Us or them.

In the mess, he could hear the others talking, Ritchie's boisterous laughter prominent over everyone else's. He caught the smell of food and realised he was starving, his stomach growling like a caged tiger. He hadn't eaten since grabbing something quickly before getting to the docks.

"Hungry is good. Hungry is progress, isn't it?" he muttered to himself in the dark.

Taking one last deep breath with his eyes closed, he willed the guilt and the doubt out of him. He couldn't be weak. Not now. He had to concentrate and continue moving forward.

Did Mum and Dad have to kill anyone?

"Not now!" he said sharply.

He stood up and opened the door into the mess, where everyone was sitting around a table listening to a story Ritchie was telling about a mix-up he had at a wedding of a mate.

"And then I said, 'Matey, I may have slept with her, but I ain't crazy enough to marry her!'"

Everyone around the table burst out laughing.

"Anyway," Ritchie continued, "we sorted it over a pint or two and—well, look who decided to join us!"

Andrea and Hannah turned and greeted Ethan. Around the table, empty plates and cups were scattered around, dinner having already been served.

"You hungry, lad?" Ritchie asked.

"Starving," he admitted.

Hannah stood up. "Let me get you something," she said. She walked over to the kitchenette and opened the fridge.

Ethan followed her. "Please, don't go to the trouble. I can make something."

"Don't be silly," Hannah said. "It's part of my job."

She started grabbing plastic containers from the fridge, placing them on the stovetop. "How does chicken salad sound?"

"Right now, I could eat a horse."

"Sorry, I left the horse on the other boat. Chicken is all I have," she said with a grin.

Ethan chuckled. "I suppose that will have to do."

He left her to it and took a seat around the table, listening to Ritchie telling Andrea another one of his tales. He felt grateful for the normalcy. He realised he hadn't sat around a dinner table with people for a long time, not since he last had dinner with Peter Miller and his family. After that, he shut himself off from the world and his friends, who had since moved on without him. Maybe that's why he slept with Andrea—not because of some overwhelming desire for her, but some sort of companionship.

Thinking about Andrea made him realise he needed to talk to her about last night and what it meant. But maybe a better time to do that would be when this was all over.

Mind on the prize, Ethan!

Hannah placed a bowl of chicken salad in front of him, and he nodded his thanks and dug into it.

"So Ritchie, you've been to these islands before?" Andrea asked.

"I have. A while ago," he said, taking another swig from his bottle and glancing at Ethan, who noticed he was swaying slightly.

"What were you doing there? I gather it isn't a place people want to visit."

"It's not, really," he admitted. "But it's home to a flightless bird, the Inaccessible Island Rail, so you get the bird watchers. Otherwise, it's those daredevil types with more money than brains who just want to go to a place because no one else has and post it on their facetwitter."

"Is there anything else there?" she asked.

"The islands are part of Tristan da Cunha, a cluster of volcanic islands owned by your mob," he told her. "The other two islands are liveable, but the Inaccessible Island are inhospitable, with jagged rocks, sheer cliff faces, and only one way in and out. It was explored centuries ago by the Dutch, I think—they called it Nachtglas Island—but if there is anything interesting there, no one has found it."

He said this, looking pointedly at Ethan, and tossed his bottle into a trash bin and got another from the fridge. "Aside from the birds, there's not much else to see. I've been on the actual island once or twice, otherwise I get as close as I can, and whoever I'm taking swims to the beach from the boat. Which, on that subject, is our plan for getting ashore. But we can talk about that when we get there."

"Sounds positively fascinating," Andrea said. "I can't wait until we see it." Then she stood up, yawning. "I think it is time I get some beauty sleep."

"Aye, you won't need much of that, lass. However, I must get me own beauty sleep so I'll see you all next month," he said, guffawing loudly and slapping Ethan on the back.

He left, with Hannah following.

Andrea kissed Ethan on the cheek. "I'll see you in the morning."

He nodded, but said nothing.

"Are you okay?" Andrea asked, frowning.

He shrugged. "I guess so. Just a lot on my mind."

She rubbed his shoulders. "We'll find something there, Ethan. I know we will."

He gave her a weak smile, and she squeezed his shoulders one more time before heading into the cabins.

Grateful for the alone time, he finished his dinner and took the plate to the kitchenette, washing and drying the plate and utensils and putting them away. He wondered about what he expected to find on Inaccessible Island.

"You didn't have to do that."

Ethan spun around to find Hannah standing in the doorway.

"Sorry," she said, "I didn't mean to startle you."

Breathing heavily, the image of a man in a suit holding a gun flashed before him. Ethan shook his head. "It's okay. I was somewhere else."

She took the glass he was drying and put it in the cabinet next to the sink. "Are you not going to bed?"

"I don't think so," he said. Then he saw her books on the table and added, "But I can go elsewhere if you need time alone."

Hannah shook her head and headed back to the table. "Not at all. I could use the company."

"It must get pretty lonely, just the two of you," Ethan said, taking a seat across from her. He pulled the device from his jacket and started pressing the stars.

"Sometimes we get a crew on for bigger jobs, or if we go fishing. But it's not so bad with the two of us," she admitted. "I have a lot of spare time, which allows me to get work done, but when it is just the two of us on long treks, I can go a bit stir-crazy. There are only so many things you can do, and only so much of Ritchie you can take on a boat."

Ethan laughed, welcoming the good feeling. "How did you

get this job, anyway?"

"Ritchie was a friend of the family, and after my parents died, he became like a surrogate father to me. With his job as a boat captain, he needed someone to help him, so it just made sense for me to tag along. Eventually, it became a job."

"You've lost your parents? I'm sorry."

Hannah nodded. "They died in a car accident twelve years ago. Drunken driver." She smiled. "It's why I am so hard on Ritchie and his drinking. But I've made peace with their deaths and accepted that they are gone. I still have happy memories of them, and that's what is important to me now."

Ethan pondered her words, 'accepted that they are gone'. *Is that my problem? Am I in denial? Am I unwilling to accept that they are dead?*

"Do you have any brothers or sisters?" he asked.

She nodded again. "One of each and both older. They did their best to look after me, but they had their own lives to lead as well. It wasn't an easy time for any of us."

"My parents are—" he paused. *Dead? Missing?* "—gone as well," he said.

"Ritchie told me. I'm sorry to hear."

"Thanks."

"How did it happen? If you don't mind me asking, of course."

Ethan let out a sharp puff of air. "That's what I am trying to find out."

"Oh?"

Ethan wasn't sure why, but he felt comfortable with Hannah. There wasn't any risk telling her, not out here in the middle of the ocean, and she wasn't involved in any way. She didn't know his parents, nor had any connection to their past, aside from Ritchie.

"They were archaeologists and…" he paused, not sure if *black market dealers* was an appropriate description, "…explorers. They were in England, exploring a potential discovery just off the coast of Norfolk when they didn't return. The police ruled it a diving accident, and my dad's body washed ashore not long later."

Hannah gasped and put her hand to her mouth. "Oh, my, Ethan… I don't know what to say. That's horrible."

Nodding, Ethan continued, "Yeah, it was. But I never really believed it was an accident. They were experienced divers, and the idea of equipment malfunction just never sat right with me— one of the first things you're taught is to check your gear before diving. But… I had no evidence to prove otherwise…" He paused, and the cabin went silent except for the hum of the engine chugging along.

"And now I wonder if I've been in denial for the past decade."

"Did you ever see anyone? Talk to anyone?" Hannah asked. "Friends? Family? Professionals?"

Ethan shook his head. "I had no one. Or I thought I didn't. My grandfather was drinking his grief away and Peter, who was a local cop and family friend, he and his family tried to help as much as they could… and I thanked them by getting into trouble and spending time in and out of jail. I push them away. Friends too. Really, I pushed away anyone who tried to help because I thought all they wanted was the goss on my family. For me to spill the Jackson's dark secrets." He gave Hannah a lopsided smile. "Anger, denial. I suppose you don't happen to have a DSM with you?"

Hannah laughed. It was light, like a wind that whipped away storm clouds, and Ethan felt a little better.

"Anyway," he continued, "a couple of days ago, I found some information in Dad's journal that led me to believe they were in England for something more than just that Norfolk dive. So, I went there, found some more clues about what they were doing, and that's where we are going now."

"You found something the police didn't?"

He nodded.

"What was it?"

"I don't think you'd believe me if I told you."

"Try me. I'm pretty open-minded."

Grabbing his diary, he flipped it open to the page where he sketched St. Martin's Church and showed it to her. "Like I said, my parents were archaeologists and explorers and found a lot of things lost in time."

Hannah nodded. "Ritchie has told me about his past and being involved in such things. It sounds… dangerous."

"It does," Ethan agreed. "The last thing they were investigating had something to do with an old British naval officer named Robert Maynard. They… acquired his diary, which mentions a cursed treasure he'd hidden. One of the last things my parents wrote in this diary was about St. Martin's Church in England, and they referenced some things Maynard wrote in his diary."

He was getting excited about reliving this part of his journey. "So I went to the church and discovered that Maynard had a secret bunker underneath it. It didn't look like anyone had been in there for a very long time, but I did find this."

He flipped to the page with the star map.

"Constellations?" Hannah asked.

Ethan nodded. "Yeah, a star map. It's why I came here. I couldn't read it, and I found Ritchie's name in my dad's contacts. Ritchie told me it leads to the Inaccessible Island. If my parents found the bunker, then they would have found the star map, and if they did, maybe they came this way."

"But you said they died in England?"

"My dad obviously did, but I met someone in England who knew my parents and may have been involved in what happened to them, and he implied it was only my dad who died."

That's what you hope, at least.

Hannah gazed at him, her green eyes twinkling in the cabin light. "How does that make you feel?" she asked.

He looked at her, confused. "What?"

"Discovering the possibility that your mum is still alive."

Blowing out a long breath, he said, "I don't know. Excited? Hopeful? The person who told me isn't a good man. He could be lying or trying to play me to get the information I have. I'm trying to keep it realistic, knowing it's been ten years. If Mum was alive, I should have heard from her, right? But I can't help thinking she is alive. I'm trying not to get my hopes up, though, because then I'm just setting myself up for disappointment."

"Ethan, I do know how you feel, at least to some degree. I tried to find ways that confirmed my parents somehow survived. I don't think there is anything wrong with keeping a little hope alive, even if you are aware of how fragile the reality of that hope is." She pointed to the star map. "I don't know anything about this kind of thing. But even finding something like Maynard's bunker and what was in it would be historically significant, right?"

Ethan nodded. "I would think so."

"Then I would imagine they would have been proud of you for coming this far."

She pushed the diary back to Ethan. "One way or another, I truly hope you find out what happened and get some closure."

Ethan smiled at her, tears and emotion threatening to overcome him. "Thanks," he said, but his voice caught and it came out as a whisper. He cleared his throat and showed her the five-sided device. "I also found this in the bunker."

She looked at it. "What is it?"

"The million-dollar question. I don't know, I can't open it. I need to figure out the sequence of these stars."

"It's like a pushbutton lock?"

"Exactly."

"Any hints?"

He shook his head. "Not one."

Hannah opened one of her medical books and said, "You'll work it out."

"I'm not sure that I will," he said with exasperation. "I have no reference to the code, and I've gone over his diary a thousand times."

"Maybe it's not in the diary," Hannah suggested. "Maybe it's mentioned somewhere else."

"Maybe."

Ethan fiddled with the device while Hannah studied, and they made idle chit-chat through the night. He learned about what she liked to do in her spare time, where she grew up, and the travelling she had done—especially to less-fortunate countries, which helped form her desire to help people and get into the medical field.

They had been silent for a while, each doing their own thing, when Hannah let out a growl of frustration.

"What's up?" Ethan asked, looking up from Maynard's diary.

"I've spent the last five minutes looking for something and just realised this isn't the textbook I need. I must have accidentally taken the wrong one when I packed for this trip."

Right then, it was as if the final piece of a gigantic puzzle had fallen into place. "How could I have been so stupid!" Ethan exclaimed.

Hannah looked at him. "What?"

"I've been looking at this the wrong way."

"What do you mean?"

He held up the device. "I've always assumed this was Maynard's, that he had always owned it." He flipped it over. "But it never made sense why it had these initials scratched on it, especially since they don't look like an 'R' or 'M', unless he took it from someone else."

Hannah looked at the device casing. "I can't make out what it says."

"No, it's faded and not very clear," Ethan agreed. "I thought it might be an F or an I, but it's not either. What he did was he scratched over it to make it look like F.I. instead of it being the real initials—E.T."

"Who is E.T.?" Hannah asked, clearly confused.

"E.T. is Edward Teach, better known as Blackbeard, the pirate. Maynard was the one who killed him back in 1718." He was getting animated now, speaking as the thoughts came to him. "In his diary, Maynard wrote: '*I rue that day thirty-three years ago when I came across that brigand*'—which I think means Blackbeard—'*and finding that infernal contraption.*' He doesn't mention what that was, but I think it was this," he said, holding up the device. "*This* is the infernal contraption."

"What's so special about it?"

"So, it was rumoured that Blackbeard had a vast treasure hidden somewhere that has never been discovered. Maybe there is a connection between Blackbeard's lost treasure and the cursed treasure Maynard said he moved. If so, this makes a lot more sense now."

"It makes no sense to me," Hannah admitted.

"Do you have a book on constellations here?" he asked.

Hannah got up and left the mess without saying a word. She returned a few minutes later with a book in her hand. "Ritchie used to show me the constellations when we'd do overnight trips."

She handed it to him, and while he flipped through the pages, he kept talking. "Now, if Maynard found this on Blackbeard's body, then the code must be related to something important to him. It could be his birthday, but that's too obvious. The only other thing that mattered to him was his ship, the *Queen Anne's Revenge*, which he captured from French privateers on November

28, 1717, in St. Vincent."

He looked up at her. "Do you know how to tell what constellations are visible in certain places at certain times of the year?"

She held out her hand for the book. "You want to know what constellations are visible in the Caribbean in November, right?"

He nodded.

Hannah started flipping through the book, dog-earing pages, while Ethan waited impatiently, his leg shaking restlessly. Finally, she handed him the book. "These four would be visible, I think, but I'm not sure if they could be seen from St. Vincent."

Ethan took the book from her and checked the pages she dog-eared: Andromeda, Cassiopeia, Cetus, and Cepheus.

"Let's find out," he said.

Using the book as a guide, he located Andromeda on the device by following one star to another via the straight lines that connected them, kind of like joining a dot-to-dot. He pressed all sixteen stars, hoping there was no particular order needed, but nothing happened. He pressed the switch to reset the stars and went on to the next one, Cassiopeia.

Hannah watched with interest while he pressed the six stars of Cassiopeia, but had the same result.

"Crap," he muttered.

"You still have two more chances," Hannah pointed out.

Ethan located and pressed in the stars for Cetus, the thirteen-point constellation, and when he pressed the last star, the device clicked open.

"You did it," Hannah breathed in awe, moving next to him.

Ethan popped open the lid, revealing a compass rose with the four cardinal directions written in thick black letters, and the four ordinal directions set between each cardinal direction in smaller red letters.

"It's a compass!"

"Why is the needle moving like that?" Hannah asked.

The compass needle was swinging wildly, going one way and then the other sporadically.

"Maybe something in here is interfering with it."

He took it outside, the night silent except for the lapping of the waves and wind blowing through the crevices and holes in the boat. He expected it to right itself, but it kept on circling wildly. With Hannah trailing behind him, Ethan moved around the boat, shaking and banging the compass on his palm, but the needle kept moving wildly.

It was broken.

"GOD DAMN IT!" he shouted into the night.

Twenty One

Inaccessible Island, South Atlantic Ocean

Ethan spent the rest of the voyage angry at the broken compass for possibly ruining any chance he had of finding out what happened to his parents. He spent the majority of the trip in his cabin, fervently working from Maynard's diary and the information he had on hand to see if there was anything else that might help. He was certain the compass was key to finding Maynard's treasure, and maybe even helping on the island, but if it didn't work, then it seemed pointless. While Andrea tried to cheer him up, telling him that the compass may not be needed, Ritchie was oddly quiet and aloof.

They finally arrived on the outskirts of the main island.

Ritchie dropped anchor in a sheltered area on the south side of the island. They were away from the worst of the waves and far enough from the jagged boulders that he would have time to manoeuvre around if needed.

Ethan joined the others on the deck, looking out at the island in the fading light. From where they anchored, the island loomed above them and reminded Ethan of a right-angled triangle. It started at sea level but gradually rose at a steady incline to the highest point, Cairn Peak, on the left.

"We'll make for land tomorrow morning, I assume?" he said.

Ritchie nodded.

"Where's the volcano?" Andrea asked, looking out at the dark, flat form of the island in the fading light.

"It's a volcanic island," Ethan explained. "Below, on the seabed, when the two tectonic plates pull apart, lava spews out and forms layers. It keeps building until eventually you get islands like this one."

"There's no risk of it erupting, then?" she asked.

He shook his head. "No, it went extinct six million years ago."

"Well, that's a relief," she said with a smile.

The next morning was stormy. Even in the sheltered area the water churned and the waves rocked the boat so much that Andrea spent the morning in the toilet, vomiting up the contents of her stomach.

Ethan stood on deck, looking out at the distant island, ignoring the sea spray from the crashing waves. Ritchie came up to him and said, "As soon as this weather blows past, we'll make our way in."

"Good."

"Laddy, you know we don't have to do this. We can turn around."

"What about your money?"

"I'll find another way."

Ethan thought of the broken compass. He shook his head. "We're here. May as well see what we can find."

Ritchie sighed. "All right, lad. I'll let you know when we're ready to go."

It was almost noon when the seas calmed enough to move closer. Ritchie lifted anchor, and the boat rumbled toward the island. Ethan still stood on deck, watching the island grow larger and larger, as the boat rocked side-to-side on the waves. Ritchie took the boat across the southern side of the island, following along the sheer cliff face where waterfalls fell from as high as three hundred metres into the ocean. The boat rumbled along until they reached the dogleg at the southernmost point of the island.

"That's the bay we'll be landing in, lad!" Ritchie shouted down to Ethan from the wheelhouse. He was pointing to a crescent-shaped bay just beyond, on the southwest part of the island. Passing around the dogleg and steering for the bay, the boat rocked as the powerful waves hit the boat with all they had. The boat crested the waves but was suddenly hit with a violent one that threw Ethan off balance. He grabbed hold of the handrail, his hair soaked, and watched, frozen, as the boat crested up another wave and then crashed down, salty sea water spraying on the deck.

"Jesus Christ," he muttered, holding tight to the railing.

The boat moved closer to the bay, riding the waves and avoiding the jagged rocks that barely peaked through the whitecaps. Ethan was watching in stunned awe at the power of the ocean while admiring Ritchie's navigation skills. They passed by sharp rock stacks rising out of the water that were taller than the boat. Here and there Ethan saw rocks hidden in the waves and wondered how many ships had struck them and sunk to the bottom of the ocean.

The island loomed closer, the sheer size of it almost taking up his entire view. The boat powered on until they were finally past the rock stacks and boulders and in the protection of the bay.

He heard a loud roar and looked up to see Ritchie cheering and shaking his fist, yelling, "You can't get the best o' me, ya bastards!"

Moments later, Ritchie dropped anchor about thirty metres from shore, unwilling to get any closer. He tossed Ethan a wetsuit. "Time to swim, me boy," he said cheerfully, still riding the high of winning the battle against the sea.

He held one of his own suits and Ethan asked, "You're coming?"

"That's right."

"Why?"

He shrugged. "Gotta make sure you don't do something stupid and get yourself killed. You still owe me the other half."

Ethan sighed, "I don't have the other half."

"What's that?"

"I lied to get you to bring me here."

Ritchie weighed Ethan's words and then a grin broke through his red beard, "I'm still coming, lad."

"Why?"

"Can't have tourists getting killed on my watch. It's bad for business." He pointed the island before them. "Besides, like you said, could be plenty o' more than eighty grand in there."

Ethan scowled and spun on his heels. He headed back to the cabin, charging past Hannah without saying a word, where he found Andrea sitting on the bed, looking paler than usual.

"You okay?" he asked, taking off his jacket and unzipping his pants.

She shook her head. "Planes are fine, roller coasters are fine. Surging waves? Not fine."

He gave her a grin. "Feeding the fish, eh?"

Grimacing, she nodded but said nothing.

"You're not coming, then?"

She shook her head. "Sorry, Ethan, even standing up will set me off. I can't imagine what swimming to shore would do."

He stuck his leg in the wetsuit, struggling to get it on. "Don't be sorry. It's probably a wild goose chase, anyway. I doubt we will be long on the island."

"You need to have a little more faith," she said, standing up on wobbly legs. She grabbed the wetsuit zipper and pulled it up.

"I always hate putting these on," he muttered, moving his arms every which way to loosen the suit. The smell of neoprene wafted into his nose and it made him nauseous, as it always did.

Ritchie appeared in the doorway and tossed him a dry bag. "Ready when you are." Then he looked at Andrea. "Feeling any better, lass?"

"Not really," she said.

"Always happens to landlubbers," he chuckled. "Hannah will be here, so if you need anything, give her a shout."

"I will, thank you."

Ethan packed a change of clothes, his shoes, a torch, and emergency supplies in his dry bag. Then tossed in his journal, Maynard's diary, and the coins, and slung it over his shoulder. "Let's go."

"Why the coins?" Andrea asked.

"For luck," he said. "Lord knows I need it."

She gave him a quick kiss when Ritchie was out of sight. They hadn't shown any sort of affection while on the boat, the both of them seeming to have an unspoken agreement to keep their relationship—whatever it was—quiet.

He found Ritchie on the aft deck where he was told that the swim shouldn't be too hard, but the water was deep right until the shoreline, so be prepared for anything. Ethan tightened the dry bag across his shoulder and was about to jump in when…

"Ethan!"

He turned around to find Hannah running their way, waving the compass.

"Look!" she said excitedly, pointing to the compass rose.

"What?"

She thrust the compass toward him. "It's stopped spinning."

"Huh?" Ethan looked at the compass and, sure enough, the compass dial had stopped swinging wildly and was now pointing toward the island, swaying slightly.

He looked up at her. "When did this happen?"

"I don't know. I was heading out to watch you guys leave, and I noticed the compass on the table. I thought you might need it, and when I picked it up, the needle wasn't moving."

She handed it to him and he put it in his dry bag. "Thanks," he said.

"Good luck," she said, and then looked over his shoulder at Ritchie. "Don't do anything stupid, Ritchie!"

Ritchie was standing on the outside of the railing, black wetsuit tight-fitting around his stomach. He tightened his own dry pack over his shoulder and said, "Lass, have you ever known me to be anything but sensib—whoa!"

He fell backward off the boat and splashed into the water.

"Please look after him," Hannah said to Ethan.

"You got it," he said. Then, with a mock salute, he leapt over the railing.

Less than fifteen minutes later, they had waded through the freezing ocean water to the rocky beach surrounded by the high, almost vertical cliffs. They got changed, and Ethan left his wetsuit on a large rock to dry out in the scant sunlight. Ethan secured his dry bag across his shoulder, everything he'd gathered so far safely inside—everything except for the compass, which he held in his hand.

"Where to, lad?" Ritchie asked, the wind blowing his damp hair in his face.

He showed him the compass, the needle pointing toward the

dogleg they passed by earlier. "That way, I guess."

Ethan led the way, traversing the loose, rocky shore toward the dogleg. The waves lapped at their feet like eager puppies, and Ritchie grumbled the entire time as he slipped and tripped, trying to follow. While they walked, Ethan watched the compass, wondering why it stopped spinning all of a sudden. The anger he held for the last six days had melted away when Hannah showed him the now-working compass, renewing the hope that he was back on the right track.

"Great," Ritchie muttered, bringing Ethan's attention back to the situation. "Now what?"

Ahead of them, where it turned back in toward the island, was a cylindrical rock stack that rose sharply, blocking their way.

"The compass is still pointing this way," Ethan said.

"You're going on the advice of that thing?"

"Do you have any better ideas?"

When Ritchie said nothing, Ethan said, "Let's look around and see if there is a way through."

They spent the next ten minutes searching around the peak of the island, trying to find a path around the stack. But they found nothing, not even the hint of a trail.

"Nothing here, lad," Ritchie said.

Ethan leaned against a rock, studying the surrounding area. Ritchie was right, there was no way through. He looked at the compass, the needle stubbornly pointing toward the tall stack blocking their way. While he sat there watching the needle, hoping it would show them the way, words from his dad came unbidden to his mind: *People tend to focus on what they can see. You*

miss out on a lot if you just think everything is happening in front of
your eyes. Look up from time to time.

He told Ethan this one day when he was very young and they
were playing hide and seek in the yard. His dad had hidden up a
tree and Ethan couldn't find him for more than an hour,
eventually breaking down and crying in the grass. His dad came
down and told him that sage advice, reminding him to look in the
most unexpected places, including up. It reminded him of the
Sherlock Holmes quote: *Once you have eliminated the impossible,*
whatever remains, no matter how improbable, must be the truth. Or in
this case, once they have eliminated the impossible paths, the only
remaining way is…

"We go up."

"What?"

Ethan pointed to the top of the stack. "It's the only way."

Ritchie looked up at the rock face and said, "Lad, be serious.
You're not going up there."

Studying the rock face, Ethan believed he found a climbable
path that would take him to the top. "Did you bring any rope?"

Ritchie nodded, and Ethan said, "Give it to me. I'll climb up
and secure it somewhere and toss it down."

"You're gonna climb that? Lad, you falling and breaking your
neck would be the *best-case* scenario."

Frustrated with Ritchie's lack of help, Ethan said, "You've got
two options: give me the rope and come with me, or wait here.
Either way, I'm going up."

Ritchie chewed his lip, as if contemplating saying something,
before he relented and pulled a coiled length of rope out of his dry

bag and handed it to Ethan. "You better be bloody careful, lad. I don't want your death on my conscience."

"I'll be fine," he said, taking the rope and putting it in his own dry bag. "I've done this a hundred times." He approached the stack, and rubbing his hands together, grabbed hold of a protruding piece. The piece was rough enough to get a good grip, and he put his foot on another and started climbing.

Grateful for all the tough climbing he did back home, Ethan took a route that went straight up until about halfway, where he ran out of handholds and had to move sideways. A narrow ledge ran around to the right, and Ethan shuffled across it until he was on the southeast side of the stack. Below him was only the ocean, with jagged rocks poking up and waves crashing into the stack. The wind seemed to have picked up, blowing through the cracks and crevices, sinisterly whispering at him, telling him he was going to fall.

Despite the hard soles of his shoes, he could feel the sharp rocks pocking through like an uncomfortable foot massage. Ethan swallowed, taking a moment to gather himself for the next part, before continuing.

The rock face here was damp with ocean spray, and Ethan was halfway across, taking care moving across the ledge, when it crumbled beneath him. Crying out in surprise, he dropped past the ledge, the cliffs a grey blur as he fell. His hands shot out reactively and he grabbed onto a handhold. He came to a sudden stop and his arm jerked awkwardly. Ethan cried out in pain but held on, and his body dangled over the jagged rocks and water below.

"Holy crap," he breathed, looking around for another handhold. The wind blew in his face, making his eyes water, and he tried to blink the tears away. To his right, just out of his reach, was another hold, a wide piece of rock sticking out like a wall shelf. Grabbing onto the handhold with both hands, he put his feet on the cliff face, bracing himself in a hanging crouch. Rocking his body from side-to-side, he pushed off with his feet, releasing his hold and leaping across the gap to grab onto the next hold. He held on as his body swung with the momentum and he scrambled his feet until they gripped onto a rough part of the rock face.

Breathing heavily but satisfied he was safe, Ethan pulled himself up to another hold and continued his ascent. After what felt like an age, he finally pulled himself up and over the ledge and on top of the rock stack. He rolled away from the ledge and lay there, panting and staring at the cloudy sky, the wind still whipping around him.

Finally, he got up and looked around. The top was flat, though leading inland it gradually rose to a pointed peak with basketball-size rocks scattered here and there. A natural path led inland, where the landscape changed from barren rock to tussock grasses.

Ethan pulled out the compass and checked the needle. The point now swung to a north-northeast direction, toward the centre of the island. He headed back to the edge and looked down to find Ritchie leaning against a large boulder. Ethan waved to him and he waved back. He then grabbed the coil of rope from his dry bag and tied it around a car-sized boulder and tossed it over the edge. Sitting on the edge, he watched Ritchie scale the rock face.

When he got near the top, Ethan could hear him cursing, and he reached out to pull him up and over the edge.

Hands on his knee and breathing heavily, Ritchie said, "Maybe Hannah is right. I need to cut down on the beers."

Ethan chuckled while untying the rope. He coiled it and put it in his dry bag. "Ready to go?"

Sucking in some more breaths, Ritchie nodded. Ethan took the lead, letting the compass guide him.

They headed inland, following the compass, which stayed pointing at the island's centre. They hiked at a steady incline along unsteady terrain, getting higher as they went. Soon the tussocks gave way to fern bushes, the dark green fronds a stark change to the pale green grasses behind them.

Two hours after they had left the shore, they took a break-in a clearing that was surrounded by ferns. Ethan sat on a rock looking at the compass while Ritchie took swigs of water from a canteen.

"Has that thing changed at all?" he asked.

Ethan shook his head. "Nope. Still heading straight."

"How do you know it's not just gonna to lead us to the other side of the island?"

"I don't."

"But you're going to follow it anyway?"

Ethan nodded. "Like I said, if you don't want to come, go back to the shore and wait for me. But I'm going ahead. If Mum and Dad came this way, I want to know."

Putting his canteen back in his pack, Ritchie stood up. "I can't let you go alone. If your ma and da are somehow alive, they'd kill me."

Packing away his own canteen, Ethan stood and said, "Then let's get going."

Rain was falling while they made their way uphill through the prickly ferns. Ritchie grumbled as he trailed Ethan, who moved with a purpose he hadn't felt in years. Suddenly, the needle swung sharply, pointing in a north-northwest direction. Ethan stopped and looked: ahead of them was Cairn Peak, the highest point of the island. It rose sharply out of the ground, as if it had been pushed from below, and the face of it ran in waves like corrugated iron.

"That way?" Ritchie asked.

"Looks like it."

"There doesn't look to be anything there, lad."

"We might need to go around them. Maybe it's leading us to the other side."

Ritchie sighed. "This is a wild goose chase."

"Like I said—" Ethan started.

"I know, I know," Ritchie said, hands up placatingly. "If I don't like it, I can go back."

Ethan nodded and headed towards the cliffs.

After ten minutes of moving in the gradually increasing rain, the needle swung again, this time toward true north and heading straight for the cliff face. Ethan expected Ritchie to complain, but he was silent as they made their way toward it, brushing past the wet ferns. As they got closer, the ground levelled off, and the route became more stable. Ethan trudged ahead, following the needle with Ritchie right behind him. Despite his size and love of the drink, Ethan was impressed with the Irishman's stamina as he kept up.

Four hours and several needle swings later, the rain had stopped, and they were at the base of the cliffs, which loomed over them like a rock tidal wave. It was mid-afternoon, and Ethan estimated they were at least two hundred and fifty metres above sea level. The needle pointed north again, which was straight up the cliff side.

"That ain't possible to climb, lad," Ritchie said, staring up the cliff face. Ethan reluctantly agreed. It was basically a flat face. There were some handholds here and there, but nothing that would get him to the top.

"We must have missed a step," Ritchie said.

Ethan shook his head. "No, this is definitely the way."

He was certain he followed the directions correctly and even if he hadn't, it should have adjusted his course. If the compass was pointing this way, then it was the way they had to go. This island had been here for centuries, and everything was natural. So, if up is impossible and the way forward is impossible, then…

"It's down."

"What's that?"

"The way isn't forward or up—it's down!" he said excitedly. "Look around. See if you can find a path or a way down."

They went their separate ways. Ethan pushed past fern fronds as he headed right, one hand shielding his eyes from the rain and the other running along the cliff face, when he found a gap in the wall.

He studied the rock face and realised it had a fold which created the illusion that it was a straight vertical wall, but here the fold led into a seam in the cliff.

"Ritchie!" he called. The boat captain was a good distance away, but the wind carried Ethan's voice and he turned around. Ethan waved for him to come over. While he waited, he stared at the wall, trying to discern the seam in the greys and whites and blacks of the cliff. The effect was wreaking havoc on his eyes, like a Magic Eye, and he moved forward, arms out, until he was in the seam. It was narrow, just as wide as him in some spots, while in other areas he had to crouch under or draw his shoulders in.

"Ethan?" he heard Ritchie call out behind him.

"In here!" he shouted, turning his head as much as he could in the narrow space.

There was a pause and then, "Where are you, lad?"

"Just run your hand along the wall until you find the gap," Ethan called back, and then moved forward.

"Jaysus Christ." Ritchie's head appeared, and he looked around. "How the hell am I gonna fit in here?"

"Suck in your gut, big boy," Ethan told him.

Ignoring the grunting and swearing from Ritchie, Ethan continued forward until the light faded and he emerged into a gloomy cavern. From above, thin beams of light penetrated the cracks in the walls and roof above. There was enough light to see a couple of metres ahead.

"Crap!"

"Shyte!"

"Aww, me head!"

Ritchie stumbled out of the seam. "Lad, you in here?"

Ethan was kneeling on the ground, rummaging through his dry pack, until he found his flashlight. He turned it on and swung it around the cavern.

Ritchie grumbled about the scrapes and bumps he'd picked up on the way in until Ethan grabbed his arm.

"What, lad?"

Ethan pointed to the opposite side of the cavern where, set into the wall, was a door.

Twenty Two

Ritchie flicked his flashlight on, and their lights illuminated an open, empty cavern with columns of volcanic rock stretching up from the ground. Water dropped from gaps in the roof and walls, making a gentle *plop, plop* as the water fell into puddles.

Ethan directed his light to the ground. "Look at this," he said. His light played over timber tracks, square-cut and laid in front of one another. They created a path, weaving its way through the columns to the door on the other side of the chamber.

"These have been laid," Ritchie said, stating the obvious.

Ethan nodded excitedly. "And look here."

He pointed his beam of light to the wall behind them where the seam was reinforced with a timber frame and a rotting door lay on its side nearby. The door was covered in rocks and stone, and Ethan ran his fingers over them. "They've been attached to the door."

"Camouflage?"

Ethan nodded. "Probably to stop anyone from finding their way in here. Either deliberately or by accident."

"Didn't look like it worked," Ritchie said. "See those splinters in the timber? Looks like someone took an axe to it."

"You think someone found it?"

"Or Maynard forgot the keys."

Ethan stood up and followed the timber path toward the other door. This door was made of thick wood with iron bands along the top and bottom and a diagonal band running from top left to bottom right. Etched into the middle of it was Robert Maynard's 'R' symbol.

"Lad, you found it!" Ritchie exclaimed excitedly.

Ethan ran his hand over the door again and tried to imagine what it was like for the people who worked here, who laid the path and installed the door.

"Looks like they tried here as well," Ritchie said, pointing to cracks in the door and splintered panels. "But this door fared much better."

There was no door handle on it—only a pentagon-shaped hole where a keyhole would be.

"Looks like the same shape as that compass you got," Ritchie said.

"Only one way to find out," Ethan said, and he placed the compass in the slot. It fit perfectly, and he turned it like a key.

There was a click, and he pushed the door open. The next room was brighter, with daylight flooding in through square holes in the walls high above them. They were in a large circular room, the floor laid with timber, with a void in the middle. There was timber scaffolding built over the gap and, hanging over it, was a square platform. The platform was suspended by a rope that knotted in the middle. From the middle knot, the rope broke into four pieces, each piece attached to a post in the platform's corner. The central piece of rope was threaded through a pulley installed on a beam high over the gap and connected to a windlass bolted into the ground. Attached to it was a simple wooden lever.

"An elevator," Ethan said. Of all the things he expected to find, an elevator wasn't one of them.

"Why would they have an elevator here?" Ritchie asked.

Ethan shrugged.

"Where do you think it goes?"

"Down," Ethan said simply, and looked around. To the left of them were timber stairs that circled around the room to a second floor. And to the right was a set of stairs that circled around the void going down, deeper into the island.

Ritchie pointed to where the daylight shone through the open spaces. "Don't they look a little too square?"

"Almost too perfect," Ethan agreed. "Looks like everything in here is man made, except the cavern itself."

Ritchie nodded and took the stairs up to the next level. The timber creaked and groaned, and Ethan could hear the thudding of his boots as he disappeared above.

"Lad!" Ritchie called out moments later.

Ethan hurried up the stairs, taking them two at a time until he emerged on the second floor and skidded to a stop. The second floor was stacked with wood and crates with a half-built staircase that continued to wind its way up to a partially built third level. On the far side of the room was a long table that sat in front of a rectangular opening, looking out over the island and the Atlantic beyond. There were cots spaced around the room and a thick layer of cobwebs in the corners and on the furniture. Ethan weaved his way around the cots and chairs until he reached the table. There were plates, cutlery, mounds of what Ethan assumed used to be food, and metal goblets.

"Looks like they were living here," Ethan said, picking up a goblet and brushing away the cobwebs. "Or at least preparing it to be liveable."

The goblet was made of a cheap metal, rusted and worn, with holes that poked through the bottom. He tossed it aside with a dull clang.

Ritchie nodded. "Aye, lad."

"Look around. See if you can find anything useful."

They split up and searched, but all they found were rotted furniture and books destroyed with rot, damp, and mould.

"Not a damn thing," Ritchie said, kicking over a chair in frustration, and Ethan thought about the man's debts.

"There'll be something," he said half-heartedly. His priority wasn't Ritchie's debts, but he had to keep him on track. "Let's go."

They headed back downstairs and cautiously approached the edge of the platform to peer down, their flashlights failing to penetrate the inky blackness.

"How far down do you think it goes?"

Ethan picked up a fist-sized chunk of rock and tossed it into the void. They were silent for ten seconds, waiting to hear any kind of noise, but heard nothing.

"That far."

"What's down there?"

Ethan moved his light to the elevator. "Only one way to find out," he said.

Ritchie groaned. "I suppose there is no point in talking you out of it?" he asked.

Ethan didn't bother replying. He hurried back to the door, grabbed the compass, and approached the elevator. He tested the platform with his foot, causing it to wobble and sway a little. He pressed down a bit more. It creaked but otherwise seemed firm.

He shone his light on the rope. It looked strong enough, the elements not having had a visible effect on them, and he stepped onto the elevator platform. Ritchie let out a gasp, as if expecting it to break, but it held and Ethan gave him a grin. "Come on," he said.

Ritchie shook his head. "Not a chance in hell, laddy." He pointed to the stairs. "I'll take those."

"Suit yourself. I'll meet you at the bottom," Ethan said. He grabbed the lever and pulled. It was stiff and resisted, but he finally got it down with a grinding protest, and the windlass started rotating, letting the rope out as the elevator descended.

Ritchie sighed and walked to the stairs. The elevator was slow, so Ritchie didn't have trouble keeping up as he thudded down the rickety staircase.

"I wouldn't trust that thing," Ethan joked. "Looks a bit dodgy to me."

Ritchie huffed as he continued down the stairs, keeping close to Ethan. His light swayed as he moved, and dirt and dust motes puffed with each step he took. As they moved down, the elevator swaying slightly, Ethan studied the structure. The stairs wound their way around the elevator, a basic design of scaffolding and planks of wood for the steps. The stairs were bolted into the side of the cavern wall, but aside from some missing planks, it looked indistinguishable from any makeshift set of stairs he'd seen at construction sites. Ethan felt elated at making another discovery, and excitement ran through him at the prospect of what waited for him below.

"What do you think they used it for?" Ritchie asked, trudging down the staircase, still able to keep pace with the slow-moving elevator.

"Moving stuff."

"That's a given, lad."

"Moving heavy stuff."

"You and your da share the same dry sense of statin' the bleedin' obvious," Ritchie said.

"It looks like they were getting ready to settle in that room upstairs, and I can't imagine they could have brought the materials the way we came in. It would have been to time-consuming. I wonder if there is another way in, an easier way to offload goods from the ships."

Before Ritchie could reply, there was a crack—the sound of timbers snapping. The elevator dropped suddenly, causing Ethan to lose his balance. He grabbed hold of the railing, but it snapped, and he tumbled over the side. He cried out in surprise and flung his arms out, hoping to grasp anything he could. Luckily, his hand knocked against one of the railing posts, and he grabbed hold of it.

"Ethan!" Ritchie cried out. His flashlight swung wildly as he searched for Ethan, who held the post with one hand while his legs dangled over the emptiness below.

Heart pounding in his chest, he called, "I'm here!"

Ritchie's light swung around to the platform, trying to find him. Finally, it stopped on his legs and Ritchie said, "Hold on, lad. I've got you."

"No, wait!" Ethan called out, but it was too late. Ritchie leapt across the gap and landed heavily on the platform. As soon as he did, the platform jolted and dropped another foot, making Ethan almost lose his grip.

"What happened?" Ritchie asked.

In response, the ropes holding the platform groaned and Ethan said, "We need to get off this thing quickly. Help me up!"

Without another word, Ritchie took three long strides to the other side of the platform, which was now swaying even more wildly. Ethan knew they didn't have much time to waste. On his knees, Ritchie leaned over the edge and held out his hand.

Ethan took it and Ritchie pulled him onto the platform just as a corner rope snapped. The corner of the platform dropped suddenly, and Ethan nearly tumbled off it again. He grabbed hold of a post as the now-lopsided platform swung wildly on three ropes, crashing into the staircase and dislodging timber planks.

The planks fell away into the darkness below.

"Hold on, lad!" Ritchie called out as the platform hit against the wall again and twisted. They swayed in all directions now, the elevator platform twirling on only three ropes.

Then another one snapped.

They both fell, but Ethan still had hold of the post, while Ritchie held on to the top lip of the platform. The elevator was now attached by two ropes, hanging vertically in the shaft. It swung back and forth, slamming into the staircase again and again, dislodging more pieces of wood.

"You right, Ethan?" Ritchie called down.

"Yeah," Ethan told him. "We need to get off this thing. Don't wait for me, just go if you can."

"Ethan, I can't—"

But Ethan cut him off, "Just do it, I'll be fine."

He'd been in precarious positions before, having slipped or fallen off old walkways when exploring places he shouldn't.

"All right, lad," Ritchie said, and he pulled himself up and grabbed the post to keep his balance. He stood on the edge of the elevator platform, and when the staircase was close enough, he jumped off and landed on it with a heavy thud and a puff of dust.

Meanwhile, Ethan reached out and tried to grab the staircase when the platform swung close enough, but it was just out of reach. Above, he heard Ritchie hurrying down the stairs.

"Hold on, Ethan!" he called out just as the third rope snapped. The platform fell and then shook almost immediately. Ethan was swinging wildly, trying to hold on as the platform twisted on its one rope and smashed into the staircase. Ritchie hurried down the stairs, and Ethan heard the rope straining. He was running out of time.

As the platform made another pass at the staircase, he reached out for a crossbeam but it slipped out of his hands. The platform swung around again, causing the single rope above to fray. He knew he had one last shot at this. Just as the platform reached its peak, Ethan let go, letting the momentum carry him just as the last rope snapped. The platform crashed against the staircase before tumbling down the shaft. Ethan sailed through the air, cleared the railing, and crash-landed on the stairs, rolling until he hit the wall.

He groaned, pain shooting up his side and elbow. Ritchie finally reached him, panting.

"Christ, lad, you right?" he asked, bending over to catch his breath.

Ethan nodded and pulled himself up. "I must have taken a knock to the head," he said.

"Why?"

"Feels like everything is shaking," he said, closing his eyes as the world around him rocked.

"It's not your head, lad. The stairs are shot."

Ethan opened his eyes. Ritchie somehow still had his flashlight and was pointing it down the elevator shaft. There was a giant gash in the staircase where the platform had crashed into it, destroying the timbers and scaffolding.

Above them they heard a metallic screech and then a loud crack, followed by another, and Ritchie shone his light up. The light failed to penetrate much, but pieces of timber planks and railing fell and disappearing into the abyss below.

There was another metallic clang and the sound of wood splitting. The staircase shook more, and Ethan's eyed widened as he realised what was happening.

"Run!" he shouted.

They turned and ran down the stairs as fast as they could as pieces of wood rained down on them. There was a thunderous crash, and they dove out of the way just as the windlass smashed through the staircase, the heavy iron destroying the stairs like they were matchsticks. It then clanged off the wall and disappeared into the darkness. The staircase swayed away from the wall as they made their way down, leaping over the gaps caused by the fallen windlass.

Ethan's heart was hammering in his chest, and his limbs were shaky as he pushed himself on and made sure Ritchie followed. Finally, Ethan saw the bottom.

"There!" he called, pointing over the side. "We're almost there!"

They rounded another section of the stairs when suddenly the whole staircase broke free from the wall and fell away, taking Ethan and Ritchie with it. They cried out as the stairs sailed through the air, crashing into the opposite wall and flinging them into darkness. They fell a short distance, and Ethan crashed to the ground and rolled.

Nearby, he heard Ritchie swear as he landed with a heavy thud.

"Come on!" Ethan shouted, getting to his feet.

Ethan hurried to Ritchie, dodging debris that rained down on them, and helped him up. They ran until they reached the safety of an alcove, protected from the still-falling stairs.

After a minute or two, things settled, and the only sound heard was their heavy breathing.

"You okay, lad?" Ritchie said, as he used his flashlight to scan the area.

Ethan checked himself over and nodded, and then after another deep breath said, "Yeah, just a few more scratches and bruises."

"That was insane," Ritchie told him.

"You're not wrong there," Ethan replied. He walked back to the chamber and looked around. The ground was littered with chunks of timber and stone, and the windlass lay on its side, bent and twisted, nearby. He scanned the wall with his flashlight, which somehow survived the treacherous descent. Here and there, fragments of stairs were still attached to the wall.

"Safe elevator, huh?" Ritchie said, his voice laced with accusation.

"Oh yeah, like those stairs were any better."

"We almost died, lad!"

"But we didn't and we're here now," Ethan shot back.

Ritchie sighed. "We don't even know where *here* is."

"The elevator and stairs started down here for a reason. There must be a way through," Ethan said, and headed back into the alcove, leaving Ritchie to fume.

Twenty Three

The alcove was actually a tunnel that led them down a straight path until they reached a circular landing. It was cool and damp in the room, with barrels and crates stacked against the wall to the left and piles of timber lying next to them.

"That must be what they used the elevator for," Ethan said, pointing to the crates.

"I wonder what's in them," Ritchie said. They walked to the crates, noticing that they were all different sizes. Some were knee high, while others were quite tall. Ethan grabbed the lid from one crate and pulled it off. The wood, long rotted from the damp, pulled away easily, revealing cloth wrapped packages. Ethan picked one up and opened it. Inside was a lumpy grey mound.

Whatever it was, it was long expired. He opened another, but it was the same.

"It's food," he said. He opened another crate and then another. "Crates of food. Whatever Maynard was doing down here, he was planning on being here for a long time."

"Clothing in here," Ritchie said, looking in his crate. He held up a shirt and a wool coat that were in surprisingly good condition.

They looked through more crates, revealing more food and clothing, as well as tools, rope, and building materials.

"Was Maynard planning on living here for good?" Ethan wondered aloud. He thought about the room upstairs and its cots, dining table, chairs, and perfectly cut windows. Why was it unfinished? Then he thought about the destroyed door. Someone had taken an axe to the door, and it made him wonder if Maynard's hideout had been discovered.

Or did his crew commit mutiny?

"Lad," came Ritchie's quiet voice.

Ethan looked at him. He was standing at a long, rectangular crate, holding a musket rifle. Inside the crate were piles of similar guns. Ethan checked the next crate. It was filled with flintlock pistols. The next two crates had more muskets and flintlocks with barrels of gunpowder beside them.

"What the hell was he doing down here?"

"Looks like he was preparing for war," Ritchie said.

"Against who, though?"

"That's the million-dollar question," Ritchie said, examining a flintlock. It was about thirty-five centimetres long and made of wood, with a brass and steel hammer, and frizzen. He put it in his dry pack, along with a bagful of gunpowder and lead balls.

"Have you ever used one of those before?" Ethan asked.

"Nah, lad. But I've always wanted to try."

They continued searching, finding more food and weapons, including a crate of sabres and bayonet attachments for the muskets.

"He was really stocking up, wasn't he?" Ritchie commented, pulling out a belt and strapping it around his waist, sheathing a sabre in it.

Ethan raised an eyebrow and Ritchie said, "Might be worth a bit of quid."

Ethan made a face and moved past him into another tunnel. This tunnel continued straight ahead, their light bouncing off the rough walls, and they emerged into another room. This room was empty and there was a door on the opposite side.

Ethan crossed over to it. Like the other doors, it was made of thick timber and banded along the top and bottom with an iron ring for a handle. Ethan tried the handle, but it didn't budge. Thinking it was because of centuries of corrosion and rust, he twisted it with more force, but it held still.

"Ethan," Ritchie said.

"What?" he asked, turning around.

Ritchie illuminated the wall with the beam of his flashlight, and Ethan followed the light as it probed the wall before him. Ethan stepped back and saw there were designs carved into the wall. It was hard to make out, but then he noticed there were torches in iron brackets set on the walls.

"Do you have a lighter?" Ethan asked.

Ritchie fished one out of his dry bag and handed it to Ethan. He lit the first torch, the soaked oil catching easily, emitting a warm, orange flame. He tossed the lighter to Ritchie, who lit the remaining seven torches that surrounded the chamber.

The lighting was dim but did enough to illuminate the wall before them. It was flat with flames carved into it that were rising from the ground and surrounding several treasure chests. The flickering light twisted and writhed around the carvings, making the shadows dance ominously among the flames. Rising from the flames were dozens of featureless devils painted a deep red. They had long horns and held three-pronged pitchforks.

"What the hell is this?" Ritchie asked.

"Hell might be right," Ethan said.

Above the flames and devils was a depiction of the sea with a ship cresting the waves. It was heading toward an island.

"Hmm…"

Above the ship were stars scattered across the sky, and Ethan recognised several constellations.

"What is it, lad?"

He pointed to the ship and the island. "I think this is Maynard's ship, and the island is this one." He examined the chests. Front and centre of all of them was one that looked familiar to him. He shrugged off his dry pack and opened it. "I think this is the cursed treasure," he said as he pointed to it. "The flames and the devils might be an analogy for the evil surrounding it." He grabbed the journal and flipped it open to the picture of the chest that his dad had drawn. "It kind of looks like this, doesn't it? With the flames around the chest."

He showed the picture to Ritchie, who squinted at it in the poor light. "It does a little. Does that mean the treasure is behind this door?"

"Could be," Ethan breathed, trying to keep his hopes from rising. *And my parents? Did they make it this far?*

"Well, let's get this door open," Ritchie said, a noticeable spring in his step.

"I'm working on it," Ethan replied.

He approached the door, testing the iron ring handle again. There was no give in it, but Ethan was certain it wasn't stuck or rusted shut. No, there had to be another way in. He stepped back and examined the mural. The dancing flames made it seem like the waves were moving and the ship flowed with them while the faceless devils danced among the chests.

It was a disturbing image, but nothing stood out to Ethan as being a key to opening the door. He ran his hand along the carved flames, trying to find any false walls or recesses hidden like the entrance in the cliffs above, but there were none.

He moved back some more, trying to get the whole mural in view, when his foot got caught in an uneven part of the floor and he fell backward.

"Shit," he muttered, and then paused. He didn't trip over an uneven part of the floor. No, it was a wooden platform in the shape of a pentagon inset in the floor. There were circular indents in each corner of the pentagon, and in the middle of the platform was a smaller pentagon-shaped hole. "Hey, look at this," he called to Ritchie, who was examining the far side of the mural.

"What is it?" he said, walking over.

Ethan touched the hole in the floor. "Want to bet that this will open the door?" he said, grabbing the compass from his pack. He slotted it into the pentagon-shaped hole in the floor. It fit perfectly.

"Here goes."

As with the other door, he turned the compass like a key, and immediately the circular indents fell away and five posts emerged from them. Each post was topped with a different statue: a chariot, a lion, a bear, an eagle, and a jar.

"What is this, now?" Ritchie asked.

Ethan examined the statues. They were made of intricately carved ivory and had pockmarked holes all over the front of the bodies. At the base of them was a hollowed-out chamber with a candle in it.

He smiled. "It's our way in," he said.

"How?"

"I'll show you. Can I have the lighter?"

Ritchie tossed him the lighter and Ethan flicked it on, holding it to the wick of the candle on the eagle statue. The candle flared to life, and from the holes in the statue, pinpricks of bright light shot out, shining on the wall. *Whatever was inside the statue must focus the light into these tiny beams,* Ethan realised. Maybe curved glass or crystal?

He pointed at the ten pinpricks of light shining on the wall among the stars. "Does that look familiar?"

Ritchie nodded. "Aye, that's the Aquila constellation."

Grabbing the statue, Ethan rotated it. It moved as if on a

gimbal and the pinpricks of light moved with it. He turned the statue around until each light touched a star, highlighting the Aquila constellation. The stars on the wall changed from yellow to a bright, glowing blue.

"Well, I'll be," Ritchie whispered in awe.

Ethan moved to the lion statue and lit the candle. As with the eagle statue, pinpricks of light shone on the wall, and he rotated the statue around the wall. With Ritchie's help, he was able to line up the ten lights to the stars.

The next two—Aquarius and Auriga—were done in quick succession. Ritchie's knowledge of the constellations made the job much quicker for Ethan as he moved on to the last one, Ursa Major.

"Uh oh," he said.

"What?"

"There's no candle in this one."

Ritchie cursed. "What do we do?"

Ethan thought for a moment, ideas floating in his head until…

"Maybe…" He grabbed his flashlight and placed it in the hollow with the light facing up through the focus of the statue. Nineteen beams of bright white light shot out of the holes in the bear statue onto the wall.

"Well I'll be…" Ritchie whispered.

Ethan quickly moved the statue around at Ritchie's instruction until it landed on the constellation of Ursa Major. The stars turned blue, and moments later, the chamber echoed with the sounds of gears turning from beneath the platform. Dust bloomed as the pentagon in the centre of the platform rose, revealing a sixth statue, this one a centaur.

Ethan didn't need Ritchie's help for this one as he lit the candle underneath. He rotated the centaur statue until the lights were sitting right above the island. The stars turned blue as the light highlighted the twenty-one stars of Centaurus.

There was a click, and Ritchie hurried to the door. He turned the handle and pushed, swinging the door open.

"Let's go, lad!" he said, all worries about the dangers forgotten as he disappeared through the door.

Grabbing the compass from the top of the centaur statue, Ethan packed it in his dry bag and followed Ritchie through the door.

Twenty Four

It was dark in the next room, and the first thing Ethan noticed was the faint sound of lapping water. He shone his light around, seeing that they were in a cavern. It was so cold that he could see his breath misting in the light as it probed around the room, revealing the remains of crates, desks, and chairs. He went to examine them, but they disintegrated under his touch. After further exploration, he let out a little yelp of surprise.

"What's wrong?" Ritchie called.

Ethan's eyes were wide as his light shone on a row of gibbets hanging from the roof. The gibbets were barely half his height, but inside each of them were skeletons. Some skeletons had crumbled into a heap at the bottom of the small cage, their bones sticking out of the gaps, while others had skeletons still sitting there, legs hanging out, as if waiting for someone.

"Jaysus," Ritchie exclaimed when he saw the gibbets. "Were they pirates?"

Ethan examined the clothing on the skeletons—or at least, what remained of them. Some skeletons wore blue coats and black trousers, and others wore shirts and breeches in a combination of red, white, and black. Ethan pointed to the first lot. "They're navy men, probably Maynard's."

"Deserters?" Ritchie asked.

"Could be. Wouldn't be easy living down here, so I expect some may have wanted to leave."

"Harsh," Ritchie commented.

"If Maynard really thought this treasure was cursed, he would have done anything to keep this place a secret. The pirates, though… I don't know why they're here."

They searched on in silence while Ethan's mind wondered at their latest discovery.

"We need more light," he said.

He found an unlit torch on a bracket on the wall, grabbed it, and used Ritchie's lighter to ignite it. Once it was lit, he found another one and put the torch to it. Handing one to Ritchie, Ethan followed along the wall, lighting a handful of torches as he went until the room was half-lit in fire light. Ritchie finished his half of the room, and they met in the middle. The lighting was still poor but bright enough to see that the cavern was long and wide with a ceiling that disappeared into darkness. There were chandeliers hanging from chains attached to the roof, but it was impossible to get to them.

"What happened here?" Ethan asked.

The room was destroyed, with holes in the cabins and chunks of stone taken out of the wall. And strewn all about the ground were…

"Are they bodies?"

Skeletons littered the floor haphazardly, some wearing the blue of the Royal Navy, while others wore an assortment of clothing like the ones the pirates in the gibbets were wearing.

"I guess that explains the pirates," Ethan said. Though he wasn't totally sure, as they weren't wearing the same colours as those in the gibbets.

"There was a hell of a fight here," Ritchie said, looking around with his flashlight. He knelt next to two skeletons that were tangled together and pulled a sabre from between the ribs of one of them. The blade was rusted and dull, and he tossed it away and wiped his hands on his pant leg. "Pirates must have found a way in."

Ethan looked around. "Looks like it."

They moved toward the middle of the room where there was a wooden wall divider that split the room in half. There were more football-sized holes, and parts of the divider had collapsed completely. Strangely, a desk and chair were set against it and looked untouched, unlike everything else in the room. To the left of it were more crates, some still standing, while others destroyed, and to the right were bookcases and tables in various forms of rot and disrepair. Shredded and burned tapestries depicting nature scenes and naval ships lined the walls, and tattered rugs covered the floor.

"Look at this," Ritchie said. He bent down and picked through a pile of rubble, retrieving something heavy. He held up something that looked like a shot put.

"A cannonball?" Ethan asked.

"Aye."

"How were they firing them down here?" he wondered. "I don't see any cannons."

"No idea, lad," Ritchie admitted, dropping the cannonball with a heavy thud and walking to some crates in the corner.

"It looks like a war zone," Ethan added, walking past skeletons with flintlocks, swords, and muskets resting next to them. Ritchie was at the crates, breaking them open. He looked up when Ethan arrived. "More weapons and food," he said.

"He was definitely preparing to move it upstairs, hunker down for the long term," Ethan said. "But why the fight?"

The sound of lapping water grew louder as he moved closer to the divider. He opened the door and passed through. It was dark on the other side, so he grabbed a torch from the wall and lit two that were attached to the wall on either side of the door. He walked around the perimeter to light the room again, and when he lit the last one, he was standing on the edge of the cavern. Before him, black water stretched out into the darkness beyond. It appeared to be a wharf, with a timber walkway and jetty built for boats to dock. There were half a dozen rowboats tied to the jetty posts, and more skeletons lying about.

Before he could investigate further, he heard Ritchie calling to him.

"Lad!" he shouted from the other side of the room, his voice echoing in the vast space.

Ethan hurried to where Ritchie was standing by several rows of cabins lined up along the cavern wall. Most of them were destroyed, or collapsed, except for one row that managed to avoid both the destruction and rot. Ritchie was standing at the entrance to the first one and stepped back when Ethan arrived. He pointed inside and said, "Take a look."

Ethan poked his head in. It was a bunk room with four cots lining the walls and a small table in the middle. Slumped face down over the table was not a skeleton, but an actual body!

Ethan's heart leapt into his mouth. His first thought was that it was his mum, but he realised the body was dressed in a blue coat with white pants and stockings, and beside it was a tricorn hat. He calmed himself and entered the room, but finding it empty of all but the cots and table, he focused on the body. "Another of Maynard's men," he said.

"Looks like it," Ritchie said from the doorway.

Ethan picked up a metal fire stoker and used it to pull the body away from the table. It resisted at first, stiff as a board.

"Strange it's still in rigour," Ethan said. "It's been almost three hundred years. It should be a skeleton."

"Maybe the cold air?" Ritchie suggested. "It's like a freezer in here."

Ethan hooked the stoker into the coat and pull the body away from the table. The body rolled over and landed on its back, and both Ethan and Ritchie let out a yelp of surprise.

"What the hell?" Ethan exclaimed. The body was shrunken,

about the same size as a child, but the head was the size of a baby with ash-coloured skin and wrinkled like a prune. Empty sockets stared back at them. The eyes long gone.

"What on God's green earth happened to him?" Ritchie asked. "He looks like he spent far too long in the bath."

Ethan pointed to the body. "Look at his arms and legs." The arms were bent like a praying mantis, and the legs were twisted at odd angles. "Is this a result of being left down here for centuries?" Ethan wondered. He turned around and left the room, Ritchie following him.

"I've seen some bodies before, lad, some older than that one, but none of them looked like that," Ritchie told him. Ethan went into the next cabin. It was laid out the same with four cots, but it was empty, as were the next two. In the fifth one, he found three more navy men shrunken to the size of children.

"Lad… this place is weird," Ritchie murmured, as Ethan left the cabin and went into the final one. He stopped at the door, shining his light on a familiar symbol etched into it. It was Maynard's, the same one as he saw at St Martin's Church.

"It's about to get weirder," he called out.

Ritchie appeared from behind him and looked at the five bodies that were sprawled on the ground. They were in the same condition as the others, with shrunken heads and shrivelled bodies, but these men were not wearing navy uniforms. They wore similar clothing: black jackets, white pantaloons, and red bandanas, and there were cutlasses laying near them.

"This was Maynard's quarters," he said.

Ritchie pointed to the bodies. "They were pirates."

"How did pirates get here?" Ethan wondered. "Did they follow Maynard? Did they come down the stairs?"

But then he shook his head, remembering the second door was still secured and dismissed it.

"There's a lot of mystery to this place, lad. Maynard living here, pirates, these shrunken bodies."

"There's no treasure either."

"Aye, that's true," he said, disappointment evident in his voice.

"If it was here, it was moved," Ethan said. "We know these pirates didn't get hold of it based on the last entry in Maynard's diary. He said he'd successfully hidden it."

"This cabin is giving me the creeps," Ritchie said. "I'll keep looking around." He left the cabin while Ethan remained to continue his search. This cabin was slightly larger than the others and only had a single cot rather than four. There was a simple wooden desk against the far wall and a chest sitting against the cot. He tried to open the chest, but it was locked. Leaving it for now, he moved to the desk to see if there were any keys. The tabletop was scattered with faded parchment, brittle and unreadable, and an upturned inkwell lay upturned near the edge.

Stacked to the side were some books. Ethan browsed through the titles, but they all seemed to be fiction—personal preference of Maynard, he guessed. He pulled open the only drawer in the desk. There were no keys. Instead, there was a leather-bound diary with Maynard's symbol imprinted on it.

Ethan opened it to find loose pages tucked neatly inside. Cautiously, he flipped through the pages. They were stiff and yellowed, but in good condition, having no exposure to the elements. He read page after page filled with Maynard's writing and realised they were the missing pages from the diary he found in the bunker. He turned to the last entry:

10 June 1726

Today is the day we leave. We have spent six years in this fortress, supplying and building up its defences, trying to make it a liveable situation for the men. I regret that we must abandon the plans to build the living quarters above, but the relentless assault from the pirates has forced my hand. I refuse to look at that evil, so I ordered the men to load the ship with the cursed treasure and prepare to sail.

The final straw was when that blackheart Philip Lyne's ship appeared in the cavern, taking us by surprise. His ship appeared from the darkness, and he fired on us before we could react, sinking one of my ships. We were lucky there were some men aboard the other ship to return fire and sink Lyne's ship just as he was landing. He still landed, though, and decimate my crew, but it could have been worse.

I don't know how Lyne found the way in, but if Spriggs and Low found us, then Lyne was never going to be far behind. Neither of those two pirates attacked from the water, but Lyne found the way. If he could, then others can.

The constant attacks from these pirates have left me ill at ease. We have spent too much time filling the waters with the bodies of pirates and my crew, who fell defending Blackbeard's treasure.

He said those things were his men, but they were no longer men — they were mindless creatures and we were forced to kill them.

But, if not for the curse of that treasure, then Lyne would have possession of it. Fortune favoured us when they opened that chest.

After that last attack, I ordered the men to pack the ship while I pondered my next destination. They realise what is at stake and, despite the company we keep and those we had to hang in the gibbets, I am sure I have their loyalty. They understand what is at risk if the treasure should fall into the wrong hands, and I have rewarded their families handsomely. They understand we must move the treasure to a more secure location and continue protecting it, keeping it out of the hands of anyone who might come looking for it.

I cannot bring myself to destroy it, but I have gone to great lengths to hide the existence of this treasure by creating diversions and laying a trail of false breadcrumbs. If I bury the treasure completely, the legend will live forever, but people will continue to look for it. But if I could plant fake clues in the right places, people could learn for themselves that it never existed and it will be forgotten by all but those who follow my path.

However, that did not fool everyone. Some focused on me and my disappearance and, thus, discovered this site. Now it is time to move.

And we must take his ship.

I know wHere we wiLl sAil tO nexT: a place that wILl Provide us saFEty and SHelTer.

-   rM.

"So, he *did find* Blackbeard's treasure," he breathed.

Whatever that treasure was, Maynard feared it. He was scared of it falling into the wrong hands, scared of looking at it himself. But why?

He thought about the two coins he found in the bunker, specifically "El Mal," the evil coin with the crossed out eyes. Is that why Maynard was scared? Because he believed the stamp meant the treasure was evil? Or was there something more to it?

Ritchie returned. "There's nothing else," he reported. "What's that there?"

Ethan turned the diary around. "The missing pages from Maynard's diary. Read this."

He waited while Ritchie read it.

"Blackbeard's bloody treasure," Ritchie breathed, his eyes going wide, and Ethan could see a greedy glint in them.

"It will wipe away your debt," Ethan said. A part of him was glad his initial promise to Ritchie seemed a possibility—it would keep the man focused.

Ritchie nodded. "And then some, lad. And then some." He paused and then said, "I always thought that treasure was a legend."

"That's what Maynard intended to happen. That treasure frightened him, but he still saw it upon himself to hide it from the world."

"What about the chest?" Ritchie asked, pointing to the one at the end of the cot.

"It's locked."

"Not a problem," Ritchie said, and pulled the sabre from his belt. He slid the tip of the blade into the seam as far in as he could and then, leaning all his weight on the handle, he pushed down on it. After giving it three hard pushes with all his weight, the lid splintered and opened a crack, but the sabre blade snapped.

Ritchie looked at the handle forlornly. "Well, there goes that," he said.

"It was for a good cause," Ethan said with a grin. "Help me with this."

Together, they ripped open the lid, revealing an empty chest. "Great, I broke a good sword for nothing," Ritchie complained.

"No, not nothing," Ethan said. He reached into the chest and pulled out...

"Two rods?" Ritchie said.

Ethan studied them. They were straight, as thick as the handle of a cricket bat, and made of wood stained a dark oak colour. One of them had a dozen notches in the shapes of squares and rectangles running all the way around it. They were imperfections in an otherwise perfectly straight and smooth piece of wood. The other had a carving of a man attached to one end. He was standing and wearing a featureless mask. He held his arms raised above his head, and he was holding a rough-cut yellow stone, about the size of a tennis ball, which seemed to glow in the light. Ethan stared at the stone, getting lost in the lines of the rough cuts and shades of yellow.

"Lad?"

Ethan blinked, pulling his gaze away from the stone, and noticed a hole in the top of one rod. Looking at the other, he noticed it narrowed, and he realised they joined together.

He slid the narrow end into the hollow and twisted it until it was secure.

"What is that?" Ritchie asked.

"I'm not sure. It's a sceptre of some kind. West African I think, but I'll need to study it in better light."

Ritchie handed it back to Ethan. "What is a West African sceptre doing here?"

Ethan shrugged. "Everything Maynard does leads to more

questions. But I think it's important."

"If not, it might be worth something," Ritchie added.

"I don't think there is anything else here," Ethan said. "Let's go. We can talk on the boat."

Ethan followed Ritchie out of the cabin and crossed the cavern back to the underground wharf as Ethan thought more about the sceptre.

"We should be able to take one of these boats out of here," Ritchie said, walking out on the jetty. He stopped suddenly, and Ethan almost ran into him.

"What is it?" he asked.

Ritchie hurried past the rowboats and stopped at the end of the jetty. He called back, "Look at this, lad."

Pointing his flashlight out to a far corner, it trailed up the dark water until it passed over the body of a ship. It was half in the water, from the rudder and stern to the mainsail, and looked as if it were easing itself into the ocean. The tattered remains of the Union Jack flag hung limply from the bowsprit while the ships' masts had all snapped and were lost to the depths. Ropes and sails were tangled and ripped, laying over parts of the ship like a poorly laid shroud.

"That must be Maynard's ship," Ethan said.

"Aye, lad. A fourth rate, I would guess. Probably fifty guns or thereabouts. But look behind it."

He pointed his flashlight through the gaps in the ship, where they spotted another one. This one was painted black, with black sails. It was also destroyed, listing on the port side and leaning against the fourth rate. The bowsprit had snapped and was hanging by fragments of splintered wood, but it was the Jolly Roger hanging off it that caught Ethan's attention. The flag depicted a front-facing man holding a cutlass in one hand and a pistol in the other.

"That's Philip Lyne's ship," Ethan said.

"He was mentioned in the diary, wasn't he? Famous pirate, then?"

"Notorious one who was associated with Edward Low and Francis Spriggs. Cruel men they were, and all three of them followed Maynard here at different times while Maynard was holed up here."

"A diary, a stick, and no treasure. I'm not sure if this is a win, lad."

Ethan shrugged, untwisting the sceptre and attaching both pieces to his pack. "It's better than nothing. Let's get out of here."

"Best idea you've had since I met you."

Twenty Five

They unhooked the sturdiest-looking rowboat and rowed into the darkness. Ritchie was on the oars, and Ethan provided minimal lighting with his flashlight. The tunnel was wide enough for three ships and high enough that the light didn't touch the roof, but it was tough going. The water was gentle, but the currents were against them, and with so little light, they bumped into unseen walls and shallow rocks. By the time they saw the first pinprick of daylight at the far end of the tunnel, Ritchie was wheezing.

They rested the boat in a shallow bend against the wall where the current couldn't push them back so Ritchie could catch his breath and rest his sore muscles. Ethan offered to row, but the big Irishman declined, telling him he was fine.

When he was ready, Ritchie announced, "Right, off we go," and he picked up the oars and began rowing. As they moved out, the light grew brighter and revealed more rocks in the water, which forced them to slalom through the tunnel. They could see the outline of the tunnel entrance when the water became choppy, the boat cresting the small waves. It was a struggle to manoeuvre the small boat over the waves and around the rocks, and soon they were soaked in icy-cold water. Ethan was pointing the way, but the power of the waves caused them to crash into rocks. The force of the impact made Ethan worried the boat would spring a leak.

"Hold steady, girl," Ritchie cooed after they knocked headlong into a pair of rocks rising out of the water. Ethan crawled to the bow and pushed the boat away, helping Ritchie row around them. They were less than one hundred metres from the entrance now. The wind was howling in the tunnel, sounding like evil spirits telling them to go back, and the waves were growing choppier, rocking them from side-to-side and threatening to capsize them. The boat crested the waves and came crashing down, spraying sea water all over them as Ritchie laboured, moving them forward. Here the rocks emerged from the water like jagged fingers ready to grab the boat and pull it down, but Ritchie was able to guide them through it, more or less unscathed, until they emerged out of the cave and into the fading afternoon light.

"Where are we, lad?" Ritchie shouted over the wind.

The sun was setting ahead of them. "West side of the island," Ethan called back.

Ritchie turned the boat and began rowing parallel to the coastline. With the tide coming in, the waves were higher and seemed to be trying to throw them against the island's rock walls. Ethan looked back to the cave entrance, but it was gone, the entrance blending into the seam of the cliff face like the entrance to Maynard's hideout above.

"I'm not surprised no one found a way in," Ethan called over the roar of the waves. "It's completely camouflaged, plus the rocks… you would need to be an expert navigator to get past that. Lyne was lucky."

"Aye lad, I was—WATCH OUT!"

Ethan grabbed hold of the sides just as an enormous wave picked up the boat and tossed it aside. Ethan was dumped into the freezing water, his muscles immediately seizing up and his breath freezing in his lungs. Water surged around his ears, and he braced his head with his arms as he was tossed around like clothes in a washing machine. Frantically kicking, his head broke the water, and he took in a deep lungful of air. He looked around for Ritchie, but he couldn't find him in the pulsing waves.

"Ritchie!" he called out. He looked around and saw the boat. It had been carried toward shore. Ethan swam to it, the power and momentum of the waves helping him. Within a minute, he had hold of it.

"Ritchie!" he called out again.

Nothing.

Ethan pushed himself away from the boat and headed to land, riding the momentum of the waves. He hoped Ritchie had made it there already. His feet touched the rocky ground, and he slipped and tripped his way out of the water and onto the rocky shore. Shivering, he walked along the shoreline north of where the *Jibboom* was anchored, calling out Ritchie's name. Something caught his eye floating in the water, riding the waves toward shore. It was too small to be Ritchie, and when he realised what it was, his hands instinctively shot to his chest to where his dry bag used to be. He waded into the water and grabbed his bag, grateful the sceptre pieces were still attached to it. He cursed himself for not noticing he'd lost his bag when he was tossed overboard.

Strapping it over his wet clothes, Ethan walked back to shore and continued along the coastline. He tried calling out Ritchie's name, but the howling wind was blowing his words away. He trudged forward with his head down against the wind and arms hugging his body, eyes searching the rocky shoreline for any sign of his companion.

What was that?

He raised his head, thinking he heard a sound on the wind.

There it is again.

He squinted and through the gloom and saw someone charging his way.

"… *an!*"

"Ritchie?"

The Irishman was scrambling over the rocky shore toward him, waving his hands.

"What?" he called out, but his words were lost in the wind.

Then he saw them.

Someone was chasing Ritchie, and it looked like he had a gun. Ritchie was warning him!

Ethan dove behind a large boulder and peered out. Ritchie ran past the boulder—whether or not he knew Ethan was behind it, he didn't know—but the gunman was close behind. The pursuer was wearing black fatigues, and if not for the watery backdrop and fading sunlight, he would be impossible to see. He passed the boulder, still in pursuit of Ritchie. Ethan grabbed a melon-sized rock and followed the man as quietly as he could, though the wind and the waves already provided him cover.

The man suddenly stopped about ten metres away, and Ethan tensed, waiting for him to turn around. Instead, he raised the gun and took aim at Ritchie's fleeing back.

Shit!

Ignoring stealth, Ethan moved as fast as he could and once he was close enough, he swung his weapon, but the man heard Ethan kicking rocks and ducked at the last moment. The rock skimmed his head. It was enough to divert his aim, though, and the gun fired harmlessly into the air. The man turned, blood from a cut trickling down the side of his head, and he raised the gun again, this time at Ethan. Ethan swung the rock once more, but the man ducked under it, giving Ethan just enough time and space to grab the gun. They wrestled. Ethan was taller and tried to use his height to his advantage, but the man was stronger and well-trained. The man forced the gun to the side and then, using the momentum and a well-placed leg, flipped Ethan onto his back. Ethan let go of the gun as he crashed into the rocky ground, the air exploding from his lungs.

The man wiped the blood from his eyes and pointed the gun at him.

Ethan instinctively raised his hands. "Whoa!" he said, as if that would persuade the man to not shoot him.

A roar suddenly sounded over the waves and wind. The man froze, and Ethan waited for the gunshot. But instead, the man swayed and fell face first to the ground, a hole in the middle of his back.

Ethan looked up to find Ritchie approaching, still holding the smoking flintlock.

"No idea how those bastards used these," he said, tossing it aside. "Slow to load and handles like a trolley."

"Who is he?" Ethan asked.

"No idea, lad, but I assume he was looking for you," he said. "Unless it's a coincidence that another group of gun-wielding maniacs just happened to land on this island when we did."

"Graves," Ethan spat. "How did he find us?"

"No idea, lad."

Ethan's eyes went wide. "Oh shit. The girls!"

Ritchie picked up the fallen handgun, a Heckler and Koch VP9, and handed it to Ethan. "Know how to shoot one of these?" he asked.

Ethan nodded. "Yeah, but..." he looked at the dead body and images of the men in Cape Town flashed before him. He swallowed, "...maybe you should have it."

Ritchie shook his head and showed him another handgun, a SIG P229. "I got his backup. Let's go."

Ritchie took the lead, and they followed the coastline south toward the bay. Night was falling as they scrambled up a sharp rise in the southwest corner, which gave them a view of the bay and beyond.

"Oh, that's not good."

There was a patrol boat anchored next to the *Jibboom,* a spotlight lighting up Ritchie's boat in blinding white light. Near the patrol boat were two smaller boats. They were slowing moving back and forth, shining their own lights along the cliffs and shoreline, while black Zodiacs were sitting on the rocky shore, just out of the surf. Along the shoreline, a dozen or more men dressed in the same black fatigues were patrolling the beachfront. They were holding machine guns with lights attached and were swinging them from side-to-side as they searched.

Ethan and Ritchie ducked back behind the rise. "What are we going to do?" Ethan said.

"We have to get to the boat, make sure the lasses are okay, and then get the hell out of here," Ritchie replied matter-of-factly. He had a serious expression on his face as he peeked back over the rise, searching the area for an idea. "All right, lad, I have a plan. First, we're going to steal a Zodiac and head straight for the patrol boat nearest the *Jibboom.*"

"Right."

"Then we climb aboard, take out anyone there, get to the *Jibboom,* and then get out of here before they notice."

Ethan looked at him. "Ritchie, that's a terrible plan."

Ritchie sat back and crossed his arms over his chest. "Well then, lad, you come up with something better."

Ethan peeked over the rise. The sun had fully set now, and he studied the moving lights. It was quiet except for the sounds of the waves crashing against the rocks and shore. "I suppose we can't swim to the boat?"

"Nay, lad, the tide will throw us back in."

Sighing, he said, "Fine. We'll do it your way, then."

Ritchie chuckled. "There's a good lad," he said. "First thing we do is take a couple of them out along the beach—the ones closest to the Zodiacs. The others should be far enough away that we can get on and get away before they notice us. The sound of the waves should cover the noise, and those things are designed to be quiet. Use rocks if needed to knock the men out, but *don't* hesitate. Got it?"

"Sure," Ethan said with a confidence he didn't feel.

"Right then. Off we go," Ritchie said. He crept around the rise and headed down the rocky decline to the shoreline, with Ethan following close behind. The nearest Zodiac was just under a hundred metres away, and two guards stood nearby, looking out at the patrol boats. They seemed relaxed, guns hanging by their sides, and were chatting and pointing to the *Jibboom*.

Ritchie tapped Ethan and handed him a fist-sized rock. "You get the one on the right. I'll take the one on the left."

"Got it," he whispered. He weighed the rock in his hand. It didn't feel heavy enough to knock out a toddler, let alone a fully grown man.

As he approached the man on the right from behind, his foot slipped off a rock, dislodging a couple of others. The clacking of the rock sounded like a gunshot to Ethan, even with the noise of the waves.

He wasn't sure why, but he froze. The two men turned around and froze as well, one of them letting out a grunt of surprise, and then they raised their guns.

Two shots cracked out over the sound of the waves, and both men fell before they could get a shot off. Ritchie appeared at Ethan's side. "Time for Plan B, lad."

"What's Plan B?" Ethan said as bullets started whistling past them.

"Shoot back!" Ritchie shouted, firing his gun at a group of men hurrying toward them.

Ethan raised his weapon and looked around, trying to find someone to shoot at. The buzzing of the bullets and the sound of waves and the million scenarios running through his head about how he was going to die overwhelmed him, causing him to fire randomly, not even sure if he was aiming in the right direction.

He fired until the gun clicked and then he tossed it. He crouched down, trying to make himself smaller.

"Here, lad!" Ritchie said, thrusting a machine gun into his hands. It was an SA80 assault rifle and felt surprisingly light.

"Either shoot the lights or shoot someone!" Ritchie called out, peppering a couple of approaching gunmen with bullets. They fell, the gun lights whirling around before falling to the ground as well.

A bullet shattered a rock near Ethan's foot, and he realised he was essentially invisible in the darkness while they were lit up like a Christmas tree because of their lights.

Holding the SA80, he fumbled with the safety until he thumbed it off. He took a deep breath and aimed down the scope.

There were three figures approaching. He aimed at the nearest one, about fifteen metres away, and pulled the trigger. The gun roared and the muzzle flash looked like fireworks in the darkness and the light on the gun he was aiming at fell. He turned, searching for another, and fired. This time he missed, but the gunman dove out of the way.

Ritchie tapped him on the shoulder. "Save your bullets, lad. Let's go."

The gunmen had all taken cover behind some large rocks. Taking advantage of the gap in battle, Ethan and Ritchie hurried along the shoreline, firing bursts of bullets at any light that appeared from cover.

They reached the closest Zodiac and Ethan pushed it into the water, while Ritchie fired on the remaining boats. With the other Zodiac's out of commission, Ritchie climbed in and started the motor, bullets whizzing by as the shouts of the men echoed behind them. Ethan climbed in, returning fire in the dark. The motor quietly hummed to life, and Ritchie grabbed the tiller and hit the throttle. The Zodiac lurched into the water, heading for the patrol boat near the *Jibboom*.

Ethan fired a final burst of bullets as Ritchie guided them over the waves, distancing themselves from the shoreline. They were jerked around as the boat skimmed the waves, catching the air and slamming down hard like they were on an out-of-control drop-tower ride. Ethan's stomach was somewhere back the way they'd came, and he turned away from the shoreline satisfied they were out of danger. He shimmied up to the front, watching the patrol boat ahead.

"Hold on, lad!" Ritchie shouted and jerked the Zodiac hard to the right just as one of the boats from the bay zoomed past, the waves almost forcing the Zodiac to capsize.

The second boat whizzed past, crossing their path, and Ethan shouted, "What are we going to do?"

The two boats were side launchers that were just under ten metres long and fast in the water. They had searchlights and were turning around the Zodiac, trying to corral them back to the shore.

Suddenly, everything turned bright, as if the sun suddenly appeared out of nowhere, and Ethan was momentarily blinded. He ducked below the gunwale and rubbed his eyes, spots dancing in his vision.

"Shoot the lights!" Ritchie screamed, jerking the Zodiac around a launcher.

Blinking away the spots, Ethan brought his gun up and found the source of the light: the patrol boat. Its spotlight was following them.

Squinting in the harsh light, he sighted it and fired his SA80, the muzzle flashing. Bullets slammed into the side of the patrol boat but missed the spotlight.

Cursing, Ethan took aim again and almost fell out of the Zodiac when Ritchie turned sharply to avoid a launcher speeding past them.

"Shit," he muttered, getting back to his feet.

He wiped sea spray out of his eyes and sighted once more, doing his best to stay level as they flew over the waves, and fired again. This time he hit true, and everything went dark.

"Good shot!" Ritchie shouted. "Now hold on."

Ethan grabbed hold of the rope attached to the gunwale and braced himself as Ritchie manoeuvred the Zodiac in and out of the launcher's wake. He passed by the first one as the second was bearing down on them from the side. Ritchie turned the tiller hard right, and the second launcher zoomed past them. They were now heading out to sea, away from the island and the *Jibboom*. One launcher was hot on their stern while the other was turning in a wide arc. Ritchie turned the Zodiac so it would cross paths with the turning launcher.

"What are you doing?" Ethan called out to him, but Ritchie either didn't hear him or ignored him.

The Zodiac zoomed in closer to the launcher, bouncing over the waves, and the other one was still chasing in their wake. Ethan tensed, wondering what the hell Ritchie was doing aside from trying to get them killed. Ritchie jerked the Zodiac right, barely passing along the launcher's port side.

"Brace yourself!" Ritchie yelled out. Behind the Zodiac, the launcher's horn blared in warning, but it was too late. The launcher rammed into the port side bow of the other, tearing through the hull and ripping the boat in half.

Ritchie laughed maniacally, and they watched as both launchers sank into the ocean, their twisted remains tangled together in a last embrace. They passed by the launchers, seeing half a dozen men jumping off the boats into an inflatable life raft, and headed for the patrol boat.

Ritchie brought the Zodiac to the stern of the patrol boat. "Quick, lad," he said, signalling to the ladder bolted to the port side of the boat. Ethan nodded and checked that he still had his dry pack and sceptre. Then, looping the strap of his gun over his head, he grabbed hold of the ladder. The out-of-sync rocking of the boat and the waves made it difficult, but he awkwardly pulled himself onto the ladder and climbed up. When he neared the top, he peered over, and seeing no one on deck, he looked down at Ritchie and said as quietly as he could, "It's clear."

He clambered over the side onto the deck, shrugging the SA80 around and watching for any signs of movement. Moments later, Ritchie was aboard and taking the lead, his own SA80 in front of him as Ethan trailed behind.

This patrol boat was much bigger than the launchers, roughly sixty metres long. Dim lights lit up the superstructure, which took up most of the main deck. As they moved ahead, Ethan saw a man appear from the starboard side with his gun drawn. Ethan pointed his SA80 and froze, his body seizing up as he saw his own life leaking out in the waters of Cape Town.

The man's eyes went wide when he saw Ethan. He cried out in shock and aimed his gun at Ethan.

Before he knew what he was doing, Ethan fired. The gun roared as a burst of bullets peppered the deck before one hit the man square in the chest and he fell.

Ahead of them, Ritchie took down another man, and they proceeded forward until reaching the door into the superstructure cabins. Ritchie turned to Ethan and said, "All right, lad, we need to get to the bridge on the upper deck. There should be some stairs at the back there. I'll go this way, and you go around back and up the stairs. If we can corner the remaining men in the bridge, we can disable this boat and get out of here."

Ethan nodded without any confidence. He'd just killed another man.

Subconsciously, he knew it was killed or be killed, but he now had more blood on his hands. Blood he could never wash off.

Would he be able to live with that? Was it something his parents had to do?

Worry about it later! He chided himself. *We need to save Andrea and Hannah and get away from here.*

He knew that the rest of Graves' men would be in the Zodiacs and on their way by now.

"Good lad," Ritchie said, patting him on the shoulder. "Let's go."

He pulled open the hatch door, and with his SA80 raised, went inside. Ethan moved further down the deck toward the stern, wondering what the hell he was doing.

How did I go from a couple of sessions at the shooting range to overtaking a patrol boat like I'm friggin Schwarzenegger?

He passed the boat's antenna array and found the stairs leading up to the bridge. He was halfway up when he heard the unmistakable sound of gunfire. Rushing up the stairs without thought of his safety, he hit the landing and found Ritchie standing over two lifeless bodies. Ritchie, having heard Ethan's footsteps on the stairs, had his rifle raised.

"Whoa!" Ethan said, his hands raised.

Sighing, Ritchie put the rifle down. "I'm gonna have to teach you a few things, laddy," he grumbled.

He pointed at the bridge door. "I don't know how many are in there, so be ready."

Ethan nodded and took a position to the side of the door. Ritchie nodded to him and pushed the door open, staying back. Gunshots fired out, pinging off a bulkhead behind them. When the shooting stopped, Ritchie rushed in, with Ethan right behind him.

"Drop it!" Ritchie commanded.

Inside was a heavyset man with a weathered face and greying brown hair. He looked to be in his forties and was dressed in the same black fatigues the others wore, though he had a captain's insignia attached to a sleeve. He dropped the handgun and put his hands up.

"You can lower your weapons, Mr. Richardson," he said calmly. "I am the only one here."

Ethan lowered his weapon, but Ritchie kept his raised.

"You have my word," the captain added.

Ritchie scanned the bridge and, seeing no one else, lowered his weapon. The bridge was spacious, with numerous terminals and seating for the operation of radar and communications.

"Lock the door," Ritchie told Ethan.

"How did you find us?" Ritchie asked the captain when Ethan returned.

The captain smiled. "Did you really think you could come back here without us knowing? This island has been under our surveillance since the last time." He turned to look at Ethan with cold blue eyes. "Though this time you brought the progeny."

Confused, Ethan furrowed his eyebrows. "Last time? What is he talking about?"

Ritchie said nothing, and the captain chuckled. "You haven't told him?"

"Told me what?"

Ritchie grabbed the captain by the arm. "Doesn't matter. We need to lock him up," he said, leading him away from the console and to the exit. "Then we can get out of here."

"He brought us here just after he brought your parents," the captain called out.

"What?" Ethan asked. "What do you mean?"

Ritchie stopped, his shoulders slumping. "We'll discuss it later. Once we are off this bastard island."

Suddenly, the captain shook loose from Ritchie's grip. Before either of them could react, he pulled a long, silver, cylinder-shaped object from his pocket and held it out in front of him.

"Now let me tell you the situation, Mr. Richardson. Your boat is wired with explosives. The boy will tell me everything you found on the island. You will give me everything you have on Maynard's treasure, otherwise," he indicated a button on the top of the cylinder, "I will sink your boat, and its two occupants, to the bottom of the Atlantic."

Ethan started to shrug off his pack when Ritchie said, "No, lad."

"But the girls! We can't endanger them."

"I'd listen to the boy, Mr. Richardson."

"I said no," Ritchie growled.

The captain turned to Ethan with a knowing smile that wrinkled the corners of his eyes, "Give me everything you've found and I will tell you what your friend here hasn't," he bargained.

"They're not on the *Jibboom*," Ritchie said, his gun pointed at the captain.

The captain's smile widened as he set his gaze on the big Irishman. "How can you be so sure?"

"He's right, Ritchie," Ethan said. "We can't take the chance on this."

"They said the boy was smart."

"He's delaying us, lad. He's waiting for backup from the island." He looked at the captain and said, "I could shoot you before you press the button."

The captain smiled wolfishly. "But could you ensure a clean death? And besides," he pressed the button but kept his thumb on it, "it's a dead man's switch. Are you willing to take the risk, Mr. Richardson?"

"Aye. I am," he said.

"Ritchie!" Ethan demanded. "What about the girls? The boat!"

Ritchie smiled grimly. "We already have a boat."

"But—"

"Just trust me, lad."

"Have it your way," the boat captain shrugged. He held the detonator up, but before he could lift his thumb, Ethan shouted, "Wait!"

He shrugged off his pack and slid the sceptre pieces out. "Here," he said, and tossed it to the captain, who caught one piece and his eyes followed the other as it landed and rolled along the floor.

"There's a good bo—"

The echo from a single shot rang throughout the bridge, and the captain slumped to the floor, a hole in the middle of his forehead. Ethan's breath got caught in his throat as he watched the detonator roll out of the captain's lifeless hands and across the floor. The silence was deafening and seemed to hang in the air for ages. Just when Ethan thought the captain had been bluffing, an explosion rocked the boat.

Ethan's eyes went wide, and he ran out of the bridge. He took the stairs two at a time and charged around the superstructure to the bow of the boat, where the blazing fireball of the *Jibboom* lit up the night.

"Holy Jesus," he breathed, his breath misting in front of him. The force of the explosion was still rocking the boat as Ritchie approached from behind. Ethan turned to face him.

"What have you done?" he snarled.

Ritchie put a hand on his shoulder. "They'll be fine," he said.

Ethan shoved his hand away. "You better be damn right," he said. "Otherwise, their blood is on your hands."

"Trust me, lad," Ritchie said with a level of calm that infuriated Ethan even more.

Resisting the urge to punch him, Ethan said, "You better tell me what the hell is going on here."

"Once we put some k's in between us and this island," Ritchie said. Then he walked past Ethan and returned to the bridge. After one last glance at the sinking *Jibboom*, Ethan followed him. He watched as the Irishman picked up the lifeless body of the captain and took it outside to dump into the ocean.

Twenty Six

Hours later, they were heading back to Cape Town. Ritchie had the boat set on autopilot, and it was cruising over the gentle waves when he joined Ethan in the mess. The mess was steel and sterile, functional with no personalisation, unlike that of the *Jibboom*, which was probably at the bottom of the ocean by now.

He was exhausted and felt like he could sleep for days, but the entire day kept playing back in his mind. With all that happened, including killing more men, he felt numb. Then there was what the captain said about Ritchie's involvement. What did he mean when he said Ritchie had brought them here after his parents? His mind whirred with thoughts faster than he could grasp them.

Despite Ritchie's insistence they were alive, he worried about Andrea and Hannah. Even if they were alive, it was his fault they were in this situation, his fault they'd been captured because he got them involved.

I should have made them stay in Cape Town.

A pang of guilt rose within, and he wondered what was going on with him.

Two days ago, I was a relatively normal kid. Now I'm killing people, watching people die, and seeing boats blow up, but I don't feel a thing. What am I turning into?

"You hungry, lad?" Ritchie appeared from another room.

Ethan shook his head.

"Well, you need to eat. I'll fix you something."

He went into the galley, and Ethan watched him through the viewer as he opened cupboards and banged pots and pans until he found something to cook. While he was busy cooking, Ethan asked, "How can you be so calm?"

"What do you mean?" Ritchie replied, looking up from the burners.

"They could be dead." They'd had this conversation numerous times, and Ritchie always replied with a calm, "They're not."

"You need to explain everything that is going on, Ritchie," Ethan said. "I need to know what happened to Mum and Dad. I need to know who these people are and why the hell you're so confident that they didn't kill Andrea and Hannah."

He remained silent while he cooked, the smells and steam wafting into the mess, and Ethan stared at him, waiting for him to say something.

Finally, he finished cooking and came out of the galley with two plates of pasta. "It's not much, but you need to eat," he said, putting one plate in front of him.

"Are you not concerned for your first mate?" he asked.

Ritchie didn't reply, instead he forked some pasta in his mouth and chewed.

"Forget this!" Ethan said, frustration reaching a boiling point. He got up to leave when Ritchie put out a hand to stop him.

"I am concerned for Hannah," he said quietly, "more than you could ever know."

"Then why aren't you doing anything about it?" Ethan asked. "Why are you acting like everything is normal when it's anything but?"

He was quiet for a long time, and Ethan was about to leave when he sighed. "He was right."

Ethan looked at him. "Who? The captain?"

Ritchie looked up at him sorrowfully, but there was something else there—maybe guilt?

"What's going on, Ritchie?"

"I—uh—I wasn't entirely honest with you, lad." He nodded at Ethan's dry bag. "Maynard's compass, I have seen it before… ten years ago… when your parents showed it to me."

Ethan blinked. "What?"

"They came to me right after visiting St. Martin's Church."

"How did—" Ethan began, but Ritchie held up his hand. He stirred more of the pasta around his plate.

"I told you I knew your parents, that I did jobs for them. You

288

saw in the photos that I went along on the hunts with them. It wasn't one or two, but quite a few. I was in the game as much as they were—and still am, to a degree—which is why I am eighty grand in the hole. Anyway, we met through a mutual acquaintance… Felix Graves."

Ethan's eyes widened.

Ritchie saw his face and nodded. "Aye, lad. I told you I knew him. But he also knew your parents, in fact we worked together. He was on the expeditions, and some of those photos you saw, well… he was the one who took them."

Ethan thought back to the torn photo of his parents and Ritchie in Jordan, the arm around his dad. "He was in that photo at the Umayyad Mosque, wasn't he?"

Ritchie nodded. "Aye."

"What happened?"

"He got too big for his britches. I mean, he was always a prickly little asshole, but in the beginning, he was actually useful. He had access to places we couldn't get to by normal methods, and he knew people who would pay a premium for what we found. Not long after that Jordan discovery, he branched off on his own. We came across him in Pakistan one day, on the hunt for some treasure or another. We beat him to it, of course, and he was not happy about it. It was his first chance to prove himself to his buyers, and he got desperate, got involved with the wrong people. We met him after we made the discovery. He begged us to help him out, otherwise they were going to kill him. Eventually your parents agreed, but that little shyte pulled a gun on us and acted like he made the discovery. He threatened us, warned us to keep away from him."

"Why?"

"He's a cold-hearted, greedy bastard, that's why." He laughed. "Your da was so mad I was sure he was going to hunt him down. Anyway, that day was pretty much the end of our little foursome. Your parents and I drifted apart after that."

Ethan couldn't believe it—his parents and Graves working together. He couldn't imagine them with a person like that.

"Then what happened ten years ago?"

Ritchie nodded. "Ten years ago, your da got in contact with me, telling me they were on to something big and needed my help. I hadn't heard from them for a few years, and I was looking after Han at the time, but rumours said they were out of the game. They knew about my situation with Han and understood I wanted to keep quiet for a bit. They respected my wishes with no issues, so I knew when they contacted me, it was serious.

"We met in Cape Town, and they told me they had come from St. Martin's Church. They said they'd made a huge discovered. That some bloke named Maynard hid something valuable somewhere in the Inaccessible Island and they offered me money to take them there. I figured it was easy money. They didn't need me to do anything but take them there and wait for them to come back. So we set sail, and they showed me everything—the compass, the coins, the diary—just like old times. We arrived, and I settled the boat in the bay like we did, and they swam ashore just like we did. They followed the same trail we did. And that was the last time I saw them."

Ethan was shocked. His world was tilting as he tried to

process what Ritchie was telling him. "What do you mean? What happened to them?"

Ritchie threw his hands into the air. "I wish I knew, lad. I waited until I was out of supplies and then some more. I even went ashore, but I had no idea where they went. I thought they were dead."

Ethan frowned. "This doesn't make any sense. They were last seen in Norfolk—Dad's body washed up in Norfolk."

"I know, lad," Ritchie said, shaking his head. "And that's the thing. Not long after I got back, I learned they died there. And a week after that, I got a package in the mail. It was everything they brought with them: the compass, the coins, the diary, and ten thousand dollars. And there was a letter from your ma. She gave me instructions on how to get into Maynard's bunker and told me to return everything and forget any of it ever happened."

"Did... did it say anything else?" Ethan felt his body trembling, like he was about to collapse.

"Aye, lad. It said that if you ever came looking for it—and they knew you would—not to tell you anything about it. Not what they were doing, not about their disappearance. Nothing. They wanted to keep you as far away from this as possible."

"Why?"

Ritchie shrugged. "No idea, lad. I don't even know how they got off the island or why they didn't contact me. I honestly thought I had lost the plot, thinking they never came, and I dreamed it all... But I couldn't explain the package. Everything was crazy... crazier than usual, anyway. I did what the letter asked me and, for some reason, I expected to hear from them despite their reported deaths. A few weeks later, Graves showed up in Cape Town. He asked me about your ma and da and what they were doing. I told him I had no idea what he was talking about and that I hadn't seen or spoken to them for years. He didn't buy it. To keep it short, I had debts, and he offered to pay them off in exchange for the information. I told him to piss off, but then he threatened Hannah. I had to take him."

He looked at Ethan with pleading eyes, as if seeking forgiveness. But Ethan couldn't focus. It was all getting to be too much.

Ritchie continued, "I took Graves to the Inaccessible Island, where his men kept me under guard. We spent a few days there. Graves came back to the boat angry and tried to get more out of me. I was grateful to your ma and da then and there for not telling me more or taking me ashore, because I had no more information to give him and, eventually, he gave up. We went home, and that's the last time I ever heard from him, your parents, Maynard, all of it—until you showed up."

Ethan felt like his head was going to explode. With everything that was happening, it was too much for him to process. He wanted to go into a quiet room and just think. But he asked, "Then why did you help me?"

"You know me debts, lad. Even with transporting artefacts once in a while, I have no way of paying them off," he said, eyes downcast. "I figured it was ten years ago. You're an adult now and you found Maynard's bunker on you own. You obviously knew what you were doing. Besides, I'd brought two people here, and no one had found anything, so I thought…," he paused. "I could take the money, you'd find nothing here, and we'd be going our separate ways."

Ethan knew he should be pissed at Ritchie, but he couldn't feel anything. His mind was focusing on the facts, and what he said all made sense. It explained why the compass and the diary were in the bunker. But if Ritchie was telling the truth, how did they get back to England from the island? Why wasn't there any record of them entering South Africa or leaving and returning to England? There surely would have been a record of their comings and goings. But then again, they were involved in the black market, so of course they could get their hands on fake passports. His mind whirled at Ritchie's revelations, but one point stuck out to him more than any other.

Going through all that, they must have known they were in danger—that's why they went back to England. Why did they send Ritchie to take everything back, and why did they tell him to keep me away from it? Why didn't they warn me?

The thought left him feeling empty, and sadness overcame him. He knew the answer, he just didn't want to admit it.

"Lad, you all right?"

Trying his best to hide the tears that were forming in the corner of his eyes, he nodded and said, "I… I just feel like this is the first time I truly believe they're dead. I know Dad is, but I held hope Mum was still alive, but now… gone without a trace?" He paused. "Then again, what did I know about them? I didn't even know they were criminals."

Tears rolled down his cheeks, and he felt ashamed to be crying in front of this man—a man he should be angry at for doing what was asked of him—but it wasn't his fault. It was his parents, and all his anger was directed at them for lying to him his whole life.

"Lad, I can't act like I knew what they were thinking, but what they did, they did with your best interests in mind. Whatever they were working on, they decided it was more than just treasure."

Ethan sniffed, wiping tears from his cheek. "What do you mean?"

"I've been in this game a long time. While hunters don't advertise what they are looking for, this is beyond normal. What Maynard did—hiding the treasure, calling it cursed. There must be something else to it. Maybe—"

Whatever he was about to say was cut off by an alert over the sound system.

"What's that?"

Ritchie got up from his seat. "A communication has come in," he said and hurried out of the mess. Ethan got up and followed him to the main deck, up the stairs, and into the bridge, where Ritchie sat at a terminal and hit a button. On the wall, a large television screen flickered to life, and the grim features of Felix Graves appeared. He looked down at them with that same unnerving calmness he had in Camden Town. His dark eyes were void of any emotion.

"Mr. Jackson," his voice carried clearly over the bridge's sound system. "Once again you have beaten me to the punch, and once again I find myself asking you to hand over what you've discovered about Maynard's treasure."

"What makes you think I discovered anything?" Ethan snarled.

Graves smirked. "Don't play me for a fool, Mr. Jackson. It didn't work last time. We followed you to the island, and you disappeared, even from satellite imagery. I know you found something that led you to Blackbeard's treasure, and I want you to hand it over to me."

"Piss off!" spat Ritchie. "You're not getting anything, Graves."

"Mr. Richardson, eloquent as ever," he said, turning his head slightly to acknowledge him.

"You blew up our boat and killed Andrea and Hannah. Why should we tell you anything when we can just go to the police?" Ethan said.

Graves seemed to find this threat amusing. "The police? The police wouldn't believe a word you'd tell them—remember, you're the son of two discredited thieves. On the slight chance you found some up-and-coming officer looking for his big break and he believed you, you don't have any evidence. And if they did happen to stumble across some evidence tying us to anything, we would simply kill them and hide the bodies just as well as Maynard hid the treasure."

The way Graves casually mentioned murdering someone sent chills up Ethan's spine. He found himself at a loss for words.

"But, if you must insist on being a morally righteous pain in my ass, then maybe this will persuade you."

The screen cut away from Graves to another room. This one was dark, with steel walls and dim lighting that made Ethan think it was an engine room or hold in a ship. In the middle of the room were two men dressed in the same black fatigues as the men on the beach. They each held handguns pointed at two people in front of them who were on their knees with their hands behind their backs, staring into the camera.

"Andrea!" Ethan exclaimed.

"Hannah," Ritchie said at the same time.

Andrea seemed calm. Her hair was down and messy and there was a minor cut on her cheek that was already yellow with bruising, but otherwise, she seemed unharmed. She was looking at the floor, head turned away from the camera. She was a stark contrast to Hannah, whose face was pale and tear-streaked. Her blonde hair hung in wet, ragged clumps around her face. Her body was rigid, and her green eyes were wide open, bright and terrified as they stared into the camera. Ethan felt his heart leap at the sight of her and anger welled up inside of him.

Both were gagged.

"That's right," Graves' voice came out from the speakers. "It would be silly not to use all the bargaining tools at my disposal. Now, I will ask again. Tell me where Maynard took the treasure or I will kill them right here, right now."

"We ain't telling you anything," Ritchie growled.

Ethan was stunned by the events unfurling before his eyes. His mouth tried to work, to get out words that would make everything better, but it seemed clamped shut.

"Have it your way," Graves said. "Kill the blonde."

The man behind Hannah cocked the hammer on his gun and held it against her head. Hannah's eyes seemed to open even wider and a single tear trickled down her cheek.

It was all Ethan needed to break out of his shock. "Wait!" he shouted.

The screen flickered back to Graves. "Yes, Mr. Jackson?"

"I don't know where Maynard went after the Inaccessible Island."

"Ethan, no," Ritchie growled under his breath as Ethan pulled out Maynard's missing pages and opened it to the last page. He turned it around and showed it to the screen, not even aware if Graves could see them or not.

"But he left a clue."

Graves squinted at the page for a minute and then looked at Ethan. "You believe it will lead to the next location?"

Ethan nodded. "I'll need an hour to decipher it."

"You have fifteen minutes, Mr. Jackson, and not a second sooner."

"But—" Ethan began, but the screen went blank and they were alone in the bridge, the humming of equipment and the engines the only sound in the room.

"Shit," Ritchie muttered. He followed Ethan to a desk with a laptop on it.

Ethan took a seat and put Maynard's diary down in front of him.

"Can you decipher it, lad?"

"I need a piece of paper," Ethan said, grabbing a pen.

Ritchie handed him a page from a printer, and Ethan set to work.

"I think it's a Bacon Cypher," he said. "Sir Francis Bacon

invented it in the early seventeenth century to encode messages."
He pointed to the last lines in Maynard's diary:

I know wHere we wiLl sAil tO nexT: a place that wILl Provide us saFEty and SHelTer.

"See how this line is written strangely? It's completely different from the rest of his writings. Each capital letter represents one specific letter, and the lowercase represents another. In this case, lowercase letters are 'r' and upper is 'M'."

"How do you know that?"

Ethan pointed to the bottom of the entry. "He signed off with 'rM'. I think it's the cypher key."

He turned to a laptop and pressed a key on the keyboard. The screen lit up, and he opened a browser, searching for "Bacon Cypher key."

"So, we have to replace the capital letters in Maynard's sentence with an M and the lower cases with a R. Then we need to remove the spaces and split it at every five letters. Each set of five will represent a different letter."

Ritchie looked at him like he was speaking a different language. "You lost me, lad."

"Just watch," he said and started converting the letters. When he finished, he turned the page around. "First, I converted each letter in that sentence to an M or an R, like this:"

Mrrrr rMrrr rrrrM rrMrr rMrrr Mrrrr rrrrr rrMMr Mrrrr rrrrr
rMMrr rrrMM rrMrr

"Now, I need to remove the spaces and split them into groups of five." He quickly converted the letters and showed Ritchie the piece of paper:

mrrrr rmrrr rrrrm rrmrr rmrrr mrrrr rrrrr rrmmr mrrrr rrrrr

rmmrr rrrmm rrmrr

"Still looks foreign to me."

Ethan turned to the computer screen. As he compared the blocks of letters to the cypher, he said, "Each block of five represents a letter of the alphabet, and if I am right, it will tell us where… we… are… going… next." He drew out the words as he converted the cypher.

He turned the page again and showed Ritchie:

mrrrr rmrrr rrrrm rrmrr rmrrr mrrrr rrrrr rrmmr mrrrr rrrrr rmmrr

rrrmm rrmrr

R i b e i r a g r a n d e

Ribeira Grande

"Ribeira Grande?"

"Now known as Cidade Velha. It's in Cabo Verde."

"Okay, good work, lad. But *where* in Ribeira Grande?"

Ethan was busy typing on a computer, verifying a thought he had. He'd never been to Cabo Verde, but he knew about its history. In 1456, Portuguese sailors discovered a cluster of ten volcanic islands west of Senegal, naming it Cabo Verde. Ribeira Grande was settled six years later on Santiago Island. It was later home to Jews exiled from Portugal during the Spanish Inquisition and then slaves from West Africa. Population and interest declined after slavery was abolished, and the only economic benefit was as a place for ships to resupply. Ribeira Grande's name was changed to Cidade Velha in the late eighteenth century.

"Ribeira Grande was the capital city when Maynard sailed there," Ethan said, reading off the screen. "It frequently came under attack from pirates, including Sir Francis Drake, and the only defence they had was a fort on the south side of the island: Forte Real de São Filipe. The fort was built in the late sixteenth century. If I were Maynard, that's where I would go. It would have provided him with protection from any pursuing pirates."

"Aye," Ritchie said, leaning over his shoulder at a photo of the fort. "Looks pretty secure. Do you think that is where the treasure is?"

Ethan shook his head. "I doubt it. Compare it to his bunker and the hideout in the Inaccessible Island. He wrote about hiding it for forever, and the fort is too exposed. If he hid it there, it would have been discovered by now, I'm sure. No, I think it's just another breadcrumb."

Ritchie sighed. "What do we tell Graves?"

"I don't know," Ethan admitted as he stood up from the desk and began pacing the bridge. "We have the information, but he has the girls. We can't let him kill them, and he knows that. So we just have to do what he wants and hope he'll give them back."

Ritchie grumbled, but said nothing.

The call from Graves came five minutes later, and his stern, sallow face filled the monitor screen. "Time's up, Mr. Jackson."

"First, I want to know if they're okay," Ethan said, his voice steadier than he felt.

Graves smiled coldly. "You're in no position to make demands."

"And without me, you'll spend another ten years *not* finding the treasure."

Graves was silent, and Ethan felt his palms slicken with sweat. It was a calculated risk, one that Ritchie insisted on. The idea was to give him as little as possible so they could withhold any information for later... if it came to that. Ethan disagreed with the decision, but what the hell did he know?

Finally, the screen flashed to the same scene as before: Hannah and Andrea on their knees, staring at the ground with two guards behind them. But this time, the guards' handguns were holstered.

Graves' voice came out of the speakers. "There. They are safe—for now. Now tell me what you found."

"Velha City," Ethan told him.

"Where?"

"It's in Cabo Verde."

"I know where it is," Graves said shortly. "*Where* in Velha did Maynard go?"

"He didn't say."

"Harris, you may shoot the girl."

The man named Harris was standing behind Hannah, and Ethan watched as he pulled his gun out of its holster. Ethan saw her stiffen with fear, her eyes wide as she looked pleadingly into the camera once again.

"Wait!" Ethan said, louder than he intended. His grip on the situation was tenuous at best, and he knew it could crumble in an instant.

The screen flicked back to Graves. "Yes?"

"Maynard didn't write where he was going, but I think I know where he went."

"Where?"

Before Ethan could reply, Ritchie cut in and said, "He'll tell you where once you release the girls."

"Then it looks like we are at a stalemate."

Fearing he might order the men to shoot, Ethan cried out, "Wait! What if we compromise?"

Graves raised an eyebrow. "I'm listening."

"What are you doing, lad?" Ritchie whispered, but Ethan ignored him.

"Winging it," Ethan whispered back, then turned his attention to Graves. "We meet in two locations on the island. You let the girls go, somewhere Ritchie can get them, and I'll meet you at Maynard's next location."

Graves considered the proposal. After a minute, he said, "I will meet you in Velha City—"

"Alone."

"Alone. And my men will take Miss Gatting and Miss—I don't believe I've had the pleasure of knowing this young lady's name—to another location of my choosing."

"Good—" Ethan began, but he was cut off.

"But," Graves continued as if Ethan hadn't spoken, "they will be released on my orders *after* we have accomplished our goal."

"Don't do it, lad," Ritchie said. "It's a bum deal."

Ethan didn't see that he had any other choice. "Fine," he said to Graves. "Where will Ritchie meet your men?" he added.

Graves looked somewhere off screen and then said, "My men

will take your companions to Juncalinho, on the island of São Nicolau, in six days' time. Mr. Richardson will get the details of where exactly when I meet you."

Looking at a map on the computer screen, São Nicolau was a good distance north of Santiago. It wasn't ideal to be so far away from each other, but it was their only choice.

"I'll be at the Sé Cathedral ruins," Ethan told him.

"I will see you in six days, Mr. Jackson," Graves said, and cut the connection.

Silence filled the room, and Ethan let out a breath that he felt he was holding for the entire conversation with Graves.

"What the hell was that?" Ritchie boomed. "You're going to see him on your own?"

"I have to."

"You know he isn't going to release the girls to us. He's probably going to kill you once you discover the next location."

Ethan nodded. "Probably, but this isn't our only play here."

"What else?" Ritchie asked.

"I'll tell you once I can get confirmation. Can this boat get us to Cabo Verde?"

"As long as we have enough fuel reserves," Ritchie confirmed.

"Okay, good. You drop me off at Velha while you head to Juncalinho. Once we get confirmation of where they are, I'll take Graves into the fort. I'll delay him as long as I can while you try to work out a way to free the girls."

Ritchie held up his hands. "Since when are you giving the orders?" he asked with a lopsided smile.

"If you have a better idea, I am all for it."

"Oh no, lad. It's about as good as this shitty situation will get."

Ethan couldn't help but chuckle. "Can you check on the fuel and see if we can get to Cabo Verde? I have a phone call to make."

"Aye aye, captain," Ritchie said, giving him a fake salute.

Twenty Seven

Cidade Velha, Santiago Island, Cabo Verde

The afternoon was hot and dry, the air still, and the sky an azure blue with the sun bearing down on the islands of Cabo Verde. Ritchie dropped Ethan in Cidade Velha, armed with his pack and the sceptre and, despite Ritchie's protests, no gun. Ethan argued that Graves would have him searched anyway, so there was no point. Ritchie grumbled and piloted the boat away while onlookers watched on in amazement at seeing the sixty-metre-long patrol boat. He confirmed his arrival about an hour after departing, with no sign of Graves' men—or the girls.

Now it was a matter of waiting. Ethan sat alone in the shade of the ruins of the Sé Cathedral, a long, double-transept, renaissance church made of stone. Construction started in 1556 and, though it started being used in 1640, it was officially completed in 1705. It stood for seven years before French privateer Jacques Cassard pillaged it in 1712, destroying it. Today, only the stone walls, entrances, windows, and pilasters remained of the once-grand church.

The ruins overlooked the southern coast of Santiago. The blue water sparkled in the sunlight, and with no one around, Ethan was watching the fishing boats sail along the coast enjoying a moment of peace.

His phone buzzed: *I'm here.* It was Ritchie.

Still waiting on Graves. Once you get the location, get them out. Don't wait for me.

Roger that was the reply, and Ethan put his phone away.

"Lovely day, isn't it?" Ethan jumped as Felix Graves emerged from behind one of the stone inner walls of Sé Cathedral.

Ethan got up, picked up his pack, and took an involuntary step back. Even in this heat, Felix Graves wore a black suit, his skin almost ghostly in contrast, but he looked comfortable. He eyed the sceptre attached to Ethan's pack but said nothing.

"Graves," Ethan intoned. "How's Grassi doing?"

"Stand still, Mr. Jackson," Graves said, ignoring the question. "I need to search you for weapons."

Ethan sighed and stood up. "Bit hot for the suit, isn't it?" he asked Graves while he was patting him down. Graves ignored him as he checked his pack, so he continued, "Are the girls on Juncalinho?"

"I have kept my end of the agreement, Mr. Jackson," Graves

said.

"I need proof."

Graves sighed and pulled a phone out of his pocket, dialled a number, and said, "Put them on the phone."

Graves pressed some buttons and showed Ethan his phone, where a live video showed Andrea and Hannah sitting on chairs in front of a dusty building. Two men stood beside them, wearing suits like their boss, but there was the unmistakable bulge of guns under them. The sign above them said *Bar Juncalinho.*

Andrea looked calm, if not haggard, and Hannah looked pale but seemed to be over the shock of what was happening. Her eyes were darting all over the place as if trying to find a way to escape.

"Andrea!" Ethan called out, but Graves turned his phone away and said, "I'll be in contact," to whomever was on the other end and then put it back in his pocket.

"What's the address?" Ethan asked.

"Not until we find where Maynard went," Graves said. "I have upheld my end of the bargain until now. Now, it is your turn. Where are we going?"

Ethan let out a breath, unwilling to take this man any further, but he knew he had no choice until Ritchie freed Andrea and Hannah. He looked at a cobblestone road that ran north between the cathedral ruins and a bright yellow stone wall. "That way," he said.

Graves raised an eyebrow and followed the road with his eyes as it ran uphill, and in the distance, he could see the stone wall of the Forte Real de São Filipe. While Graves was distracted, Ethan quickly pulled out his phone and sent Ritchie a message:

Bar Juncalinho.

Graves turned back to him just as he put the phone away. "The fort?" he asked.

Ethan nodded. "It's the logical choice. It existed when Maynard was looking for a safe spot once his hideout at the Inaccessible Island was compromised. And it provided defence against any pirates giving chase."

"It was compromised?" Graves asked, clearly surprised. "How?"

"Come on," he said and began the steep walk up the cobblestone road toward the fort. He told Graves what happened on the island, finding the hideout, the missing pages, the attacks, and the bodies.

"There were bodies?"

"Yes."

"Skeletons or bodies?"

"Uhh… both," Ethan said, unsure where this was going.

"Describe them to me," Graves demanded.

Ethan did, telling him how their bodies were shrunken and contorted, their skin wrinkled like prunes. Questions Ethan couldn't answer, and by the time he finished recounting what happened, they were almost to the top. The cobblestone road had made way for a dusty gravel one that lead into the fort's parking lot.

"If this leads us to the treasure, then your friends will have nothing to worry about," Graves said.

"Is it true that you worked with my parents?" Ethan asked as they crested the rise.

"Yes," he said simply.

"And you left them? To branch out on your own?"

"Yes."

"Were you friends?"

Graves hesitated only for a moment, but long enough for Ethan to catch it. "Yes."

"Then tell me what happened to them," he pleaded. It was the question he'd wanted to ask since they'd met in Camden Town.

"What happened to who?" he replied coyly.

"You know who, asshole."

Graves stopped and faced Ethan. "Let me be clear, Mr. Jackson. I do not need to answer your questions. You do not get to know me. I am here for one thing and one thing only. If I get what I want, then I might tell you what I know. But until then, I would keep my mouth shut if I were you. My patience can only go so far."

Ethan fumed as they entered the parking lot. With the day almost over and the fort closing soon, the lot was empty of all but two cars.

"By the way, I will want *my* diary and those pages, Mr. Jackson."

"I left it on the island," Ethan lied. In actual fact, Ritchie had it. One more bargaining tool they had if needed.

Graves lashed out, grabbing Ethan on the shoulder so quickly he didn't have time to react. The man squeezed his shoulder so hard it felt like his bones were breaking, and it was all he could do to not cry out. "I do not have time for your nonsense nor your lies. I know you have it, and the reason I know is simply because you are not stupid enough to leave it there. Once we are done here, you will get me the diary, or I will kill both the girls and that Irish drunk you have watching over them."

Shit.

Ethan tried to shrug free from his vice-like grip, but Graves showed incredible strength considering his size.

"Do you understand me, Mr. Jackson?" Graves whispered.

He grunted his affirmation, and after one final squeeze, Graves let go.

"It means a lot to me that you don't think I'm stupid," Ethan said, rubbing his shoulder and following Graves across the parking lot toward the fort.

Overlooking Cidade Velha, Forte Real de São Filipe was a structure of no definable shape. It was two stories high and made of stone and sharp corners. The ocean-facing walls were lined with crenellations for cannons and had lookouts on the corners to spy approaching ships.

Ethan followed Graves to the ticket booth, where a young lady greeted them. She informed them, in heavily accented English, the fort would be closing soon and they consider returning tomorrow for a better experience.

"That won't be necessary, Miss," Graves told her, handing over some Cabo Verde escudo to her.

She handed him a ticket and looked at Ethan expectantly. Ethan looked at Graves and snorted. "I'm not paying."

Graves turned to the attendant with a smile. "And one for the child as well," he said drily.

The attendant handed him another ticket, and they passed

through the stone archway into the open courtyard. The courtyard was dusty, its ground made of dirt and stone, with some areas chained off. They crossed the courtyard and head up a set of stone-laid stairs, where they were greeted with a vista of Cidade Velha and the sparkling ocean beyond. Graves turned to Ethan. "Okay, Mr. Jackson, here we are. What are we looking for?"

Ethan shrugged. "I don't know. There are no official records of Maynard ever being here. That means that anything he did here, he did it privately. He probably paid off the officials. But he has left clues everywhere else, so I guess we just need to look for something that's out of place."

"Something out of place? That's the best you can do?"

"I've done more in a week than you have in a decade," Ethan shot back. "Yes, Ritchie told me everything," he added when Graves raised an eyebrow.

Graves said nothing, just stared coldly at Ethan, who continued, "It's not as if they would advertise it with a big sign saying 'Hey, Robert Maynard was here!' So, yeah, find something 'out of place'."

Before Graves could answer, Ethan spun around and walked the length of the crenellations, running his hand over the dormant cannons still standing guard over the city. He thought about Graves' threats. He knew Ritchie was watching over the girls, which probably meant he had someone watching Ritchie as well.

Ritchie would expect this, so he wasn't too worried about him. The best thing he could do was to give Graves what he wanted, but he didn't have the slightest idea of what to look for. For all he knew, Maynard never came here. Maybe he went somewhere else.

Continuing around the fort, Ethan came to another set of stairs that led down into the main building. He took them, and just as he passed the doorway, he stopped and stepped back.

Chiselled in the stone next to the doorway was a pattern of dots. For the average person who didn't know anything about stars, it looked like an irregularity in the stone, but Ethan had seen this pattern before. It was the six-star constellation of Auriga.

Did Maynard do this?

"What is it?" Felix Graves appeared at the top of the stairs, his body cast in the shadow, making him look like a grim spectre.

"I think I found something," Ethan told him.

Graves descended the stairs and stood next to him, looking at the constellation.

"This is the first constellation Maynard used to follow the route from England to the Inaccessible Island," he explained. "It can't be a coincidence that it is now etched into the stone here."

"You think Maynard did it?"

Ethan nodded. "It would be a ridiculous coincidence otherwise."

He went inside, with Graves following closely. They found themselves in a large room with tables and chairs set about, and glass cases with artefacts. Paintings and maps hung from the walls, and in the middle of the room was a scale model of the fort. This room was empty of everyone but themselves, and Ethan pointed to the right side and said, "Look for anything that might look like a constellation on that side. I'll take this side."

They split up. Ethan scanned the wall and stone floor looking for signs, and after a couple of minutes, Graves called him over. He'd found the constellation of Leo etched on stone next to the third door with a 'Do Not Enter' sign written in half a dozen languages attached to it. Looking around to see if they were still alone, Graves pushed the door open, and they entered a dark hallway. Ethan pulled a flashlight from his pack and turned it on. The walls were bare and various footprints disturbed the otherwise dust-blanketed floor. There were doors set into either wall, some open and leading into other rooms or halls.

They found Ursa Major next to a door with a sign that said 'Strictly No Entry' in multiple languages.

Ethan tried the handle, but it was, unsurprisingly, locked. He rattled the handle and pushed the door, but it didn't budge.

"Well, it's locked. Guess we'll have to go home," he said.

"Move aside," Graves said.

Ethan moved away from the door, and Graves positioned himself in front of it. With a snap of his leg, he kicked the door and splintered the lock.

"After you."

"Jesus," Ethan muttered, pushing the door open. They were on the landing of a set of wide stone stairs leading down into darkness. The air was cool and stale. Judging by the dust on the floor, Ethan figured no one had been here for years. He probed the bare walls with his light before heading downstairs. Graves, with his own flashlight, followed behind, and as they descended, he wondered why this part of the fort was closed off.

They reached the bottom, which opened into a large square chamber with multiple doors on all three walls. Each door had a constellation etched into the stone next to it, and it took Ethan a couple of minutes to find the next one in the sequence of Maynard's route: Aquila.

"Are you sure this is the right way?" Graves replied.

"He did say to follow his path," Ethan said, opening the door. They were in a tunnel dug into the earth, the ground sloping slightly down as Ethan led the way. The tunnel meandered left and right multiple times before they saw the exit ahead of them.

Ethan took a step and felt the ground sink. He looked down and caught a glimpse of metal in the dirt floor. Suddenly, the ground shook and there was a rumbling sound echoing through the tunnel and dirt rained down on them. They looked at each other before both shouting, "Run!"

Graves, who was deceptively quick, took the lead, but Ethan was hot on his heels as the tunnel caved in on them. Clumps of dirt and stone fell around them, battering them on their shoulders, and nipping at their heels like puppies. Graves made it to the door first, passing through without looking back, while Ethan dove through just as the tunnel collapsed.

"Shit," Ethan said, panting heavily. "He installed a damn pressure plate."

He coughed, breathing in dust and dirt, and he tried to settle his racing heart.

"Are you all right?" Graves asked, hands on his knees, trying to catch his breath.

"Yeah," Ethan coughed. He stood up, dusting himself off. "Thanks for your concern," he said drily.

"I wouldn't want your friends to die for nothing," Graves

replied coldly. "How will we get out of here?"

Ethan shook his head. "No idea."

"Let's keep going then," Graves said and before he turned around, he added. "And do be careful where you stand."

Ethan scowled at him while the dark-suited man explored the chamber. It was another square chamber with even more doors than the previous one. Some doors had rotted away or collapsed because of a cave-in behind it, but each one still had a constellation carved into it.

"Well, that explains why they never found anything down here," Ethan said. "This place is a maze. Without knowing the order of the constellations Maynard used, there is little chance people found what he hid down here."

"So it seems," Graves agreed. "What is the next constellation?"

"Aquarius," Ethan told him. "Just look for anything with twelve stars," he added when Graves stared at him blankly.

They split up, Ethan taking the right side and Graves the left. Thinking about their situation, Ethan realised they were both at a stalemate. Graves wouldn't be able to proceed any further or find his way out without Ethan's knowledge of the constellations Maynard used, and Ethan couldn't do anything to stop him with Andrea's and Hannah's lives at risk. He didn't know if Graves had orders for his men based on whether he came back at a certain time, but it was best to assume that he did, and without phone reception, Ethan wouldn't know if Ritchie rescued them. He didn't trust Graves to keep his word, so his only hope was to give Ritchie as much time as possible to rescue the girls and be ready for when Graves makes his own move.

"Here's one," Graves' steady voice called out in the gloom somewhere on the other side of the chamber. Just as he was about to follow Graves, Ethan noticed one door had a picture of a ship on it, which differed from every other door he'd seen so far. He made a mental note of it and walked to where Graves waited near the corner of the chamber.

Graves pointed above a door, and Ethan shone his flashlight, revealing the Aquarius constellation.

"That's it," Ethan confirmed.

Graves opened the door. "After you," he said again.

"So courteous," Ethan said sarcastically, and walked through. The passage sloped down, taking them deeper under the fort, and Ethan wondered just how far below it they were. They must be close to being level with the city.

They avoided another pressure plate, and the passage opened up into yet another chamber with even more doors. More of them had collapsed or been destroyed and Ethan worried their way would be blocked for good. While he searched for the fourteen-star Centaurus constellation, Ethan idly wondered what was behind the other doors.

Booby traps? Passages to nowhere? Bottomless pits? A dragon?

He chuckled.

"Something funny, Mr. Jackson?"

His musings stopped when he found the constellation. As his light played over the etching, he felt an almost all-consuming temptation to go through and leave Graves behind.

Let him wander this maze forever.

But before he could act on the urge, Graves was next to him. "Is this it?"

Ethan nodded. "This should be the last one… I think," he said, and pushed open the door into a smaller, square chamber. Opposite them was a single wooden door banded in iron. The floor and walls were made of stone except for a slab of timber just before the door. Ethan tested the timber, thinking it was an obvious trapdoor, but it held his weight. He grabbed the door handle and tried to open it, but it was locked.

"I thought you said this was the last one," Graves growled.

"Maynard didn't intend to make this a walk in the park. He was frightened of this treasure and wanted to hide it forever," Ethan shot back. He noticed some torches in brackets and said, "Light those." When Graves didn't move, he added, "Please."

Graves did what he was asked without a word, and soon they were bathed in the warm glow of firelight. It was still gloomy but better than the pitch black they'd been in for the last hour.

"What are these?" Graves asked. He was looking at two shrouded figures standing on either side of the door. Ethan approached the one on the right and ran his fingers over it. It was dusty but soft and smooth and made of silk.

"It's a shroud," he said. He grabbed it and pulled it away. A dust cloud billowed into the air and he coughed, waving the dust away. When the dust cleared, he saw that before him was a twelve-foot-tall statue standing on a metre-high pentagon base. The statue was of a man wearing a coat and a bicorne hat. He held a sword in one hand and had a stern face that gazed out into the antechamber.

Ethan ran a hand over its leg, feeling the slightly sandy texture.

Limestone.

On the floor around the base were arced scratches with deep grooves. "Interesting," he murmured.

"There's one here as well," Graves said, pulling the shroud off to uncover a second statue standing on a similar base. This one was of a different man in a long, open coat, revealing four holsters. In one hand was a cutlass and in the other was a flintlock, but what dominated the statue was the thick beard hanging down to his chest. He was looking to his left, at the other statue.

Graves ran a hand over the statue. "Who is it?"

"Are you kidding me? That's Blackbeard," Ethan said.

"And the other?" Graves asked, ignoring Ethan's chiding.

"Robert Maynard."

Graves raised an eyebrow. "This is all very nice, but how does it get us in?"

"I'm working on it," Ethan said. He ran his flashlight up the statue of Blackbeard, the light giving him a better look. He stopped at his midsection. There was a faint line running along the midriff of the pirate, just below his long beard.

"Does that look like a seam to you?" he asked Graves.

Graves pointed his light at it. "It does." His light moved up the statue. "There's another one there, at the neck."

Ethan followed Graves' light to where it was shining on a bare spot on Blackbeard's neck. Ethan moved to the statue of Maynard. "There are more on this statue," he said. "Elbow, shoulder, and head."

"What's this?" Graves asked as he was crouching by the base of the Maynard statue, examining a small hole midway up. He was shining his torch on it, trying to get a look inside while Ethan went back to the Blackbeard statue.

He crouched before the base and examined it. He expected to find markings on the stone floor or another hole, but he found a pentagon-shaped relief, with timber edging carved into it.

"Hey," he said to Graves, who was still studying the hole. "Check this out."

Graves came over while Ethan grabbed the compass from his pack. "What is it?"

"I think it's the way in," Ethan said. He showed him the compass and then slotted it into the relief. It fit perfectly.

"Now what?"

"Watch," Ethan said, and he turned the compass like a dial. Above him, the statue of Blackbeard moved. As he turned the compass, the Blackbeard statue bended at the waist, while his head turned to face down, looking at the ground. He looked as if he were bowing in reverence to the statue of Maynard.

"Incredible," Ethan breathed. "They must have worked on the mechanism and built the statue around it. This... I can't even begin to describe how significant this is."

"The door is still closed."

Ethan frowned. "But this has to be it."

"You are wasting time, Mr. Jackson."

"No. There's no reason for this to be down here. No one creates something like this and leaves it hidden forever. It must be the way in."

He walked to the Maynard statue and looked it over. It was made of the same limestone and had seams, so it must have moving parts, too, but there was no spot for a compass.

He shone his light on the hole. It was circular, but there were notches cut into it, like it was made for the teeth of a key.

For a rounded key…

"The hole—it's a keyhole."

"What's the key?"

Grabbing his pack again, Ethan untied the sceptre pieces and studied the square and rectangular notches along the lower shaft. "It's this," he said.

"What is that?"

"A sceptre we found in Maynard's bunker," he explained, connecting the two ends, and twisting it together to form the full piece.

"And you think that will open it?" Graves asked, scepticism clear in his voice.

Ignoring him, Ethan pushed the end of the sceptre into the hole in the statue's base, rotating it until the notches aligned with the gaps in the hole, and pushed it in. The sceptre slid in until it met resistance halfway up the shaft.

"Nothing is happening," Graves said impatiently.

Pointing to the ground around the base, Ethan said, "Don't they look like tracks to you?"

Graves squinted at the markings. "I suppose so," he admitted.

"Then watch this," Ethan told him. He grabbed the sceptre's shaft and pushed it like a capstan. It resisted for a moment, and

Ethan had the fleeting fear that he was wrong, but then it gave a little. The sound of stone grating on stone filled the antechamber as he pushed and the base rotated, dust falling on him. As the base turned, the statue of Maynard moved. The head turned to face the bowing Blackbeard while his sword arm raised into the air until the base reached the end of its tracks.

Now the statue of Maynard stood facing Blackbeard with his sword held up high. Between them was the door.

"Well?" Graves asked.

Ethan pulled the sceptre out of the lock, and Maynard's sword swung down. Graves jumped back as the sword swung through Blackbeard's head and the head fell off, crash-landing on the wooden plate, and the door swung open.

Graves moved toward the door while Ethan examined the head, marvelling at the engineering. He examined the square timber section of the floor. "It's a pressure plate," he said. "It unlocks the door when Blackbeard's head falls on it. Morbid."

He looked at Blackbeard's head. A chain was attached to it and connected it to Blackbeard's body.

"There must be a winch in the torso to wind it up and reset it. Absolutely fascinating."

"Indeed," said Graves, who sounded bored. "Get a move on."

Ethan sighed. "I bet Mum and Dad got tired of your shit very quickly," he said, grabbing the compass and the sceptre.

Twenty Eight

Ethan poked his head through the door, seeing that the new room was larger but similarly designed to the antechamber. It had stone walls and floor, and thick timber beams running across the roof as support. Seeing no danger or risk of a cave in, Ethan entered the room with Graves following behind. His light traced a path toward the middle of the room, where he found a brazier. Sitting at the base of it was a pool of liquid, which Graves knelt beside and sniffed. "It's oil."

"Light it."

Graves tossed Ethan the lighter. "You light it."

"Don't trust me?"

"Not particularly."

"I'm hurt," Ethan said. Next to the brazier was a pile of rags. Ethan picked one up and dipped the tip into the oil. Then he flicked on the lighter and held it to the rag. The rag flared up in red hot flames, and Ethan dropped it into the brazier.

Fire roared as the oil caught and lit up the immediate area. Shadows danced among four stone pillars, and Graves came over with a torch, putting the tip in the fire to light it. Ethan watched him walk to a corner of the room and put it to a smaller brazier, and it flared to life. He walked to the other corners of the room until he lit all of them and then lit torches that were sitting on the four pillars.

The lighting was bright enough that Ethan turned off his flashlight. The room was covered in rugs, and against one wall was a cot and against another was a desk. On the furthest wall was a giant map of the world carved into the stone. Africa was positioned on the left and the Americas on the right. It was meticulously detailed, with the oceans recessed deeper into the stone and the mountains raised at different heights. There were rivers, lakes, and forests carefully stencilled into it.

"This is incredible," Ethan said, running his fingers over the map. "The amount of detail in this is simply astounding."

"Yes, it is all very fascinating," Graves said, boredom lacing his words. "Let's get on with it."

Ethan sighed. "You have no appreciation for history, do you?"

"I have an appreciation for what history can bring me," Graves replied, moving off to search a set of bookshelves near the desk. Ethan followed him, checking them as well. "That's what your parents and I disagreed on."

Ethan raised his eyebrows. "How so?" he prodded.

Graves turned to him, holding a book in his hand. "They were hypocrites. They were nothing but treasure hunters. Yet they wanted to lecture me on the value of history when they would raid tombs and desecrate sacred sites for their cut. I just wanted a bigger cut."

"Is that all this is about?" he asked. "Blackbeard's treasure?"

"Something like that," Graves muttered.

"So that's how my parents are connected to this," Ethan said. "You were both looking for it."

"We weren't both looking for the treasure, Mr. Jackson." Graves said, replacing a book he pulled out that wasn't helpful. "They were working *for* me."

What! Ethan felt like he'd been punched in the guts. *They were working for this slimeball!*

"No… they wouldn't. Ritchie told me you left them to chase your own opportunities."

Graves put away another book. "Oh, but they did, Ethan. They didn't know it at the time, but they stole Maynard's diary from my client, who put in the winning bid. They thought they got away with it, but I worked out that it was them and… forced them to work for me."

"Forced them how?"

Graves gave him a wicked smile. "I threatened the one thing that mattered to them over everything else."

Ethan swallowed. "Which was?"

"This isn't a coffee date, Jackson. Find where Maynard went, or else."

The urge to strangle him growing, Ethan walked off, taking deep breaths to calm down, and reminded himself that he was not the only one at risk here. He walked to the desk on the other side of the room and sat on the rickety wooden chair. The desk was bare except for a strange contraption sitting on it. It was a wide square box with a circle of glass in the middle that was set at a forty-five-degree angle. Ethan picked it up, discovering that it was heavy and solid, with no moveable parts.

"What is this?" Graves' voice came from the middle of the room. Ethan turned around to find him looking at a chain hanging from the roof.

"Pull it and find out," he joked, and to his shock, Graves did.

"No! Wait!" but it was too late. Graves pulled the chain, and in the centre of the room, above the brazier, a small trap door opened up. Dust and dirt fell into the room, smothering the fire, and the room dimmed. Ethan thought the entire roof was going to cave in on them, and he was halfway to the exit when the dirt stopped falling.

From somewhere in the cloud of dust and dirt, Graves coughed and called out, "Jackson?"

Ethan paused. Could he take a chance here? Leave Graves here or try to take him out?

"Jackson?"

No, you don't know if the girls are safe.

"Jackson? I'm warning you."

"I'm here," Ethan said, turning on his flashlight.

Graves emerged from the cloud of dust, his face stained, and his formerly immaculate suit rumpled and covered in dirt.

"That was… pleasant," he said evenly. "What is the point of such a thing?"

Ethan shrugged. "So they can bury suit-wearing dickheads under a pile of dirt?" he suggested.

"Amusing," Graves said with the tone of someone who thought it was anything but. Ethan didn't care because the dust had settled, and piercing through the gloom was a pinprick of light.

Graves noticed it, too. "Where is that coming from?" he asked.

Ethan walked to the light. It was pale and faded and seemed to be getting dimmer. He waved his hand through it. "It's sunlight," he said.

"Sunlight? All the way down here?"

"It must be a shaft or tunnel. All the dirt that fell was just built up over the years." He examined it closer. "It looks man made."

Graves peered up at it. "How do you know?"

Ethan shone his flashlight around the hole in the roof. "It's almost perfectly round and smooth."

"That could be from water," Graves said. "I imagine water would run in here if dirt did."

Ethan shrugged. "Could be, but why have a trap door? Why not just patch it up? Unless…" He noticed the brazier had a shelf attached to it. He turned to the desk where the contraption was sitting. He picked it up and returned to the brazier.

"Here, grab this end," he told Graves, passing over one side of the contraption. "We need to place on this shelf so the light hits the reflector in the middle."

They manoeuvred the contraption over the brazier and placed it down. It didn't seem right, so they adjusted it slightly until the beam of light hit the reflector at a forty-five-degree angle and cast a single point on the map on the wall. They left the contraption and approached the map. They tried to find the point of light in the ebbs and flows of the map, but the fire light was too bright, and the faint sunlight disappeared before it hit the map.

"Put out the fires," Ethan instructed.

"Why?"

"So we can see the map."

"Fine." Then he grabbed Ethan by the forearm and squeezed. "Remember, Mr. Jackson. No funny business. Their lives depend on it."

"Yeah, yeah," Ethan grimaced, yanking his arm free.

They split up and extinguished the torches on the pillars by butting them out on the ground and then tossed handfuls of dirt into the corner braziers. Cast in total darkness, they returned to the map and could now see the beam of sunlight on it. It was pointing right in the middle of the Pacific Ocean, with no islands or any discernible landmarks to be seen.

"He dumped the treasure in the middle of the ocean?" Graves asked.

Ethan shook his head. "No, I don't think so. He wrote about how he should have dumped it, but never did."

"Then I suggest you find out where he *did* hide it," Graves said, pulling a Beretta handgun from his shoulder holster. He turned off the safety and pointed it at Ethan's head. "You have five minutes."

Ethan gulped, admonishing himself for letting his guard down around this man. The excitement of the find, the information about his parents… it side-tracked him, and he suspected Graves deliberately did it.

"You won't find this without me," he said, his voice cracking as he spoke.

"Then I'll find someone else," Graves said. "Four minutes."

Shit!

"You haven't gotten a sniff of it in ten years. You need me."

"You're wasting time, Mr. Jackson."

Ethan desperately looked around with his flashlight, trying to find what he'd missed. He was certain that the contraption was in the right spot. It was designed to redirect the sunlight onto the map, and he was also certain the treasure wasn't at the bottom of the ocean.

There must be something missing.

He shone his light around, passing over the pillars, the beams, the desk, and the bookshelves, but he found nothing out of the ordinary.

"Three minutes," Graves said monotonously, his gun following Ethan as he walked around, searching for something. Ethan's light was probing the floor when it stopped on a hole in the tiling.

Wait a minute…

He knelt beside it, brushed away some dirt, and ran a finger around the hole. It was smooth, definitely not a crack or irregularity in the stone. It was directly below the beam of light, which was fading to almost nothing now and it looked like a hole for a post... *Or sceptre.*

"Two minutes," Graves announced.

Ethan flipped his backpack around and unclipped the sceptre. Graves' gun followed him as he stood up and down.

"Can you stop following me with that thing?" Ethan snapped.

"One minute," he intoned.

"Asshole," Ethan muttered. He lined up the sceptre and slotted the base into the circular hole in the floor. He expected resistance, but it slid in until it hit the bottom.

"Twenty seconds."

Ethan rotated the sceptre until it clicked in, and the yellow stone lined up with the fading beam of light.

"Ten... nine... eight..."

The light from the sun focused through the back of the stone, passed through, and emitted multiple pinpoints of yellow light on the map. Ethan hurried over and saw that the points of light formed a route from Cabo Verde, or *Insulae Capitis Viridis* as it was stencilled, to...

"Seven... six... five..."

"Here!" he said, pointing to somewhere in West Africa.

Graves stopped counting and walked over, his gun still on Ethan. "Where is it?" he asked.

Ethan traced the route with his finger. "This map is old. The borders were different back then. It looks like he went from here toward the west coast of Africa. He headed down and around eighteenth-century Guinea. Then he followed a river from the

329

eastern border of Guinea, heading northward to…" his finger traced the route through Guinea and stopped at a lake, "here. This lake in… Negroland. Geez, they weren't even trying back then, were they?"

Graves, unconcerned about Maynard's racism, asked, "What lake is this?"

Ethan pulled his phone from his pocket and took a photo of the lake just as the beam of light faded away. He turned on his flashlight and moved back until he was next to the sceptre and took a series of pictures, trying to get the entire map so he could cross-reference it. Satisfied that he had enough to work with, Ethan was about to pocket his phone when Graves pointed his gun at him. "Where is the lake, Mr. Jackson?"

Ethan held up his phone. "I need to cross-reference it with a map."

Graves moved closer, putting the gun to Ethan's temple. "Tell me where it is!" he snarled, his face sinister in the shadows of the torchlight.

"I don't know!" Ethan shouted, his voice echoing around the chamber.

"Give me your phone," he demanded.

"You won't find it without me," Ethan said, trying to stall as he handed him the phone.

"I'll manage," he said, cocking the hammer on the gun.

Before Ethan knew what he was doing, he flashed the light into Graves' eyes and ducked. Graves reflectively turned his head, blinded by the light, and fired. The gunshot boomed around the room and Ethan grabbed the sceptre, yanked it out of its holder, and swung it around, catching Graves on the gun-holding arm. The blow caused him to cry out in pain, and he dropped the gun. Ethan swung the sceptre back, trying to catch Graves in the temple, but he ducked just in time, tumbling out of the way. Ethan bent down and picked up the gun just as Graves lunged for it.

Ethan awkwardly held the gun, sceptre, and flashlight, and backed away.

"Just stay there," he commanded, his light swaying all over the place. Graves complied, his hands in the air.

"Give me the gun," he growled.

"Put my phone over there," he said, pointing a table nearby and ignoring his command.

Graves complied, and Ethan told him to back away.

"You won't ever escape from me, Jackson," Graves said, his voice menacingly low, and he backed away until he was in the corner. "There is no where on this planet where you can run from me."

Ethan ignored him, grabbed his phone, and pocketed it. He stumbled backwards, almost tripping over the brazier in the middle of the room, and bumped into a pillar, but he reached the exit. "Don't move," he warned.

Graves stared back at him in the dim light, his eyes glowing with rage.

Ethan pulled the door open and moved into the antechamber, closing the door behind him. Immediately, there was the sound of metal cranking and grinding as the head of Blackbeard lifted into the air, being pulled back on his body. When the head was back in its rightful place, both statues moved back to their original positions and the door locked. As quick as he could, he clipped the sceptre to his pack and slipped his pack back on.

Then he took off, trying to create as much space between himself and Felix Graves as he could.

Twenty Nine

With Graves' gun in one hand and his flashlight in the other, Ethan hurried back down the hall into the Centaurus chamber. He entered the Aquarius door and sprinted down the tunnel, careful not to trigger any pressure plates. Once he arrived, he looked for the etching of the ship that he saw before.

He couldn't believe Maynard would only have one way in and out of here. It would be too dangerous considering the risk of a cave in, or if one of the pirates had found him like they had at the Inaccessible Island. No, he would have to have another way out, and Ethan had a hunch it was the ship that would lead the way. He found it and opened the door with his light directed ahead, revealing another tunnel, and he hurried down it, closing the door behind him. He felt the ground gradually rise as he continued forward, moving as quickly as he could. Soon, he entered another chamber. This one was just a hollowed-out section of the underground with no supports, and Ethan was surprised it was still standing. On the opposite side were three tunnels, but they had no doors, signs, or evidence that they had any supports either.

"Shit!" he growled. He examined each exit, looking for any hint of which might be the right one, but they all looked the same. With time running out, he took the right path. With the unknown head of him, and his flashlight his only safety measure, he forced himself into a slow jog.

Despite the air being cool and damp, Ethan was sweating as he made his way forward. The path twisted and turned, but it was gradually heading up, and he considered it as good a sign as any, given the current situation. Hearing nothing behind him and certain he was safe for the moment, he slowed his pace even more to conserve energy. It surprised him at how calm he felt wandering these underground tunnels, where even the slightest misstep could be deadly.

His mind turned back to everything that had happened. How finding a journal in a locked drawer led him all over the world, trying to find out what had happened to his parents.

Killing people.

They were trying to kill you.

You could have incapacitated them, instead.

It was self-defence.

They're not innocent people.

Them or you.

The words warred in his head, and the pit in his stomach deepened. He turned his mind to other things in an attempt to forget about it. He thought about what he knew so far, piecing it together from what Ritchie and Graves had told him.

His parents, Ritchie, and Felix Graves all worked together before but had a falling out, and Graves struck out on his own. Later, his parents took an interest in Maynard on a hunch and stole the diary from the people Graves was working for. Graves figured out they stole it and threatened Mum and Dad to help him recover what Maynard had hidden. They went to England and used the Norfolk dig as a cover so they could head to St. Martin's Church and then on to Cape Town, where Ritchie took them to the Inaccessible Island. Presumably, they had escaped Graves' notice at this point. Somehow, they disappeared from their and reappeared in England without Ritchie knowing. They dove at the Norfolk site for some unknown reason, possibly to keep up appearances, and then disappeared. Dad's body washed up later and Mum's was never found.

Meanwhile, Graves must have found out they slipped away to the Inaccessible Island and went to Ritchie. He paid Ritchie to take him to the Inaccessible Island, which he did, but Graves found nothing. Ritchie received mail from Ethan's mum telling him to return Maynard's things and to never let her son get involved, and the trail goes cold.

Until I found the journal.

And what was Maynard scared of?

"Why did he think it was cursed?" he wondered aloud. That

was the thing that had him most confused. Maynard clearly believed it was cursed, and he believed it so much that he went to almost insane lengths to hide it. Twice.

He took a left turn where the ground levelled out, and ahead of him something glinted in the light of his torch. Hurrying ahead, he came to a set of rusted metal gates. On the other side was a concrete and brick tunnel with a channel of water running down the centre.

Ethan gagged as the smells hit him like a smack to the face. "Great. A sewer," he grumbled.

He pushed on the gates and they opened slightly before resisting, squealing on hinges that hadn't been used in decades. It was then that he noticed the thick chain and padlock circled around the two gates.

"Why can't just one thing be unlocked?" he asked, shaking the gates harder.

The gates were rusted, but still strong. He moved the light to the hinges. The gate was mounted to a rotted timber frame that looked hastily built, and Ethan guessed this tunnel had been explored, then closed off because of the potential dangers. He kicked at the side of the gate, trying to break the hinges. The metal rattled like gunshots in the silence, and after the third kick, the wood cracked.

With a final kick, the gate broke away from the frame and dangled listlessly, only held up by the lock and chain. Ethan crossed into the sewer. The rancid smell seemed to intensify, but Ethan didn't care. He was out of the underground and, at this stage, away from Graves.

He followed the sewer on the elevated path, dim light filtering through cracks in the ceiling. He dodged piles of waste and squeaking rats until he stopped at a metal ladder bolted into the wall. Seeing no better option, he put the gun in his waistband and grabbed the first rung, but he immediately pulled his hand away.

The rung was slimy and Ethan retched at the thought of what was growing on it, but he forced himself to grab it, and he climbed as quickly as he could until…

Crack!

"Ow!"

His head bumped against a solid wood trapdoor.

He pushed against it and the door rattled but wouldn't open.

He tried again, this time wedging his back against the trapdoor. It was awkward, but he pushed against the rung with his legs and tried to force it open with his back, but it remained firmly in place.

Ethan let out a snarl of rage and thumped the heavy door with the side of his fist.

"Ola?"

Ethan was so startled at hearing a voice that he almost fell off the ladder. He pointed his flashlight around, but saw no one. "Hello?" he called out.

He waited.

Just as he was wondering if he'd imagined it, he heard it again.

"Ola?"

The voice was muffled, and Ethan realised it was coming

from the other side of the trapdoor.

"Hey!" he shouted, banging on the heavy wood. "Open up!"

He heard some fumbling and then the trapdoor slowly lifted up a crack, and Ethan peered into the dim light at the wrinkled face of an elderly man.

"Hey," Ethan said casually, pushing the door up on its hinge with the man's help and climbing out. The man looked to be in his seventies, with wispy white hair and vivid blue eyes. He wore slacks and a button-up top, and he carried a lantern. Ethan helped him lower the trapdoor, and then he flipped the latch over a U-bolt, bolted into the floor and pointed to the padlock in the man's hand. "You might want to lock that," he told him, and then headed up a set of rickety old stairs.

The man let out a burst of Portuguese that Ethan didn't understand. He left the confused man behind and took the stairs. At the top, he entered a small room with a stone arch to his right, which took him to a narrow, rectangular nave with wooden pews on either side. It was empty, and Ethan crossed the nave in fifteen steps and exited the small church.

Outside, the sun was below the horizon, and Ethan found himself in a small stone courtyard with tall trees surrounding it. He crossed the courtyard and left through an opening in the surrounding stone wall, disappearing into the trees. He was in a valley. On either side of him, the earth rose sharply, and he caught sight of Forte Real de São Filipe on top of the crest to his left. He moved as quickly as he could in the darkness, his feet crunching the leaves underfoot, until he came to a road. There was a sign on the side of the road, pointing back the way he came, that said

"Convento de Sao Francisco."

Ethan pulled out his phone and found he had multiple missed calls and texts from Ritchie. Most of the texts were variations of 'Call me now!' but the first was more in-depth:

Couldn't get the girls. It was a trap. Managed to escape. Following them now. Call me.

He called Ritchie, who picked up on the second ring. "Ethan? Where the hell have you been, lad?"

He could barely hear him with the sound of wind blowing into the phone's microphone. "Long story. Where are you?"

"I'm in Praia, tailing the girls."

"They brought them here?" Ethan asked.

"Aye, lad. Probably to give that ratbag a quick escape."

Ethan nodded. "All right, I'll head there now. I'll call when I arrive. We'll get the girls and get the hell out of here."

"Good lad," Ritchie said, hanging up the phone.

Pocketing his phone, Ethan hurried down the road where the lights of Cidade Velha twinkled in the dusk. There were very few cars out, but he passed a dozen or so people by the time he reached R. Calhau, the main road in Cidade Velha. He was near the Sé Cathedral when he rounded a corner and immediately ducked back. Glancing back around, he saw two black sedans parked in the middle of the road out the front of the cathedral. There were three men in black suits waiting around it, while another was on the phone.

"Shit," he muttered.

The man on the phone hung up and spoke to the others. Two of them nodded and hurried towards the ruins of the cathedral, while the other two headed towards Ethan, their jackets flapping in the breeze, showing off their holsters and guns.

"Not exactly subtle," he muttered. A fifth black-suited man got out of the driver's side of one sedan and Ethan recognised the mountain of a man.

Grassi.

Ethan felt some satisfaction watching the man limp around the sedan to open the rear door.

"What is he doi… Oh, you have got to be kidding me!" Ethan grumbled.

Emerging from a side street in his rumpled and dirty black suit was Felix Graves.

"Damn, how did he get out so fast?"

All of those doors past the ship must lead out of the fort.

Silently cursing Maynard, Ethan moved out of his hiding spot and joined a group of people crossing the road to the seaside, heading for a restaurant. He kept them between himself and Graves, and watched as he got into the car, Grassi getting into the driver's seat. The car sped off, heading toward Praia. Ethan branched off, heading behind the restaurant and a row of single-story buildings coloured in yellows and pinks and reds. He took stairs down and hurried along the rocky coastline, passing by palms and stone fencing.

He was wondering how he was going to get a car when he heard someone shout, "There he is!"

Ethan turned around, and two of the men in black suits were hurrying down the stairs, guns drawn.

"Crap!" Ethan dove behind the trunk of a tall tree just as shots rang out. He pulled Graves' SIG P229 out. People screamed and ran as Ethan peered around the trunk just as a bullet slammed into it, splintering the bark. Ignoring all the doubts that screamed at him to stop, Ethan aimed and fired back, missing the mark. One man hid behind a low stone fence, but the other was caught out in the open near the water's edge, and Ethan fired again, catching him in the chest. He cried out and splashed into the water.

Ethan fired again at the stone fence and ran up another set of stairs toward the main road, where he entered the town square.

The square was filled with a dozen people looking around in tense confusion, wondering if the sounds they'd heard were actually gunshots.

Ethan waved his gun in the air, shouting for them to get out of the way, as he headed for the main road.

The people screamed and scattered and he crossed the square.

Once he reached the main road, he heard horns blaring and watched cars moving around the idle sedans. He sprinted to one sedan, and just as he reached one, a gunshot cracked in the air and a bullet thudded into the car door. Ethan pulled the door open, tossed the gun and backpack on the passenger's seat, and dove in. More bullets slammed into the car, shattering the window on the passenger's side. Ethan pulled the door closed and, grateful that the keys were still in the ignition, started the car. The engine roared to life, and he put it in gear and slammed on the accelerator.

The car lurched forward, nudging the other sedan out of the way, and he set off down the highway toward Praia. Checking the rear-view mirror, he saw no one behind him. By the time he reached Costa D' Achada, he let off the accelerator, deciding caution was best on this unfamiliar, windy road now that night had fallen.

He overtook a sauntering pickup and turned, skirting around the town. Suddenly, the roar of an engine and dazzling bright lights flooded the car's interior, and Ethan was side-swiped by an SUV coming from a side road.

The sound of screeching tyres and twisting metal filled the inside of the sedan as it spun and Ethan tried to regain control of the car. Eventually, the sedan skidded off the road and came to a stop on the shoulder. Dust filtered through the car's headlights, and Ethan saw that the SUV that hit him had careened off the road and was trying to turn around. He put the car back into gear and floored it, the dented metal groaning and tyres kicking up the gravel, and he was off like a shot. Behind him, the SUV skidded back on the road and gave chase.

Ahead of Ethan, the sprawling lights of an expansive town came into view: Praia. He'd reached the outskirts, and he gunned the engine, blasting over a roundabout and swerving around the increasingly busy traffic. Horns blared and people flashed their lights, but Ethan kept his focus ahead. He could sense the SUV coming at him from behind, so he floored the accelerator. The car jolted as it rocketed forward, the wind from the shattered passenger's window roaring in the interior.

The SUV was right on his tail when he swerved around a slow-moving sedan and then immediately cut back in, narrowly avoiding an oncoming truck. The SUV following Ethan wasn't as quick and collided head-on with the truck. He looked in the rear-view mirror and saw the crumpled hood of the SUV sitting halfway across the road, debris scattered over the road like children's blocks.

Suddenly the back window shattered, and Ethan ducked, swerving the sedan. He fought to regain control of the steering. He peeked at the side mirror and saw two more SUVs bearing down on him. A man was hanging out the side of the window of one of the SUVs, aiming a machine gun at him.

Ethan ducked again as a hail of bullets slammed into his car, thudding into the trunk and headrest.

"Shit! Shit!"

He came up to another roundabout and, at the last moment, took a hard left, hoping to get away from his followers. The leading SUV zoomed past, mounting the roundabout before skidding to a stop, but the second made the turn in time and gave chase.

They were in the middle of Praia now, the colourful buildings a blur of blue and green and yellow and pink as he sped past them. Car horns blared, and people in the streets shook their fists and protested, watching as the two cars raced along the main roads.

Ethan took a hard right and then another and was now driving along a road circling the Porto de Praia. Just as he reached another roundabout, the blue and red lights of a police car came hurtling down the opposite side of the street. The police car banked the roundabout and slammed into the SUV.

Ethan looked in his side mirror and saw the smoking police car had T-boned the SUV. The driver's side caved in so much it almost wrapped itself around the police car.

Taking another right, Ethan headed back toward Praia, driving at a casual pace as police sirens blared and cars zoomed past, heading back to the crash. He picked up his phone and dialled Ritchie's number.

"Lad, where are you?"

"Had some trouble, but I think I'm in the clear now. Are you still following them?"

"Aye, lad. They took them to the airport, but I don't know how long they'll be here for."

"All right, keep an eye out for Graves. He'll be there soon and it won't be long before—"

Ethan was cut off as the second SUV tore out of a side street and rammed into the rear passenger's side of the sedan. The car spun out of control, mounted the exposed roots of a tree, and launched into the air. It flipped and landed with a crash on the roof and skidded along the road until it crashed into the side of a building.

Thirty

Blaring sirens brought Ethan back to consciousness, and he groaned. His head pounded and he very much wanted to go to sleep, but he felt strange, like he was falling. His eyes fluttered open, and he turned his head sideways, trying to work out why everything looked strange and why his head felt so heavy.

Weird.

He tried to undo his seatbelt, but his hands were resting on the roof of the car, which was now the bottom of the car.

"What in the hell?" he groaned and closed his eyes again, trying to figure out what happened.

He remembered the chase from Cidade Velha and the SUV crashing into him, hitting the tree and…

He opened his eyes and looked around. Even upside down, he could see that the sedan had crashed into a night market of some sort. He saw stalls and single-story buildings with bright lights, and the thumping of music over speakers vibrated through his seat. Police cars and fire trucks skidded to a stop nearby. Their blue and red lights flashed and reflected off every surface, attracting locals like moths to a flame.

I've got to get out of here before they arrest me.

Fumbling for his seatbelt again, he pressed the button and tumbled awkwardly on his head, wrenching his neck.

"Ow," he complained, and rolled around until he was the right side up. His leg hurt but he was otherwise ok, and he tried to open the driver's side door, but it wouldn't budge.

"Ola! Você está bem?"

Ethan looked through the shattered windscreen and saw three police officers approaching with an EMT. More were approaching the SUV, which had crashed into the corner of another building. The front and side crumpled with one headlight glaring off the tree trunk. Ethan watched the officers moving toward the SUV when the door opened and Felix Graves stumbled out. The two EMTs hurried to him, but he reached into his jacket and pulled out a handgun. He aimed and shot one of the EMTs point-blank in the head.

The other one stopped and froze, but Graves ignored her. Instead, he aimed his gun at the approaching police officers. He fired three times, and each bullet hit their mark.

The officers fell, and there was a silence in the cool night air, as if people were trying to process what had just happened. Then someone screamed and chaos ensued. The crowd of people scattered, while the police officers who were approaching Ethan's car turned and pulled their weapons. Graves shot one of them, and he fell while the other two ducked and moved away. He fired at them but missed.

Ethan tried to force his door open again, but couldn't move it. He rolled around to get in a better position and kicked again. The door moved slightly, and he tried again, and the door gave a little more. He kept kicking as hard as he could, pain lancing up his leg with each kick, but the door wouldn't open. Then he tried the window, but the glass was too strong and he was too cramped to get much force behind his kicks.

He looked out the windshield and watched as Grassi and other men in suits poured out of the destroyed SUV. They spread out and joined the fight against the two outnumbered police officers.

Ethan knew he didn't have long. He growled, kicking at the door, and remembered the passenger's side window had been shot out. More sirens wailed in the distance, blaring out over the screams of people and gunshots in the chaotic street.

Turning around so he was on his stomach, he crawled across to the passenger's side and then peaked out. Graves' men and the police officers were distracted, focusing only on each other. He grabbed his pack with the sceptre and crawled out. He got to his feet in a crouching position, wincing in pain and, after securing his backpack, hobbled to the back of the car just as someone cried out. Peering around the rear of the car, he saw an officer on the ground in the middle of the road, blood pouring from his shoulder. He had been using his own car for cover, but the shot must have turned him, as he was lying a few metres away from it, exposed to Graves and the others.

Ethan rushed to him, grabbed him by the collar of his uniform, and pulled him back behind the police car just as Graves' men spotted him. They cried out in surprise and fired at him, bullets pelting the police car.

He propped the officer back against the car and reached out to grab his fallen handgun, a Walther P99. He turned to the officer and said, "You're going to be okay. They're after me."

He didn't know if the officer could understand him, and he didn't wait around to find out. Backing away from the police car, Ethan moved in a crouching position until he was near the corner of a stall. He stood up and aimed his gun at the men. He pulled the trigger three times, and two of them hit their mark, catching one of the black-suited men in the shoulder and then neck. He fell, and Ethan ducked away from a hail of bullets that splintered the stall's timber sign.

Well, now you have their attention. What's next?

The market was set up in a wide square area with brick buildings around the perimeter and stalls placed wherever the owners could find space. It was tight, and Ethan wondered how people could move about. The market was poorly lit, with only string lights providing any illumination, but it was perfect cover for Ethan. He moved past the stalls and away from the pursuing men until he reached the other side of the market.

It was a dead end.

"Shit," he whispered. The market backed into a row of two-story buildings. Each had a door, and he tried a couple of them, but they were locked. He doubled back, crouching behind a stall selling brightly coloured dresses, and watched the three men sweeping the stalls, guns held out.

He thought about his options. He could try to take them on in a gunfight. The stalls would give him a lot of cover, but as soon as he fired, they would be on him quickly and try to surround or corner him. Plus, in this light, there was no guarantee he would even hit his target.

He decided against a direct gunfight and focused on trying to get out of the market. He raised his head and chanced a look around the stalls, searching for the best way out. The front of the market where they had crashed through was the most direct and open route. But he could only see two of the three men, and it was likely the third had doubled back and was waiting at the entrance in case he did exactly that.

Moving from stall to stall to keep away from Graves' black-suited goons, Ethan continued searching for an escape route. He moved to the perimeter, following along a row of buildings until he came to a large trash bin. He peered over it and saw another bin about thirty metres away, and above it was a ladder bolted into the wall leading to the top of the building.

Wiping blood from a cut on his forehead, he scanned the area and saw one man on the far side of the market, but the others were out of view.

Without waiting to see where they were, he hurried along the wall in the shadows, his body tense. He expected to hear shouts and gunshots but, to his surprise, they didn't come. The ladder was rusty, but it looked sturdy, and with one last look to see if he was in the clear, Ethan put the gun in his waistband and climbed onto the bin. The rumpling of the metal as he climbed onto it sounded like thunder to his ears.

"Hey!"

Ethan didn't bother looking back. This was his only chance of getting out, and he was either going to get out or get shot in the back. He grabbed the rungs and climbed, quickly making his way up. Just as he reached the top rung, the first gunshot sounded and a bullet thudded into the clapboard next to him. More followed, each one a hollow thud as they slammed into the wall, but Ethan rolled over the side and onto the tin roof. The shooting stopped, and Ethan heard running footsteps.

Ethan got to his feet and hurried along the rooftop, the banging of his shoes on the corrugated iron a beacon for his pursuers. More sirens sounded in the distance, but Ethan would be long dead before they got here if he didn't keep moving. He pulled his handgun out of his waistband, turned, and fired at the first man as he climbed onto the rooftop. The man cried out in pain, and there was a barrage of returning fire from the ground. Ethan sprinted to the edge of the building, leapt off it, and landed on the hood of a car, the rolling momentum carrying him on to the road.

The road was empty of all but a handful of confused pedestrians, wondering what was going on and gasping at the sudden appearance of the ragged and bloodied Ethan. Ethan hurried down the street, weaving between parked cars while he heard the shouts and screams of pedestrians behind him. He chanced a glance behind him and saw two men jumping down from the rooftop. He stopped and fired twice, hoping to surprise them. Both shots were off the mark, but it bought him some time as they ducked behind a car, and he sprinted down the street and rounded a corner. He was now in a street of colourful buildings lined with various shops and businesses. The street was far enough away that no one had heard the gunfire, and it was busy with people getting in some last-minute shopping before closing.

Hoping to get lost in the crowd, Ethan put his gun in his waistband and mingled as best as he could, sliding in and around groups of shoppers and trying not to draw attention to himself.

Three gunshots cracked into the night air, and a collective cry sounded from everyone in earshot. With no other way to go, the crowd panicked and funnelled up the street away from the shots. Ethan tried to go with the tide of people, but in their panic, they moved erratically, trying to get away that he was at risk of being trampled. He saw a parking lot to the side and headed for it, moving perpendicular to the rushing crowd. It reminded him of swimming across a rip tide to avoid being taken out to sea. Eventually, he found a gap and crossed into the parking lot.

The lot was an unsealed, uneven parcel of dusty land full of cars and, thankfully, empty of people. Ducking behind a station wagon, Ethan watched the tidal wave of people thin out until the two gunmen appeared. They were walking slowly, as if in no hurry. Once they passed the parking lot, he could double back behind them and get away.

But one of them stopped and said something to the other. The other seemed to argue, both of their voices raising a little, but

Ethan couldn't make out what they were saying. Finally, the second nodded and the first continued moving forward while the other headed toward him.

Damn it!

Ethan watched the man move from row to row, searching between the cars. He was hurrying, as if he was doing it because he was told to rather than he believed Ethan could be in here. As he got closer, Ethan circled around a car and moved down two more. He hoped to circle around the gunman and exit without him knowing. The gunman switched back, heading down a second row of cars toward the entrance, and Ethan followed him from the other side of the cars. Just as they reached the last of the cars, Ethan stood on a soda can. The crushed aluminium sounded like shattered glass, and he rolled aside just as the man leapt over the hood of the car and landed where Ethan was.

The man pointed and fired, but Ethan had rolled under a pickup truck, the raised vehicle giving him just enough room to roll to the other side. He got up as quick as he could and the gun fired again. The shot pinging off a car frame. Ethan remembered he had his gun and pulled it. He fired. It was a wild shot that missed everything, but the gunman instinctively ducked and Ethan dodged out of the way, hiding behind another car.

They dodged and weaved through the parked cars. Ethan knew this game of cat and mouse had to end soon, otherwise the gunman's friend would arrive and he'd be cornered. He decided he'd try to flip the script. Instead of moving to the next car behind him, he moved to the one in front of him. The gunman, expecting Ethan to be at the next car, rounded on it and pointed his gun.

"Huh?" he said.

Ethan sprang up from behind him and put him in a chokehold. The gunman struggled and tried to bring his gun up, but Ethan grabbed his arm to keep it away and dropped to one knee, bringing the gunman down with him. Graves' goon dropped his gun and his free arm was flailing, trying to grab Ethan, to pull his arm away, to scratch his eyes, anything to break free, but Ethan held firm. The flailing slowed as the oxygen flow to his head was cut off, and then he finally stopped struggling. Ethan held on for a bit longer before releasing him, and his assailant slumped to the ground.

He sat back, huffing. He knew he had to get up, to keep moving, but his knee throbbed and he felt so tired, as if he had expelled the last of his energy.

He didn't even consider the idea he might have killed another man. Even thinking about thinking made him want to lie down and go to sleep.

After a few more deep breaths, Ethan reluctantly got up, swaying a little on unsteady feet.

"Put your hands up."

Shit.

Thirty One

Ethan put his hands up.

"Turn around."

He did and found himself face to face with the other gunman. He must have heard the shots and came back. He searched Ethan but found nothing. Ethan's gun was on the ground, having dropped it when he was strangling the other man.

The gunman nodded to his fallen colleague. "What did you do to him?"

"Nothing, he's unconscious," he said, unsure if that was actually true.

"Fine. Turn around."

"You going to shoot me in the back?"

The gunman shrugged. "It's nothing personal, kid. Orders are orders."

"You know he won't find the treasure without me," Ethan said, desperately trying to bide time and come up with a way out of it. His mind was racing, but all his options either had slim chances of working, like diving behind a car, or were impossible to do, like charging the man and grabbing his gun before he got a shot off.

The man shrugged. "I get paid whether or not he finds it, so I don't really care. Now turn around."

"If you're going to shoot me, then you can do it face-to-face," Ethan said, unsure where this bravado was coming from. Perhaps exhaustion and delirium were mixing together to make him braver than he felt.

Sighing, the gunman said, "Fine," and aimed the gun at Ethan's chest.

Ethan tensed, ready to dive.

The gun went off and Ethan dove, way too late for it to be any good. He landed on his belly behind a car and scrambled to his feet. He checked his body, trying to find where he'd been shot, but he found nothing—no hole, no blood, no pain.

He missed?

Ethan peered around from the front of the car, ready to fight or run, and saw the gunman lying on the ground in a pool of blood.

What the?

"We have to stop meeting like this."

Abigail Myers stepped out from behind a car, gun drawn but

pointed down.

"What?" Ethan said, dumbfounded.

She pointed to the body on the ground. "Second time this week I've saved your ass."

"Oh…" Ethan snorted. "I had it under control."

A hint of a smile crossed her lips. "Yes, you were really convincing him to not shoot you."

"I need to get to the airport," he said, ignoring her jibe. He picked up the dead gunman's gun and headed toward the parking lot exit.

"No, you're not going anywhere," she said, putting a hand out to stop him.

"I have to!" he argued, trying to push past her.

"First of all, put the gun down," she said.

He batted her hand away and hurried on. "I need to save my friends!"

"What friends? What is going on?" she asked, following him.

Ethan stopped just before the exit. "Later. I need to get to the airport."

"Ethan, you called me, remember? Tell me what's going on."

"I have to get to the airport before Graves leaves."

"Wait, Felix Graves? He's here?"

Ethan nodded.

"You're sure?"

"Considering we had a casual stroll through a secret underground maze before he tried to kill me, I'm pretty sure."

"What?"

"Look, I'll explain it to you later, but I need to get my friends back before he takes off. In fact, I could use your help."

"Lead the way," she said without pause.

Ethan left the parking lot with Abigail behind him and ran into the street. Lights from the shop were still on, and sirens blared in the distance, but they were alone.

"Boy, the police are really slow around here," Ethan commented, looking both ways. "Do you have a car?"

"They're not really equipped to deal with this. They'll be waiting on BAC. And yes, I do."

"Where is it?" he asked.

Abigail signalled for him to follow. "Near the market," she said. "I had to follow your trail of destruction."

"Hey!" Ethan protested, falling in step with her. "I'm responsible for maybe a quarter of that."

They reached the market, the streets busier than before as people crowded around. More police cars had arrived at the scene to investigate and question witnesses. Abigail led him closer to the market, and he asked, "What if someone recognises me and they detain me?"

"Don't worry about it," Abigail said.

They reached the roped-off area, and Abigail spoke in Portuguese to an officer manning the cordon. The officer nodded and lifted the police tape, and Abigail gestured for Ethan to follow. They passed under the tape and walked by the market entrance where a handful of officers were standing with firefighters and EMTs, probably discussing the events of the night and what they were going to do. Nearby, the crashed SUV sat amongst the rubble, a hazy smoke drifting from the smashed front. They passed the bodies of the police officers and Graves' men covered in sheets.

"Who are you? Really?" Ethan asked her once they were past the bodies and through to the other side of the market where the streets were empty. They rounded a corner, walking along a side street lined with parked cars.

"I told you," she replied vaguely.

"Yeah, Mossad," Ethan said. "But I don't believe it."

"I don't care what you believe, Ethan. I care about you telling me all you know about Graves and helping me catch him."

"Hey, I'm with you on that. Well, at least to the point of finding out what he knows about my parents, but—"

The screeching of tyres behind them cut him off, and they both looked around to see a black SUV sitting in the middle of the road. The doors opened, and men in black suits, armed with submachine guns, poured out of them.

How do they just keep showing up?

"How close is the car?" Ethan asked.

"Not close enough. Run!" Abigail aimed her gun and fired. The black-suited men scattered, buying them both enough time to round the corner of the street before they could fire. Abigail and Ethan sprinted down a busy main road, cars flashing past while they dodged unaware pedestrians. Ethan looked behind him and saw the first of the gunmen round the corner, the others, and the SUV following closely behind.

"Keep going!" Abigail huffed.

Ahead of them, another black SUV skidded into view from a side street and stopped in front of them. The window wound down and the muzzle of a machine gun poked out. Ethan and Abigail stopped, eyes wide. Seeing an alleyway to his right, Ethan pulled her in it just as bullets peppered the stone buildings, tearing away chunks.

"How many cars does this guy have?" Ethan said, following Abigail down the rubbish-strewn alleyway. Thankfully, the alley was too narrow for the SUVs, and he knocked over garbage cans as he passed them, hoping to slow down their pursuers. They turned down another narrow alley sandwiched between two tall buildings before emerging on to another street. Abigail pressed herself against one side of the wall while Ethan did the same on the opposite. He watched her peek down the alley they just came from.

As soon as the first pursuer emerged, she fired. The man cried out and clutched his chest, then fell. There were shouts coming from behind him, and Abigail fired again and then turned and ran, with Ethan following behind. The street they were on was quiet, and they passed multi-story factories shut down for the night. Sparsely placed streetlights provided dim yellow light. They passed by a row of buildings with scaffolding attached to the front, and ahead of them was another main street. They could see bright lights and cars passing by.

"This way," Abigail said, aiming for the street. "We might be able to double back and get to my car."

"Can't you call for backup?" Ethan asked breathlessly.

"No."

"Why not?"

"I'm not supposed to be here."

"Great."

"I'm here at your request," she said. "And you gave me very little information, so I couldn't bring a team."

They were near the end of the street when another SUV skidded to a stop, blocking the road. The doors to the SUV opened, and Abigail fired at it. The doors closed as her bullets hit the SUV. The car turned and headed back down the street.

Black-suited men emerged from the alley and Abigail fired at them until her gun clicked.

"You got a gun or a water pistol?" she shouted.

It took a moment for Ethan to realise he was still carrying the SIG he picked up from the parking lot. He raised it and pulled the trigger. Remarkably, he hit one gunman. The man fell to the ground, clutching his leg, while the others took cover behind parked cars and garbage cans, or backed into the alley.

"Scheisse!" she said, reloading and firing back at the men coming from the street. "We're cornered!"

Ethan fired until his gun was empty, then tossed it aside. He ducked behind a car with Abigail, a constant barrage of bullets thudding into it.

"I'm empty," she said. "You?"

"Same," Ethan said.

"Got any ideas?"

"Wait for the police?"

Abigail shook her head. "BAC won't get here in time."

Ethan looked around. Both sides of the street were covered by approaching gunmen. If they could get over them, they would have a good shot at getting to the next road. Directly across the road from them was a factory. Scaffolding ran the length of the building and continuing on to the adjoining buildings toward the main road.

"I have one," he told her. "How well can you climb?"

"I'm not going to like this idea, am I?"

"No. But it might work," he said.

"That's good enough for me," she said after another flurry of bullets thudded into the car. "I can climb well enough."

He pointed to the scaffolding. "If we can get on top of that, we might be able to pass over them and get to the main road."

"That's a horrible idea," Abigail told him.

Ethan couldn't help but smile. "This whole venture has been nothing but horrible ideas. Yet we're still alive. So really, they're good ideas disguised as bad ideas."

Abigail gave him a look that said she didn't agree.

"When they stop firing next, run like your life depends on it… because it does."

The barrage of bullets relented moments later and Ethan cried, "Now!"

They both sprinted from their position behind the car, circled it, and crossed the road. Ethan arrived at the scaffolding first and leapt onto the horizontal steel beams. He climbed as quickly as he could, shuffling along a diagonal beam, and then pulled himself up and onto the timber planks. He expected to see Abigail right behind him, but she wasn't there. She was still climbing as he peered over the edge. He reached down. "Give me your hand!" he shouted just as the bullets started flying again.

Abigail reached up and grabbed his hand, and he hauled her

up and onto the boards. She rested on top of him as bullets pinged off the beams around them and they were showered with splintered wood.

"You know how to show a girl a good time," she said, rolling off him and hugging the wall. Ethan got up and ran along the boards, following Abigail. Bullets zipped all around them, hitting poles and brick, and splintering planks as they ran.

"Up here," Abigail said, climbing a ladder up to the second level of scaffolding. Ethan followed her up, and they continued running along the scaffolding. They were getting further away from their pursuers, who had to weave around parked cars and trucks, while Ethan and Abigail had a straight run toward the end of the road.

They reached a large, abandoned factory that was covered in graffiti and had broken windows. Graves' men continuing firing and the street was filled with the sound of gunfire and ricocheting bullets, and on top of the noise, Ethan heard the roar of an engine. The third SUV came tearing out of a side street and rammed into the scaffolding below them. The scaffolding shook, and the support beams began collapsing in a chorus of squealing metal. Ethan cried out as the planks beneath him slipped and broke away from their supports. He fell, slamming into the scaffolding below. The air was knocked out of his lungs and he groaned.

"You okay?" Abigail's head appeared from above.

"Yeah, I'm fine. Just go," he groaned, waving his hand. Behind him, the SUV reversed out of the wreckage and smashed into the scaffolding again. Ethan felt the scaffolding beneath him rumble and shake more violently. It wasn't going to hold much longer. Groaning again, he got to his feet and ran just as the boards started collapsing beneath him. He ran as fast as he could, staying just ahead of the crumbling steel and wood, but the SUV followed him, ramming through the posts like a bull in a China shop.

Ethan leapt over a gap between two sets of scaffolding and continued running as the SUV chased him. A loud pop and a screeching of metal echoed out over the sound of gunfire as the SUV hit a post and veered too far right, slamming into the factory wall.

Everything shook, and the scaffolding came loose from the bricks. Ethan stumbled, his footing uneven, and he fell sideways, smashing through a window and landing on a metal catwalk inside the factory.

Covered in, and cut by, shards of glass, Ethan sat up. The factory was dark, the streetlights outside and dim night lights suspended from the roof high above him being the only sources of light. The catwalk was bolted to the wall, and there was a set of stairs leading down just ahead of him. Outside, he could still hear the constant sound of bullets, while below him the SUV revved its engine and tried to back out of the hole in the wall it had created. The half-destroyed car rocked back and forth, the chassis caught on something, while bricks and metal crumbled around it. Taking advantage, Ethan got up and ran along the catwalk, heading down the stairs and onto the ground floor.

As he hurried toward the rear of the factory, passing by large machines and conveyor belts, the SUV finally got loose and backed away, leaving a gaping hole in the wall. Four black-suited men appeared, scrambling over a pile of broken bricks and metal poles and into the factory. Ethan made it to the end of the factory where two wide barn-like doors were. He pushed on them, but they were locked.

"Give me a break!" he mumbled.

He looked around for another way out. There were windows evenly spaced along the catwalk on the upper levels, but the ground floor was solid brick.

"Spread out. Find him and end this before the police arrive," he heard one man instruct the others.

Ethan ducked behind an enormous machine that fed out a conveyor belt, and his foot brushed against something. He looked down and in the dim light saw a piece of metal pipe about a metre long. He picked it up, weighing it in his hand, and decided it was a better weapon than nothing. Peering around the side of the machinery, he saw one gunman was approaching. He was walking the length of the conveyor belt, while the other three had spread out, searching other areas of the factory floor. Ethan tensed, took a deep breath, and gripped the pipe as hard as he could.

Ethan saw the machine gun first, the muzzle poking around the machinery. He swung the pipe as hard as he could and connected with the man's stomach. The gunman let out an "oof" and doubled over, and Ethan forcefully brought the pipe down on his head. Even through the sound of sirens in the background, he could hear the sickening crunch of his skull fragmenting into pieces. The man slumped to the ground and Ethan crouched waiting for the shouts or gunfire to come, but after three breaths, there was nothing. He looked down at the man's form, unsure if he was dead or unconscious, but right now, he didn't care. He couldn't pull the machine gun strap over his body, so he pulled a SIG P229 from the man's shoulder holster.

Feeling like he had a slight chance now, he moved down the factory to look for another way out. He spied a glowing green exit sign on the other side of the factory. He wondered where Abigail was and a sick feeling forming in the pit of his stomach at the thought of her being shot and bleeding out on the scaffolding.

Shaking his head to remove the vivid imagery from his mind, he told himself that overthinking and carelessness would get him, and Abigail, killed.

And she can take care of herself. Moreso than you can.

He moved between machines and conveyor belts, avoiding the searching men while heading to the exit. He could still hear sirens blaring out in the night, but they still sounded far away.

What's taking them so long?

"Watch the exits," one man suddenly called out. Then asked, "Has anyone seen Marco?"

Shit!

Ethan hid behind a vertical shaft and watched one gunman move towards the exit.

Now what?

"Holy shit. Marco!"

"What is it?"

"He's down."

Damn it!

There was a pause and then, "The kid's in here somewhere.

Find him!"

Ethan considered trying to shoot his way out. He could take one out without the rest knowing at first, but they would be on him in a matter of seconds. Dismissing the idea, he saw the stairs that led to the catwalk nearby. He crept to them as his eyes remained locked on the nearest gunman, who was searching near the exit, facing away from him. As quietly as he could, Ethan ascended the stairs. His feet tapping on the steps, though quiet, sounded like the banging of metal drums to his ears. He was near the top when he kicked something. It was hard and metallic and it rolled off the catwalk, clanging to the ground. Before he even knew what he was doing, he fired on the closest gunman, who had turned around to see what the noise was. Ethan didn't know if the shot was fatal, but the man cried out and fell to the ground.

He ran along the catwalk while the other two gunmen were firing on him. Sparks from the bullets striking the metal lit up around his feet, and he felt them whiz by his ear. He reached a second set of stairs and climbed them two at a time, figuring the more distance between them, the better his chances. He blindly fired as he climbed, trying to get the men to duck into cover and give him more time to get out of there. As he ran, he glanced out the windows he passed. He was on the back side of the factory and there was nothing to climb out on—just a long drop into an open work area, and he certainly would break his legs if he jumped.

He hurried forward, bullets clanging off the walkway and walks, until he reached the end of the factory. Turning right, Ethan crossed the width until he was on the front side of the factory. Ahead of him were stairs leading to the first level and then to the ground floor.

Ethan pointed his gun over the railing, waiting for the gunmen to appear from their hiding spots.

Both gunmen appeared at once from the shadows and fired a volley at him. Ethan ducked and fell back against the factory wall.

"Go! Go!" one of them shouted and kept firing.

Bullets pinged off the catwalk and bricks in a constant cacophony, pinning Ethan down with nowhere to run. A feeling of helplessness and desperation overcame him, and he considered taking the risk of running to the nearest window when the shooting stopped.

Over the ringing in his ears, Ethan heard sirens screaming and the screeching of wheels as cars skidded to a stop. Voices shouted and below he heard one of Graves men call out, "Shit! It's the police!"

"What do we do?"

"Graves said not to get caught."

While they were talking, Ethan crept over to the nearest windows and looked out. Outside, a new gunfight had begun between Graves' men and the heavily armed police officers who were pouring out of a troop truck with 'BAC' written on the side.

Finally!

They took up positions behind the truck and opened fire on Graves' men, who were caught out in the open. Five of them were down in no time, and the rest quickly retreated behind cars. The two gunmen in the factory exited through the hole in the wall, joining the fight. Ethan was about to follow them out when a hand clamped over his mouth.

Thirty Two

"Follow me," Abigail whispered into his ear and then removed her hand from his mouth. She was banged up, her jacket and pants torn, and she had a cut just above her brow.

She turned and climbed out a nearby window, with Ethan following behind. They climbed out onto the scaffolding that was still standing in this section, having avoided the destruction from the SUV.

The scene on the road was a bloodbath. The gunfight was still going, though the BAC had the upper hand and had surrounded Graves' men. Only two of them were fighting back, since the others lay on the ground either too injured or too dead to help.

Sirens wailed as more police cars skidded to a stop near the

BAC truck, their flashing lights turning the street into a red and blue disco.

Abigail and Ethan moved quickly until the scaffolding ended at a ladder on the back side of the factory. They climbed down, keeping to the shadows, and fled from the scene.

They exited the road into a crowd of people who were milling around, curious to watch the events unfold, but not willing to get any closer. All eyes were fixed on the scene, and despite Ethan and Abigail looking like they had just come out of a war zone, no one took notice of them as they squeezed their way through.

Once they were alone, Ethan said, "Where's your car?"

"Back the way we came," she told him, leading him down a narrow alley lined with chain-link fencing. A dog barked behind a fence, and they both froze, thinking the sound could attract attention. After looking and seeing no one around, they exited the alley into a dark, narrow street.

"Here," she said, approaching a dark sedan.

She unlocked it with the press of a button and got in the driver's seat. Ethan got in the passenger's side and immediately felt pain shooting up his side.

He hissed and grabbed at his ribs.

"What's wrong?" Abigail asked.

"Nothing, just my ribs," Ethan told her.

"I'm not surprised. You look like shit," she said, starting the car and pulling out on to the street.

Ethan flipped down the sun visor in front of him and examined himself in the little rectangular mirror. There were minor cuts around his forehead and one on his lip, raised welts around the cheek and left eye that would no doubt bruise, and his face was haggard and drawn.

"Definitely not winning any beauty pageants today," he muttered.

"To be fair, you weren't beforehand, either," Abigail said with a small smile.

"Ha. Ha."

She turned the car onto the highway, heading for the airport.

"You're sure Graves will be at the airport?" she asked him.

"Yes. He's heading to West Africa."

"Why?"

"He's after treasure."

"Blackbeard's treasure?"

Ethan was surprised. "How did you know?"

"Your parents."

"What?"

Ethan felt his phone vibrate from his pocket and cursed the timing. He pulled it out. It was Ritchie. He looked at Abigail expectantly. She glanced at him and said, "You better get that."

Cursing again, he answered the phone. "Ritchie?"

"Aye, lad. Where are you?"

"We got held up."

"We?"

Abigail drove along Circular da Praia, where the Nelson Mandela International Airport loomed ahead of them. "You'll find out soon," Ethan told him. "We're near the airport. Where are you?"

"In the parking lot opposite the terminal."

Ethan could see the open-air parking lot to their left where a dozen or so cars were parked. He pointed it out to Abigail, and she nodded. "I see it. We're driving in now."

"I see you."

Ethan hung up the phone.

"Who are we meeting?" Abigail asked.

"Ritchie. He's a… boat captain."

"Just what we need at an airport," she replied. "Can we trust him?"

"Yeah, he's been with me since Cape Town."

Ritchie appeared from between two cars, and Abigail parked in a free space nearby. Ritchie opened one of the rear doors and got in.

"Who's this?" he asked.

"This is the phone call I made back on the boat. Ritchie, this is Abigail Myers, from…?" he let the question hang in the air, waiting for her to answer, but she just sat there looking at him with the hint of a smile on her face. Sighing, he continued, "And Abigail, this is Ritchie."

"Lass," Ritchie said with a nod of his head.

"Ritchie," she said back.

"Right, enough small talk," Ethan said. "Where are they? What happened?"

Ritchie nodded at the airport terminal. "The bar was a bust. They knew I was coming. After they tried to take me out, I followed them here. They took the girls into the terminal. I tried to get in to follow them, see where they are going, but they have men posted around the building, and it's locked up tighter than my pa's wallet on Christmas."

"Have you seen Graves?" Ethan asked.

"Not yet."

"Are you sure he'll be coming this way?" Abigail said.

"The girls are here," said Ritchie.

"And he needs a way off the island," Ethan added.

Abigail considered this, then asked, "Where in West Africa is he going?"

"Oh, right," he said. With all that had happened since the fort, he forgot he knew the next destination. He pulled out his phone and opened his photos, viewing those he took of the map.

"Here," he said, flipping the phone around to show Abigail and Ritchie.

"Where is it?"

"Somewhere in West Africa. Can I borrow your phone?" he asked.

Abigail handed him her phone, and he pulled up the maps app, using it to cross-reference the photo from his own phone. It didn't take him long to discover the location. "Lake Faguibine," he whispered. "Maynard must have taken the treasure along the Niger River."

They both looked at him blankly.

"Mali," he said. "And it explains this," he added, pointing to the two sceptre pieces attached to the pack at his feet.

"And he knows it's there?" Abigail asked.

Ethan nodded. "He can figure it out based on the map."

"Good. I can work with that. Can I have my phone back?"

Ethan handed her the phone.

"I'm going to make a call," she said, and left the car.

When the door shut, Ritchie asked, "Do you trust her, lad?"

"She's saved my life twice. I don't have a reason not to."

"Who the hell is she?"

Ethan shrugged. "She has a Mossad badge."

"Lad, if she is Mossad, I am the Loch Ness Monster's left testicle."

"I suspect she is Interpol."

"Then why doesn't she say so?"

Ethan shook his head. "No idea."

The door opened, stopping any further conversation, and Abigail got in.

"Okay. I have spoken with my bosses. We think it's unlikely Graves will submit a flight plan. So we are going to plant some people at Malian airports near Lake Faguibine, and organise a team to intercept him at the lake if need be."

"Can't you ground the planes or something?" Ethan asked her.

Abigail shook her head. "I told you, no jurisdiction."

"What about tipping off the airport? Say there's a bomb or something."

Ritchie sighed. "Won't work. Graves' men basically took over the place. Once they arrived, everyone else left."

"Jesus, who is this guy?"

"Someone with a lot of money and a lot of influence," Abigail replied.

"We have time," Ritchie said. "I had a snoop around to see if I could find the girls. I don't know where they are in the terminal, but I noticed there aren't any planes on the move right now. They're all in the hangars."

"Maybe they don't have a pilot," Abigail suggested. "Show me where you saw them."

They all got out of the car and crossed the dimly lit lot. Ritchie led them to the northern end of the airport and past the terminal.

Ethan was surprised to find that the airport building's security lacking. The admin buildings weren't guarded by fencing, and their only hindrance was a boom gate into an employee parking lot. They circled around a low-lying building, which opened to a view of the runway. They approached a mesh fence running parallel to the runway, and Ritchie said, "See, no planes."

He was right. There were no planes on the runway and only one at the gate, a Beechcraft 1900 twin-propeller plane.

"Could they use that one?" Ethan asked.

"No," Abigail said. "That plane wouldn't have the range to make it to the coast of Africa, let alone Mali. They must be waiting for one to arrive."

Toward the terminal, they saw a handful of Graves' men casually walking around, submachine guns strapped over their shoulders. If they were expecting trouble, they weren't showing it.

"How many men did you see?" Abigail asked Ritchie.

Ritchie thought for a moment. "At least a dozen," he told her. "Maybe more."

"What do we do now?" Ethan asked.

"We wait for Graves and his plane," Abigail told him.

"What about Andrea and Hannah?"

Abigail turned and started back to the car, with Ethan and Ritchie in tow. "There is nothing we can do," she said. "We don't have the firepower to take them down right now."

"What about the police?"

"They're stretched thin as it is. And BAC is busy with everything else that has happened in the city. We can't afford to get into a gunfight, not with your friends' lives at risk."

Ethan cursed. "So we just wait?"

"Yep."

Great.

Thirty Three

It was just past two a.m. when Ritchie nudged Ethan awake. He'd fallen asleep in the passenger's seat just before midnight, exhaustion finally setting in.

"Wha?" he slurred.

Ritchie pointed toward the airport entry, where two black sedans and three jeeps were driving in, followed by what looked like an army troop truck.

The three of them got out of the car and headed to the terminal. The night was clear and warm and they crouched in the shadows between two cars parked near the terminal and watched.

The doors of the first sedan opened and Grassi got out, opening a rear door to reveal Felix Graves. From his vantage point, Ethan thought the usually stoic man was looking haggard and strained. Despite Ethan's clenched fists, he felt a grim satisfaction at the idea that Graves was uncomfortable.

"Does this guy just pack suits when he travels?" he growled, noticing he'd changed into a pin-stripe. Graves walked to the sedan behind him and opened the passenger door. Out stepped a tanned, middle-aged man with salt and pepper hair and a greying beard.

"Son of a bitch!" Abigail swore.

"Who's that?" Ethan asked.

"That's Farid Abboud."

"Who?"

"He's a terrorist based in Yemen and basically the reason for the atrocities going on in the Middle East. He was believed to be dead."

"What's he doing with Graves?"

"I don't know," she grumbled.

From the other side of the car, Ritchie whispered, "Incoming plane."

Ethan and Abigail looked around and saw the red, green, and white flashing lights of an incoming plane. They circled around the perimeter, avoiding the guards, and returned to the spot near the fence along the runway and watched the plane land.

The first thing Ethan noticed was the size of the plane. It was huge, with a fuselage that looked as big as a train tunnel and wings that spanned almost forty metres. Twin propellers lined each of the wings, and it had a rudder like the tail of a whale.

As the plane came to a stop, a ramp slowly opened at the back and three men emerged. They hurried into the terminal, passing a fuel truck driving the other way to refuel the plane.

"Why do they need such a big plane?" Ethan wondered.

It was another twenty minutes before his question was answered. While the plane was being refuelled, a forklift departed a shed on the far side of the terminal and drove up the ramp into the plane's hold. Meanwhile, the troop truck drove out on the tarmac and parked nearby. A few minutes later, the forklift emerged carrying a long, rectangular crate. They watched men part the canvas covering the back of the truck, and the forklift placed the crate into it.

"Oh, no," Abigail gasped.

"What?"

"If that crate contains what I think it does, then I know why Farid is here."

"What's in it?"

"A bomb."

"What!"

"Intelligence suggested Farid was looking to buy one. Among other things, Graves brokers black market deals for weapons."

"So the little bastard has branched out, eh?" Ritchie grumbled.

"This changes everything," Abigail continued. "I have to call this in."

She moved away from the fence and back around the buildings.

"Mossad, huh?" Ritchie said.

"Don't worry about that. We need to get Andrea and Hannah

out of there before BAC, Mossad, Interpol, or whoever the hell Abigail works for, comes in and they're caught in the middle of a gunfight."

"I don't think you have to worry about that, lad," Ritchie said, pointing at the plane.

A group of people, led by Felix Graves, were walking toward the plane's cargo hold. There were more than a dozen of his men following behind, two recognisable faces in the middle of them: Andrea and Hannah.

A swell of anger rose in Ethan, and it was all he could do to stop himself from charging in, guns blazing. Instead, he seethed as he watched them march up the ramp into the plane.

"Shit! This complicates things. The plane will be gone by the time Abigail's people get here. We have to do something."

"What can we do, lad?"

Ethan was silent, his mind racing while he watched the forklift unload more crates from the plane and lift them onto the truck. While the forklift was busy, the three jeeps drove on the tarmac and lined up, ready to go up the ramp and into the plane's hold.

An idea suddenly came to him.

"Think you can create a distraction?" he asked Ritchie.

"Why?"

"I have an idea."

"Is it a good one?"

"No."

"Is it going to get you killed?"

"Probably."

"You're gonna try to get the girls, aren't you?"

"Am I that transparent?"

"Like a window, lad."

"Good," Ethan said. "Give me ten minutes and then create a distraction. Doesn't need to be for long—just enough to get them looking the other way."

"Rightio."

Ethan turned toward the terminal when Ritchie stopped him. "And lad—"

Ethan stopped and looked at him. "Yeah?"

"Good luck."

Ethan nodded and hurried to the terminal. On his way there, he ran into Abigail, who was coming the other way. "I've spoken to my boss—where are you going?"

Ethan didn't answer as he ran to the car. He opened it, grabbed his pack, and then made his way to the south side of the terminal. He hid behind an air conditioning unit and peeked around the corner. Two guards were standing at the gates leading to the tarmac. Beyond them, Ethan saw the forklift put the last of the crates in the truck, and Farid's men started securing the load.

He was about to move forward when someone grabbed his arm. He turned, about to draw his gun, but stopped when he saw it was Abigail.

"What are you doing?" she hissed.

"The girls are on the plane. If I don't get them off, then we may lose them, or worse, Graves kills them once he discovers Blackbeard's treasure and has no use for them."

"Ethan... I can't help you here. If you get on that plane,

you're on your own."

"I know."

"But you're going to do it anyway."

"They're in this because of me. I can't just leave them and hope it works out."

Abigail chewed her lip and said, "What do you need me to do?"

"Ritchie is about to create a diversion. I need your help getting over the fence."

"Got it."

Just then they heard the roar of an engine and a loud crash coming from near the terminal entrance. The blaring of a horn followed, disturbing the otherwise quiet airport. Ethan and Abigail watched as Graves' men ran towards the commotion, while the gate's guards watched the scene unfurl from their station.

With them distracted, Ethan and Abigail hurried until they reached the perimeter fence. They moved along the fence, away from the gate, until they were in an unlit section obscured by shrubs and bushes.

"You sure about this?" she asked.

"Let's do this before I chicken out," Ethan said, already feeling the bravado leaving him and doubt replacing it.

Abigail stood with her back to the fence. "Come on, then," she said, crouching and cupping her hands.

Ethan put his foot in them, and she lifted him. He grabbed hold of the top of the fence, pull himself over, and land on the concrete ground without making too much noise.

Behind him, the fuel truck had finished refuelling the plane, and Farid's men had finished covering the troop truck, which was now driving to the gates.

Meanwhile, the plane's engines coughed to life and the propellers slowly began turning.

"You better hurry."

Ethan nodded. The jeeps hadn't been loaded on the plane yet, but he knew he didn't have long.

"Thanks for your help," he said to her. "Maybe once this is over, you could come find me again and tell me what the hell I got myself into?"

She smiled. "Deal."

Ethan was turning to go when she added, "Good luck, Ethan."

He gave her a casual salute, secured the pack and his gun, and, before he could talk himself out of it, hurried toward the third jeep. The driver had left the car and was standing a few metres away, yelling at the crowd of people looking through the fence who were trying to see the car crash.

As quietly as he could, he opened the back of the jeep and climbed in, then shut it without making any noise. He settled between boxes of supplies as the jeep idled.

Palms sweating, he pulled his gun out and held it at the ready. He felt on edge and was rethinking his decision when the driver's side door opened and someone got in. The driver slowly edged the jeep closer to the cargo bay of the plane, then finally climbed up the ramp and moved into the cargo hold. The driver drove deeper into the plane's belly until he stopped just behind another jeep. He killed the engine and got out, slamming the door shut behind him. Ethan let out a long breath. It was dark, but he was alone, the interior lights dimmed as the plane readied to take off.

He heard the man talking to some others, and they circled the jeep. Ethan waited and gripped his gun tightly, expecting the back to open at any moment. He realised he didn't even check to see how many bullets he had left and cursed himself even more for this foolish idea. Luckily, the men finished what they were doing and left, their voices fading away. Once the ramp ascended and closed, he relaxed a little.

A short while later, he felt the plane lurch forward and taxi around the tarmac. There was a slight pause before the engine revved louder and took off down the runway. The roaring of the engine and the propellers filled the cargo hold, and Ethan was pushed back by inertia and then at an angle as the plane took off. His stomach dropped when the plane levelled and then banked around as it set its course for West Africa.

It was pitch black in the jeep, and he carefully got up and peered through the windshield. He was at the back of the plane near the raised ramp with the jeeps lined up, one in front of the other. A dim red light cast a haze over the hold, but he couldn't see anyone around. Ethan figured they were elsewhere on the plane, having no need to guard a few stationary jeeps.

He sat back and worked out what to do next. Getting on the plane was essentially the only solid part of his plan. From here on out, he was winging it. He thought about his options. He could try to sneak the girls off the plane when it landed, but it was risky with how many of Graves' men were onboard. He had no chance in a gunfight, and that brought additional risk to the girls. No, sneaking off was their best chance. Otherwise he would have to somehow make a deal, which is why he brought the backpack with the sceptre.

Just wing it like everything else you've done so far.

He figured the flight would be close to six hours, so he sat back and tried to get as comfortable as possible to rest his aching and weary body. It felt like every time he moved he discovered a fresh cut or bruise or ache, and he tried to remember if his parents went through the same punishment on their bodies.

He was nine years old and in a hotel room in Tajikistan. His parents told him it was a family holiday, and he remembered wondering why they couldn't go somewhere cool, somewhere he knew. He didn't even know where Tajikistan was. He was getting into a taxi at the airport and driving past buildings with letters he didn't know and asking his dad what they were.

"It's Tajiki, Ethan. Similar to Farsi."

Ethan didn't know Tajiki or Farsi. He just looked out the window, trying to spot anything familiar, but aside from a sign advertising Pepsi, nothing was recognisable. Before arriving at their hotel, they drove past white-walled mosques, and women in colourful clothing and men wearing kallapush hats.

His parents left him in the room that night, leaving on a cartoon that he couldn't understand because it was in Tajiki. So, he read the books he had brought with him until he fell asleep.

He was startled awake by his mum and dad crashing through the door in the middle of the night. Dad's shirt was bloody, and Mum had a cut along her arm and shoulder. Ethan remembered how scared he was as he asked what happened to them..

They told him they were mugged on their way back from drinks, and he believed them. Why wouldn't he?

But now…

Ethan startled awake, the memory of his bloodied parents slipping away. He looked around in confusion and then remembered he was in the back of a jeep in the middle of an outrageous plan that had little chance of working. Light started filtering in around the jeep, and he saw through the small windows that the sky was a hazy white, the sun beginning to rise.

Yawning, he checked his watch. He had been in the air for over five hours now and figured they must be beginning their descent soon.

I guess now is as good a time as any, he thought with no enthusiasm. He walked through the plan again. Depending on where the girls were, he figured he had enough time to find them and free them when the plane landed. Or he could take Graves by surprise and force his way off by gunpoint.

Or there would be parachutes on the plane. He could find the girls and they could jump out.

Otherwise he could try to make a deal with Graves, the girls for the sceptre.

None of the ideas seemed like good ones, but it was all he

had, and he had to get them back.

If jumping out of the plane is your best idea, then you're in trouble.

As quietly as he could, he pulled the latch and opened the back of the jeep. He climbed out, his body stiff and sore, and grabbed his pack. He slung it over his shoulders, making sure it was secured properly. Then, with gun in hand, he crept along the narrow gap between the jeep and the fuselage. At some point during the flight, the lights had changed from a dim red to a bright white. He passed by the first jeep into a wide storage area where there were wooden crates secured by nets piled to the left, and to the right was—

"Andrea?"

Andrea was sitting in a seat bolted to the wall of the plane. Her head whipped around so fast that she might have gotten whiplash.

"Ethan! What are you doing here?"

"I thought I would channel my inner superhero and save you," he said with a grin. "Where's Hannah?"

Andrea pointed to a door. "Upstairs," she said.

"Okay, wait here and I'll see if I can— wait, why aren't you cuffed?"

"What?"

"You're not cuffed or guarded."

"They're preparing for landing and I guess... where am I going to go?"

"Well, that's a good start," Ethan said.

"Ethan, how did you get on the plane?"

"I snuck in on the jeep."

"How do you plan on getting us out of here?"

Ethan blew out a breath. "I have no idea. I'm kind of just seeing how it goes."

He looked around and saw a row of parachutes hanging from hooks opposite them. "How do you feel about skydiving?"

Andrea's eyes went wide, stretching her scar. "You must be joking."

"We can't shoot our way out. So it's either that or hide and hope we don't get caught. If you have any better ideas, I'm all ears," he said. He pulled one parachute off the hook and tossed it to her, grabbing another two and putting them on the seat beside her. He took off his pack and pulled out his journal, the compass, and the coins, and zipped them into pockets in his jacket, along with his phone. He leaned his pack with the sceptre against the fuselage and slipped on the parachute, securing the buckles.

"Why are you separating them?" Andrea asked.

"Insurance." He helped Andrea slide into her parachute. "If this goes to shit like I think it will, then we need to get ready to jump, and quickly. Hannah is going to need help, so I need you to grab the pack and go. Don't worry about us, we won't be far behind. As soon as you're clear of the plane, count to ten and pull on this," he said, gently tugging on the pull cord at her hip. "Got it?"

Andrea nodded apprehensively, and Ethan put his hands on her shoulders. "Hey, you got this, all right?"

She swallowed and nodded.

"Good." He handed her his pack.

"What's this?" she asked, indicating the two sceptre pieces.

"A sceptre I found at the Inaccessible Island," he said. "Yet another of Maynard's clues." He turned around and saw the jeeps, and an idea came to him. He hurried across the hold to open the door of the first jeep and released the parking brake and put it in neutral. He did the same for the other two and then returned to Andrea and said, "Wait here. I'll get Hannah and be back as soon as I can. Just be ready to jump."

She nodded again, and Ethan clicked off the safety of his gun and headed to the door.

Just as he reached the door, it opened and Hannah stumbled through, followed by the man he recognised as Harris.

Hannah gasped in surprise and Harris started to shout, but Ethan clubbed him with the weapon before he could get a word out and he slumped to the ground.

"Ethan!" Hannah cried out and hugged him.

"Hannah," Ethan said with relief, hugging her back. When they pulled away, he said, "Come on. We have to get out of here," and he led her to where Andrea was waiting and grabbed a parachute from the seat.

Heavy bootsteps thudded on the roof above and Ethan turned to Andrea. "Help Hannah get her parachute on," he ordered. "Things are about to get hectic. I'm going to try to hold them off in the stairwell, but we're gonna need to get out of here quickly."

Andrea nodded and, with his gun ready, Ethan headed back to the door. He had almost reached it when it slammed open and he was thrown back into the cargo hold. His gun flew out of his hands, skittering to a stop a couple of metres away. Half a dozen men flooded into the hold, followed by Grassi and then Felix

Graves.

"Mr. Jackson. Why am I not surprised to see you here?"

Ethan sat up. "Oh, I just enjoy pissing you off," he groaned.

Graves snorted. "If only I thought so much of you."

"Now that's just mean," Ethan said, getting to his feet.

"Were you planning a dramatic escape, Mr. Jackson?" Graves said, walking over to him. He was calm and relaxed, as if he had everything under control.

"Planning on kicking your ass!" Ethan said, taking a swing at the man. Graves was expecting it though, and ducked the right hook and buried his fist in Ethan's stomach. His ribs exploded in pain and he fell to his knees, gasping for air.

Jesus Christ, this guy can hit.

He coughed and slowly got to his feet again. "Maybe I was a bit premature on the 'kicking your ass' thing," he wheezed.

Graves said nothing, just moved in. He jabbed twice with his left, which Ethan dodged. Ethan then ducked under his right and planted one on Graves' midsection with his own right and then caught him on the cheek with his left. Graves stumbled back and Ethan smiled, satisfied to see the glowing red welt on his cheek.

The other men raised their guns, but Graves put up a hand and they lowered them.

"Very good, Mr. Jackson. Very good," he said. "I assume your parents got you some lessons?"

"Yeah, something like that," Ethan said. While he had had some boxing and self-defence lessons growing up, most of his fighting—or brawling, as the police called it—came from the schoolyard and, later, pubs.

"I'll tell you what, Mr. Jackson. You land one more hit on me. I'll let you and your friends go."

"Sounds fair to me," Ethan said, not believing a word the man said but savouring the idea of landing some more punches on this man.

He held his hands up as Graves moved in. He blocked Graves' first jab and went for his own, but Graves rotated and his blow glanced off his shoulder. Using the momentum of his turn, Graves rolled around and he caught Ethan with a hook that rattled his brain. He followed it up with a jab to the nose, a jab to the jaw, and a punch to the stomach, and Ethan was on the ground before he knew what was happening.

Blood dripped from his nose, which he was sure was either broken or pasted to his face. For good measure, Graves kicked him in the stomach, and Ethan recoiled, rolling away, coughing.

Graves crouched before him. "What was the plan here, Jackson? How did you think this was going to end?"

He grabbed Ethan's shoulder and squeezed, his thumb digging into the sensitive spot near the joint.

Ethan clamped his mouth shut, trying not to give the man the satisfaction of seeing him cry out. Graves' cold, dark eyes locked with his own and pressed harder.

The sharp pain built and built and Ethan screwed up his face. Tears formed, and he groaned until the pressure became unbearable and he cried out in ragged pain.

"Stop it!"

It was Hannah who screamed, surprising everyone. Ethan felt the pressure on his shoulder ease and, taking advantage of the distraction, rolled away and grabbed his fallen gun. He was back on his feet and attacked the nearest gunman, knocking his gun aside and getting him in a chokehold. He used him as a human shield and fired blindly. He hit one man, and he cried out and fell while the rest scattered, taking shelter where they could in the hold.

"Come on!" he called out, but his breathless voice came out in a rasp. Hannah was frozen with fear, her parachute half on, and Andrea pulled her over to Ethan.

Putting himself between Graves' men and the girls, Ethan moved back towards the ramp, pulling the struggling man with him.

"Put down your weapon, Mr. Jackson," Graves said casually. He indicated to Harris, who had just gotten to his feet, and the others to spread out. "You are cornered and outnumbered."

"Tell your men to lower their weapons!" Ethan rasped. His stomach and ribs hurt with each breath he took, his shoulder throbbed with pain, and his nose was leaking blood.

Graves chuckled as he stalked towards Ethan. "Where are you going to go, Mr. Jackson?"

Ethan was next to the last jeep, and he saw the switch for the ramp. He checked on Hannah and Andrea. They'd taken cover behind a jeep trying to get Hannah's parachute on. Ethan reached out and pushed the green button. The lights in the hold dimmed as warning sirens blared and red lights flashed and the ramp slowly opened. Air rushed in, and Ethan was almost thrown off balance by the force of it as it tried to pressurise the hold. Anything not nailed down was blown out of the plane, and the last jeep in line started to shake.

"It seems like we are at a stalemate, Mr. Jackson," Graves yelled over the wind. "Time to push the odds into my favour."

He pulled the trigger, and Ethan's captive jolted and slumped to the floor, leaving Ethan exposed.

"Kill them," Graves said.

Ethan ducked behind the last jeep just as gunfire rang out over the sirens. Bullets pinged off the shaking vehicle, and he cursed himself for his stupidity.

He peered out from behind the jeep. Graves' men were closing in on them. He fired, trying to keep them at bay.

"Shit," he muttered. Behind him, the ramp had fully opened, morning light glowing, revealing blue sky and wispy white clouds. Ethan fired at Graves' men. He hit two of them, and they again took cover. Taking advantage of the situation, Ethan hurried to one of the fallen men and checked his pockets. He fired the remaining shots of his weapon, forcing Graves' men to stay in cover, and then grabbed a spare clip from the man's belt. He also found a grenade. He took it and ducked back behind the second jeep just as more bullets rang out around the hold.

Replacing the clip, he returned fire, forcing Graves' men back, and checked on the girls.

Andrea was sitting with her back to the jeep's grill, while Hannah was struggling to get her parachute on. But she was wide-eyed and panicking and her shaking fingers fumbled with the clips.

"We need to get a move on!" he yelled, firing at Graves' men. "Andrea, help her!"

Ethan moved out of cover, moving forward and firing, forcing the men back, giving Hannah time to get her parachute on. Ethan was taking aim at one of Graves' men, who had been caught out in the open, when…

"Drop your weapon, Mr. Jackson!"

Ethan turned with his gun raised and saw Felix Graves, silhouetted against the morning light, with his arm around Hannah's neck, using her as a shield. His gun was pointed at her head.

Ethan, his gun still on Graves, circled toward the ramp, trying to get a shot, but Graves circled with him, keeping Hannah between them. Ethan knew he didn't have the shot. He knew he was just as likely to shoot Hannah as he was Graves.

"Let her go!" he said, though he knew he had no leverage and Graves' men were moving forward, guns raised as they surrounded him.

"I'm a reasonable man, Mr. Jackson," Graves said. "Give me everything you have and I'll let her go."

Ethan glanced around. Behind him and the men circling him, Andrea stood on her own, as if forgotten. Ethan chewed his lip as he tried to think of a way out of this. The hold had pressurised, but the wind still whipped at his clothes. And he still had the grenade cupped in his other hand. He put his thumb in the ring.

"I only have the sceptre," he said. "It was my bargaining tool. Let all of us go and you can have it."

Graves turned and looked at Andrea, who was holding his pack with the sceptre. She stiffened slightly and Ethan wondered if Graves was going to shoot her, but instead, Graves turned back to Ethan and raised his gun. "It's over Mr. Jackson. I have the sceptre and whatever else you have, I can simply take off your dead body."

Ethan dove aside as Graves pulled the trigger, the shot echoing around the hold, but the bullet disappeared into the sky above West Africa. Ethan landed hard and rolled. Pulling the pin on the grenade, he tossed it, arcing it towards Graves. The suited man ducked as it sailed over his head, thumped against the back of the second jeep. It landed on the ground and rolled back.

Graves took aim again but, just as he was about to fire, the grenade beneath the last jeep exploded. The jeep flipped it into the air, slamming into Harris and another man, and they disappeared out of the plane, followed by the ruined jeep.

Ethan's ears rang from the explosion, while black smoke poured out of the second jeep, which caught some of the grenade's blast.

The hold was a cacophony of sirens blaring and people shouting and moving into position. Ethan, still on the ground, watched as Graves' men took aim. In the billowing smoke, he saw something move, and he rolled out of the way just as the second jeep rolled past and down the ramp, tumbling over the edge.

"Ethan!" Hannah screamed.

He turned around just in time to see Graves pulling Hannah to the edge of the ramp, her parachute held uselessly in her hands. "I've had enough of this, Jackson!" he yelled over the rushing wind.

Ethan glanced around. The smoke had cleared, and he was surrounded by Graves' men, all with their weapons drawn.

Andrea stood behind them, watching the event unfold with no emotion. She could run and jump off the plane since she had her parachute strapped on, but Ethan thought she was caught up in the moment. Meanwhile, he was cornered, with no escape and nothing but a handgun and a couple of bullets to protect him. Graves wasn't going to let them go, even if he gave him what was in his pockets. There was no way to MacGyver his way out of this.

It was over. He'd doomed all three of them.

"Don't hurt her," he said, his body tense but his voice defeated.

"I gave you the chance to leave it alone," Graves said coldly, his grip still tight on Hannah's arm, who was fighting uselessly to break out of it. "I gave you the chance to walk away."

"I'll give you everything," Ethan said weakly. "All I have on the treasure… just… please… don't."

"But you pushed it and you pushed it and there is only so much I am willing to take," Graves continued, like Ethan hadn't said anything. His eyes were burning, and Ethan felt a chill run down his spine. "This isn't a game, Jackson. People get hurt. Your parents. Your friends. This is the reality." He looked at Hannah. "This is *your* reality and with it comes consequences you have to live with."

"Don't," Ethan took a step forward just as Graves yanked the parachute out of Hannah's hands and, without another word, shoved her out of the plane.

Thirty Four

Somewhere over Western Africa

"Hannah!"

Ethan fired the remaining bullets in his gun. There were only three, but it was enough to scatter Graves' men. The gun clicked, and he tossed it away.

"Come on!" he shouted to Andrea. He ran to the edge of the ramp and, without a second thought, dove out of the plane, hoping she would follow his lead.

The sun was just above the horizon, the golden hour casting a pinkish-purple haze in the sky, but Ethan had no time to enjoy it. He scanned the sky, trying to find Hannah. He blew through a cloud cluster and was greeted by green fields and forests, brown mountains, and a yellow-orange desert in the distance. Wiping away the condensation, Ethan squinted against the wind tearing at his eyes and kept his head on a swivel, searching for Hannah.

He knew he didn't have much time—maybe somewhere between ninety seconds to two minutes—before he had to pull his chute. It wasn't going to be enough time and desperation set in.

The wind ripped at his clothes and roared in his ears. He wiped his eyes, blinking out the tears, and finally spotted her.

Hannah was thrashing about, spinning out of control and helplessly trying to slow her descent. She was about three hundred metres away and Ethan focused on her flailing body. He sped up his descent by tightening himself into a ball, reducing his body's surface area, and tried to angle himself so he could cut her off. The ground seemed to race toward him, getting alarmingly close as they fell, and Ethan knew he had one chance at this. If he overshot, he wouldn't have the time, or ability, to try again.

He'd halved the distance between them when he opened up, slowing his descent a little. He tried to call out for her, but if Hannah saw or heard him, she gave no sign. He readjusted and tightened himself again and dove toward her, hoping he was on the right trajectory. As he got closer, he heard something else over the roaring of the wind: Hannah's screams.

He watched her, still spinning wildly in the air and swinging her arms as if she was trying to fly.

Almost there.

He was close enough now he could see the fear on her face, her eyes wide open as she screamed and flailed, but she still hadn't seen him.

Almost! He reached out to her, trying to grab her and pull her in, but he was going too fast and they collided. He grabbed hold of her, but the impact of tackling her in mid-air caused him to tumble as well, and he lost his grip. They were both spinning wildly out of control now, like they were on a tilt-a-whirl, the view switching between the sky and ground as they fell.

Ground.

Sky.

Ground.

Sky.

Ethan reached out and grabbed at Hannah again while she was clawing at him, grabbing hold of anything her hands could find: arms, legs, face, hair, anything.

Finally, he grabbed hold of her arm and pull her toward him, embracing her in an awkward bear hug.

"Hold on!" he shouted, and he felt her grab his jacket. He pulled her closer, encouraging her to wrap her arms around his body and loop them between the pack and his back until she held on fiercely. He freed one hand, grabbed hold of the ripcord handle, and once again shouted, "Hold on!" and pulled.

The parachute burst from the pack and spread out above them, catching in the air.

There was a jolt as their descent slowed suddenly.

Hannah's grip was jerked free, and she screamed as she slid, and only Ethan's hold on her prevented her from slipping away. She grabbed his legs as tight as she could. He told her to grab the harnesses, that he needed his legs free for the landing, but she either didn't hear him, didn't want to risk letting go, or was too scared to move.

Whatever the reason, Ethan wasn't going to force it. There was still a risk of slipping.

They were a close to a hundred metres from the ground, and Ethan relaxed a little. His heart was pounding in his chest and he tried taking deep breaths while he navigated with the steering lines. He took in their surroundings, looking for an open area to land. They were following a river that snaked north, which Ethan thought was the Niger. Around the river were green areas that gradually turned rocky, dusty, and hilly as they moved away from the river. The river fed into a lake that was surrounded by green trees and grass, and continued north toward the sandy desert. Deciding it was the softest place to land and that he needed to get Hannah down safely, he pulled on the handles and aimed for the desert west of the snaking river.

They had just cleared the last of the treetops from the lake when Ethan told Hannah they were about to land. She didn't respond, just kept holding on to his harness and legs, her face buried in his thigh.

As soon as Hannah's feet touched the sandy ground, she let go, falling into a heap on the soft sand. Ethan carried on for another thirty metres before he landed. He slid to a stop, and as quickly as he could, he unbuckled the harnesses and shook himself out of the pack, letting the breeze blow it away.

He hurried back to Hannah. When he got to her, he found her lying in the sand, curled up into a ball, her body shuddering, and he heard quiet sobs escaping from her tight cocoon.

"Hannah," he whispered, putting a hand on her shoulder.

"Hannah. It's ok. You're safe now."

Hannah's body shook, but she didn't react.

"Hannah," he tried again. "Hannah… Han…?"

Suddenly, Hannah lunged for him and buried her face deep into his chest.

"Thank you," she whispered, repeating it over and over. He felt her hot tears soaking through his jacket as the shock and adrenaline of all that happened wore off.

They were safe, but he knew she would no doubt relive the last week on repeat.

How does anyone recover from this?

Ethan felt guilty and ashamed and sad for her all at once. It was his fault that she was in this situation. His fault that she got kidnapped. His fault that she got tossed out of a plane. And it was his fault they were stuck in the middle of nowhere in West Africa.

"I'm sorry," he said, feeling the first tear trickling down his face. "I am so, so sorry, Han."

They sat on their knees in the sand, embracing each other as he ran his hand through her hair, trying to calm her.

Trying to calm himself.

He didn't know how long they were like that, but he watched the sun continue to rise over the horizon through blurry eyes. Eventually, Hannah pulled away, wiping her eyes with the sleeve of her jacket. Ethan looked at her, taking in her red-rimmed eyes, her ragged blond hair, and her dirty clothes from days of travel without change.

"Did Graves hurt you?" he asked.

She shook her head. "No. No, he just questioned me and

Andrea. He's obsessed with finding this treasure."

Andrea!

Ethan looked to the sky, as if expecting Andrea to be landing any second now, but he saw only blue sky and puffs of white clouds. He looked back at Hannah, who was looking at him with a puzzled expression.

"She should have jumped after me," he explained. "I guess they stopped her." He sighed. "We need to get going," he said, getting to his feet.

"Go where?" Hannah asked, remaining on her knees.

He looked at her. "I need to find the treasure."

Hannah sighed. "Of course… the treasure. I should have known."

"What?" he asked.

"First Ritchie and now you."

"What?"

Hannah ran a hand through her tangled hair. "Ritchie was the same—consumed by finding lost treasures, selling them on the black market for riches—and look where that got him."

Ethan looked at her blankly and she continued, "Why do you think he's in so much debt?"

"Bad investment choices?" he said lamely.

"Trying to fund these stupid hunts of his, and thinking he can get that one find that will set him up for life."

"Look, I get it. But I'm trying to find out what happened to my parents, trying to finish what they started. I owe it to them. It's what they would have wanted."

"You told me on the boat that your parents tried to hide

everything they found. They wanted you safe and happy, not doing this."

She's right.

"I still need to save Andrea," he protested.

"Then call the authorities."

"Look around, there's no phone coverage. We're probably closer to the treasure than a working phone, and I need to stop Graves before he gets to it."

"Why?" Hannah sat back in the sand, and Ethan took a seat beside her.

"Look, I just need to do right by you and Andrea. Han, I—"

"Don't," she interrupted. She swallowed and continued, "Don't do that, Ethan. Don't lie. Not to me and, certainly, not to yourself."

"Listen, Han—"

She gave him a look.

"—nah," he amended. "I got you both into this mess, and I need to get you both out of it. I owe you that much."

"I've heard this all before, Ethan. Ritchie told me that exact same thing a hundred times, and each time it was a lie. An excuse. It was always about the treasure—the 'big score', as he put it. Something to pay for his debts and my college and a better life and many other things. They're all lies, Ethan. All of them. They're justifications to ease your conscience and ignore what it really is: greed."

"But—"

"The funny thing is," she continued. "I never wanted him to do that. I just wanted him to be around. I wanted to have someone there for me since I was all alone. But I guess even that was too much to ask for."

Ethan was stunned, shocked by the raw emotion coming from her, and his protestations died in his throat. Here she was, revealing to him, a stranger, someone she had known for just over a week, someone who had come into her life and turned it upside down, something she must have had held inside of her for a long time.

He reached out and put his hand on hers. "I know I've said this before, but I truly mean it: I'm sorry," he said, as if those two simple words could fix everything that happened. It felt hollow, even to him.

She pulled her hand free and stood up. "Which way?"

"The Niger River is east of us. If we follow it north, we should get close to Lake Faguibine."

"Let's go," she said and began heading towards the river.

Ethan stood and watched her walk away.

Ethan, you utter fool.

The terrain had changed from desert to rocky to hilly to green and lush before they reached the Niger River an hour later. The Niger River was the longest river in West Africa. It started in the Guinea Highlands and travelled through Guinea, Mali, Benin, and Niger before discharging in the Niger Delta in Nigeria.

Using the photos he took of the map in Cabo Verde as a guide, Ethan led the way along the clear, silt-free river. They marched in silence for the better part of the day, not only to save energy, but they seemingly had nothing to say. Ethan was grateful for the silence since he could focus on the task at hand: trying to get Andrea back before Graves hurt her. He knew they had to get there before Graves to give himself a chance to scout the area or even find the treasure first and trade it for Andrea's life.

Hopefully, destroying the jeeps would delay Graves a little.

His mind turned to the treasure. He couldn't lie. The idea of finding appealed to him. Who *wouldn't* it appeal to?

He glanced back at Hannah. She was only half a dozen steps behind, sweat pouring off her brow, and he got his answer.

But it was secondary to making sure they survived this. He wasn't lying when he said he had to get them both and Andrea out of this.

Or are you?

His mind wandered, and he imagined himself discovering the treasure. Imagined himself being the first person in almost three hundred years to lay eyes on Blackbeard's famous treasure. There was definitely an appeal to it, and he could see why Ritchie, and even his parents, did it.

It was something he needed to think about it when all this was over.

If you get out of it alive…

They walked on. The sun was on its way down when Hannah, trailing behind him, broke the silence. "What's that?"

Ethan stopped and turned around. Hannah stood a way behind him and was pointing to the trees away from the river. He walked back to her to see what she was pointing at.

"I can't see anything," he said, looking into the green foliage.

She pulled him closer until they were almost cheek-to-cheek. "Follow my finger. You see the clearing between those two tall trees?"

Ethan followed her finger and saw what she was pointing at. There was a cluster of branches and what looked to be straw or long grass high up, but angling down towards the ground. "It looks like a hut."

"Let's go look," she said. Without waiting for him, she began trudging through the bushes and grass, making enough noise to alert anyone within earshot of their presence. He sighed and followed in her tracks until they emerged into the open space a couple of minutes later.

"Whoa," said Ethan, looking around. They were in a village. In front of them were ten huts with mud walls and thatched roofs of straw set in a semicircle. Some huts had collapsed, their walls and roofs fallen in.

"You were right," Hannah told him. "It is a hut."

"*Was* a hut," Ethan corrected. He walked around the village circle, passing shelters made from thick tree branches and roofs of straw. He saw a rock outline for a vegetable garden, and pens made of thick branches for livestock.

"It looks abandoned," he said, approaching a stone well in the middle of the clearing. He looked down, but it was too dark to see anything. There was a rope attached leading down into the well, so he grabbed it and pulled, realising he hadn't eaten or drank anything since arriving in Cabo Verde.

That feels like an age ago, he thought as he kept pulling, feeling the weight of something as he did. He pulled up a metal bucket, sloshing with water. He grabbed the handle and pulled it out, resting it on the ground.

The water looked clear and clean, and he dipped his hands into the bucket, cupped them, and brought them to his lips. He took a sip.

"Tastes good," he said to Hannah. "Metallic. But that's normal, isn't it?" It was then realised he had no idea what tainted water tasted like, so he continued to drink it, savouring the coolness as it travelled down his dry throat.

"You sure that's safe?" Hannah asked.

"At this point, I don't care," he said. "But it tastes fine, and you must be thirsty."

He moved aside, allowing Hannah to take a seat next to him. She cupped her hands in the bucket and brought out some water. She hesitated and then put her hands to her lips and drank it, deciding it was better than dehydration.

They sat there drinking it for the next ten minutes. Once finished, Ethan explored the huts. The ones he could access had one room with tattered animal hides or straw for beds. Some had buckets and stools and tables, but all were deserted, and based on the thick layers of dust and the cobwebs in the corners, they had been for some time. Finding nothing useful, he exited the last of the huts and returned to Hannah, who was sitting with her back against the well, watching the sky turn from yellow to orange.

"When I was a little girl," she started as he sat down next to her, "my dad would take me to the park after he finished work. He'd push me on the swings and watch me play on the slide.

After what felt like hours, we'd sit on a park bench and watch the sunset, seeing the colours change like they are now. I asked him why they changed, and he told me that ending the day with these beautiful colours was a reminder that no matter what happened, there was still beauty in the world."

"Do you think it helped?" Ethan asked.

Hannah considered and then said, "I think so. It helped me accept my parents' deaths. It helped me mourn and move on. I don't live wishing I could have them back, or wishing I could tell them I love them one last time, because it wasn't possible."

Ethan thought about this. He'd wished for the same things with his parents many times over, but he didn't voice this. Not because he didn't want to, but because he didn't want to ruin the moment. Hannah continued, "I don't believe you when you say it's not about the treasure, but I think you are right about trying to save Andrea. If we left it up to the authorities to help her, I don't think they would believe us, and even if they did, it might be too late." She shuddered. "That man is evil, and I don't think he would let her live if he does find the treasure."

Ethan nodded. "Felix Graves is a cold, ruthless killer who has an incredible right hook."

"You are sporting quite the shiner there," Hannah said with the hint of a smile.

Ethan put his hand to his eye and winced at the pain around his eye and cheek.

"Wait here," she said, getting up and hurrying to the huts. She returned a minute later with a piece of cloth. "Lie back," she said, and Ethan did as instructed, lying on the dusty, rocky ground.

"This is not very comfortable," he complained.

"Shush," she admonished.

"Gee, if this is going to be your bedside manner when you're a doctor, I'll take my injuries elsewhere," he teased.

"Put your head in my lap then, you big baby," she shot back, though there was a faint smile on her lips. She put the cloth in the bucket of water and pulled it out, wringing it, and then dunked it again and put it on his sore eye.

He hissed in pain.

"It won't do much," she said. "But it might help the swelling a little."

"Is this what those big text books teach you? How to tend to a swollen eye?" he said with a grin.

Hannah smiled. "Something like that."

Ethan lay there, watching her with his good eye while she dabbed at his other. "You know, you have a really nice smile," he said and closed his eyes.

Ethan lay there enjoying the rest as Hannah dabbed at his eye and cheek, wiping away the dried blood. It felt nice. He had almost dozed off when Hannah asked, "Do you think you will ever find out the truth about what happened to your parents?"

Ethan mumbled something, and Hannah nudged his leg. He opened his eyes to find her staring at him intently. He avoided eye contact with her and watched the darkening sky, which was now a deep purple, and then said, "Dad is dead, Mum probably is as well."

It was a tough thing for him to say, and he didn't want to

believe it, but he knew it was the truth. No matter where this journey took him, he knew they were not coming back. "When or where or how doesn't really matter anymore. They died searching for this treasure, and I think Graves had something to do with it. That's what I need to find out."

"Just don't let it consume you, Ethan," Hannah said as she put the cloth in the bucket to rinse it and then put it back on his eye. "I've seen what it did to Ritchie. I don't want it to happen to you."

"It won't. Look around. Turns out I'm not very good at this treasure hunting crap."

"On the contrary, you have gotten further than anyone else has, including your parents. It pains me to say it, but you might be great at it."

Ethan snorted, but said nothing.

"I got the impression it was more than just treasure to him."

"Who?"

"Graves."

"What do you mean?"

Hannah moved her head from side-to-side as if trying to shake loose something in her mind. "I don't know exactly, but he spoke of it as if he was going to sell it."

"Sell it?" he repeated. "I figured he'd use it to buy weapons. His group does fund terrorists, or at least provide them weapons."

"He does?"

Ethan nodded, dislodging the cloth. "The man he dealt with at the airport in Cabo Verde is Farid Abboud, a terrorist from Yemen."

Hannah put the cloth back on his eye. "How do you know that?"

"Abigail told me."

"Abigail?"

"Oh, right, I suppose you wouldn't know about her." He explained how she saved his life in Cape Town and Cabo Verde and helped him get on the plane. He finished by telling Hannah that Abigail was following him because she had an interest in Felix Graves.

"Who does she work for?" Hannah asked after Ethan finished talking.

"Mossad, apparently."

"'Apparently'? You don't believe her?"

Ethan shook his head, dislodging the cloth again. "Not really. Neither does Ritchie."

"Why?"

"For one thing, she's German. When we were being shot at in Cabo Verde—"

"Shot at?"

"—she said *Scheisse,* which is German for—"

"Shit."

Ethan smiled. "I think she works for Interpol."

"Why wouldn't she tell you that?"

"No idea."

"And you still trust her?"

Ethan nodded. "As much as I can, I suppose. She plays her cards close to her chest and is a bit miserly when it comes to information, but she's saved my life twice."

"Maybe she has a crush on you," Hannah teased.

"There are much easier ways to get my attention," he said with a drowsy chuckle.

Hannah laughed. "Lost treasure. Terrorists. Interpol. What the heck have you gotten me into, Ethan Jackson?"

Ethan chuckled with her. "I seriously have no idea."

She stood up, dropping the rag on his face. "I think I am delirious if I find this life-and-death situation funny."

"Laughter is the best medicine, doctor."

"Yeah, ok Patch Adams."

Ethan got up, tossing the rag aside. His eye was damp and tender like a raw steak. "I think we should sleep here tonight. No one has been here for a long time, and there are some mats in the hut. We should be safe."

"What about Andrea?"

"Graves is going to need to new vehicles since the jeeps fell out of the plane. It may give us some time. Either way, it's too dangerous to go walking around at night and we need the rest."

Hannah nodded in agreement, and they walked back to the huts, finding the most suitable one for them to sleep in as night descended.

Thirty Five

Somewhere in Western Africa

They woke at sunrise the next morning, stiff and sore. Ethan didn't have a great sleep on the rough, uneven ground, and Hannah spent the night tossing and turning and crying out in her sleep. Ethan felt a pang of guilt, wishing there was something more he could do to help.

"Your eye is looking better," Hannah said, touching it and causing Ethan to flinch.

"Funny, it doesn't feel better."

The day was cloudy and promised rain as they headed back to the river, where they disturbed a herd of Dorcas gazelle drinking on the other side of the riverbank. The reddish-brown animals brought their heads up from the water and looked at them as if deciding whether or not they were a threat. Determining they were not, the gazelles went back to drinking, and Ethan and Hannah continued following the river north.

At mid-morning, the river turned sharply to the east, forcing them to leave the lush green riverbank and enter the arid, dusty landscape. They trudged on, passing mesas that looked like floating islands in a sea of rocks and dust.

It was an hour later when they found another abandoned village. The huts were similar to the ones from the day before, but bigger and spaced out among the open plain. There was no well and nothing in the huts.

"Another abandoned village," Hannah said.

"Yep, looks like this one has been abandoned longer than the other one."

"I wonder why."

Ethan had no answer, and his best guess was that it was no longer viable to live here, so the community moved on. "We better keep going," he said. "We still have a long way to go."

It was raining heavily when they found another abandoned village. Ethan's phone battery died hours ago and with no map, they decided it was best to rest and wait out the rain.

They hurried into the closest hut and wiped the rain off their faces and shook out their hair.

"Naturally, we get the rainiest day in the desert," Ethan joked, watching the rain pool around the huts. When Hannah didn't say anything, he looked over to her to find her backed up to the wall, standing rigid with her mouth wide open.

"Hannah? What's wrong?" Ethan asked.

She pointed behind him, and he spun around and jumped in surprise. "Jesus!"

There were two bodies at the back of the hut, one of them on a mat and the other sitting against the wall. Ethan approached them while Hannah stayed back.

"What's—what's wrong with them?" she asked.

He knelt beside the one on the mat. "I'm not sure," he said, then went over to the other one sitting against the wall. Both bodies wore the tattered remnants of blue clothing, torn and moth-eaten over the years. "But I've seen this before," Ethan told her.

Both bodies were shrivelled up, their skin aged like leather and a dark ash-like colour. Their heads were the size of a baby's, which looked somewhat comical on adult-sized bodies, and their limbs were drawn in, bent at the elbows and knees at odd angles.

"You have? Where?"

"Ritchie and I found some pirates and Maynard's men in a similar condition at his hideout in the Inaccessible Island."

Hannah gathered up her courage and walked to him. "They look like shrunken heads."

Ethan nodded. "They do, but they can't be. It's not something practised in Africa. It's a South American thing, more specifically in the Amazon."

"Then what happened?"

Ethan shrugged. "You know more about this kind of stuff

than I do. What do you think?"

Hannah seemed reluctant to get any closer, and Ethan said, "Have you not seen a dead body before?"

"Of course I have! Just… didn't expect to find one in a hut in the middle of Africa looking like a prune."

"Well, then consider this a medical find of a lifetime. Something to put you on the front of the New England Journal of Medicine." He spread his arms out like he was displaying an imaginary sign. "Hannah Coetzee, medical archaeologist."

"Medical archaeologist? Seriously?"

Ethan smiled at her. "It's a thing."

"It's not."

"But it could be."

She rolled her eyes. "Fine," she said and knelt beside him. Ethan watched as she looked over the body, unwilling to touch it without any gloves or protective equipment. "Based on bone structure, I would say they were adults, both men. The limbs at that angle… it's like the muscles shrunk and not just in their arms and legs but their whole body. The head, I'm not sure, but their skulls have been crushed."

She pointed to a spot at the back of the head of the one sitting against the wall. "You can see fractured parts of the skull poking through the skin."

"What could cause something like this?"

Hannah shook her head. "I've not read anything like this before. I've read about muscular dystrophy and stiff person syndrome, even amyotrophic lateral sclerosis, but nothing to the extent that it would shrivel them up and crush their skull."

"You will not find it in any of your medical books," said a heavily accented voice from behind them.

Both Hannah and Ethan spun around in fright to find a man standing in the doorway. He was wearing a rain-soaked blue robe with a tagelmust covering his face. Through the gap in his veil, he had dark eyes and weathered, dark skin. Leaning on his shoulder was a Winchester 1912 shotgun.

"Fear not, friends," the man said when he saw them eyeing the shotgun. "I use this only for protection."

"Well, you have no need to fear us," Ethan said cautiously.

"It is not you I fear," the man said.

Ethan gestured to the two bodies behind them. "What happened to them?"

"Best not to talk here," he said, looking around like he thought they were being listened to. "Come with me. I will take you to my village. It is not far."

"Thanks for the offer, but we're kind of on the clock here," Ethan said.

The man looked at him, and Ethan could hear the humour in his voice when he said, "Do not worry, my friend. The treasure can wait."

Thirty Six

"What happened to them?"

"Where are you taking us?"

"What is your name?"

Despite the questions, the man was true to his word. He would not answer any question, which frustrated Ethan as they followed him away from the abandoned village. No matter what Ethan asked him, he would simply tell him to wait until they got to his village. The only thing that stopped him from telling the man to shove it was that they were heading north, which meant they were getting closer to Lake Faguibine. The rain continued to pour, and they were all soaked to the bone by the time they reached his village just before midday.

Like all the others they had visited, this one consisted of several mud huts with thatched straw roofs. But this village was clearly occupied. There were vegetable patches and goats and sheep penned behind fences as well as clothes hanging from lines attached to the huts.

Despite the rain, children wearing blue tops and pants ran about playing soccer, while adults in similar blue clothing tended to the needs of their livestock. The man greeted others speaking a language that Ethan thought sounded like Tamasheq or Berber.

"This way, my friends," the man said, pointing to a central hut that looked to be slightly bigger than the rest. Inside, they were greeted with simple but colourful furnishings; mats and hangings, cushions, and rugs, in greens, yellows, reds, and blacks, but the predominant colour was indigo blue. In the middle, a pot was sitting over a fire, and the smells made Ethan's stomach rumble. He glanced at Hannah, who looked like she was ready to dip her hands into the pot and eat whatever was inside.

"Please sit and warm yourselves," the man said. He handed them metal dishes and a ladle. "Help yourself, it's Alabadja."

Ethan took the ladle and spooned out a mixture of rice and beef on a buttery sauce and his mouth watered at the strong, spicy aroma. He served some on Hannah's plate and then his own. He offered some for the man, but he shook his head. "I'll have some later."

Ethan ate a small sample of beef and decided it was delicious, so he dug in, using his fingers. While he wasn't sure about the prudence of eating food from a stranger, he doubted the man would have brought them here just to kill them.

"So, who are you?" Ethan asked between mouthfuls of rice.

"My name is Amastan. I am what you would consider an elder of the village," he said.

"Ethan," Ethan said to introduce himself, and then pointed to Hannah. "And this is Han... Hannah."

Amastan nodded his greeting and said, "So, you are looking for the treasure of Blackbeard?"

"You know of it?"

"I do."

"Do you know where it is?"

"I know where it rests, yes."

"In Lake Faguibine."

Amastan nodded. "That is correct." If he was surprised that Ethan knew the location, he didn't show it.

Ethan and Hannah exchanged glances. "How did you know we were looking for it?"

"There would be no other reason for you to be here, and your arrival was certainly... strange," Amastan said, handing them a clay cup. It was then that Ethan noticed his hands. They were stained blue, and it triggered a memory.

"The Blue Men of the Desert," he said.

"You have heard of us?"

"To some degree. Your people helped Robert Maynard hide the treasure."

Amastan nodded again. "We are of the Tuareg people, nomads wandering the desert. Maynard came to my ancestors asking for their help to hide it. At the time, they did not know what it was, but they helped him."

"Can you take us to it?"

"No."

"Why?"

"That treasure has been cursed by vodun."

"'Vodun'?" asked Hannah.

"You Westerners might call it 'voodoo,'" Amastan said.

Ethan put his dish down. "Maynard said the treasure was 'voodoo-cursed.' What did he mean?"

"I think he translated 'vodun' incorrectly," Amastan said, and he fished for something in his pocket and held it up for them to see. It was a Spanish gold real, stamped 1508.

"These are the coins Robert Maynard brought to my people."

Ethan fished out the coins from his pocket and showed them to him. "I know, I have two of—"

"No!" Amastan shouted, jumping back in fright. In a flash, he had his shotgun and was pointing it at Ethan.

Hannah cried out, ducking out of the way while Ethan raised his hands. "Whoa! What the hell?"

"Where did you get that?" Amastan asked, his eyes wide with terror.

"I found it."

"Where?" he demanded.

"In England."

"How long ago?"

Ethan was perplexed. "I don't know. Why?"

"How *long?*"

Ethan swallowed. The man was on edge. "A week or so," he said.

"Have you been feeling okay? Any feelings of weakness or pains? Anger issues?"

"No. Why would I?"

Even under his tagelmust, Amastan looked visibly relieved. He lowered the shotgun and leaned it against the wall. "I am sorry, my friend. But what you are holding is a vodun-cursed coin. When a person comes into contact with one, they go weak. It could affect a person immediately or after a day, but anyone afflicted with the vodun will go into a rage, becoming violent as their body changes. Then, after some days, a week, the body wears down, changes, and they die."

Ethan thought about this. He remembered the bodies he found at the Inaccessible Island, which were like the ones in the village. Both groups had access to the coins.

"The muscles atrophy and the head shrinks, cracking their skull, right?" Hannah said.

Amastan nodded.

"Fascinating," Hannah whispered.

"How do you know all this?" Ethan asked.

"My people helped Robert Maynard hide the cursed treasure. The knowledge of this and the location was handed down to a select few of my people, and for generations, we lived as if it never existed. But when I was a little boy, some of my people discovered the location, purely by accident, and brought handfuls of the gold coins into the villages.

"They handed them out to their family, sharing them with each other. They thought we were rich, that we could live a life of luxury, but some coins were the vodun coins. Not long after bringing it to the village, they suffered the curse. They raged throughout their village, killing others, and then turned on other villages, attacking them. I was just a little boy when they came, but I remember it so well. I was playing with my brothers when they attacked like a pride of crazed lions. They would punch, kick, claw, pull, rip at anything they could grab at, all the while screaming these inhumane sounds of pain.

"My father pulled me away and passed me to my mother, and she ran with me and my brothers and another family. We returned at nightfall hoping to find any sign of those who attacked us, but instead, we found homes destroyed and bodies beaten and bloodied, mashed to a pulp—including my father."

"The village you found us in?"

"That was my home."

Ethan closed his eyes. *So many families destroyed because of this treasure.*

"I'm sorry," he said. "What causes this to happen?"

"I do not know," Amastan said, shaking his head.

"That doesn't seem possible," Hannah said. "You're saying this disease is transmitted by touching these coins—coins that have been around for centuries—which reduces a person into a rage before shrivelling their bodies? Something like that would be known in the medical world."

Amastan shook his head. "The world is full of medical mysteries. Western medicine doesn't believe in vodun or curses, but you have seen the bodies and even admitted that you yourself cannot understand it."

"Well, yes, but I'm not a doctor."

"Yet you have seen it with your own eyes."

"But there must be an explanation!"

Ethan interrupted before the argument got heated. "Amastan, dangerous men are coming for the treasure."

Amastan looked at him through the slit in his tagelmust. "There are always greedy men looking for treasure."

"Not these men. They don't want the treasure—they want the disease that comes with it."

"What are you talking about?" Hannah asked.

"You told me yesterday that Graves wanted to sell the treasure, which didn't make much sense to me. But he was particularly interested in the bodies we found at the Inaccessible Island. I thought he was just being a creep, but what if he wants to weaponise whatever this disease is? Create a disease or virus or whatever that causes these people to go into a murderous rage, killing others, and sell that on the black market? Think about it. Abigail said he was an arms broker, and just last night he provided Abboud with a bomb. But if he can weaponise this disease, then he stands to make a hundred times more on the black market than what the treasure alone could get him."

He turned to Amastan. "I cannot let these people get their hands on it. They can't be far away. Either you can take us there, or we go alone. I won't ask you to come with me, but I must get there before they do."

Amastan was silent for a long while before he asked, "If I take you there and you find the treasure, what will you do then?"

Ethan glanced at Hannah and then blew out the breath he had been holding. "I have no idea. I just know Felix Graves can't take it."

The Blue Man of the Desert looked at him as if trying to decide his intentions, and Ethan gave it one last attempt. "Look, if we don't get there first, then what we saw at your villages could happen on a global scale. What if it gets into the hands of people who would happily use it against you or your family, unleashing a genocide on your people? What if they do it for no other reason than to use you as political fodder? A point to be made so others get what they want? We can't let that happen."

Amastan sighed and walked to where his Winchester was sitting against the wall. He picked it up and slung it over his shoulder. "Come on."

Thirty Seven

The rain finally stopped when Amastan brought them to a halt near the lake.

"Rare to have such rain here," he said, looking up at the sky.

Water had settled on the arid land, creating puddles and miniature waterfalls poured off the mesas that surrounded them.

"This is as far as I will take you," he told them.

"Where is the entrance?"

Amastan shook his head. "I do not know. We have kept this hidden from everyone, even ourselves, to resist temptation."

That wouldn't stop Felix Graves, Ethan knew. He would tear this place apart until he found Blackbeard's treasure.

"All right, we'll take it from here. Thank you for your help,

Amastan," Ethan said, holding out his hand.

Amastan shook his hand and said, "Allahu ysalmak." Then he let go, turned around, and returned back the way they came, Winchester still dangling from his shoulder.

They watched him leave and Hannah said, "That might have been the strangest encounter I have ever had."

"He could have let us borrow his shotgun," Ethan muttered.

They turned and headed for the lake, splashing through the puddles of water. They passed trees, those closest to lakes still with green leaves, and mesas and buttes that rose out of the ground like natural columns. They walked along a narrow track between a mesa on the right and a depression on the left. The depression was where Lake Faguibine, and surrounding lakes, connected with the Niger River. Ethan took a right, Hannah close behind, and they crested a rise that gave them an elevated view of the lake.

"There's no way we can search all of this before Graves gets here," Hannah said when they saw the size of the lake. She was right, the lake was huge. The shape of a right-angled triangle, the lake measured seventy-five kilometres at the longest point and fifteen at the widest. The lake was partially full, and dotted around the shore were locals who were using the lakebed to grow burgu millet, whose seeds they used for food and other crops.

Ethan agreed. "We can probably eliminate most of the area since it's wide open with heavy traffic and, clearly, no treasure about."

"Then where do we start?"

Ethan scanned the lake and the surrounding area. It was

mostly desert, the dusty Sahara expanding out in front of them. There were small lakes to the right of them, and mesas and rocky ground surrounded them on all other sides.

"This is a needle in a haystack," he said, shielding his eyes against the sun.

"Do you still have Maynard's compass?" Hannah asked.

"Good thinking," Ethan said and pulled the compass from his pocket and opened it. The needle was pointing west to a cluster of mesas at the head of the lake.

"This way," he said.

Walking along the lake, they rounded the shoreline, letting the compass lead them, until they reached the mesa cluster.

"The needle is pointing to the interior of this mesa," Ethan said as they walked. "The way in must be here somewhere."

They searched for an area, trying to find the way in, but all they found were rocks and dust.

"Well, that's no surprise," Ethan said, wiping sweat from his forehead. The humidity had risen, and with the cloud cover, it felt like a sauna. "If it were down here, then someone would have stumbled upon it."

"Then what do you suggest?" Hannah asked, her hair matted to her head.

Ethan looked at the compass, "It says it's here. At this cluster."

"Maybe it isn't here," Hannah suggested. "Maybe the compass is wrong."

Ethan shook his head. The compass hadn't been wrong yet. Why would that change now? He looked around and then up, and idea coming to him.

He turned to Hannah, "How do you feel about climbing?"

Sweat was pouring off them when they reached the top of the mesa. It wasn't a hard climb. There were plenty of handholds and ledges to rest on, but exhaustion from the past week and the heat made for slow progress.

"Graves can't be too far away," Hannah said, resting against a large rock.

Ethan agreed. It had been well over twenty-four hours since they had landed, and even with minimal rest, they would have to be a couple of hours away by now.

"Hopefully Abigail could do something at the airport to stop him. Or, at least, delay him."

"Do you remember if the map had the entrance on it?"

Ethan shook his head. "I don't think so. It just pinpointed the lake as the location."

"So it's a needle in a haystack?"

"Pretty much."

Hannah sighed and got up. "Let's keep looking then."

They split up. They searched the top of the mesa. Ethan lost track of time as followed the compass, searching around the Lake Faguibine side. Hannah was working her way toward Lake Kamango when she called out, "Ethan!"

He looked up and saw her waving to him near the far end of the mesa. He hurried over to her.

"Look at this," she said when he arrived. She was kneeling

next to a large boulder running parallel to the mesa edge, and underneath it, in the shadows, were markings. The markings were faded, but there was no mistaking the familiar indigo blue they'd been painted in.

"Doesn't that look like a constellation to you?" she asked.

Ethan knelt beside her to get a closer look. There were fifteen points in the shape of a sea monster. "I think you're right. In fact, I think it's—"

"Cetus," Hannah finished.

He looked at the compass and then back at her and smiled, feeling the excitement rise within him. "This must be it! Let's see if there is a way in."

They each circled the boulder, taking a different direction and looking for anything out of place, but by the time they met halfway, they had found nothing. They continued, double-checking if the other had missed something.

"Anything?" Ethan asked when they met at the Cetus mark.

"Nothing," Hannah said.

"It *has* to be here."

"Ethan, it's been decades since anyone has been here. For all we know, it's buried under a pile of rocks or in the sediment or a flood carried it away. We don't even know what we are looking for."

Ethan sighed, acknowledging her point. He looked out over the lake and to the Sahara beyond, wondering if the treasure was buried under an impossible amount of sand.

It has to be here. All this way for nothing, it just can't be, he thought and leaned back against the boulder.

"Whoa!" Ethan cried out as he felt the sensation of falling and instinctively shot his hands out to grab something.

"What's wrong?" Hannah asked.

"I... I think the boulder just moved."

"What?"

The boulder towered over him and he pushed on it, feeling it rock slightly back and forth. "Yeah, it's definitely moving. Give me a hand."

Hannah put her hands on the boulder, and on Ethan's count, they pushed. It moved forward and then rocked back like a pendulum. They continued pushing it, going with the momentum until it reached a tipping point and fell over with a heavy crash and kicking up a cloud of rock dust and sand.

"The underside is curved like an egg," Ethan said, looking at the base of the boulder. "It's like a cradle—give it enough of a push and it will rock. Fascinating."

"Ethan, look at this," Hannah said. She was looking down at where the boulder used to be, and in its place was a hole with a rope attached to the side that led down into the gloom.

"You found the entrance!"

Thirty Eight

They looked in the hole. Crisscrossing pinpoints of light filtered through the cracks in the mesa and provided them with enough light to see that it opened into a vast cavern.

Ethan grabbed the rope, and as he was about to go climb over the lip, Hannah grabbed his arm. "Are you sure it's safe?"

"Sure. Why wouldn't it be?"

"Because it's a centuries-old rope that has been somewhat exposed to the elements for the entire time. It could easily snap."

"It'll be fine. Rope back then was basically indestructible." Before she could protest, he slipped over the edge and slowly let himself down the rope. After a minute, his feet hit the ground, and he called up, "Told you it was safe," his voice echoing in the vast cavern. "You can come down."

Hannah called out something he didn't catch, but he was certain it was nothing flattering. He watched her easily shimmy down the rope. When she landed next to him, he looked at her expectantly. "Well?" he asked when she stared back at him.

"Well, what?"

"Something to say?"

She rolled her eyes. "You got lucky."

"Not at all," he said, grabbing the rope and giving it a couple of hard tugs.

On the last tug, he felt the rope slacken as it snapped somewhere above them. The rope coiled at his feet until the broken end landed on the ground, and Ethan stood there holding the useless length of rope in his hand.

"Don't make them like they used to, huh?" Hannah said sarcastically.

"I don't know the first thing about ropes," Ethan admitted. "I just needed you down here."

She punched him in the shoulder. "You're an ass."

"Ow," he mocked, rubbing his shoulder. He looked around. The cavern disappeared into the darkness, with a steep drop to their left and a path ahead of them leading away, deeper into the mesa.

"Let's go. Watch where you walk," he pointed to the drop next to them. "Don't want to fall down that."

"What about light?"

"We'll be fine," he said and led the way. Hannah was following him so closely that he could hear her every breath. The guilt he felt for getting her into this situation arose again.

Somehow, I'll make it up to her. And Andrea. We just have to get out of this first.

The path led them downward, and if Ethan's sense of direction was correct, they were heading towards the lake.

Suddenly, there was a loud crack that reverberated off the walls of the cavern.

Hannah grabbed his arm. "What was that?" she whispered.

A rumbling sound followed soon after, and Ethan realised what it was. "Thunder," he said. "I guess more rain is on the way."

She let go of his arm and said, "Sorry."

Ethan chuckled. "No need. Scared me, too," he lied.

They continued forward, guided by the light that was getting fainter the deeper they went. The path widened as they walked, and Ethan felt safer as it did.

"Do you think we can make our way back?" Hannah asked after they had walked in silence for a while.

"Maybe, why?"

"Well, we are running out of light, and we can't bump our way around here hoping to find the treasure, can we?"

"We won't bump into any—"

Ethan walked face first into something solid, smashing his forehead and nose.

"Shit!" he groaned, rubbing his nose. His eyes watered, and he dabbed at his nose with his hand, expecting blood.

"You okay?"

"Yeah, just great," he said, his voice nasally as he pinched his

434

nose closed with two fingers. "What the hell did I walk into?"

Hannah moved past him, and in the darkness, he could barely see that she had her arms out. "It feels like... wood... a door."

"A door? Good. Doors are good."

"Doors *are* good," she agreed. "But how are we going to get in?"

"I don't know," he said, stepping back. As he did, his heel caught on something and he fell backward, landing on his backside.

He sighed while Hannah laughed. It was a genuine laugh that echoed around the cavern, and he liked the way it sounded.

"I'm having a good run," he grumbled. It was too dark to see, and his hands searched the rough ground until they came upon something long and narrow but lightly rough to touch, like fine sandpaper. He followed it upward until it changed direction, leading up and away from him. He continued to feel along the length until he felt something else— a different texture.

Cloth?

He rubbed it between his fingers. It was coarse and thick, definitely a cloth of some kind. Continuing up and following the cloth, his fingers found empty space and then something else. Whatever it was, it felt similar to what he felt before, but it wasn't as fine, having a lot of little bumps and dips and sharp corners.

A rock face?

"What is it?" Hannah asked, kneeling beside him.

Ethan said nothing as he continued to touch it, his fingers running along a smooth surface into dips and across bumps before finding a small hollow. He ran his finger around it, and

435

when he realised what it was, he pulled his hand away like he'd touched a hot stove.

"Oh, God," he muttered with an involuntary shiver.

"What?"

"I just picked the nasal cavity of a skeleton."

"Eww."

"These last few minutes have not been great for me," Ethan replied lamely.

"Who is it?"

"Despite my intimate connection with him, he refused to tell me his name. You know, on account of him being a skeleton."

"Okay, okay, sorry. Silly question."

Letting out a breath to calm his nerves, he reached out for the skeleton again and began searching around the cloth that he now knew were clothes.

"What are you doing?"

"Searching him."

"You're robbing him?"

"Robbing? Not at all. I pick his nose for him. We're great mates," he replied sarcastically. He found some buttons and unhooked them, opening what he hoped was a coat. The material was too thick to be a shirt or pants. He ran his fingers around the inside until he found an inner pocket.

"Bingo!" he said, pulling a contraption out of the pocket.

He held it up, despite it being too dark for her to see.

"What?" she asked.

"If this is what I think it is…" he said, running his fingers over the tube-shaped device until he found a piece of thin rope attached to it. He followed the rope to the other end, where there was a circular piece of metal attached. "It's a tinderbox."

He found the lid and popped it open. After turning it over, a piece of stone rolled into his palm. "And he still has the fire starter."

"Good, but what will you use to start a fire?"

He handed the tinderbox to her and reached for the skeleton's clothing. Finding the undershirt, he ripped a length off and balled it up, putting it on the ground and grabbing the fire starter and stone from Hannah. Looping the fire starter around his fingers, he held the stone in his other hand near the ball of cloth.

He struck the stone with the metal fire starter at a downward angle. It took a few strikes, and a few curses when he missed the stone and cut his fingers, but the first sparks came and caught on the dry fabric.

Ethan blew on the flames, encouraging them to grow until the fire took. When it did, it provided enough light for Ethan to see the skeleton slumped against the wall. Wasting no more time, he told Hannah to rip off a piece of the skeleton's shirt while he grabbed it by the arm.

"Sorry about this," he said, and he put his feet against the skeleton's body and pulled hard until the shoulder popped out of the socket with a hollow *thock*. The fire was fading quickly, and he pulled the arm through the shirt sleeve while asking Hannah for the cloth. She handed it to him, and he wrapped it around the skeleton's fingers until it was tightly secured around the hand.

With the fire almost out, Ethan put his makeshift torch to it. After a few breaths, the fire caught on the cloth, spreading quickly. Soon, the surrounding area was lit in a warm orange light.

With enough light, he looked at the one-armed skeleton properly. It was dressed in a navy-blue waistcoat with brass buttons and black knee breeches, and beside him was a tricorne hat. Ethan examined the waistcoat closer and found a small burn hole on the coat over the breast.

"He was shot," Ethan said, standing up.

"Who would have shot him?"

"Best guess is Maynard."

"Maynard? But why?"

"He wrote in his diary that he had done away with everyone who knew of the treasure, except the Blue Men of the Desert. I assume this meant he murdered all of them."

Ahead of them was the door Ethan walked into. It was a double door made of thick timber, and carved on both doors were ships.

On the left were two sloops, each with three masts and a single gun deck. With the sails unfurled and the Union Jack flag flying in the wind, the sloop was following another ship on the right door. The other ship had two decks and was a square-rigged, fourth-rate warship armed with forty-two guns. In the distance beyond the second ship was what looked to be a landmass or an island with another ship docked there as well.

"What's this?" Hannah asked. She was pointing at the door. There were no door handles, instead four pentagon-shaped handles were sticking out of the doors.

Ethan grabbed the inner left handle and turned it. The handle turned without any resistance, but when he tried to push the door open, it remained closed.

"Look!"

Hannah was pointing above the ship, where in the dim firelight he saw a small rectangular panel had opened, revealing the word *Ranger*.

He rotated the handle again, the word disappearing and another taking its place: *Lyme*.

"Maynard and his bloody puzzles," Ethan grumbled.

Rotating it again revealed the word *Scarborough*, and then one more rotation exposed a blank plate. He tried the outer left handle and rotated it four times, revealing the words *Pearl*, *Ranger*, and *Jane* before returning to a blank plate. He tested the inner right handle and was given *Bedford*, *Pearl*, and *Lyme*, while the outer right handle gave him *La Concorde*, *Adventure*, and *Queen Anne's Revenge*. Both right handles ended in blank plates, just as the left handles did.

"Ship names," Ethan said. "Specifically, they are ships Maynard had some involvement in."

Hannah caught on. "So we just have to match the nameplate with the right ship?"

"That's right."

"Should be easy enough."

"Should be, but we don't want to get any of them wrong. Just in case."

"Just in case what?"

"I don't know. Maybe the door is locked forever, or a trapdoor opens and we fall to our deaths, or the mesa caves in and we are trapped here forever, or the skeleton comes to life and strangles us, or—"

"Okay, I get it," Hannah said.

"Just saying, it's better to be safe than sorry."

"You just climbed down a rope that was hundreds of years old."

"Yeah, but that was no risk to you…" he said, trailing off.

Hannah looked away, absently scratching her arm.

Idiot! He groaned inwardly. *Now is not the time!*

They stood in awkward silence until she asked, "Do you know what ships they are?"

"I think so," he said, relieved to move on. "Here, hold this." He held out the torch, but she didn't take it.

"There is no way I am holding that."

"What? Why?"

"It's an arm, Ethan."

"Humerus, actually."

"No."

"It's not going to hurt you."

"No."

"Fine, then."

He held the light up high and focused on the right door with the depiction of the larger ship. Ethan was aware of Maynard's history and was reasonably sure he could eliminate *Bedford* as an option. *Bedford* was a ship that he was a lieutenant on before the fight with Blackbeard.

"This island here," he said, pointing to the one in the distance with a ship resting next to it. "I think it's meant to be Ocracoke

Island, where he killed Blackbeard. He served on the *HMS Pearl* when they approached Blackbeard's ship." He rotated the handle until the plate above the ship said *Pearl,* and then pushed the handle in until it was flush against the door. Then he turned to the two handles on the left. "He was given command of two sloops, which attacked Blackbeard's ship." He pointed to the ship near the island on the right door. "They were named—"

He turned the outer left handle.

"*Jane* and—"

He turned the inner handle.

"*Ranger.*"

"*Jane, Ranger, and Pearl,*" Hannah read out while Ethan pushed the handles flush with the door. "And the last one? That's Blackbeard's ship, isn't it? So it would be *Queen Anne's Revenge,* right?"

"Yep," Ethan agreed and turned it to *Queen Anne's Revenge* before pushing in the handle.

Silence laid heavy in the cavern.

"Anything?" Hannah asked.

"I—" Ethan started, but before he could say anything else, the ground started to shake and rumble.

"What's going on?" Hannah yelled over the noise.

"I'm not sure, I— watch out!"

Ethan tossed the torch aside and grabbed Hannah, pulling her out of the way just as a huge boulder rolled past them. Rocks rained down on them, and Ethan lay on top of her, shielding her as they both watched the boulder roll toward the chasm and disappear over the edge.

"That was lucky," he breathed, adrenaline coursing through his body.

"Yeah," Hannah said, letting out a nervous, breathy laugh.

"Did you also think the mesa was collapsing on us?"

In the faint firelight, he saw her smile, "What happened?"

Ethan was so close to her he felt her breath on his ear and was acutely aware that he was on top of her.

"I'm an idiot, is what happened," he said, rolling off. He dusted himself off and stood up, his back sore from the rocks that had fallen on it.

"Why?" she asked, accepting his outstretched hand.

"Because the ship Blackbeard used when he died wasn't the *Revenge*." Ethan said, pulling Hannah to her feet. "He lost it when he ran it aground elsewhere in North Carolina." He grabbed the handle and turned it. "No, his last ship was called…" He rotated the plate until it showed *Adventure*. Then pushed the handle in until it was flush with the door and braced himself, waiting for another boulder to try to crush them. Instead, there was a faint click coming from behind the door.

"Just like a vault door," he said, and he pushed the doors open.

Thirty Nine

The door opened to a wide platform which narrowed into a crossroad at the far end. Ahead of them were stairs leading deeper, while the left and right branched off into tunnels.

"Which way?" Hannah asked.

Ethan looked at each option. "No idea," he admitted. "Maynard wanted this to be as difficult as possible, so only he would have known the way."

"What about the compass?"

"Good idea." He pulled the compass from his jacket, pressed the code, and opened it. The compass needle was pointing to their right. "This way," he said, and they went down a long tunnel that ended in a set of stairs.

The stairs were narrow and roughly cut out of the stone—nothing like the intricate work he had encountered in the bunker and the Inaccessible Island. He wondered if Maynard built this in a hurry, or if he just wasn't concerned by it. They descended deeper, and Ethan was certain they were under the lake by now. The air was cool, and they splashed through pools of water as he led the way, with Hannah close behind. They came to more branching tunnels and followed the compass needle as it helped them make their way through the maze. They walked on in silence, feeling as if the darkness was closing in on them. They were descending another set of stairs when the tunnel opened into a vast cavern. It was impossible to tell the size, but there were pockets of light seeping in from cracks above, and on either side of the entrance were torches that Ethan lit. The cavern was empty for all but some fallen rocks and large boulders. With the compass pointing straight, they forged ahead, lighting torches as they passed them. They continued on, splashing through puddles and skirting around large pools of water, which confirmed to Ethan that they were actually under the lake, or at least water from the lake trickled down here. As they moved on, the cavern shrunk in on them until it formed a narrow path that they had duck-walk to get through.

"Are you sure this is the right way?" Hannah asked, groaning and shuffling behind him.

"I'm not sure of anything about this," Ethan admitted. "But the compass is pointing this way, so I guess we are heading the right wa—whoa!"

He stopped suddenly and Hannah bumped into him, almost

444

knocking him off a ledge.

"What is it?" she asked.

Ethan was on his knees and bracing himself against the tunnel wall, and Hannah poked her head under his armpit. When she saw what was before them, she pulled back quickly.

"You expect us to cross *that?*"

Before them was an open chasm, the firelight doing a pitiful job of penetrating the darkness. A bridge so narrow that it would hardly be more than the width of his feet side-by-side, reached out over it and disappeared into the darkness beyond.

"Unfortunately, I do."

"There's no guarantee that the bridge goes anywhere or that it won't collapse the moment one of us stands on it," Hannah said.

"The compass is pointing this way."

"It's not the compass that's the problem. I don't trust the bridge."

"Do you have any better ideas?" he asked.

"Yes! Let's go back and find another way around."

"We don't have time! If Graves isn't here by now, he will be soon, and he won't be as slow as we have been."

Hannah was silent, so Ethan pressed his case. "Look, I'm going ahead. You can wait for me, but we have only one light and I will need it. And they might be coming this way."

She was silent for a long time, and Ethan worried she was actually going to stay. He didn't know if he could do it alone— not in here, at least. He started this adventure alone, but he'd relied on Andrea, Ritchie, and Hannah to get him this far. Without them, he would likely be back home having given up, or dead.

445

"Okay, let's go," she said softly.

Relief flooded through him. "Thank you," he said just as softly as he tried to capture her eyes with his own, but she was looking down, avoiding him. He put the compass in his pocket, turned around, and crawled onto the bridge. Standing up, he said, "Let's take this slow."

He spread his arms out for balance and shuffled out sideways a little and then stopped. He turned his head as best he could while trying to keep his balance and waited for Hannah to follow. He watched her stand, arms bracing herself against the walls, and peer over the edge. She moaned and retreated into the tunnel.

"Focus on the path," he said. "That's the way across. Don't worry about anything else but your balance and the path. Take your time. I'll stick with you."

She put a foot out on the path and said to herself, "I can do this. I can do this," repeating the mantra as she shuffled out. She stiffened and tried to crouch once she was out in the open, but then instinct took over and she had her arms out for balance like Ethan had.

"Let's go. Slow and steady," Ethan said.

Taking a deep breath and letting it out, he slowly shuffled across, facing sideways, and found that once he had the rhythm of 'left foot, next foot over,' he was confident. In the dim firelight, he saw the pointed ends of stalagmites below, standing there like silent soldiers waiting for him to fall. He swallowed and kept going, stopping frequently to let Hannah catch up if he felt he was going too fast. Before he knew it, they were at the peak of the arch.

"Halfway there," he announced. "Just a bit more to go."

They continued moving, the path widening in parts and narrowing in others, the inky black chasm wreaking havoc on their depth perception. Finally, Ethan could see the end of the path extending into a platform.

"There it is," he said. "Not far now!"

"Oh, thank God," Hannah said with obvious relief. "Though, you know, this hasn't been so bad."

Ethan laughed, his voice echoing off the cavern walls when he heard a loud *crack*.

The bridge rumbled and ripped, and without thinking, he took a step forward and leapt just as a section of the bridge disintegrated beneath him. He sailed through the air, still holding the torch, and hit the lip of the platform. The air exploded out of his lungs. He held there for a moment before he started sliding back over the edge. Tossing the torch onto the landing, Ethan flailed his arms about, trying to grab something to hold. His feet scrambled on the cliff face, finding a protruding ledge just as he was almost over, stopping his fall.

"Ethan!" Hannah shouted out.

Still holding on, he called out, "Are you okay?"

There was silence.

"Hannah!"

"I'm here," she said, her voice was shaky.

"Just hold on," he said. Grasping the rocky ground, he used his feet to hoist himself up until he could plant his elbows and lift himself over the edge. Without time to think, he grabbed the torch and turned to Hannah. In the faded light, he saw she was on her knees with her arms wrapped around the bridge, hugging it for dear life. Between them was a gap where the path had broken off. The gap was too big for him to reach over, and a quick look around showed him nothing he could use to help her across.

CRACK!

It sounded like a gunshot around the cavern and… *is the bridge swaying*?

Hannah cried out in fright. Even in the gloom, Ethan saw she had her eyes squeezed shut, and she was gripping the path with all her strength. He got on his stomach, leaning over the edge with his hand out.

"Hannah!"

She didn't react.

"Hannah, look at me. I can help you, but you have to look at me."

She opened her eyes slowly and looked at him. Her green eyes were wide with fear, and he heard her murmuring "I can't do this" over and over.

"Hannah. I need you to stand up. You're going to have to jump—"

"*What!*"

"—but don't worry, I'll catch you."

She shook her head and cried out again as the bridge let out another loud crack.

"Hannah! Please. You have to trust me." He could feel the desperation in his voice, trying to get through to her. She was on borrowed time as the bridge swayed and threatened to collapse. "I can't lose you," he pleaded.

Something in Hannah seemed to click, and she slowly got to

her knees, her palms on the bridge in front of her.

"Good. Good," Ethan encouraged her.

She moved to rest on her haunches and got to her feet, her whole body trembling.

"Okay, just jump and I'll catch you," he instructed.

CRACK!

The bridge shook and jolted again, and Hannah almost lost her balance. "I can't!"

"You can, Hannah. Just jump to me and I'll do the rest."

"I can't!" she repeated, and she squeezed her eyes shut.

The bridge shuddered and chunks of the roof were falling, narrowly missing the bridge and crashing to the darkness below.

"Han. Look at me."

Hannah opened her eyes and locked them with Ethan's and he saw the abject fear in them. "I *will* catch you," he said. "I *promise!*"

The bridge shook violently and dropped, and Ethan's heart jumped into his mouth. Hannah took a step and leapt off the bridge moments before it collapsed, disappearing into the black depths below with an echoing crash.

Hannah sailed through the air, arms and legs flailing about. She wasn't going to make it to the ledge, dipping just below it, but Ethan adjusted and caught her arm. Hannah held on and crashed into the wall, while Ethan's shoulder wrenched, and he cried out in pain. Hannah swung around until she grabbed Ethan's arm with her free hand, and Ethan, rallying a strength he didn't know he had, dragged her up and over the ledge. She fell beside him, both of them panting heavily while the echo of the crashing bridge still reverberated around the cavern.

Eventually, the sound died away, and they lay in the darkness. Only the flickering fire from the torch provided Ethan enough light to see the combination of fear and adrenaline and gratitude in Hannah's eyes. There was something else there, too. Pity? Anger? Resentment? She didn't say anything, but that was enough for him. He feared that if she spoke what was truly on her mind, he might break down then and there and give up.

He didn't know why he needed her support. Maybe it was because he knew he couldn't do this alone. Or that he feared the answer to the question of what happened to his parents—a question whose answer had sent him spiralling for most of the last decade.

Or do you seek her approval?

Whatever the reason, he was grateful Hannah was with him, though it still didn't dim any of the guilt he felt for putting her, Andrea, and Ritchie in danger.

After another minute of wrestling with his thoughts, he got up, helping Hannah to her feet and picking up the torch. "You good?" he asked.

"This treasure…" she started, but whatever she wanted to say, she kept to herself. "I want to get out of here."

"I know, Hannah. Just a little bit longer, ok?"

She nodded, and in the light, he saw her face was streaked with dirt and that a fresh cut had formed along her hairline, near the temple. He reached out, brushing a strand of hair away from the cut, and wiped the blood away. The cut was minor, but she still winced, and he could see the area darkening. He looked her in the eyes and found hers were already on his. Their gaze held for what felt like both a brief second and an eternity before he swallowed the lump that had formed in his throat and said, "Let's go."

With the torch held high, Ethan pulled out the compass and led them away from the fallen bridge.

It was more than an hour of walking through twists and turns, narrow tunnels and wide open expanses, of climbing up and down rock faces when Hannah asked, "Do you hear that?"

"Yeah," Ethan said. There was a roaring sound, faint at first but getting louder as they moved forward, the compass leading the way.

"The temperature's dropped as well," Ethan noted. The previously dry air was now cool and wet.

Ahead of them they saw a dim light, and they looked at each other, excited to see some natural light, and hurried forward. The roaring sound reached a crescendo when they emerged from the tunnel into a wide chamber with a path that led to a set of doors similar to the ones at the entrance. Natural light was filtering through cracks and crevasses high above them, light angling in where motes of dust danced in it.

No, not dust… mist.

"Wow," Hannah breathed, hurrying into the chamber.

What had captivated her was not the doors or the light filtering through, but the source of the noise. To their left, torrents of water poured down from a ledge above them and disappeared into the darkness below.

"An underground waterfall!" she said. She turned and looked at him with a huge smile on her face.

Ethan watched her from the other side of the chamber. She was standing in a puddle, beams of light from above highlighting the mist dancing around her hair, and he couldn't help but smile back.

Careful now.

Shaking his head, he looked around and found rusted lanterns lining the right side wall, evenly spaced and holding puddles of oil. He went to the closest one and pulled open the door with a rusty squeak. He thought that the dampness in the room and the mist from the waterfall would have made it impossible to light but he put his torch to the oil and it flared to life. He walked the length of the wall, putting his torch to each lantern. By the time he reached the end, he had almost all of them lit.

What was that?

Ethan strained his hearing, trying to listen over the sound of the waterfall. He thought he heard something crashing or banging. Maybe more rocks falling?

He walked over to Hannah, who was still enraptured by the waterfall, her hair damp with mist. He touched her shoulder.

She turned and smiled at him. "This is so beautiful," she said.

"Yeah, it is," he replied, not looking at the waterfall.

"It's almost worth being thrown out of a plane for," she said.

Ethan smiled weakly and dropped his gaze. He left her to watch the waterfall while he examined the doors. Like the entrance, these doors were made of thick timber, though it was damp from centuries of mist and probably rotted. They had no handle and were banded with iron across the top, bottom, and middle.

Etched across both doors was a ship cresting giant waves. It was a fully rigged, square-sailed, forty-cannon ship with raised forecastle and quarterdeck. Flying at the back of the ship was a black sail with a skull on it and written beneath the scene was *'Queen Anne's Revenge'*.

Blackbeard's ship.

He pushed on the door, hoping it would be that easy. The wood was wet and slimy underhand, but they didn't budge.

"Figures," he muttered.

He stood back and Hannah came over. *"Queen Anne's Revenge,"* she read.

Ethan nodded and his eyes passed over the helm—or at least, where the helm should have been. Frowning, he stepped back, trying to get a better look at it since it towered over his head. He thought he saw an indentation where the helm should be.

"Look at that," he said, pointing to it.

Hannah stood next to him, noticing the problem right away. "It's missing the helm."

"Yep."

"And another one here," she said, pointing to the rudder of the ship.

She was right. There was another circular indentation in the ship's rudder.

"I wonder…" he said slowly and then put his hand in his

pocket. He fished out the two coins and showed her.

She looked at him expectantly. "You think…?"

"May as well try it." He knelt by the rudder and held up the El Mal coin next to the depression, but it looked too big. He tried the other and thought they looked the same size. "Here goes nothing," he said and pushed the coin in, profile facing out.

It took a few rotations to get it in the right spot, but then the coin slotted in perfectly. The king and queen facing upright, like they were looking at him behind those crossed out eyes.

"It fit?" Hannah asked.

"Like a glove. Here, I'll boost you up to the helm."

He handed her the remaining coin and squatted down with his back to the door. He cupped his hands together and Hannah stepped into them. Ethan, pushing from his thighs, groaned as he lifted her, and she put her feet on his shoulders. He felt her fidgeting up there and he was on the verge of complaining when she said, "Done," and dropped off his shoulders.

They stood back, waiting for something to happen.

They waited.

And waited.

Nothing happened.

"Should something be happening?" Hannah asked.

"I think so."

"Nothing is happening, Ethan."

"I see that."

Am I hearing things?

Ethan thought he heard a strange noise again. Similar to before, it sounded like something crashing or falling. "Did you hear—" he asked. As he turned around, he caught sight of the bowsprit.

"Hear what?" Hannah asked.

Ethan didn't reply.

"Ethan, what is it?"

He pointed at the bowsprit. "Notice anything missing?"

While she was looking, Ethan thought he heard the noise again, louder this time, and turned around, frowning

"The figurehead is missing," she said, drawing his attention back to the door.

He nodded. "It looks like there is a spot for something to go in there," he said, noting the long indentation that ran just below the bowsprit.

"Like what?"

Ethan was staring at it and turned his head slightly. The figurehead looked like the outline of someone standing with their arms raised and holding something above their head.

"The sceptre," he sighed. "The sceptre goes in the bowsprit."

"We don't have the sceptre, though."

"That's right."

"So we can't go any further?"

"Correct."

"Then if we can't go any further, neither can Graves. Not if we take the coins."

Ethan shook his head. "He's not going to let this stop him. It might delay him, but it won't stop him."

"Then what do we do?"

"I—"

He was interrupted by people shouting over the crashing noise of the waterfall. They both turned around to see a group of armed men approaching and, behind them, wearing an immaculate navy-blue suit, was Felix Graves.

Forty

The cavern was a war of noises as Graves' men shouted over the cascading waterfall to put their hands up. Hannah tried to run, but Ethan grabbed the rudder coin from the wall before the armed men surrounded them. They were wearing black fatigues with combat boots and were carrying a mix of SA80 Assault Rifles and SIG P229s, all of them aimed at Ethan. Ethan noticed Grassi standing next to Graves with the sceptre in his meaty paw.

He mentally kicked himself. The sounds he heard before were from Graves and his goons. The waterfall covered most of it, allowing him and his men to catch up with minimal detection.

Tears in her eyes, Hannah moved next to him with her hands up while Ethan kept his down. He had no weapon, and they had the upper hand. There were a dozen or more men, plus Graves, and behind them all was…

Andrea.

She looked up at him and he was relieved to see she was no worse for wear, though she was now wearing nylon hiking pants and a jacket. Her face was clean and bruise-free, a stark contrast to Hannah when she was in Graves' company.

Ethan frowned, but Graves spoke before he could say anything. "You are rather resilient, Mr. Jackson," he said. "I thought I was done with you and your services, but you not only saved Miss Coetzee from what seems like the impossible, you also beat me here. Your parents would be most proud."

Ethan knew he was trying to bait him, but he took it anyway. "Screw you, asshole."

Graves smiled, though it didn't reach those cold eyes of his. He turned his head slightly, looking at the door behind them. "The *Queen Anne's Revenge*, Blackbeard's ship. Interesting that Maynard used this for the motif, but I guess it is where it all started."

Ethan didn't bother correcting him, and Graves turned back to his men. As soon as he did, Ethan took a giant leap sideways and landed near the edge, seeing water flowing into the dark abyss like an open mouth drinking its fill. He swallowed and held his hand with the coin over the edge.

Every gun in the room followed him and the sounds of safeties being released simultaneously would have been comical if not for the situation.

"Guns down or I drop it," he said.

Graves looked at him with an obvious lack of concern. "Why should I be concerned about a trinket?" he asked.

"Because it's the only way in," Ethan replied, showing him the coin. "You shoot me, I drop the coin."

Graves lifted his gun and pointed it at Hannah. "Give it to me, or I shoot the girl."

Well, this is going sideways quickly.

Ethan swallowed. "Shoot her and I drop the coin," he said, hedging Hannah's life on that one simple comment.

Hannah looked at him wide-eyed, and the fear on her face was as easy to read as a children's book. But there was more than fear there. He'd just told them all that he valued the treasure, the coin, and everything about this sordid affair over her, despite having said otherwise.

What could he say, though? Giving Graves the coin would mean he had no other use for them, and he wasn't going to let them get away, not again. The only way to save both Hannah and himself was to be useful to the man and buy some time.

No one said anything, and only the roar of the waterfall filled the cavern.

Then, out of the corner of his eye, he saw Andrea make her move. She was standing behind everyone, forgotten, as all eyes were on Ethan. He watched her pick up a fist-sized rock, creep over to the nearest gunman, and bring the rock down on the man's head. The man cried out, but it was drowned out by the waterfall, and he slumped to the ground. She pulled his handgun out of his thigh holster and, before anyone knew what was happening, had it pointed at Felix Graves.

"All weapons down," she said, loud enough for everyone to hear.

Graves spun around to look at her. He looked as if he was about to say something, but thought better of it and put his gun on the ground. He looked at his men, who had their guns trained on her, and nodded his head. All of them engaged the safeties on their assault rifles and placed them on the ground.

Andrea circled them, her gun still pointed at Graves, until she passed Hannah and was standing next to Ethan.

"All right," Ethan said, feeling like they had a shot of getting out of there alive. "Here's what's going to happen. You let the three of us go, and I take the coin. Once we are at the entrance, I leave the coin there and we all go on our merry way. Deal?"

He expected Graves to negotiate, to argue, maybe even agree, but what he didn't expect was for him to smile.

"No."

"No?"

"You're not going anywhere, Mr. Jackson."

"Then say goodbye to the coin."

"He's right, Ethan."

It was Andrea who spoke, and before he could even process what she said, she swung the gun at his head. The blow caught him near the temple, and his vision clouded. She yanked him away from the edge, throwing him to the ground, and pointed the gun at him.

"What are you doing?" Hannah cried.

Andrea ignored her and held her free hand out to him. "Give me the coin," she said coldly.

Ethan lay on the ground, his mind still in a daze from the blow to his head. He was sure he was bleeding, but his mind was reeling from Andrea's betrayal.

"Now!" she ordered.

He thought back to his time with her: the mysterious phone call in the hotel room, how Graves knew he'd been to the church in Great Mongeham, how he followed them to Cape Town and the Inaccessible Island, why she was roaming free on the plane. Even thinking about his parents and how she was the last person they were meant to see. So many suspicious individual acts that, in hindsight, made it obvious there was more to her story.

Hell, she's wearing new clothes!

"God damn it," he grumbled as another fact came to him. "I should have known when you said you didn't know Graves, but you called him by his first name in the hotel in Cape Town, even though I never mentioned it. You said, 'Felix Graves cannot be trusted', I should have realised it then."

"I must admit that I worried about that slip, but then again, it was so easy to occupy you with other, shall we say, *physical* demands." She gave him a salacious smile.

She played you like a fiddle.

She looked pointedly at Hannah. "It's amazing what men will tell you once you sleep with them."

Hannah looked at Ethan incredulously, and her features darkened and she turned away.

"Bitch," Ethan muttered, glaring at Andrea, and handing her the coin. The upper hand he thought he had, brief as it was, was now gone, and his mind turned to working out what he could do to protect Hannah's life, and perhaps his own. He touched the spot where she had hit him, wincing as he felt the bump, and his hand came away with blood.

Graves walked over to him wearing a smug smile, and Ethan wanted nothing more than to strangle him. Andrea handed him the coin, and he examined it in the light before he said to Ethan, "Nothing personal, Mr. Jackson."

Ethan glowered at him, watching as he knelt by the door and slotted the coin into the spot near the rudder.

Andrea, Graves, and all their men watched the door expectantly, waiting for something to happen.

"Open it," Andrea said, her gun still pointed at him.

"Let Hannah go."

She pointed her gun at Hannah. "You are a child in an adult's world, Ethan, and you do not have what it takes to live in it. Nothing is stopping me from shooting you both, except my benevolence. Now open it, or she dies."

"What's stopping you from killing us is that you need me to ensure you find it. I know that without the treasure, you go to Farid Abboud empty-handed, and I don't think he would like that one bit."

He didn't know if Abboud was the one they were working for, but it was worth a guess.

"It could be just past these doors."

"It's not," he hedged. "It might not even be here at all."

"We'll see," she said, and she cocked the hammer on the pistol. "Well… I will."

"Andrea, wait," Graves interjected. "Abboud is getting

impatient."

"Who cares about Abboud!" Andrea spat. "That short-sighted fool doesn't have the first clue what we're actually doing. He just wants his split of the treasure to fund his little tantrum."

"I understand that," Graves said evenly. "But Abboud is not a man we want on our bad side. We've already had to appease him with the bomb. Let's not make this situation worse. The boy got us through the fort quicker than it would have taken otherwise. There's no risk in keeping him around. He's outnumbered, with no weapon and nowhere to go."

Andrea considered his words, and Ethan noticed how different she was. There was a sinister look about her now. Her face was harder, with sharper cheekbones and emotionless, narrowed eyes. He wondered how he could have missed that before.

"Fine." She turned to Hannah. "But she doesn't."

Hannah closed her eyes and let out a cry as Ethan jumped in between her and Andrea, hands held in a placating gesture. "You will have to kill me first."

"Andrea, we will deal with it later."

"Fine," she growled, lowering her gun. She turned back to Ethan. "Now open the door."

Realising he had no other option, he said, "Give me the sceptre."

"Why?"

"Because I need it."

Andrea nodded at Grassi. "Give it to him." Then she turned back to Ethan. "I'm watching you."

"Yeah, yeah."

Grassi glared at him as he handed him the sceptre, then stood back while Ethan turned. As he did, he locked eyes with Hannah, who also glared at him but didn't say anything.

He sighed and turned back to Grassi and said, "Give me a boost, big boy."

Grassi grunted something negative, and Ethan looked pointedly at Graves and Andrea.

"Just do it, Hugo," Graves told him exhaustedly.

Grassi grunted again and approached the door.

"How is the knee?" Ethan asked him as he slowly got down to one knee. The man scowled at him, and Ethan gave him a smug smile and climbed onto his shoulders. Once he was there, Grassi stood up and Ethan placed the sceptre along the bowsprit, the figure holding the yellow gem becoming the ship's figurehead.

Ethan climbed down just as there was the sound of a lock turning, and he pushed on the doors. They moved slightly, and he turned to Grassi again. "Give me a hand."

Grassi took a spot next to Ethan, and Graves told three of his men to help as well. When they were ready, Ethan said, "Push," and they pushed against the door.

It resisted at first, but then the door creaked and groaned and slowly opened. Centuries of dust build-up fell around them, but they had the door open wide enough that they could comfortably walk through it. Ethan went in first, followed by Grassi and the three others who helped open the door, then Andrea, Hannah, Graves, and the rest.

They were in a rectangular room similar to the previous one, with natural light filtering in from somewhere above and torch brackets on the wall to the right. The once-booming roar of the waterfall was now a dull buzz.

Graves instructed one of his men to grab the coins and the sceptre, and then turned to Ethan and said, "Get on with it."

"I miss that all-too-brief moment we had when you were courteous," he said, wondering why he thought giving this guy attitude would be helpful. He reached into his pocket and pulled out the compass again.

Pressing the star sequence, the lid popped open to reveal the needle pointing straight ahead.

"Which way?" Andrea asked.

"Straight ahead," he said evenly and then added, "Give me a torch."

On Graves' instruction, one of his men handed him a torch, and he pointed it straight ahead. He started walking, following the needle. Hannah appeared next to him while the others were following close behind.

The far end of the room narrowed down to a tunnel that could comfortably fit three abreast, though it was Ethan and Hannah taking the lead.

The tunnel sloped down, and behind him, he could hear Andrea and Graves talking, discussing how far below the lake they were. Ethan estimated they were at least a hundred metres below, but kept the information to himself. While they were talking, he asked Hannah, "How you doing?"

She stayed quiet for so long that he thought she hadn't heard him, and just as he was about to repeat the question, she said,

"I'm about to die and my body will be left to rot where no one will ever find it. How do you think I'm doing?"

That stung. While he knew it was a stupid question, he had to keep her from shutting down. If and when a chance came to escape, he needed her to be ready.

"I know it's not worth much, but I'm sorry. I should have realised she was working with Graves."

"You were going to let her shoot me instead of giving her the coin!" she hissed.

"No. I would nev—"

"And you *slept* with her!"

Ethan closed his mouth. His guilt was already beating at him from every which way. He didn't need to make it worse. When it was clear he was going to say nothing, she huffed.

The compass swung left, and he took them down a branching tunnel, this one full of puddles that glistened in their torch lights.

"I'm going to get us out of this," he whispered to her after they'd turned right at another tunnel.

That elicited a very unladylike snort. "How?"

Good question.

"Just be ready," he said. "First chance we get, we have to take it."

They continued moving at a steady pace, following the compass as it took them through a maze of twists and turns and branching paths.

"I can't believe you slept with her." Hannah muttered, breaking the heavy silence.

Ouch.

"In hindsight, I'm not exactly thrilled about it either," he said. "It was after they chased us in Cape Town. I just had a boat almost fall on me and I killed someone—well, multiple people—and almost got executed myself. It was just too much, and I opened up to her. We—I—got caught up in the moment."

She huffed again and walked on in silence.

They led the way for another hour before the tunnel ended at a simple wooden door.

"Open it," Andrea instructed.

Ethan pushed it open, and they entered a circular chamber with multiple doors set evenly around it. It reminded Ethan of the rooms under the fort in Cabo Verde, and he admired Maynard's repetitiveness of his designs. Each door had a thick metal plaque with a number attached to it, starting at one and ending in the door they had entered from, which read *twenty*. Between each door was a torch, and Andrea instructed the men to light them. The room lit up in an orange glow, and Ethan walked to the centre of the room, where a compass rose was painted on the smooth stone floor. The cardinal directions pointed at doors three, seven, twelve, and seventeen.

"Which door?" Andrea asked, coming up behind him.

Ethan checked the compass, but the needle was swinging wildly.

"I don't know," he said, showing her the compass.

"What about the doors this points to?" she said, pointing to the compass on the floor.

Ethan shrugged. "Seems too obvious. But don't let me stop you."

She pointed to four of her men. "Check those doors. Find out which one gets us out of here."

The men nodded, and they took the four doors the compass on the floor pointed to.

"Did Maynard mention any of this, Jackson?" Graves asked him.

"Maybe," he said, thinking back to all he read about in the diary.

"Maybe?" Andrea huffed. "Did he, or didn't he?"

"Look, it's not as if he specifically wrote 'to get through the chamber with the doors located under Lake Faguibine, go through door number whatever'. If you hadn't noticed, he was very secretive about all this stuff and left abstract clues."

A scream echoed from behind door twelve.

Everyone spun around, facing the door, and Andrea said, "Tannen, go."

The man named Tannen nodded and, with his assault rifle raised, approached the door and opened it. He passed through and the door closed behind him. They waited in silence, the air tense until, after a couple of minutes, Graves broke it, asking, "Where are the other three?"

"This is taking too long," Andrea agreed. She spoke to three other men. "Check on the others."

The men walked through doors three, seven, and seventeen, the doors swinging shut behind them. They waited some more. Ethan was trying to figure out how to get out of their current situation, especially now with fewer goons about, when door twelve burst open and Tannen scrambled out, his fatigues and face covered with blood.

"It's Rolo," he said, panting. "He's dead."

"Dead? How?" Graves asked.

"Spikes. From the wall. Impaled him." Tannen said between gasping breaths.

"Any sign of the others?" Graves asked.

Tannen shook his head.

Just then, door seventeen opened and another of Graves' men walked out.

"Did you find anything, Heath?" Graves asked him.

Heath shook his head. "Strangest thing, boss. I followed the tunnel for a bit, but then it just stopped. It was a dead end."

"What about Adam?"

"No sign of him. I circled back to see if I missed any other passages, but nothing."

Graves frowned but said nothing.

"Enough of this!" Andrea snapped. She pointed her gun at Hannah while speaking to Ethan.

"You have two minutes to figure this out, or I shoot her."

"But—"

"Do it, or she dies," she spat, and for emphasis, she flipped the safety off her gun.

Crap. Crap. Crap!

Ethan's mind ran a hundred miles a minute as he thought about what to do. He had no way out of this, so he focused on the problem. He thought back to Maynard's writings. Nothing hinted at this. He wrote nothing about a circular room, or doors with numbers, or anything like that. He wasn't lying when he told them Maynard didn't spell it out for them.

"One minute," Andrea announced.

Shit.

He eliminated the idea that Maynard had hidden the solution in his diary and instead focused on the room. There must be something in here that would give him a clue. He looked around the chamber. There were the doors numbered one to twenty. They were the key. He looked up at the ceiling and thought he saw something twinkling, so he pointed his torch at it. The powerful beam of light scanned the roof, passing circular dots that reflected the light back at him.

Stars!

Ethan followed the stars with his light, going from one to another until he realised it was the constellation of Cetus, the sea monster.

"Thirty seconds."

His heart sped up, and he looked down at the compass rose. The cardinal directions pointed at doors that led nowhere or to traps. Those door numbers were meaningless, a red herring, but the compass…

The compass!

Cetus was the constellation on Blackbeard's compass.

It must have something to do with it. But what?

Torch light probing the compass rose on the floor, he noticed the word *annus* written above the north point.

Annus is Latin for 'year'. So, we have the Cetus constellation, a compass with the word "year" written in Latin on the north point and the four points pointing to doors that lead to death.

"Ten seconds."

Maynard found the compass when Blackbeard died. Which was in—

"Five seconds."

1718. 1718.

"Four seconds."

1718 has four numbers. Maybe...

"Three seconds."

"I got it!" he shouted. "Door one."

"You're sure?" Graves asked.

No.

"Yes."

"Then off you go," Graves said. When Ethan hesitated, he raised his gun at him. "While we're young, Mr. Jackson."

Ethan glared at him for a three count and then, armed with only a torch, he entered door one.

Forty One

The door, like every other they had walked through, opened into a tunnel. Thankful for the powerful beam of his light, Ethan looked around but found nothing threatening—no obvious traps or anything that looked like it would kill him.

"Here we go," he muttered.

He checked the compass again, but the needle was still swinging wildly. It would be of no help here.

The path took him straight ahead, and he walked it cautiously, checking for any sign of traps, until it ended at another door five minutes later. He pushed it open and examined the next room with his torch. It was so similar to the previous room, with twenty numbered doors and a compass rose on the floor, that he thought he'd circled back and was surprised he didn't see everyone else waiting there.

A quick inspection of the room showed that there were no obvious traps, so he returned to the first chamber and informed them of what he saw.

"It's the right way, then?" Graves asked him.

Ethan nodded. "It is. I know the way through it."

"Tell me."

"You let Hannah and I go and I'll tell you."

"You are in no position to negotiate."

"Then good luck finding your way through."

"I've had enough of your games, Ethan," Andrea grumbled. She turned to Graves. "Kill them both and we'll work it out ourselves."

"Go ahead," Ethan said casually, though his heart thumped in his chest. "But you won't make it anywhere near the end. Past this chamber is another chamber like this, and then there will be more after that. You don't have enough men to search each one, and you've heard what happened to the others."

Graves pulled Andrea aside and said, "He's right."

"And before you threaten Hannah again, if you kill her, I won't help you," he called out.

"This is childish," Andrea muttered. "Fine. Here's the deal. You lead us to the treasure, and once it's found, you are free to go. Any arguments, any tricks, any attempt to escape before then, we shoot you and take our chances. Got it?"

It was better than nothing, and Ethan knew they were not going to let them go, but it bought him more time—though how much, he didn't know. The treasure couldn't be far away.

If it is here at all.

"Fine," he said, glancing at Hannah, who remained silent.

Graves pointed to two of his men. "Wait here and see if any of the others return. We'll mark the way through. Wait ten minutes and then follow us as quickly as you can." They nodded and then to Ethan, Graves said, "Lead the way."

He took them through door one and led them through the passage until they arrived at the second chamber.

"Which way?" Graves asked.

"This way," Ethan told them, pointing to door seven. He grabbed the door handle, took a deep breath, and said a silent prayer that he was right.

"Jay, you go with him," Andrea said, talking to a dark-haired man.

Jay nodded and pushed Ethan to the door.

"Take it easy!" Ethan said and pulled the door open. They passed through and the door closed behind them.

He expected another long tunnel, but this one sloped up so sharply Ethan was almost on his hands and knees before it levelled out into another cavern. Again, light filtered through from somewhere above, giving them enough light to see their gloomy surroundings. The cavern stopped suddenly before a sharp drop, where a timber platform about ten-by-ten metres in size sat about two and a half metres below them.

Shallow enough to jump down but too deep to climb back out.

On the other side was a plateau with ten doors set into the

cavern wall. Ethan knew they had to cross the wooden platform to get to the other side, but he knew it wouldn't be as straightforward as it looked. He noticed a perfectly square stone block sitting in the middle of the platform below him.

He turned to Jay, who was silently watching him with his hand resting on his assault rifle. "This is it. You might want to go get them."

Jay gave no sign he was going to leave, his stoic form matched by his stoic expression.

"I'm not going," Ethan continued, "and I don't think your bosses are keen on being kept waiting. Besides, look around. I have nowhere else to go."

He seemed to think about it before he grunted, "Don't go anywhere." Then he turned on his heel and ran back down the tunnel.

While he waited, Ethan studied the platform, trying to get an understanding of how it worked. It was sitting on a single narrow pillar and the square block was sitting dead centre on the platform. As he walked up one end and back, he came across a sign hammered into the ground. In faded paint, it read: *Sacrifices must be made!*

He frowned, realising what it meant. Meanwhile, Graves and the rest of the group arrived. Ethan was relieved to see Hannah, and she walked to him, followed by Graves.

"What now, Mr. Jackson?"

He pointed to the other side. "We make our way across."

"Yes, I see that. But how? I cannot imagine this is a simple platform."

475

Before Ethan could answer, he watched two of Graves' men jump off the ledge and onto the wooden platform. They landed with a loud thud, and the platform groaned as if under great stress, and then tipped.

The men cried out and hurried toward the other side, where the platform tipped in the other direction. The cavern filled with the echoes of shouting as everyone, except Ethan and Hannah, tried to give instructions on what to do. Finally, the two men stood opposite each other near the centre of the platform and it stopped tilting.

"What do we do now?" Andrea said to no one in particular.

All faces turned to Ethan, and he sighed.

"It's like a giant see-saw," he explained. "You need to balance the board so the far end is high enough that you can climb onto the plateau on the other side. I'll show you." Before anyone could object, he grabbed Hannah's hand, and they jumped down to the platform.

They landed with a heavy thud, and he quickly pulled her to the middle of the platform. The platform swayed slightly while they all sought balance in the middle of it.

Andrea, Graves, and the others had their guns trained on Ethan. "What are you doing?" Andrea demanded.

"Showing you how it works." Ethan turned to the two men on the platform with him. He pointed to the end of the platform where Andrea and the rest waited above. "You two slowly walk back that way. I'm going to push the stone to the other end. You need to time it so we are walking at the same pace so this platform doesn't tip too much. Got it?"

476

The two of them glanced up at Andrea, who nodded.

Ethan turned to Hannah. "Wait here."

She nodded.

"You better not try any funny business," Andrea warned.

Ethan pushed the stone. It was lighter than he expected, but still took a lot of effort. "A length of rope walks into a bar," he started while pushing the stone. "And the bartender looks at him and says, 'Get out, we don't serve ropes in here!' So, the rope goes outside and cuts himself in half and ties his two sections together."

Ethan was a quarter of the way there now.

"Not pleased with his appearance," Ethan continued, "he takes a comb and combs out his ends. Then he walks back into the bar and the bartender says, 'Hey, aren't you that rope I just kicked out?'"

He stopped moving the stone when it was about halfway between the middle and the far end, the platform tilting slightly in his favour.

"And the rope replied, 'No, I'm a frayed knot.'"

There was a pause before one of the men on the platform chuckled.

"Thank you," Ethan said with a nod of the head. "Now, since you laughed, you stay right where you are. You," he said to the other, "slowly move back until you're at the edge."

The man shuffled backward, and slowly the platform tilted up on Ethan's side. When he was at the end, he stopped, and Ethan told him to wait there.

The platform was now tilted up towards the far end plateau.

Ethan and the block were midway between the centre and the far end, while Hannah stood in the middle. One goon stood at the midway point and the other at end, where Andrea and Graves waited. The platform tilted back-and-forth slightly as it balanced precariously on its axis. The slightest misstep here could send them all tumbling into the dark abyss below.

He spoke to Hannah next. "I need you to move slowly toward this end of the platform."

"Okay," she said, and cautiously moved to his side of the platform. The platform creaked and groaned as she walked across it and, with encouragement from Ethan, she made it to the edge.

"All right, now you," he said to the one who laughed at his joke standing midway between the centre and the far end. "Slowly move back. You're the control."

The man did as he said and, as he moved back, the platform tilted up higher and higher. When he was about two-thirds of the way back, the lip of the wooden platform was almost even with the lip of the plateau.

"Hold it," Ethan told him. And to Hannah, he said, "Climb up."

As she climbed up, the weight favoured the opposite side, and the platform tilted even more toward the front plateau. Ethan moved the stone slab toward Hannah's end, balancing out the weight distribution. By the time she was up, Ethan had the slab far enough away from the middle that the platform was rocking slightly but stayed atop the pivot.

"Next person, jump down," he called out.

Ethan couldn't hear what they were discussing, but both

Graves and Andrea were animated. Eventually, Andrea pointed at one of her goons, and he jumped down onto the platform.

The platform tilted suddenly with the added weight of three men on one side, forcing Ethan's side to swing up. Two of the men hurried forward, desperate to balance the platform, while Ethan ran the short distance to the edge of the platform and jumped. He grabbed the lip of the plateau and pulled himself up with Hannah's help. He crawled over the side and looked back, watching the three on the platform try to steady it along with the block.

The cavern echoed as everyone shouted instructions to get the platform balanced.

"Did you deliberately do that?" Hannah asked, watching them move about.

"Had to get you over here first so they didn't use you as a bargaining tool. Now they can sort themselves out."

"Do we run?"

Ethan glanced behind him at the thirty metres of open terrain before the doors. "If we run now, they'll see us and start shooting. We need to start slowly moving back while they're preoccupied with getting across, and whatever happens, go through door number one."

They slowly moved back as Graves and Andrea sorted out who was going next, trying to work out the best way to proceed. Ethan wondered if they realised the meaning behind the sign, or if they had even noticed it.

Sacrifices must be made!

The nature of the platform design meant that as soon as the

second-to-last person was off the platform, the weight of the stone slab would shift and drop. The last person on the platform would fall, as would the platform itself.

But that was their problem. Ethan was entirely focused on getting himself and Hannah through the door. Once they were through, they might have a shot at escaping.

Though it depends on what else Maynard has up his sleeve.

That thought complicated any hopes he might have had about escaping. Regardless of what Maynard had in store for them, it was going to take time to get through it. But as soon as Andrea and Graves realised they were gone, they would give chase. He didn't express these concerns to Hannah, not wanting to worry her even more. This was the slim chance that they had, and he had no belief that Andrea would let them live once they found the treasure.

They were almost at the door when the first of the men climbed up and off the platform. Ethan saw Graves jumping down to balance the board.

"Quickly," Ethan whispered to Hannah. The gunman still had his rifle slung over his shoulder and was watching the platform instead of them, so Ethan followed Hannah toward the first door.

Just as they neared the door, someone cried out, and Ethan pushed Hannah to the door. She opened it just as the first bullets pinged off the wall near their head, and they both dove through. With the torch in one hand and Hannah's hand in his other, Ethan took the lead and they hurried through another winding, rising tunnel.

"We have to hurry," Ethan said. "They saw which door we

went through, so they won't be far behind."

It didn't take long for them to emerge out of the tunnel, huffing after the uphill run. They were in a narrow corridor and before them was another timber platform. This one spanned the width of the corridor and made of tiles, each one about two metres by two metres. The platform ran four tiles wide and seven tiles long. There were names etched into them. Etched into the first row tiles were: *'Virginia'*, *'Kent'*, *'Nachtglas Island'*, *'Kent'* again, and *'North Carolina'*.

"What's this?" asked Hannah, looking at the names.

"Look," Ethan said. There was another sign hammered into the ground. It read: *'Follow my journey'*.

"I guess we take the path he took," Ethan said, looking at the first row of tiles.

"And if we don't?"

"That." Ethan pointed to a nearby gap in the tile where it had fallen and revealed the deep dark abyss below.

"Right. Ok. So where did his journey begin? When he defeated Blackbeard, or when he was born?"

Echoes came from the tunnel behind them, and Hannah grabbed his arm. "Ethan, we have to hurry!"

He tried to look at the tiles beyond to see if he could trace a route, but the words were so lightly written that it was hard to make out what the next ones said. He decided to take a chance. "Kent," he said. "It's where he was born."

"Which one?"

He took a step toward the fourth tile from the left. "This one."

"Are you sure?"

Ethan shook his head, "Not really. I'm guessing his journey started from where he grew up." He put all his weight on one leg and tested the '*Kent*' tile with the other. It didn't give, so he added more weight until he was putting all of it on the tile.

"Looks like this is the right one," he said. "I'm going to check the next one, and you follow my lead, okay?"

Hannah nodded and Ethan looked at the next row of tiles: '*Kent*', '*Nachtglas Island*', '*North Carolina*', '*Virginia*', and '*Ribeira Grande*'. On his left was '*Nachtglas Island*', which he immediately dismissed, and '*North Carolina*' was on his right.

I can ignore 'Ribeira Grande' and the 'Nachtglas Island', so that leaves his time in America. He defeated Blackbeard in North Carolina.

He put one foot on the '*North Carolina*' tile to his right, and just as he was about to take another step...

No, wait!

The tile fell out from beneath him. Hannah shouted his name, and Ethan cried out in surprise. He twisted as he fell and grasped hold of the edge of the '*Kent*' tile. He held on with his forearms on the tile while his legs dangled in the open space below. Hannah rushed over to him, and his heart leapt into his throat, worried the extra weight would cause the tile to fall, but it held and she pulled him up. "Are you all right?" she asked.

"Holy shit, he's a sneaky bastard." Ethan's heart was pounding in his chest as adrenaline surged through his body. "And I'm a dumb one."

"Why?"

"Because I just remembered he was based in Virginia before coming to North Carolina when he killed Blackbeard."

He took a step forward onto the *'Virginia'* tile in the second row and then to the *'North Carolina'* tile directly left. He followed the rest of the path. He went from *'North Carolina'* to *'Nachtglas Island'* to *'Riberia Grande'* to *'Lake Faguibine'*, and then finishing on *'Kent'* where he lived out the rest of his days.

Hannah followed his path, and they stood on the other side of the platforms. "That won't keep them for long," Ethan told her, turning around.

They ran along the cavern, with Ethan's light leading the way, until they came to another set of ten doors, labelled one to ten.

Ethan immediately took her through door eight, guiding them into another tunnel.

"One, seven, one, eight?" Hannah asked.

"He captured Blackbeard and found his compass in 1718, which began this madness."

"That's clever," Hannah said.

Ethan agreed. "But if Andrea and Graves have any basic historical knowledge of Blackbeard and Maynard, they will figure it out."

"Just hopefully not before we get out of here."

Ethan nodded, continuing through the tunnel. This was another long tunnel, though it had dips and rises here and there. They eventually made it to another room.

"This is getting old," Ethan complained. "But at least there is only one door this time."

This room was small and square, with a door to the far end with some sort of pulley contraption attached to a ship's bowsprit above it. To their left was a pool of water that disappeared beneath the wall, possibly part of an underground river.

They hurried to the door and tested it, but it held firm.

"I suppose it was too much to ask for it to be that easy," he muttered. "All right, let's see what we have here."

They stood back, and Ethan ran the light over the contraption above the door. There were four circular boards, overlapping each other in a quatrefoil design. Every board had four hooks on it, and the bottom hook on the bottom board had something attached to it.

"Is that a head?" Hannah asked.

Ethan ran his light over it. The design was rough, but there was no mistaking a nose, eyes, and a long beard. "That's Blackbeard's head."

Running from the boards was a rope-and-pulley system that connected separately to two helms attached to the wall on either side of the door. The bowsprit was attached to the top board, and the halyard rope hung down from it.

"Let me guess, we have to move the head from the bottom board to the top board using the helms?" Hannah asked.

"Yep," Ethan replied. "Come on, let's see what controls what."

Ethan took the left side and Hannah took the right as they turned the helms, seeing which handles turned what. After a minute, they worked out that the bottom and left boards were turned by the helm on the left, and the right turned the top and right boards. It seemed simple enough, except that the helms turned two boards at a time, but in opposite directions. Turning the left helm to the left made the left board turn left, but the bottom one turn right, making everything more difficult to figure out.

After a moment of deliberation, Ethan said, "All right, we know what to do. I'll turn them and you direct me."

Hannah stood back while Ethan turned the handles. It took some time, the rotating boards confusing them for most of it, but eventually, the stone head was rotated to the top, where it was hooked to the halyard.

Ethan grabbed the halyard rope and pulled, and the head slowly moved along the bowsprit, swaying with the momentum. While he did, Hannah said, "This is a little morbid."

"It is," Ethan agreed. "But historically accurate. Maynard cut off Blackbeard's head and hung it from the bowsprit of his ship."

"Still morbid."

"Yep."

He pulled one last time, and the stone head settled into place at the tip of the bowsprit. Once there, the weight of the head pulled the bowsprit down like a lever. There was grinding as cogs behind the wall turned and the door unlocked.

"Come on," Ethan said. "We don't have much time."

They went through the door and entered a massive cavern. Light filtered through a long scar in the ceiling high above, the glare almost blinding them after hours in Maynard's dark tunnels.

The light illuminated a huge, crystal clear lake before them that was about the width of ten football fields and extended into the darkness far beyond.

"This must be centuries of run-off from Lake Faguibine," Ethan said in awe, leading Hannah toward it. But his awe for the lake was short-lived because, as they rounded a large outcrop of rocks, they came to a jetty that was partially destroyed from fallen debris.

"No way," Ethan breathed. "This is impossible."

"What is it?" Hannah asked.

He pointed, at a loss for words. Because, docked at the jetty, was a hundred-foot-long, forty-cannon ship. Fully rigged with three masts and square sails, it had a raised forecastle and quarterdeck. Hanging off the captain's cabin, and fluttering in a light wind, was a blood-red Jolly Roger.

"It's the *Queen Anne's Revenge.*"

Forty Two

"The *Queen Anne's Revenge*?" Hannah said, obviously as confused as Ethan was. "But I thought it had been found in America."

They were weaving their way along the jetty, passing fallen debris, crates, and barrels, trying to reach the infamous ship.

"That's what I thought," Ethan said. "But none of this makes sense."

How did Maynard get the ship when reports were that Blackbeard had run it aground a few months before he died and that it was discovered in North Carolina in the 1990s?

He supposed it was possible that the finding could be wrong. He didn't know much about the discovery beyond it being believed to be Blackbeard's ship, but the evidence was right in front of him.

The ship creaked, swaying slightly in the mostly calm waters as they made their way to the end of the jetty.

"How did they get the ship in here?" Hannah asked as they stepped onto the gangplank.

Ethan stopped and pointed to the other side of the lake. "With that."

Rising out of the water was an enormous, open-faced shaft that extended all the way up to the cavern's dark ceiling, and connected to long, vertical beams. Four chains, as thick as mining truck tyres and just as big, hung down from the beams and joined on to a huge rectangular platform resting just above the waterline. Built onto the platform were dozens of bilge and keel blocks of various sizes. They started small and gradually got taller toward the outer side of the platform, forming a large 'V' shape.

"Is that a drydock *elevator*?" she asked incredulously.

Ethan nodded in awe. "I think so. I think they used it to lower the ship off the lake."

"That's amazing."

"It's unbelievable," Ethan agreed.

Near the elevator was a rocky beach, strewn with debris and broken pieces of timber. Beyond it, a ladder was bolted into the cavern wall leading to a plateau. A small bridge connected the plateau to the elevator, where a series of stairs and ladders ran up the exterior of the shaft in a set of switchbacks. Ethan followed the stairs with his eyes until they disappeared into the darkness above. He pointed at it and said, "And I reckon that's our way out of here."

"Then let's go," Hannah urged.

Ethan stared at the ladder and then at the *Revenge.* His eyes lingering on the worn wood, the ripped and tattered sails and jolly roger shifting lazily in the moving air. He started walking towards it.

"Ethan…" Hannah said, but he held up a finger.

"Just… just one second," he said. Excitement welled up within him and he hurried up the rest of the gangplank. He dropped onto the deck of the *Queen Anne's Revenge*, his shoes kicking up a puff of dust as they landed on the solid timber. Hannah dropped down beside him a moment later.

"Wow," he whispered, as if speaking any louder would disturb the history of the ship. He looked around, admiring the mizzen, main, and fore masts, the topsails, pulleys and ropes, the handrails, and the crow's nest.

A rusted cutlass lay on the deck and he picked it up. It was heavier than he expected.

"Avast, ye bilge-sucking landlubber!" he called, swiping the air with the cutlass. Then he turned to Hannah. "Do you realise we are the first people to walk on this ship in over two hundred fifty years? Since Maynard himself!"

She gave him a weak smile but said nothing.

Ethan didn't notice her lack of enthusiasm. He put the cutlass down and walked along the deck, running his hand over the long-dormant cannons, the handrails and tugging on the thick ropes.

He reached the captain's cabin at the stern of the ship and pushed on the painted black double doors, but they resisted. He put his shoulder against them and pushed. He heard the snapping of the latch and the door gave a little. He shoved it harder this time, and it opened enough that he could see a desk was propped against them.

"That's strange," he said.

"What?"

"The door is blocked from the inside. Here, give me a hand."

"Ethan, we need to get out of here," Hannah urged.

"Just a minute," he said. "Come on."

She stood next to him, putting her shoulder against the door. They pushed once, twice, three times, and on the third try, they pushed the door open enough so that Ethan could squeeze through. He pulled the desk out of the way and opened the door for Hannah.

The cabin was sparsely furnished with bookshelves to the left and a tattered hammock on the right. A cobweb-covered chandelier hung from the roof, and at the back, sitting in front of multiple arched windows, was a long desk.

Ethan walked to the desk, running his fingers over the dust, while Hannah explored the perimeter of the room. There were scrolls and bowls, ink pots and quills, and sitting in the middle of it all was a thick, leather-bound book. Just as he was about to open it, he heard Hannah cry out. She was standing near the rear cabin windows, staring at something in the corner.

"What's wrong?" Ethan asked.

"There's a skeleton here."

"What?"

He circled the desk and, in the light that passed through the grimy windows, there were the remains of a skeleton sitting with its back against the wall. It wore a pair of black boots, tattered black pantaloons, and a moth-eaten dark-red coat over a stained white shirt. On top of the grinning skull was a red bandana and beside it lay a tricorn hat. The skull was cocked to the side with an open mouth smile, some teeth missing, but looking seemingly proud of his fashion sense.

"How do you think he died?" Hannah asked.

Ethan pointed to a small hole in the side of the skull. "Shot in the head."

He knelt beside the skeleton and pulled aside the coat to reveal a set of twin holsters. Three flintlock pistols remained in their holster and he found the fourth on the floor near the hand. "Shot himself," he amended.

"Suicide?"

Ethan nodded and pulled a flintlock out of the holster and examined it. The once-polished wood had faded, the gold trigger guard had dulled, and there was rust on the hammer and frizzen, but it was otherwise in good condition. An intricate swirling design had been inlaid on the metal plate below the frizzen and Ethan knew these pistols meant a lot to the owner.

"Do you know how to use that?" Hannah asked as he stood up and put the flintlock in his waistband, and pocketed a bag of gunpowder and iron shots.

"Ritchie used one at the Inaccessible Island, can't be that hard, can it?"

She nodded to the skeleton. "Who do you think it could be?"

Ethan knelt and picked up the hat, rotating it on his finger, and said, "I would say one of Maynard's men, but with the way he's dressed…" he paused. "Maynard wrote how Edward Low, Philip Lyne, and Francis Spriggs all found his hideout in the Inaccessible Island. Maybe this pirate found him here."

He tossed the hat aside and got up, returning to the desk and the book. The book was plain, with no design on the front, just a buckle and strap to keep it secure. He wiped away a thick covering of dust and unbuckled it and carefully opened it. Written on the first page were dates and numbers and supplies. It was an inventory of some kind. He carefully turned the stiff, yellowed pages and found entries detailing the amount of money spent on food, building materials, and workers.

"This must be everything they spent to get the ship down here," he said to Hannah, who was reading over his shoulder. He picked up a receipt for thousands of pounds for gears, cogs, chains, timber, and other materials. He turned the book to the last page, and, instead of more inventory, there was a written passage:
January 1749

That scoundrel has betrayed me!

I should have expected it, though. It was always his plan. He constantly spoke of the risks of letting those who knew of it live.

I can't be upset with him because I was planning to do the same. He just beat me to it.

Those things are beating down the door, but I think it will hold. They are vicious, mindless creatures, but thankfully not smart enough to get through. It gives me time to write everything down so history knows what happened… what we did… if my ship is ever discovered.

In 1717, my crew and I pillaged a Spanish ship carrying gold and spices and other cargo. We took everything they had, including a black chest hidden behind a false wall. The chest was locked, and when I interrogated the captain, he begged me to not touch it. He told me to take anything I wanted but not 'el cofre negro,' that it was 'tesoro maldito'.

Asking a pirate to not take treasure is like asking a dog to not take a bone. I took the key from the captain's dead fingers and opened the chest. Like the other chests, it was filled to the brim with gold. But even on first sight, part of me knew there was something different about it. I later realised it didn't shine like gold — it was dull, even in the brightest light.

After the raid, we took everything to the Revenge and scuttled the ship. Me and my crew opened all the chests — including the black one — and celebrated. The men eagerly dove for the gold like they were at their first whore house. As usual, a fight broke out among them, and I sent Ben, one of the cook's boys, to the cells and locked the treasure away. The men carried on with the merriment into the night.

In the middle of the night, I was awoken by my first mate. He told me that Ben was acting strange. I went down to the cells where the crew had already crowded around, and Ben was growling, screaming, and clawing at the cell bars. I thought he was drunk, but remembered he hadn't been celebrating with the boys. I asked what happened, and the men said they didn't know. They told me he started screaming and rushing at the bars, slamming into them. His face looked like beaten meat, his nose bloodied and out of shape, and he'd clawed deep scratches into his cheeks and neck. I tried to talk to him but he didn't respond, didn't even take notice of anything I said. It was as if he didn't recognise anyone.

Not knowing what to do, we left him in the cell with plans to take him to a doctor when we landed in port. We were still days away, and all day, every day, he was screaming, yelling, charging into the bars. We discussed whether we should put him out of his misery, but one morning, Ben was

493

found dead in his cell, shrivelled up like he had been left in the sun for too long.

It happened again just after Ben died. We were close to Nassau when young Jack was overcome with rage and started attacking the men. He had killed ten of them before I shot him and tossed the body overboard. The crew were spooked, wondering what curse had befouled the ship. I thought about the Spanish captain and what he had said and asked one of the men what 'tesoro maldito' meant.

He told me it meant 'cursed treasure,' and I thought about that black chest. I locked it away and told the men to stay away from it, but the curse took hold and more men fell to it.

The changes varied. Some who touched it felt fine for a few days before suddenly going into a rage, while for people like Ben, it was almost instantaneous. For some, including myself, it had no effect at all.

To make matters worse, when we sighted Nassau, we found the Royal Navy had barricaded it, led by that pain in my ass, Woodes Rogers. We turned sail and headed for Carolina before they could spot us.

I spoke with Israel about what we should do. He determined that the gold from the black chest was turning the men somehow, but I said that was nonsense. We decided to test it. I had two chests brought to my cabin, the black one, and one of the others we recovered from the Spanish ship. I ordered two of the young deckhands to take a coin. John took one from the black chest and Marty took one from the other. Marty never changed, but it was almost sunset when John turned. I shot him myself when he started screaming in pain. It was the least I could do for the boy.

It was a cruel but necessary experiment.

We now knew the Spanish captain was not lying. The gold was cursed. We set sail for the Nachtglas. I had previously used them as a hideout and employed some engineers to build me the compass. It was the safest place to hide the treasure until we decided what to do with it. We unloaded the treasure and, with my compass, it ensured only I had the direct route to finding it.

We departed the island and were immediately attacked by an English fleet. We escaped, but they had the island surrounded and while I thought the treasure was safe for now, there was a great risk that they would discover it, even without the compass.

We returned to North Carolina where I learned that Woodes Rogers was the man behind the attack at Nachtglas. He had set sail from England with a fleet of ships and was tasked with putting an end to piracy, and he was determined to track me down.

If not for the situation, I would have been flattered he cared so much about me.

Israel and I were both worried that the treasure would be found and, with the empires' focus on ending piracy, it could be used against us. We decided we had to reclaim the treasure and hide it elsewhere. Somewhere no one would ever find it. But with the island occupied by the British fleet and Woodes Rogers bearing down on us, we had to get him off our trail first.

Israel mentioned to me a man named Robert Maynard. He was a British naval officer, an honest enough fellow, but more importantly, he was God-fearing. With his connections, Israel organised for us to meet in secret. The meeting was tenuous with five of my men and five of his. A powder keg ready to explode at any moment as I explained the situation with the treasure. It was no surprise he didn't believe me and thought it was a setup. After the standoff, I offered him proof and, with gloves on, handed some cursed coins we brought with us to his men. I told Maynard to not touch the coins but find me when 'it' happened.

Maynard found me a two days later, furious, and tried to run me through. I asked him what happened, and he told me that two of his men started attacking others, killing three. They tried to subdue them, but it was as if the devil possessed them, and they were forced to kill the turned men. I explained to him what happened to my men, and Maynard demanded to know everything.

I told him all I knew.

He asked why I came to him and I told him I wanted to get rid of the treasure, but with Woodes Rogers on the hunt, I could not move the treasure from Nachtglas.

To my great surprised he agreed to work with us, calling the treasure an affront to God, and we came to an agreement.

The first thing we did was plan on how to get Woodes Rogers off my sails.

We planned the fight on Ocracoke Island, but not before I ran my ship 'aground' for Maynard to recover later. I 'marooned' some of my most trusted crew on an island and told Stede Bonnet where to find them. Unfortunately, I couldn't save them all, but I needed to sacrifice some in the battle on Ocracoke Island for 'the greater good' as Maynard put it.

Second, we needed intelligence of my whereabouts and my latest misfortune to get to the governor so he could act on it. Knowing William Howard was skulking about the taverns, I had some of my men spread the word among those that Howard frequented. If he heard I was around, he would run to the governor quicker than a young babe runs to its mother. The plan worked, and Maynard received the word from his superiors that I was on Ocracoke Island and they were planning to ambush me.

Then came the day of the battle. We planned it so Maynard would tell his men that he was to engage me on his own. He would cut me with a poisoned blade that would 'kill' me.

I must admit I was concerned he would simply go back on his word and kill me outright, but to my great relief, he didn't. After the battle was done and everyone believed I was dead, Maynard took the compass from my coat, revived me, and we replaced my 'dead body' with one of my crew, dressing him up in my clothes and adding the beard. Maynard presented my 'body' to his superiors. And to make it even more dramatic, he cut the head off the fake and hung it from the bowsprit of his ship when he sailed into Virginia. I had a good laugh when I was told about it afterwards.

The man was as ruthless as he was dedicated.

Maynard smuggled me away from North Carolina and returned me to my ship. I sailed for Nachtglas, trailing behind Maynard's ship. Maynard tried to convince Woodes Rogers to push his fleet elsewhere. He told him that with the infamous Blackbeard dead, there was no point focusing on the island when there were other pirates to capture in Nassau.

Rogers agreed and sailed off with most of his fleet. We launched a surprise attack on the remaining ships, sinking them and leaving no one alive. We landed on the island with Maynard, arriving soon after with a crew of his most trusted men, and we settled there for a time, content that we had enough protection for the treasure.

My crew and Maynard's co-existed well enough for seven years and we tried to make a living before we were discovered. We dealt with Spriggs and Low, but Philip Lyne and his crew found the passage to bring their ship in. I believe he followed one of the cargo ships we used for supplies.

We escaped, although it was a close one, with Lyne's surprise attack catching us off guard. His crew got a hold of the treasure, but they made *the mistake of opening the chest and touching the gold. Fate was on our side that day as Lyne's men turned almost immediately and turned the tide of the battle. I killed Lyne. Even without my beard he recognised me, and the surprise on his face as I ran him through is something I will never forget.*

God was with us that day, but we had been complacent, and the battle with Lyne's crew lost us a lot of our own, enough that we barely had enough to man one ship. We scuttled both Maynard's and Lyne's ship, and took the Revenge, sailing her to Cape Verde and then Western Africa. Maynard had some fool hardy notion to take her inland, insisting that no one would think to look for the treasure there. I argued with him. But he was stubborn and, since his men outnumbered mine, I acquiesced and we took the Revenge up the river, sailing for months, until we met the Blue Men of the Desert. Suddenly, our crew had doubled as Maynard brought them aboard. I had nothing to do with them. Maynard was the one who did all the talking and explained what we were doing.

They believed his story, thinking the treasure was what they called 'vodun' and led us back to a lake we passed by weeks before. The lake was enormous, but in plain view. Maynard agreed with me, but one of the blue men showed us where a section of it fed into an underground lake. Maynard had the foolish idea to lower the ship to this lake. I argued but was once again overruled, and with the help of the crew, the blue men, and some of the best engineer's gold could buy, we actually did it!

Most of my gold was spent building that contraption to lower the ship, sealing the tributary and building those infernal traps which left me with mere crumbs of my plunder.

Once everything was done, the blue men left as suddenly as they appeared. I suggested we give chase, but Maynard was unconcerned. We lived on the ship for another month, ensuring everything was working as planned and that no one stumbled onto the lake.

That was when the next part of the plan took place. When we began this endeavour, Maynard came to me one night and told me how he feared the treasure. That it was an affront to God and, in the wrong hands- like pirates - it could cause untold damage to the Empire. My argument was the opposite. That the treasure in the hands of the empire could spell the end of me and my kind. We ultimately agreed the treasure couldn't be put in the hands of any man. We decided that no one who knew of the cursed gold could be left alive. Once we had everything built here, the engineers who knew of the location were dispatched and Maynard and I took care of each other's crew until it was just the two of us. We dumped the bodies overboard and lived on the Revenge for the next two months, preparing the last resort and ensuring no one would find us.

But some did find us. The Blue Men of the Desert returned, hungry for the gold, and before we knew it, we were surrounded on the deck of my ship. I listened as Maynard, who had established a relationship with them, told them to take the gold, that it was in the hold.

I thought he had lost his mind until, as I sit here in my quarters contemplating when to use this pistol, I realised that no matter what he said, this was his plan all along. Knowing the Blue Men would open the chest and succumb to the curse, Maynard walked away as the last man alive who knew of the cursed treasure and its location. He knew that I have no way of escaping amid the violence.

I have reflected on my life many times during this quest. I spent part of my life as a pirate, feared by many, and then I spent it protecting the unknowing world from a terrible curse.

God certainly has a sense of humour!

It has been days. I still hear them out there. The ones who didn't change are undoubtably dead while those creatures bang on my door, wanting to get at me with the same tenacity of Woodes Rogers.

My stomach growls and my throat is parched.

I cannot sleep for fear of those… things getting to me.

I can no longer go on.

This is my end…

EDWARD TEACH

Forty Three

Ethan looked up from the journal and stared at the skeleton of the most infamous pirate of all time. Words could not describe what they had just uncovered.

"They were working together this whole time?" Hannah asked.

Blackbeard and Maynard worked together!

Ethan nodded. "They collaborated, put on a show to fake Blackbeard's death to hide a treasure he stole from the Spanish. It seems they put aside their differences for the greater good... well until Maynard stabbed him in the back."

"He never mentioned it in his diary?" Hannah asked.

"No way would a British naval officer admit to fraternising

with a pirate, even in his own diary. It just wasn't proper…"

He trailed off, spinning around and heading out the cabin door.

"Where are you going?" Hannah asked, following him out of the captain's quarters and onto the deck. He went down a set of stairs into the hold of the ship.

Even with his torch and light filtering through the cracks in the boards, the hold was dark. Ethan found a lantern and lit it with the fire starter. The lantern provided a dull light, and Ethan headed deeper into the hold. He passed shredded hammocks hanging from the beams, broken tables and chairs, and a mess of pots and pans. He passed by the remains of dozens of the Blue Men of the Desert. Some were skeletons while others were victims of the curse, their bodies shrivelled up like prunes, twisted and deformed. All of them were dressed in tattered blue clothing.

"They really did go all out on each other," Ethan muttered.

All around the hold were red barrels. Ethan walked to one of them and pried the lid off. Shining his light inside, he saw it was filled with black powder.

"What is it?" Hannah asked.

Tossing the lid aside, he scooped up a handful of the powder, letting it fall between his fingers and back into the barrel. "It's gunpowder." He looked all around the hold. "It's everywhere."

"They were going to use this to blow up the ship?" she asked him.

He looked around at the barrels and the skeletons and thought about Blackbeard's last words. "It was the last resort," he said. "He was going to blow the ship up if all got out of hand."

Hannah shivered involuntarily. "Can we get out of here, please?"

"Just a second," Ethan said, heading towards the stern of the ship. He came to a door and pushed it, expecting it to be locked, but with a little effort it fell off its hinges and landed with a *whump* as air kicked up centuries of dust.

Inside, the room was dim and Ethan found a lantern hanging off the door frame. He lit it and then another on the other side. The front of the room was cast in a yellowy gloom, but it was enough.

"Oh, my," Hannah breathed.

Orange firelight glinted off mountains of gold coins, bars, and other trinkets bursting from a dozen chests in the middle of the room.

Ethan stared at the gold, unable to think. Temptation told him to dive in like Scrooge McDuck, but instead, he picked up a handful and examined them. They were mostly Spanish, minted in the seventeenth and eighteenth centuries, but there was one familiar one. It was a gold coin from the sixteenth century with the profile of a man facing right, and along the outer edge were the words: PHILIPPUS ● V ● 1709.

"This is Blackbeard's lost treasure," he whispered. "The 'mere crumbs' as he called it." He turned to Hannah with a wide grin. "I found it!"

"Good for you," she said softly, and Ethan turned back, not realising her tone.

Sitting in the middle of all the gold, as if it was the most important item in the room, was a black chest. Amongst the gleaming gold, the chest looked like it was hidden in shadows, a darkness that was incapable of drawing in light, and Ethan felt uneasy looking at it. He moved closer to examine the depictions carved into the chest.

"Ethan?" Hannah called to him from the threshold. "We have to go. They will be here at any moment."

"Look at this," he said, staring at the chest. There were swirls carved into the sides and back of the chest like twirling tentacles, while the front was split into five panels, each panel depicting a scene.

He remembered the sketch in his dad's journal—the sketch that started all of this. "This is it," he said, almost in reverence. He knelt before it and studied the panels.

The first panel showed a man and a woman standing next to each other, and the next one showed the woman standing over his shrivelled body. The third was just the woman with what looked like…

"Are those demons?" Hannah asked.

"I think so," Ethan agreed. He looked at a fourth panel. It showed the woman and man standing in front of what looked like a bubbling cauldron with large coins raining down into it.

The El Mal coins.

The fifth and final panel showed dead bodies strewn about with coins scattered next to them, while others were holding the coins. They were alive but looking crazed.

Carved below the panel were the words "Juana la Loca."

"Juana la Loca," Ethan murmured, thinking. Then it came to him, "Joanna the Mad! Holy shit! It all makes sense now!"

"What does?"

"Joanna of Castile. She was a Spanish queen who went mad after her husband—" he pointed to the first two panels, "—Philip I, died in the early 1500s. She exhibited strange behaviour before he died, but afterward, she spiralled. She accused nuns of trying to kill her, spoke in tongues, and even had Philip's casket exhumed and had it follow her wherever she went."

"Creepy."

"Oh, yeah. Batshit insane," Ethan confirmed. "But there were rumours she was into witchcraft, making love potions and other concoctions to keep her unfaithful husband's interest in her."

He looked over the panels again, connecting the pieces, and the puzzle was finally falling into place. He pointed to the first three panels. "These three seem to tell us first about Joanna and Philip's marriage, then his death, and then her descent into madness." He pointed to the second last panel. "As for this panel, this is her with, who I am guessing is, the vodun shaman who invoked the curse, creating the *El Mal* coins. And the last one is the effects of the curse."

"So, she created these vodun-cursed coins?" Hannah said. "But why?"

Ethan shook his head. "Revenge, maybe? She thought people were out to kill her, that her father poisoned her husband. She was mentally ill, so it could be any number of reasons that made sense only to her."

Ethan went to put his hand on the chest, but Hannah's hand intercepted his. "What are you doing?" she hissed.

"I'm opening the chest."

"What if it is also cursed?"

"It's not."

"But what if you're wrong?"

"I'm not."

"Ethan!" she urged. "I don't want you touching it. I want us to get out of here!"

"Just… hang on a minute." He went out of the cabin and picked up a piece of cloth hanging from a broken table and returned.

"Happy?" he said.

She looked at him but said nothing, and with the cloth wrapped around his hand, he unlatched the chest and opened it.

The chest was almost full, but the gold coins were dull, like they were shrouded in a permanent shadow. The coins were stamped with the same date and had the same dual profile of the king and queen as the one in Ethan's pocket.

"This is it," he said.

"What are you going to do?" Hannah asked.

"We could take it."

"What!" she hissed.

"Carry it out of here."

"Ethan, we don't even know *how* to get out of here! We can't take it."

He shut the lid, the sound echoing loudly in the cabin. "We can. We can get it out of here before they get here. I can finish what Mum and Dad started, change the narrative of their lives."

Hannah stared at him like he was insane. "Listen to me, Ethan. Your mum and dad don't want you to clear their name and change the narrative of their life—they never did. They wanted to protect you, to keep you away from the life *they* chose to live. You are doing nothing here except carrying on their legacy."

Ethan felt a mad pull toward the treasure.

"No," he shook his head. "No. They wanted this for me. They were teaching me to become like them." He nodded at the vast treasure before them. "To be a treasure hunter."

Hannah shook her head. "No, Ethan. They didn't. They didn't want you to live like them. Like Ritchie. Like Felix Graves. They didn't want their only child endangering his life to carry on their legacy."

"Then why did they do it? Why did they teach me all they knew?"

"Because they wanted to give you a *better* life. Not one of danger. But one where you could use their wisdom and knowledge to create a better legacy for yourself."

Ethan swallowed. He wanted to take the treasure and ignore Hannah, but her words rang true. He wasn't going to clear his parents' names or their history. They were what they were: thieves, tomb raiders, black market dealers, and it was a dangerous game. Did he want to be like them? Did the thrill of discovery drive him? He thought about where he stood and felt the electricity run through him. The idea that he was standing on the *Queen Anne's Revenge*, the ship of the most infamous pirate ever, was worth everything he'd been through.

He felt something warm on his hand and he looked down to find Hannah holding his. He looked up into her pleading green eyes. He could see her desperation, her desire to get out of here.

This isn't worth what Hannah has been through.

He looked at her, and even in the dim light, he could see her green eyes were glassed over, tears ready to spill. She was scared, and not only of getting caught, but for him. He couldn't let her down. He raised his hand and brushed it against her cheek, feeling a different kind of electricity. "You're right. I'm sorry. We have to get out of here. But first, we do what Blackbeard planned: We sink the ship, send the coins to the depths."

"Are you sure?" she asked.

He nodded. "We can't let them get hold of this… disease. No one can—it's too dangerous."

He led Hannah out of the cabin, through the hold, and up the stairs to the deck.

And waiting there for them were Andrea and Felix Graves, guns trained on them.

"Shit," Ethan said, putting his hands up.

Forty Four

Six of Graves' goons aimed their guns at Ethan and Hannah, while Andrea and Graves put their weapons away and approached them.

"You led us on a merry chase," Andrea said. "But this is the end now, Ethan."

"Save me the dramatics," he huffed.

"Search them," she ordered. A guard roughly patted him down and found the flintlock, which he admired and put in his waistband.

"Hey! That's mine, asshole," Ethan said.

The guard ignored him and, finding nothing else, he stepped back.

"Where's the treasure?" Graves asked.

Ethan gestured with his elbow to the hold. "Down there."

"Check it," Graves said to one of his men. "But don't touch it."

"Yes, sir," said the man and nodded at another to follow. They disappeared down into the hold while the others moved Ethan and Hannah to the poop deck. As they moved up the stairs, Ethan noticed more barrels all around the deck. *Maynard was not taking any chances.* He leaned against the railing with arms crossed, brooding, while Hannah silently cried next to him, each tear a dagger in his heart. Grassi and another man guarded them, while another patrolled the deck and Andrea stood near the helm discussing something with Graves.

"Did you kill them?" Ethan asked.

Andrea and Graves stopped talking, and both turned to him.

"At least give me the courtesy of knowing what happened to my parents before you kill me," he continued.

Andrea looked at Ethan as if deciding whether she would grant his final request. Then she said, "Before they grew a conscience, they worked for me from time-to-time. They would pass on the information on what artefacts had been discovered and sell them to me if we had a buyer. It was a good business arrangement for all of us."

"Why though? Why did they risk everything?" he asked.

"Because archaeology doesn't pay well, and we do," she said simply.

"You're lying."

She smiled coldly. "Not at all, Ethan. There was no ulterior motive for them, no conspiracy. Just simple human greed and desires."

He glared at her, wanting nothing more than to charge at her and wrap his hands around her neck.

"After you were born," she continued, "they had less to do with us. They realised you were no longer worth the risk, especially after what happened in Tajikistan."

Ethan thought back to the dream he had on the plane, the memory of his parents coming back into the hotel covered in blood.

"What happened there?"

She smiled at him. "We decided they were too much of a risk and tried to eliminate them."

"You tried to kill them?"

Andrea looked taken aback. "Me? God no, Ethan. I don't get my hands dirty like that. Not often, anyway. No, it was Felix here who tried to eliminate them, but he failed."

"But it was enough of a message to keep them away… until they stole Maynard's diary from us. Then your father came to me, not knowing I'd tried to have him killed, and told me what they had and what he suspected. Of course, we knew all about it, but it was serendipitous that they unknowingly returned the diary to us. We could now let them lead us to it and do away with them afterward. Two birds, one stone."

"But they had other ideas, didn't they?" Ethan guessed. "That's why they disappeared from the Inaccessible Island. They worked out what the treasure was and decided it was better off left lost forever. Especially since *he* was now into arms deals." He looked at Graves. "They knew you wanted to weaponise it, didn't they?"

Andrea leaned back and laughed. "You really are too clever for your own good. You are quite correct. Yes, they eventually worked it all out and returned to England, where they thought they would be safe."

"Why?"

"They cut a deal with Interpol," Graves grumbled. "Tried to set us up, but, as you can see, it failed."

He didn't want to ask, but he had to know. "Did you kill them?"

"Your dad gave me this scar," she said, running her hand along it. "When we ambushed them in Norfolk, he slashed me with a knife, trying to protect your mother. He missed my throat, but—" she tapped the scar near her eye again.

"And I thought you said you didn't get your hands dirty."

"Oh, Ethan. This was one of those special occasions that I *had* to be there."

"It's a shame he missed," Ethan said.

Before either of them could answer, the two men returned, wearing gloves and carrying the black chest between them. They climbed up to the poop deck and dropped it with a loud thud on the deck.

"Open it," Andrea ordered.

"Be careful," Graves warned. "We don't know how those coins work."

One lifted the lid, revealing the cursed treasure.

"This is it," Graves breathed. "At long last."

They both stared at the gold as if in a trance before they were interrupted by one of their goons. "Sir, there was more down there."

Graves looked at him. "How much?"

"The entire room was full of it."

"Okay, you two," Andrea said to the two men who brought up the treasure. "Head back and find the others. We will need their help to transport it out of here."

Both men nodded and hurried down the gangplank, tossing their gloves over the side, while another man leaned in and whispered something to Andrea. She nodded, and he walked away, pulling a phone from his jacket pocket.

Andrea gazed at the panels on the front of the chest. "What's this?" she asked, looking at Ethan.

"It's the origin of your cursed coins," he muttered. They both looked at him expectantly, so he told them the story of Joanna the Mad and his theory about the coins.

Andrea laughed derisively. "All this is because of a voodoo curse?"

"Seems the Spanish thought so."

"You must think I'm an idiot."

"I think a lot worse than that."

She seemed about to throw a retort back when the man patrolling the ship returned.

"Ma'am," he grumbled.

"What?"

"There's something you should see."

While they were speaking, Ethan whispered to Hannah, "When I give the signal, distract the guards."

"You, come with us," Andrea said to one of their guards. To Grassi, she said, "Watch them." Grassi grunted his assent, and she followed the man down the stairs, Graves trailing them both.

When it was just the three of them, Ethan started fidgeting with his shirt.

"What are you doing?" Grassi grunted.

Ethan showed him a cut on his arm that he'd picked up somewhere on their journey under the lake. "I'm wrapping it.

The man glared at him, suspicious, as Ethan ripped the bottom of his shirt until he had a strip. He acted like he was wrapping his arm when he nudged Hannah and suddenly she screamed and fell.

Grassi, not expecting it, looked over at Hannah impassively, while Ethan, with the strip of shirt in his hand, rushed to the chest and grabbed a coin, careful not to let it come into contact with his skin. He turned and yelled, "Hey, Grassi!" and tossed the coin at him.

Grassi turned to Ethan and instinctively caught the coin. There was a moment of confusion as Grassi processed what had just happened, then he dropped the coin like it burned him.

He looked at Ethan with wide eyes, and before he could pull his gun, Ethan grabbed Hannah and dove behind a stack of crates.

Bullets thudded into the wood, sounding like thunder as the noise reverberated into the distance. There was the sound of thudding feet on the deck, and Ethan peered around the crate.

The second goon had joined him. "What happened?" he asked, then saw the coin. "Why's the coin here?"

Grassi laughed. It sounded like the rumbling of a cement

mixer. "He tossed the coin at me. I thought I was done for."

"You touched it?

"Yeah."

The second man had his gun up immediately, pointing it at Grassi.

"What are you doing, Thom?" Grassi said.

Thom shook his head. "Sorry, Hugo. You know what Graves said. You can't touch the coins."

"Don't be an idiot!" Grassi snapped. "We need to get the kid before Graves gets back."

"But—" Thom started. He hadn't moved or taken his gun off the mountain of a man.

"But nothing," Grassi snapped gesturing to himself. "See? Nothing happened. I'm fine."

"But Graves—"

Grassi grabbed the torn piece of Ethan's shirt, picked up the coin, and tossed it back into the chest. "There, happy?"

Thom sighed. "Let's just get this over with and get the hell out of here."

They turned toward the crates that Ethan and Hannah were hiding behind.

Shit.

Forty Five

Ethan was defeated. The coin was his last ditch attempt and he knew it was a Hail Mary.

Thom led the way, gun drawn, with Grassi behind him. Ethan scrambled, searching among the debris for a weapon, but found nothing, not even a solid piece of wood to defend himself with.

Something heavy landed on the deck with a thud.

"Hugo? Hugo?"

Ethan peered over the crates. Thom had stopped and was looking back at Grassi. The giant was standing dead still in the middle, his gun laying at his feet. He was staring out in the distance, his eyes unfocused.

Thom moved toward him with his gun held out, saying,

"Hugo? What's wrong?"

Grassi suddenly twitched. His shoulder jerked sharply, and then his head snapped up, his eyes wide open. His neck strained, the veins popping, and his hands were repeatedly balling into fists and then opening again.

Thom approached him cautiously and put a hand on his shoulder. "Hugo?"

Grassi gave an inhuman scream that bounced off the cavern walls and tackled Thom. Thom cried out in surprise as they crashed to the ground. Grassi was still screaming in pain and beating Thom, his fists flailing wildly as he pounded the man's body.

The other guards, Andrea and Graves, appeared at the bottom of the step, guns drawn.

"Hugo?" Graves said, pulling his weapon out.

Grassi, in a rage, pounded one last time on Thom, whose body was bloodied and face mashed to a pulp. Then he let out a monstrous shriek and charged at the others. He moved fast and was on another guard before anyone could react. The guard cried out and fell. Grassi landed on top of him, his bloodied fists pounding at him now.

From his hiding spot, Ethan saw <u>Thom</u>'s fallen SIG. With everyone's attention on Grassi, he crept out and picked it up. Then he saw the flintlock poking out of the dead guard's waistband. He pulled it out and snuck over to the helm. He peered over just as the first shots rang out in the cavern.

Grassi let out more inhuman roars as bullets slammed into his body. He attacked again, this time Graves, who calmly backed up, his gun firing in rapid succession. His bullets slammed into Grassi's body, but the man kept charging, backing Graves into the railing. Grassi ignored the blood flowing from multiple bullet wounds as he crashed into Graves, causing the timber railing to crack and break away. They both fell overboard, entwined in an awkward embrace, before disappearing from view. There was a splash and Ethan took advantage of the distraction by standing up, aiming the gun, and firing, taking down another of Andrea's men. He adjusted the gun slightly and fired at Andrea. He missed, the bullets thudding into the deck, and she dove out of the way, hiding behind the mainmast.

"You won't get away from here," she called out from behind the mast. "More of my men will be here any minute now."

Ethan ignored her. He ducked behind the helm and signalled for Hannah to come closer. Bullets sailed harmlessly overhead as Andrea fired at them. Ethan grabbed the gunpowder bag and poured it into the flintlock's barrel and then dropped in an iron ball. He pulled the ramrod from its spot below the barrel and tampered it down before he found some cloth and wrapped it around the flintlock. He handed the loaded gun to Hannah.

"Take this. It's loaded and ready to shoot if you need it. Just pull the hammer all the way back and pull the trigger. It should work." He pointed to the shore on the starboard side, where they saw the ladder and debris earlier. "Remember the ladder? I'm going to provide you cover. When I do, I want you to jump overboard and swim for it. Get to the ladder and go. Don't stop. I'll catch up to you."

Her eyes went wide, and she said, "Ethan, no. Come with

me!"

He shook his head. "I need to blow up this ship."

"What!"

"Listen, you saw what that curse can do. I can't let it fall into the hands of people like Graves or Abboud."

Hannah looked ready to protest, but she caught herself and nodded. "Okay," she said, and then grabbed his hand and looked him in the eyes. "Be careful."

He grinned at her. "Always am. Now when I say 'go', you run."

She nodded, and Ethan readied himself. He silently counted to three and then said, "Go!" He stood and fired three times in Andrea's direction while Hannah took off like a rocket. Ethan saw Andrea peer around the mainmast and aim her gun at Hannah, but he fired again, the bullet slamming into the mast, and Andrea ducked back behind it.

Hannah leapt over the railing and splashed into the water below.

Relieved she was off the ship, Ethan checked his clip. He had three bullets, plus the one in the chamber.

You only need one.

Water lapped against the ship's hull. The boards creaked, and the rigging strained while they waited. Ethan stood near the helm. He had the higher ground, and he watched the mast, urging her to pop her head around, to give him a target. He didn't have much time to waste. The longer they were in this stalemate, the more likely more of her men would show. He had to do something.

Moving away from the helm, he checked the body of Thom,

looking for another weapon or a clip, but he found neither. He did find Maynard's two gold coins, and he pocketed them. Standing up, Ethan circled to the port side of the poop deck, hoping to get behind Andrea, but she was waiting for him. Bullets thudded into the railing near his head, the wood splintering. Ethan hurried down the stairs, firing twice, before ducking behind a crate.

They exchanged shots, then Andrea ran toward the hold while Ethan fired at her but missed and she disappeared down the stairs.

"Shit!" he muttered. He took another set of stairs down on the opposite side of the hold.

It was darker at this end of the hold, with hardly any light filtering through and the lanterns having sat unlit for centuries. It looked like he was in a kitchen of sorts, with shelves and cabinets. There were knives in a big butcher's block set in the middle. He pulled one out. The blade was dull and rusted, but it would do. With the gun in one hand and knife in the other, he moved forward, creeping toward the middle of the hold where it was brighter from the light filtering in from outside.

The ship's creaking was louder below deck, as if it was protesting their presence, and Ethan tried to move as quietly as possible. With the gloom and the various crates and overturned tables, there were almost too many places to hide. He checked behind each one, gun ready.

He was approaching the middle of the hold, near a wall divider, when he saw Andrea out of the corner of his eye, appearing from behind an overturned table. She tackled him and they crashed into a barrel, knocking it over, before they tumbled to the ground. She grabbed his wrist and repetitively slammed it on the floor, forcing the gun from his grasp. She pushed it away, causing it to disappear into the gloom.

Slashing at her with the knife, Ethan caught her on the arm. She cried out in pain but didn't stop. She grabbed his neck with a roar, her cold hands clamping down on his windpipe.

Ethan wheezed, fighting against her while also trying to breathe, but she held tight and he started feeling faint. Only the pressure and pain on his neck and windpipe kept him alert enough to remember the knife in his other hand.

He sliced wildly, hoping to hit anything, and felt it connect. It scraped somewhere near Andrea's head and she screamed in pain, easing her grip on his throat.

Andrea clutched at the side of her face and Ethan pushed her off, coughing and gasping for air as he rolled away and got to his feet. She was already on hers by the time he turned around, her gun pointed directly at him.

Forty-Six

Andrea held the gun on him, while her other hand was clamped over her cheek, blood trickling between her fingers, and running down her arm.

"It's almost poetic," she said between heavy breaths. "A scar from the father and now the son. It's a shame your mother isn't around to see this."

Mum?

Ethan looked around desperately. He was standing next to a table with a lit lantern on it. Behind Andrea was a barrel of gunpowder that had toppled over in their scuffle. The lid had come loose, and black powder was pouring out of it.

A stupid, desperate, dangerous idea came to him, and before

he could even think about it, he grabbed the lantern and tossed it in Andrea's direction. He dove behind a thick timber post while Andrea instinctively ducked and the gun went off.

The lamp smashed and landed in the pile of gunpowder, its fire sputtering and then dying in a lazy twirl of smoke.

Andrea laughed as she got to her feet. She looked ghoulish in the dancing firelight. Shadows crisscrossed her bloodied face, illuminating a deep gash that ran across her cheek, up past her ear, and disappeared behind her hair.

She walked slowly to him, and Ethan searched for something—anything—to use as a weapon, but there was nothing around. This was it. He had relied on, and pushed, his luck too far and too often, and now it was time to pay the piper.

"We could have been a great team, you know," Andrea said lazily, like a cat teasing its prey. "I convinced Felix to let you live when we first met, that we could try to convince you to join us. I thought it would be a matter of coaxing your emotions, being there for you, making love with you. I thought I could mould you to my will, but it was clear you are not like them. You were your own man who went his own way."

Ethan's chest was heaving now. "Was it you who killed Dad?"

"No, that was Felix."

She said it with such cold emotion that he wondered if she was lying. He looked into her eyes, trying to find any hint of deception, but only found those same intense eyes she'd always had, and he knew she wasn't lying.

"What about Mum?" he asked. "Did he kill her as well?"

She nodded. "Your father tried to save her and, in the struggle, she was knocked overboard and never resurfaced."

Finally, he had the truth. Despite the situation, he felt lighter, relieved. He could die knowing his parents didn't die in a scuba accident, knowing they were actually murdered. The puzzle was complete.

Ethan let out a breath that released all the anger and pain and frustration that had built over the last ten years.

Andrea raised the gun. "Goodbye, Ethan."

Just as she raised her gun, the smoking gunpowder sparked and flames flared to life. Ethan's eyes went wide. Andrea saw his reaction and fired just as the gunpowder exploded in a thunderous boom, the concussive blast throwing Ethan off his feet.

Ethan's eyes fluttered open, and he found himself on his back, looking at the roof of the hold. He coughed and looked around. Smoke billowed through the hold and shattered timbers lay strewn about. At the far end, the deck had caved in and a fire had broken out, igniting everything in its path, making its way to him.

Get up! Get up!

He watched the fire spread, travelling toward another barrel of gunpowder.

"Oh shit!" he exclaimed. He rolled over and pushed himself up to his knees just as another explosion threw him into the wall, timber and debris crashing down on him.

Ethan groaned and felt something wet along his back. He felt around and his hands splashed in water. The ship's hull had been breached.

"Christ, that's cold," he said. "Got to get out of here. Come on Ethan, focus. Stay awake."

He tried to get up, but he was stuck. A heavy beam was lying across his legs. He tried to push it off, but it didn't budge.

"Oh come on!"

Ethan felt the ship listing. The water was rising rapidly, already past his knees, and his legs were starting to feel numb from both the pressure of the beam and the freezing water. Ethan coughed. The smoke was getting thicker, and he searched around for something to leverage the beam off him. He coughed again, and his hand brushed against something smooth and round: a metal pole with a hook on the end of it. Wasting no time, with the water now around his hips, he grabbed the pole and wedged it under the beam and tried to pry it up.

He pushed on it as hard as he could and the pole snapped in half.

"Damn it!"

He tossed the broken shaft and grabbed the lower half, wedged it back under, and pushed.

"Come on!" he yelled. The water was now at his neck, but the beam still didn't move.

He tried again, straining with all the energy he could muster, and felt it budge a little. He took a deep breath and ducked his head under the rapidly rising water. He couldn't see in the dark water, but he still held the pole in his now numb hands. He pushed, feeling the beam loosen a little more while his lungs burned, desperate for oxygen.

He lifted his head and had to turn it awkwardly to get one last bit of air. This was his last chance. The water was past his head now. With the pole in hand, he pushed with all the strength he had left, and felt the beam move some more. He kept at it, pushing and wedging the pole further underneath.

While he worked, he felt his lungs burning and his vision cloud. Even with all his free diving, he was expending too much energy, too much oxygen, and he knew time was running out.

Just when he felt like he was about to pass out, he levered the pole one more time and pushed. Suddenly, the pressure on his legs yielded, and he slid them out from underneath the beam. He kicked away to a shallower part of the ship, coughing and gasping for air as he burst from the water.

With no time to waste, Ethan searched for a way out. The hold was a complete wreck, and water was gushing in through the breach in the hull. Broken pieces of wood floated past him as he waded through the water, heading for the stairs.

Even though he was in a shallower part of the ship, the water was up to his neck by the time he reached the stairs. Ethan cursed when he found them blocked by debris and heavy beams. He swam back to the other stairs, already submerged in the water, and ducked under. It was too dark to see, and he probed along the stairs, trying to find the opening. He reached the top, but there was no way out— the door was blocked.

He banged on the door, a burst of profanities bubbling away, and he ascended until he emerged above water. There was little air space left in the hold, and it was filling fast. Ethan spun around, trying to find a way out, but it was getting darker and colder in the water.

An idea came to him. He took a deep breath and dove under, swimming against the current to the dim light where the breach in the hull was. The light got brighter the closer he got, and he grabbed hold of the edge. The breach was narrow and shaped like a lightning bolt, forcing Ethan to reposition his body to slide through. He put his arms through first and then pulled his head and upper body through at an angle. As his lower half came through, he felt his pants snag on a jagged edge. He tried to shake it loose, but it wouldn't come free.

Lungs burning, Ethan pulled himself back inside the ship and tugged at the snag. His pant leg ripped free, and he carefully manoeuvred his body through. This time he got through and, with burning lungs and clouding vision, he kicked for the surface. His head burst through and he gasped, sucking in the cool air. He turned, seeing the *Revenge* was listing sideways, and he swam along the deck. By the time he reached the stern, the ship was completely on her side now and half in the water. Sails and ropes fell in a tangled mess as the masts snapped.

As he swam away, chunks of rock, shaken loose from the blasts, smashed through the *Revenge* like giant cannonballs—one last barrage for the famous ship. Ethan turned back, watching the ship sink, and saw the black chest resting on the railing of the poop deck, its lid open and coins pouring out of it into the water.

A sudden urge to swim to the gold and grab all he could overwhelmed him, and before he knew it, he was swimming towards it.

Ethan was halfway there, desperation and desire propelling him through the water, when a boulder the size of a car smashed through the railing.

The railing disintegrated, and the cursed treasure of Joanna the Mad disappeared into the lake's depths.

Forty Seven

Ethan felt like he'd just woken up from a fever dream. He treaded water while rocks splashed all about him.

"Ethan!"

It was Hannah. She was waving at him from the shore, urging him to come and Ethan swam towards her.

"I th-thought I told you to go," Ethan said through chattering teeth.

Hannah ignored him and helped him out of the water. "What happened out there?"

"The g-gold is g-gone."

"My God, you're freezing!" she said.

Ethan shivered, the cool air blowing his soaked clothes

making him even colder.

"Y-yeah," he stuttered, wrapping his arms around himself.

"Ethan, you're bleeding!" she said.

"What?" She was pointing at the lower part of his shirt where it was soaked with blood, and he pulled it up, revealing a dark hole just above his hip.

"That b-bitch sh-shot me!"

The adrenaline and cold water must have numbed the pain during the chaos in the hold, but he knew he would really feel it once it wore off.

"We need to get you out of here," she said, looking around as if there would be a convenient exit somewhere.

All around them, the cavern was collapsing, rocks falling and splashing in the lake. Across the lake, the *Queen Anne's Revenge* had disappeared, sunken to the depths, and Ethan felt a pang of sadness for it. History had been destroyed, and no one would know the truth of what Blackbeard had done.

He looked longingly at the spot where it had gone under, as if hoping the ship would emerge out of the water. He thought about all the lost gold, now having sunk to the depths. It would have been enough to make anyone rich. He shook his head and turned his back to the lake. Above them was the plateau that was connected to the elevator by the wood bridge.

Ethan pointed at it and said, "W-we have to cross that br-br-bridge and get on the s-st-staircase," he stammered. "Th-That's our way out of he-here." He pointed to the rusty-looking ladder, having no choice but to take it as more rocks came crashing down around them. "G-Go."

"But your side," Hannah protested.

"I'll be f-f-fine, just go," he said.

She grabbed the rung and climbed. Once she was halfway, Ethan followed, taking it slowly as his side burned. Hannah was almost to the top when the rung snapped and she almost fell. She cried out but managed to hang on and pulled herself on to the plateau. Ethan followed behind, nearly at the point of the broken rung, when the ladder snapped and broke apart. He fell, but his hands shot out and he grabbed a handhold and hung on as pieces of the ladder crashed to the ground.

He dangled over the pile of debris, sharp spikes of broken wood pointing up at him, and he swallowed.

"Ethan!"

Ethan's side burned and pain blossomed from his wound. "I'm fine," he winced. His eyes scanned the face of the rock wall and followed a climbing route that would take him to the plateau.

Ethan slowly made his way up. Being cold, tired, and injured sapped his strength, and his numb fingers made it hard to grab on to the handholds. But he pushed himself, the alternative spurring him on. He was spent by the time he reached the top and Hannah helped him over, where he lay on his back, trying to catch his breath.

"You don't look okay," Hannah asked, looking at the wound with concern.

Grateful he was no longer freezing cold, he said, "I might have exaggerated when I said I would be fine."

"You should rest a little," she said, but he shook his head.

"No, we need to get out of here. Who knows how long this

place will last."

The rocks had stopped falling and the cavern seems to wait with its breath held. Ethan knew they were in a precarious position. It wouldn't take much for them to start again. While he rested, Hannah jumped over a jagged crack in the plateau and examined the bridge. It was wide enough for a cart, and she tested it by putting her weight on it. "Do you think it will hold?" she called to him.

"It's going to have to," he said simply. He stood and hissed in pain as his hip flared up.

Hannah ran back to him. "Let me help you," she said, and before he could say anything, she put his arm over her shoulder and placed her arm around his waist and helped him to the gap in the plateau.

"I can do this," he said. Taking a couple of deep breaths, he was about to leap over the crack when they heard a whistling sound.

"What's that?" Hannah asked. Before Ethan could answer, an explosion rocked the plateau and threw them to the ground.

"What the hell?" Ethan shouted over more whistling sounds. Explosions continued to shake the plateau as he crawled to the edge and looked down. "Oh, shit!"

Funnelling into the cavern were a dozen of Andrea's men, and three of them were carrying grenade launchers. There was another whistling sound, and a smoke trail followed a grenade heading in their direction. It exploded below the plateau, rocking it violently.

"Ethan!" Hannah screamed.

He turned around just in time to see Felix Graves reach down and yank him to his feet. His face was scratched and bloody, his suit crumpled and wet, and his dark eyes were full of rage.

He threw Ethan against the wall and punched him in the stomach.

The air exploded from Ethan's lungs, and he groaned and fell to his knees, coughing.

"You have cost us *everything!*" Graves snarled and punched Ethan in the head.

Ethan's head cracked against the stone wall, and his vision clouded. He groaned and spat out blood.

"You may have stopped us getting the gold, but at least I can take you away from her!" Graves snarled, punching Ethan in the side again and again, each punch making his wound erupt in fiery pain before shoving him away.

Ethan crashed to the ground, Graves words echoing in his mind.

'Take you away from her'. Her? Hannah? Or…?

Ethan was pulled roughly to his feet. His legs were wobbly, and only Graves' hold kept him from collapsing in a heap. "That all you got?" he wheezed, blinking out blood leaking out from a cut above his eye.

Graves went in for another punch, but a loud explosion caused him to stagger and clutch his own shoulder. He turned around in shock, blood blooming over his jacket.

Nearby, Hannah stood with the flintlock still pointed at him, the muzzle smoking as she continued to pull the trigger, as if expecting it to fire again. Graves took two steps and shoved her.

Ethan's heart stopped and everything went in slow motion as Hannah tripped backwards and went sprawling over the side of the plateau.

"Hannah!" Ethan cried. Adrenaline and rage spurred him, and he charged at Graves, who was still clutching his shoulder. He crashed into him, and the momentum sent Graves over the edge, with Ethan tumbling after him. Flinging his arms out, Ethan grabbed the edge, and he slammed into the rock face, pain from his hip, almost causing him to lose his grip. He gasped for air as his hip throbbed, and he hung on to the still violently shaking plateau.

"Ethan!"

Below him, Hannah was hanging from a ledge, her feet dangling over the dark water of the lake.

"Hold on!" he shouted. He could see the fear in her eyes, and he clambered down as quick as he could, trying to keep the rising panic at bay.

"Just hold on," he repeated. "I'm coming!"

"Jackson!"

Near Hannah, Felix Graves was hanging one-handed from a hold at the bottom of the plateau. Beneath him was the shoreline, littered with the remains of the destroyed ladder and split timbers. He tried to lift his wounded arm to pull himself up but couldn't and he let hang limply at his side, blood trickling down his arm and dripping off his fingertips.

Ethan turned away, his focus back on Hannah, when Graves shouted. "Save me. And I will tell you where your mother is."

He paused.

"What?"

Despite his predicament, Graves gave him a bitter smile. "I know what happened to her! I know where she is!"

"Ethan!" Hannah called out. "I can't hold on much longer."

"Jackson! I am the only one who knows!"

Ethan climbed down, his hip flaring with unbearable pain, while Graves and Hannah both called out, vying for his help.

He thought about what Graves was offering him.

The truth.

Closure.

It was everything he wanted.

It was why he was on this crazy adventure.

It was a no-brainer.

He descended to the bottom of the plateau, reached out, and grabbed…

…Hannah's arm. He pulled her up, hip still protesting in pain, and she secured her feet on the edge.

"You fool!" Graves shouted. He flailed angrily, swinging his legs as he tried to find a foothold. Another explosion rocked the plateau and Graves's handhold broke free. A look of surprise-turned-confusion crossed his face as he stared at the rock in his hand before he fell.

Ethan and Hannah watched him fall, his arms windmilling as if he could slow his descent, and he crashed onto the debris, impaling himself through the chest on a timber post. Blood poured down his suit and he gave one jerk and then stopped moving, his lifeless eyes staring at the roof of the cavern.

Ethan helped Hannah as they climbed back onto the plateau.

He tried to get to his feet, but he stumbled and fell. Hannah was next to him in an instant. "That's looking worse," she said.

"I'll be—"

"Fine, I know," she said with a lopsided smile. She examined the bullet hole and ripped a piece of her shirt off, pressing it against the wound.

He hissed in pain and then gave her a lopsided smile of his own. "You could probably claim this as a practical for your course," he said.

She hugged him, "Thank you," she whispered.

Ethan winced. In pain or guilt, he wasn't sure. "Think nothing of it."

"You could have chosen him. You could have found out the truth," she whispered in his ear.

"Not a chance. I wasn't going to let anything happen to you, and despite all they've done, Mum and Dad would have agreed. That's not the legacy they would have wanted for me.

Besides, I owed you one for shooting him."

"Thank you," she repeated and wiped a tear from her eye.

He smiled at her weakly, but before he could say anything else, another explosion shook the plateau. Ethan peered over the edge where he saw the men with the grenade launchers still firing at them.

"Boy, they're taking the loss of their bosses really hard," he said. "We need to get out of here before this plateau is destroyed." As if reinforcing the point, the plateau shook violently as it was bombarded with more grenades. Ethan stood up, wobbling. "Let's try this again, hmm?"

He leapt over the small gap and hobbled toward the bridge with Hannah's help.

"All right, here goes," he said, and they crossed the fiercely shaking bridge. They managed to keep their balance and reached the ladder. Hannah went first, and Ethan followed close behind. The ladder shook, and the rungs creaked but held, and they climbed as quickly as they could to the first walkway. Ethan reached the top of the ladder and climbed onto the narrow walkway with Hannah's help.

Ahead of them was another ladder leading to another walkway. Ethan took a step when a loud boom rattled the elevator shaft and he stumbled forward.

They looked over the railing and saw Graves' men still hammering the structure with their grenade launchers. A loud crack, like thunder, echoed around the cavern, and Ethan knew the elevator wasn't going to last.

"Shit!" Ethan exclaimed. "Go! Go! Go!" he shouted at Hannah, and she led the way forward to the next ladder. She climbed, with Ethan behind, the explosive sounds of the grenades echoing around them.

After they made it up the ladder, they ran until they reached the next platform and continued up the stairs, switching back and forth as they climbed higher. Ethan's hip stabbed at him with every step, slowing his pace and causing the gap between him and Hannah to grow. She was waiting for him at the next ladder, and just as Ethan was urging her to climb, there was another loud crack.

"Watch out!" he cried and shoved Hannah forward just as a

large boulder crashed through the platform.

Hannah grabbed hold of the ladder as the walkway disappeared beneath her feet.

The platform swayed and Ethan leapt over the gap and caught hold of the ladder just as it fell away to the lake below.

"They're bringing the whole thing down!" he yelled as they climbed.

They continued climbing amid a shower of rocks that rained down like giant hailstones, smashing through the elevator as they fell. When they were almost to the top, a rock bounced off one of the horizontal braces, snapping the timber and twisting the entire elevator shaft. A second rock slammed into the boards behind Ethan, taking the platform with it, and he fell backward.

Before he could even cry out, he crashed onto the platform below. He groaned, his hip a fireball of pain. Slowly standing up, he found the way ahead of him was gone, the platform destroyed by falling debris.

"Ethan!" Hannah called out from above. She was looking over the railing down at him.

"I'm fine," he called back. "Just go. Get to the top!"

"Be careful!" she said and disappeared.

Ethan laughed despite himself. There was nothing careful about any of this.

Ahead of him was a ladder that led to the platform above. If he could get to it, he could get back up, but the space to the ladder was too big. He knew he couldn't make the jump.

He didn't have to contemplate that idea for long, as another boulder smashed through and the ladder and platform disappeared.

"Shit!"

He looked around desperately and then saw his only hope. A thick piece of rope was dangling from a horizontal beam, swaying with the rocking stairs. It was one of the support ropes that was usually lashed to the vertical beam, but it had come loose. It was a long jump, but if Ethan could get to it, he could climb up to the next level that was, somehow, still standing.

The platform he was on dropped again, and Ethan's heart shot into his mouth as he nearly lost his footing and fell over the edge. He had no choice. It was either go down with the platform or jump for it. Backing up as far as he could, he ran, ignoring the pain in his side, reached the edge, and jumped. Just as his feet left the platform, a boulder smashed through it, destroying it. He sailed through the air with his arms outstretched and grabbed hold of the rope. Momentum swung him back and forth, but he held on tightly and wrapped his leg around it.

The crashing of rocks and the violent movements of the structure fuelled Ethan's climb, and he pulled himself up along the swinging rope. When he reached an intact platform, he used his momentum to swing the rope back and forth. Just as he was about to let go of the rope, the platform disappeared, taken out by another boulder.

Bloody hell. How am I going to get out of here?

He continued to climb, his arms shaking with exhaustion, and the pain in his side was becoming unbearable. He looked up. The top of the stairway wasn't far, and he forced himself to continue.

A course of adrenaline surged through him and sweat poured

down his forehead as he climbed higher while everything around him fell.

Come on, he urged, forcing himself on. *Not far to go.*

At the top of the stairway was a ladder that lead to another plateau, this one the size of a football field. Hannah was already there, urging him on. Above him, dozens of thick crossbeams that reinforced the entire elevator shaft were attached to the cavern ceiling. Some beams were threaded through giant gears, which held the four chains that supported the elevator platform. The chains looped over the gears and disappeared somewhere over the plateau. Ethan kept climbing, and when he was finally in range of the ladder, he swung his legs again, creating the momentum he needed to cross the gap. He took one last swing, and when he was almost at the highest point, he let go of the rope. Momentum took him the rest of the way, and he crashed into the ladder. He cried out again at the pain in his side, but he held on, wrapping his arms around the rungs.

Hannah appeared from over the side. "Hurry!" she called. "The entire roof is coming down!"

She was right. Larger chunks of rock were falling, crashing through the remains of the elevator, and splashing into the lake below. Blinding spears of light poked through the roof as the cavern collapsed.

Ethan realised they had to hurry, or they were going to be buried with it. Spurred on by the threat of being crushed, he climbed the ladder. Hannah helped him up and pulled him away from the edge just as another boulder took out the ladder.

On the far side of the plateau, shafts of light beamed through, and Ethan pointed. "That way," he said. Hannah took the lead while he hobbled toward it, hand clutching at his side, trying to stop the blood flow.

The plateau was rumbling and rocks were raining down on them as they passed the chains connected to four huge car-sized capstans bolted to the floor. A chunk of stone crashed onto one capstan and the huge machine screeched and was ripped free from its bolts by the heavy chain. The capstan disappeared over the side. With one capstan compromised, the other three groaned, protesting at the additional weight, and they were ripped free from their bolts. They smashed through the cavern walls and disappeared over the edge.

The cavern shook, chunks of the roof crashing down all around them, and threatened to cave in on them.

"Go!" Ethan shouted, giving Hannah a push. Hannah took off while Ethan followed, his legs feeling like bags of cement as he stumbled across the open ground.

Come on. Just a little further, he urged. *You cannot die here!*

He tried to push through the pain, willing himself to continue, but his body disagreed with him and he slowed, his energy sapped. He watched Hannah get further and further away.

At least she'll survive, he thought, slumping to his knees. He took one last look at her fading body and then closed his eyes and fell forward, passing out.

Forty Eight

Ethan heard an alarm ringing, and someone was tugging at his arm. He grumbled something about not going to school today and tried to turn over.

"Ethan!"

"Just turn the alarm off," he groaned.

"Ethan! Get up. We have to get out of here."

"What?" he slurred.

"The roof is caving in!"

He opened his eyes. He was on his back and there, looking down at him with concern written all over her face, was Hannah.

"You have beautiful eyes," he said dreamily.

"Let's go," she said, and pulled him into a sitting position.

A shooting pain in his hip broke him out of his fugue. He groaned and rolled over and got to his feet. Hannah put his arm around her shoulder and, supporting his weight, they headed for the exit together.

Ethan hobbled after Hannah, trying to avoid and dodge falling rocks as they moved along the shaking ground. The light ahead was getting brighter and bigger with every step, and it powered his tired body forward.

"Shit!" he said when they finally made it to the end. It was a dead end, but there was a ledge just out of reach above them with light filtering through. Ethan turned to Hannah, cupped his hands, and said, "Come on."

"But—"

"Just go," he said.

She looked ready to argue with him, but a large rock crashed landed next to her, and whatever argument she was going to make died then and there. She put her foot in his cupped hands, and Ethan strained, the pain in his hip making his vision dance, as he hoisted her onto the ledge. She pulled herself up and crawled over the side and then looked back at him, reaching down.

"Come on!"

Ethan jumped up, but he didn't have the energy to get high enough to grab her hand. He tried again, putting his all into the jump, and their fingers touched, but she couldn't grip them. The pain in his side now burning like someone had placed a hot iron on the wound, and he didn't know how much more he had in him.

"Use the rock," Hannah said, pointing to the one that had

nearly fallen on her before. It was positioned near the wall and would give him some extra height. He stood on it while Hannah adjusted her position, and then he jumped again.

This time, Hannah grabbed his hand and held on. She pulled while Ethan tried to scramble up the flat wall, but he didn't have the energy.

"Come on!" she said, struggling to hold his weight.

"Damn it. Just let me go."

"No," she said through gritted teeth. She tried pulling again, and Ethan focused all his attention on the wall, trying to find some rough patches or uneven surfaces he could grip.

But there were none. The wall was as smooth as glass, and Ethan pulled his hand free from hers and fell to the ground. He looked up at her and said, "Hannah, go. Before it's too late."

"No! I can't leave you!"

"I don't have the energy to climb up," he murmured. "It's okay, Hannah. Really. I can die knowing the truth about Mum and Dad."

More debris was falling now, and they both knew there wasn't much time left.

"I won't leave you, Ethan. If you stay, I stay. Can you have that on your conscience?"

Despite the situation, he smiled. "You are stubborn."

"South African blood," she said. "Now come on!"

Taking a deep breath, he got to his feet and jumped again, and she caught his hand. She struggled, trying to pull him up, while he tried to scramble up the face of the wall, but he couldn't get any purchase on it. He was about to pull free again, ready to insist he was done for when, suddenly, he was yanked up like he weighed nothing.

"Gotcha, lad," said a familiar Irish accent.

"Ritchie! But how—"

The red-headed Irishman put up his hand. "No time, lad. Follow me."

Behind him, Abigail was leading Hannah away, but she stopped her and turned to them. "Ritchie, he's been shot," she told him.

"Is that right?"

Ethan nodded but said nothing, only the pain from the wound keeping him conscious.

"Explains why you look like shit," Ritchie laughed. He put Ethan's arm around his shoulder and carried him forward. They followed Hannah and Abigail toward the light, weaving their way around fallen debris and a maze of stalagmites. They arrived at a crack in the wall, Hannah and Abigail climbing through first. Ethan grunted in pain as the narrow sides squeezed on his hip, but Ritchie unceremoniously shoved him forward, and he burst out of the crack and into daylight. Even though it was raining, the light was harsh, and he closed his eyes while Ritchie guided him away.

When he opened them again, he saw they were behind a mesa on the shore of Lake Faguibine, the mud dried and cracked while rainwater pooled on top of it.

"Are we–" he started, but the ground rumbled and cracked as it started falling into the newly forming sinkhole. They ran, Abigail in the lead and Ritchie and Hannah carrying Ethan, until the ground finally stopped shaking.

It was eerily silent now, and a thick cloud of dust rose into the air, creating a haze in the gloomy, rainy day. Ritchie charged up to Hannah and enveloped her in a bear hug. "God, Han. I thought I lost you, lass," he said.

Ethan watched her hug him back and he smiled. He fell to his knees and then slowly laid down on his back, staring up at the cloudy sky. It had only been a couple of hours since he had seen it, but it felt like forever. His chest was heaving while he tried to catch his breath, and his legs were stretched out, grateful for the rest. The pain in his hip was unbearable, but it only made him smile.

Pain means I'm still alive.

Every now and then, he felt minor tremors, but he ignored them, knowing he was safe. He closed his eyes, finally able to rest.

Forty Nine

Bamako, Mali

"How did you find us?"

Ethan and Ritchie were walking down a long, windowless hall. It was the next morning, and after walking kilometres along the lake's dried shore, they were met by local police, who drove them to a hospital in Timbuktu. There, Ethan was examined and patched up, the doctor decreeing that there was no threat to his vital organs or life and that the bullet had passed through. After a couple of hours, they were back in a car and driving sixteen hours to Bamako. Ethan, with the help of some painkillers, and Hannah slept the entire drive in the car's back. They probably would have slept more if not for Ritchie waking them when they had arrived at a nondescript, two-storey building in the middle of Bamako.

Now they were following Abigail, who seemed to know the place well, through the halls of the building. She greeted a few people in business attire walking in the opposite direction.

"It was just luck, lad," Ritchie said. "We arrived at the lake a couple of hours before we found you. Abi—", she turned and gave him a look but Ritchie just grinned and continued, "—called in the local police and we found a bunch of cars that we assumed belonged to Graves, but we found no sign of them. So, we just stumbled around for hours until we felt the rumbling, and we came across that gap and there you were."

Abigail stopped them outside a windowless office and told them to take a seat. "I will need to debrief you all, one by one." She opened the door. "Ethan, you're first."

He hobbled into the sterile room of dark-grey walls, a desk, and two chairs. There were no pictures or personal photos, only a security camera in the corner watching the room.

"This feels familiar," he said.

Abigail took a seat, and Ethan took one opposite her. She opened a laptop, punched some keys, and when she was ready, she looked at him.

"Right," she began. "Bit of a rough week for you."

Ethan snorted. "You could say that."

"Tell me everything you remember from when this all started."

Letting out a long breath, Ethan recounted everything to Abigail. Finding his parents' journal and deciding to look for Andrea in England. The discovery of Robert Maynard's bunker in

Great Mongeham, and the incidents in Cape Town and the Inaccessible Island, including the kidnapping of Hannah and the "kidnapping" of Andrea. He told her about the underground chamber in Forte Real de São Filipe and what they discovered there leading them to Mali. He skipped over meeting Amastan, the nomad didn't need the authorities questioning him and his people, and he recounted everything that happened at the lake, including the discovery of the *Queen Anne's Revenge* and Blackbeard's body. He told her everything he could remember, though he skipped over the fact he slept with Andrea. After he had recounted the events, she asked him to talk about the gold and to describe what it did to Grassi when he touched it on the ship.

He did, telling her that he went into a rage and started attacking his own men. That he didn't even notice being shot multiple times, and that it only ended when he took Graves over the side of the ship. Whether Graves killed Grassi, or he drowned, or he escaped, Ethan didn't know.

"What happened to Felix Graves?"

"He's dead."

"And Andrea Gatting?"

"Also dead."

"You're sure?"

He nodded.

"You saw their bodies."

"I saw Graves' body. He got impaled on some of the broken timbers."

"And Andrea's?"

Ethan remembered the door in the hold when he almost drowned. Was it debris blocking it or was it locked?

She couldn't be alive... could she?

"No. I guess I didn't see her body," he admitted. "I just hoped she'd been blown up."

After he'd finished talking, she typed some more. While she did, Ethan ran through the journey's events in his head for what felt like the thousandth time since everything ended. Even in his own thoughts, it all felt ridiculous and fantastical, but saying it out loud to Abigail made it even more so.

"If you hadn't met me in Cape Town or Cabo Verde or saved me at the lake, would you believe any of this?" he asked.

Abigail continued typing something for another minute. When she stopped, she moved the laptop aside and clasped her hands together. "You know, I never saw the bunker, the gold, or the ship, so there isn't any reason to believe you now." Ethan frowned, but she continued, "That isn't to say that I don't."

She chewed on her lip for a bit, thinking, and then asked, "Do you know who I work for?"

"Interpol."

She smiled. "They said you were bright."

"Who is this 'they' everyone keeps mentioning?" he asked.

She ignored him. "Yes, I work for Interpol. In the Antiquities Division."

"Never heard of them."

"No, you likely wouldn't have. We're not a big part of Interpol, nor considered very important, which is why it was only me and no backup. But our role is to investigate and recover

antiquities sold on the black market and, well, investigate any…
irregularities with them."

"Investigate huh? By who? Top. Men?" he said with a smile.

Abigail furrowed her brow and the smile died on Ethan's lips.
"Irregularities?" he asked.

"Things like what you saw happen with the gold. Unnatural,
unusual, or—"

"So anything weird?" Ethan said.

She smiled. "'Weird' is simplistic but correct. The admittedly
infrequent things we have come across are the result of
experiments, or alchemy if you will, like Joanna of Castile cursing
those coins. While we would have liked to have had a coin to test
and learn what it did and how she did it, we believe it wasn't
magic. We think there is a scientific explanation behind it, like a
chemistry experiment gone wrong."

"You're sure about that?" Ethan said.

"Of course. You aren't?"

He shrugged but said nothing. The truth was he didn't know
what to think and was too tired to try.

"Did you know about Felix and Andrea before Cape Town?"

She nodded. "Felix Graves was a well-known 'obtainer of
goods' on the black market. It was likely they knew about the
curse of the coins and wanted to replicate it, weaponise it, and
mass produce it to sell to anyone who wanted it. It would have
made them ten times more than Blackbeard's treasure alone."

"Sell it to someone like Farid Abboud?"

"That's right."

"And Andrea?"

"We knew Felix Graves answered to someone, but we didn't know who until you uncovered it. Andrea was high up in Provolution, which was just a front for their criminal activities. They were not only involved in the black market but also drugs, sex trafficking, arms. They have their fingers in a lot of pies. You have actually done us a great service in exposing her activities."

"And Provolution?"

"They've gone underground, and since Graves is dead and she is either dead or missing, we have no leads on them. There's no one to question, so we will do what we can with what we have. There are still others out there who will be on the lookout for dangerous artefacts and supply them to people like Farid Abboud."

"Did you get him?"

Her eyes hardened at this question. "No, he escaped."

"Bugger."

"We'll get him."

Ethan sat back in his seat and relaxed a little. "So, this is over?"

She nodded. "Your part is. Once I have debriefed Hannah and Ritchie, I will organise for you all to go home."

She stood up with him and offered her hand, which he took. "Interpol would like to officially thank you for your support."

She sat back down, returning to her laptop as Ethan turned to go. But something in his mind clicked, and he turned around. "What was their role in this?"

She looked up at him from her laptop. "Who?"

"My parents."

"What makes you think they had any?"

"Graves said they betrayed him and Andrea, and that they disappeared from the Inaccessible Island. I suspect that was Interpol's doing. What I don't understand is why they went back to England acting as if nothing happened."

Abigail sighed and closed her laptop. "What I am about to tell you is between us. It doesn't leave this room. Got it?"

Ethan made the crossing motion over his heart.

"The record is out of my reach, so what I have is second-hand information." She paused, as if considering what to say. "After your parents stole the diary, they came to Interpol with a suspicion about what was going on; that Graves wanted Blackbeard's lost treasure."

"So my parents helped you try to capture Graves in return for what?"

"Immunity. They were famous, and it would have made waves had they been arrested. But they were small fish, so they convinced the higher-ups to go after people like Felix Graves."

Small fish.

"They theorised that Robert Maynard stole the treasure. Of course, no one would have guessed that Blackbeard actively worked with Maynard and that he tried to hide it. It was hard to sell to Interpol back then, and given that your parents had sold artefacts on the black market and confessed to doing so, they were almost arrested then and there. But they promised to name names, pull in the bigger fish. Interpol worked with them on a sting operation. Interpol wanted your parents to work both Andrea, trying to catch her out on illegal activity, and Graves to recover the gold, and then Interpol would swoop in.

"At the Inaccessible Island, it appears your mum and dad worked out that the gold was cursed, and they figured out Graves' plan wasn't to take the gold, but to weaponise and sell it. At that point, they agreed with Robert Maynard that the gold should be left lost forever. They requested extraction, and Interpol was ready to toss them in jail, but they were given a lifeline."

"Interpol wanted to use them as bait in Norfolk. To draw Graves and his crew out, right?"

Abigail nodded. "Exactly."

"Then what happened?"

She shrugged. "Some say there was miscommunication, others say the strike team weren't at the right site. But the prevailing theory is that Graves knew what was going to happen, and instead of backing away, he made a pre-emptive strike… he attacked when no one was ready. Whatever it was, it was a gigantic *fehler*…"

"And as a result, my parents died," Ethan finished. He felt hollow now. This wasn't what he expected. His stomach twisted at the thought of them trying to do the right thing and getting killed for it.

"Ethan, are you all right?"

He sniffed. "It's funny. They spent years being criminals, then they were willing to give it all away so they could be in my life. And in the end, trying to do the right thing is what got them killed."

Abigail stood up and circled the desk, kneeling next to him. She put a hand on his, an unexpected act of compassion from the otherwise stoic agent. She leaned in close to his ear and said, "She said you were bright."

Ethan's heart leapt.

She.

He looked at her. "What?" he choked. "Mum *is* alive? But Graves said he was the only one…"

"It was a while ago, and this is top secret, but as far as I know, she is. She survived the attack that killed your father. When Graves attacked, your parents set off a beacon that alerted Interpol and local authorities. As I said, no one was ready, but a local police boat was nearby and intervened. Your mother was pulled out of the water hours later and taken to safety. Later on, Interpol handed her off to ASIS."

"Australian Intelligence?"

She nodded.

"Then she is in Australia?"

"I don't think so. ASIS is Australia's international intelligence agency, so she could be anywhere. It might explain why you haven't heard from her."

But why hasn't Mum tried to contact me?

He fished in his pants pocket and pulled out the cursed coin and dropped it on the table. It landed with a heavy thud. "I don't know if this will help, but I found it in the bunker in Great Mongeham. For some reason, it has no effect on anyone who touches it, so maybe Maynard worked out a way to remove the effects."

She didn't touch it, but she nodded at him and said, "I will see what I can find out about your mother."

"Thanks," he said, and left the room.

Hannah was called in next, and while she was being questioned, Ethan told Ritchie about the debrief and his parents.

"Gem's alive? Lad, that's great news! Where is she?"

"No idea. Abigail is going to see what she can find out, but we know Australian Intelligence took her."

"That's great news, lad," he repeated, though he seemed less enthused about it.

They sat in silence, waiting for Hannah to finish with Abigail. Ritchie seemed deep in thought, while Ethan stared at the clock as it approached midday. The office was warming up, and Ethan got up to get a drink from the cooler. When he returned, Ritchie asked, "What's next for you then?"

Ethan shrugged. "I guess I'll go home, find a job, wait to hear from Mum. You?"

"Dunno, lad. I'll have to put in a claim on the boat for one, but then…"

"I'm sorry I couldn't get you your money," Ethan said.

Ritchie shrugged it off. "Don't be, lad."

They waited in silence for a minute before he continued. "Maybe I'll resume the business, though it wasn't great to begin with. But I was thinking…" He trailed off.

"Yeah?"

"Back at the Inaccessible Island… I hadn't felt a thrill like that in years. Not since working with your parents. I still got some old contacts, and I'm thinking maybe I'll get back into the game... and I'll need a partner."

Ethan raised his eyebrows. "Are you serious?"

"Lad, you know your stuff, and with a little of training, you'll be able to handle yourself. Plus, you're fearless. Going after Han out of the plane like that—"

Ethan raised a hand, cutting him off. "I'm not fearless. At best, I don't think, at worst, I'm reckless."

"Whatever you say, lad. All I know is that you jumped out of a plane to save Hannah's life without a second thought."

Ethan said nothing and Ritchie continued, "You could be a real asset. Follow in the footsteps of your ma and da."

"Treasure hunting?"

They didn't want you to live like them. Hannah's words echoed in his mind.

"Look, I'll be honest with you. I still got me debts and people gunning for me. It's a dangerous world, a dangerous life, but lad..." he rubbed his fingers together.

"I don't know," he said. Though if he was honest with himself, it appealed more to him than going back to Tasmania and trying to find a job and a place to live.

To have a normal, though mundane, life.

But he had no prospects there. He'd chased all his friends away, and the house was gone. Nothing was keeping him there.

"I appreciate the offer, but I think I'll head home and wait to hear from Mum."

Ritchie nodded, but looked upset at his response. "Aye, I understand."

At that moment, the office door opened and Hannah stepped out. She looked stern and avoided looking at Ethan. Ritchie asked her how it went, but she just put her hand up and walked down the hall.

"What happened?" Ritchie asked.

"It was a traumatic experience for her," Abigail said, staring at Ethan. "Reliving it isn't easy."

With the way Hannah had avoided looking at him and Abigail was staring at him, Ethan had a feeling that there was more to it and that it was his fault.

"Ritchie, you're the last one. When you are ready."

Ritchie looked down the hall and then at Ethan. "Just give her some space, lad," he said, getting up from his seat and entering the office. Abigail gave Ethan a pointed look and closed the door behind her.

It took him all of three seconds to get up and follow Hannah. He turned a corner that ended in a wide window overlooking the sprawling city. Beyond the city was the Niger River, and he could see a handful of boats lazily moving up it. Hannah stood at the window, her head pressed against it as she watched the people outside go about their day.

"Hey, you okay?" he asked, standing next to her. She hadn't showered or freshen up since arriving, and he noticed the cuts on her face, along with some bruising and a smudge of dirt on her cheek. He reached up and brushed it away gently with his thumb, and she closed her eyes and leaned into his hand. Her skin was soft and smooth, cool to his touch, and it felt... nice.

"Han...I—"

Hannah suddenly pulled away and tears started rolling down her cheeks. He looked at her, but was unsure of what to say. Asking what was wrong seemed woefully inadequate, considering all she had been through because of him, so he pulled her into a hug. She sobbed into his chest and he held her, stroking her hair, his cheek resting on her head.

After a couple of minutes, she leaned back, allowing him to look into her eyes. They were red-rimmed and glassy with the threat of more tears. He felt his own tears coming as well, the guilt of it all overwhelming him.

What long-term effects had he caused her because of what happened?

He took hold of her hands in his. "Han, I can't… I…I'm sorry," he said, his voice cracking at an octave above a whisper. "I got you into this. Everything that happened to you and Ritchie was my fault."

Her eyes softened a little, and he felt like this was his chance for redemption. He continued, "I trusted Andrea, and…" he trailed off when he saw her eyes harden.

She pulled away from him, and he realised he'd said the wrong thing.

"You slept with her!" she hissed.

"It was a mistake," he admitted. "I wasn't in a good place."

Even to him, that sounded lame.

"She tried to kill us!" Her voice was getting louder now, echoing off the walls. Some people walking past glanced at them disapprovingly as Hannah continued, "She and Graves kidnapped me. They threatened to torture me, to shoot me. They threw me out of a plane! They said they would kill me if you didn't do what they wanted. Do you understand what that is like?"

Each point she made was like a knife to his heart. "Hannah, please," he said lamely. He had nothing. She was right, and they both knew it. He looked at her and saw fury in her eyes. He tried to think of something to say that could fix it, but he came up blank.

"I thought I could forgive you… for all that happened, but I can't. Every time I try to sleep, I'm falling out of that plane, or there's a gun to my head, or I'm hanging off that ledge. And every time you're not there to save me. Instead, you've run off to the treasure because it was more important to you. I wake up screaming… I just—I just can't," she said.

"But—" Ethan started, but Hannah interrupted him.

"I think the worst part is you lie to yourself. What we spoke about on the ship… I see the hunger in your eyes, Ethan. The thrill, the excitement, the search for treasure. The greed. No matter what I said or what happened to me, nothing was stopping you from finding that treasure."

"That's just not true," Ethan said, though there was no conviction in it.

"You can lie to me, but don't lie to yourself," she said. "I saw it in Ritchie, and I see the exact same thing in you."

She turned and walked away, and Ethan leaned back against the glass window. "I would have never let them hurt you," he whispered to her retreating back. "I would rather die than see you hurt."

Hannah passed Abigail, who was coming in the opposite direction, and rounded the corner, disappearing from sight.

"What did you do now?" Abigail asked.

"I ruined her life," he said.

She raised an eyebrow but let the comment go. "ASIS called me."

Ethan pushed off the window. "They did? What did they say?"

"You need to come with me now," she said solemnly.

"Why?"

"It's about your mother."

Fifty

Praia da Luz, Portugal

"I'm so glad I could see you one last time."

Ethan was sitting on a chair next to a bed. Machines beeped, and tubes ran from them into his mum's arm and up her nose.

After she received word that his mother was dying, Abigail organised a private charter for Ethan to get to Portugal. He spent the entire four-hour flight fretting, trying to get more information out of her, but she said she told him all she knew.

A taxi took him from Portimão Airport in Montes de Alvor to a nondescript white apartment building in Praia da Luz. Any other time, he would have admired the drive along the coast with the sparkling blue water, but he was fraught with grief.

Cancer. Of all things. After surviving countless dangerous treks, murder attempts, and going into hiding, the thing that kills his mum is cancer.

"Don't say that," he said quietly, though it was half-hearted, and they both knew it. When he arrived, he was immediately taken to her room. He was shocked. Gemma Jackson was a woman who once had fierce brown eyes and long chestnut hair, but now her eyes looked faded, defeated, and her hair was stringy and patchy. But what shocked him the most was how gaunt she looked. He could see the points of her elbows and the lines of her collarbone through her ill-fitting clothing. When he stepped into the room, he couldn't, didn't want to, believe it was her, and almost ran from the room. But when her eyes fluttered open, and he saw the tears after she recognised him, he practically flew over to her and embraced her, his own tears flowing freely.

Now he was sitting beside her, grateful for what little time they had left.

She chuckled, her laugh sounding like the rattling of an empty spray paint can, and he grabbed a drink from the side table and offered it to her. After she took a sip from the straw, he put it back.

"Ethan, we both know I look like shit."

He couldn't help but laugh. "You wouldn't believe how often I've heard that in the last week." Then he turned serious. "How long?"

"How long have I had it, or how long do I have left?"

"Both, I guess."

"They diagnosed me last year, but they said it had been in my body for years, and it was too late. As for when… days, hours… minutes. It's anyone's guess."

"Why didn't anyone tell me?"

Her eyes softened. "I wanted to, I really did, but ASIS was adamant that if we contacted you, we would put your life in danger of *those people*." She spat out the last two words.

"You don't have to worry about them anymore," he said. "They're gone."

"It wasn't me I was worried about, Ethan. It was you. But they told me what happened," she said and smiled. "Sounds like you did everything we didn't want you to do."

Ethan smiled back. "Fantastic treasures, dangerous people, wild adventures. You can't dangle that in front of your son and expect him to ignore it."

She chuckled. "No, I suppose not. Tell me about the treasure."

"It was evil, Mum. Just by looking at it, you could tell there was something wrong with it. There was no light, like it was always cast in shadow. But what it did to people—I wouldn't wish that on my worst enemy." He thought about Andrea and Felix Graves and corrected himself. "Well, that's not entirely true, I suppose."

"We saw the bodies at Maynard's hideout… it was extraordinary."

"The treasure's gone now. Buried beneath Lake Faguibine. Same with the *Queen Anne's Revenge*."

At the mention of the ship, her eyes lit up, and he saw a glimpse of her old self in there. "Blackbeard's ship. I can't believe it survived all this time. Tell me about it."

"Oh, Mum, it was incredible! To walk on the deck, to enter his quarters. I just can't… I wish you were there." He told her about the ship, what he found and how it felt to be on it, and the aftermath.

"It's a real shame it couldn't be preserved."

Ethan nodded. "I know."

"Your father would have loved it."

There it was again—his chest tightened like someone had grabbed hold of his heart and squeezed it as hard as they could. "They told me he died saving you."

A single tear trickled down his mum's cheek. "He did. Fought them off long enough so that I could get out of there. He sacrificed himself for me. And for you."

He sat back, staring out the window as more tears fell. A million thoughts and wishes raced by about his dad and how he wanted to talk to him or see him one last time. To tell him he loved him, but that had been taken away from him.

"Ethan, are you okay?"

How do I have any more tears? He looked at his mum, fragile as she was, and smiled. Whatever grief he felt, it could wait. He wanted to spend whatever time she had left with her. "I'm okay," he said.

They fell into a comfortable silence, then he asked, "Why didn't you tell me?"

"How could we admit to our only son that we were criminals?"

"It would have been a hell of a lot better than finding out from reporters on my way to school. I was fourteen."

His mum looked guilty. "We weren't perfect, Ethan."

"It's okay, Mum. I'm not mad at you for doing what you did. I can even see the appeal in it. But not knowing… it hurt. And I never got to say goodbye to Dad."

She nodded. "I know."

They were silent for a while, Ethan reflecting on life and all he missed out on until she said, "We don't have time for misery. Tell me about the last ten years. Do you have a girlfriend?"

"Nah. I'm actually married. Wife, two kids, a dog. Left them all to go on this chase."

"Really?"

He snorted and they both laughed.

Ethan told his mum about his life, the good and the bad. About Peter trying to help, about the troubles he got into. They talked and laughed and cried throughout the day and into the night. Then, at four twenty-seven the next morning, Gemma Jackson closed her eyes and was pronounced dead, the smile still on her face.

Ethan stayed in his hotel room for days, mourning the loss of his mum and dad now that he knew the truth about their deaths. Abigail tried calling him multiple times, but he ignored her. Eventually, the calls went away. The days passed, and he barely ate or drank. All he did was lie on the bed and stare at the ceiling.

Five days after his mum's death, he finally moved to sit on the beach in the sun, deciding the blue sky was a better view than the hotel ceiling. He listened to the waves until night fell and, not having the motivation to do anything more, he slept there.

The next morning, ASIS organised to have his mum flown back to Tasmania to be buried with his dad. He saw her one last time, resting on the table at a funeral home in Praia da Luz and looking at peace. He was grateful for that and stayed with her for as long as they would let him. A balding priest who didn't speak any English entered and read from a well-worn Bible as a short farewell service. When the priest finished, he walked up to Ethan and placed his hand on Ethan's shoulder. He said something in Portuguese that Ethan assumed had something to do with being sorry for his loss, a greater purpose, all the things he'd heard at the first funeral ten years ago. Then he walked away, leaving Ethan to his thoughts.

After they took her away, he just sat there, at a loss about what to do.

"How are you feeling?" Abigail appeared at his side.

He shrugged, not surprised to see her. "I'm not sure. I thought I had lost her ten years ago with Dad, but then I found out she was alive. Then I find out she has cancer, and now I have lost her again. I'm not sure what I feel right now."

Abigail put a hand on his shoulder. "The circumstances are unfair, but I think you should focus on the positives. You got to see your mum one last time. You got to talk to her and hug her and spend time with her, and that must have made her world."

"I guess so."

She continued, "Grieve as much as you need to, but don't let this stop your life, Ethan. They wouldn't have wanted that."

He nodded.

"Are you going to go home?"

He shrugged again. "She'll be buried next to Dad, but there won't be a funeral—not that anyone would turn up anyway—and I already said my goodbyes. So… I don't know."

She handed him a card and said, "If you need anything, call me."

He pocketed the card and said, "Thanks."

Abigail squeezed his shoulder and left him alone.

He left the funeral home a while later, thinking about his parents and what Abigail had told him. He had to do something because he was pretty much out of money. He could try to get a job back home, but much like with his old friends, he was sure he had burned all his bridges in Tasmania.

He sat on a park bench in the middle of Praia da Luz thinking about the last couple of weeks. His mind warred between Hannah and what she said about his parents' wanting something better for him, and the gold in Blackbeard's ship. Not the cursed gold, but the rest that was lost to the bottom of the lake and was now underneath tons of stone. But as he thought more about it, the image of the gold drowned out Hannah's words and he felt an electric thrill race through his body. He pulled out his phone and opened his contacts. His finger hovered over the number while he thought about what he was about to do. Could he do it? Would it amount to anything? But the question that pushed its way to the top was: *What more do I have to lose?*

He thought about Hannah; her face clear in his mind and his heart constricted. He'd failed her and she was gone. Gone to live her life with the nightmares of all he put her through. They were demons that would follow her for a long time.

She deserved better than that. Better than him.

He thought about how he found the bell of the *Swallow*, the secret passage in the house. How it felt when he did. It was the same as he felt at finding the *Queen Anne's Revenge* and all that gold.

He thought about the thrill, the adrenaline, the adventure. It called to him now as it did all those years ago.

He thought about how his parents did it and they made a career out of it.

The electric rush of adrenaline surged through his body as he thought about it all and he realised the truth about himself.

He was *born for this*.

Hannah's face faded from his mind, and he pushed the number and waited while the phone connected.

It was answered after the third ring.

"Ritchie? It's Ethan. That offer still open?"

Ethan Jackson will return in another exciting adventure.

About the Author

Born in 1984, Danny Gunn grew up in Melbourne, Victoria, before moving to North-west Tasmania in 2016 with his partner and daughter.

Now living on the beach, his family has grown to include two cats and the occasional penguin.

When not writing, Danny enjoys reading, hiking, kayaking, scuba diving, and spending time with his family.

He is the author of the Van Diemen's Valley horror series for children, The Gambler's Luck and the Ethan Jackson Adventures.

Social Media

Facebook: https://www.facebook.com/dannygunnwrites

Twitter: @danwritesbooks

Email: danwritesbooks@outlook.com

Goodreads:

https://www.goodreads.com/author/show/21990610.Danny_Gunn

Feel free to contact me with questions, comments, or reviews.

I'd love to hear them.

www.ingramcontent.com/pod-product-compliance
Lightning Source LLC
Chambersburg PA
CBHW061504020726
47502CB00006B/1935